Also By Stella Barcelona

DECEIVED

Praise for *Deceived*:

"Stella Barcelona's stunning debut, *Deceived*, has it all. Mystery-check. Action-check. Romance-check. A heart pounding must read, Barcelona writes for those of us who want intelligent protagonists and an intriguing mystery."
> – Cherry Adair, New York Times Bestselling Author

"Stella Barcelona's *Deceived* brings history to life in a suspenseful, contemporary tale that sends the protagonists on a research trip to a past close to their hearts. Barcelona's debut books brings an excellent author to the fore; the intrigue blends beautifully with the romance."
> – Heather Graham, New York Times Bestselling Author

"With the power of a master craftsman, Stella Barcelona takes us on an unforgettable journey in her debut novel, *Deceived*. She sweeps the reader away with whirlwind action and heart-pounding suspense, all the while sitting you beside vibrant, unforgettable characters who take root in your heart and refuse to leave. This is one book not to be missed!"
> – Deborah LeBlanc, author of Voices

SHADOWS

Stella Barcelona

To Bob, my own blue-eyed hero, thank you for your constant encouragement, for making me laugh, and for sharing with me the luck of the Irish.

Prologue

They'll kill me when they realize I'm not cooperating.

With that thought screaming though his mind, Richard Barrows' fingers shook as he typed commands. Sweat dripped into his eyes. He swallowed his growing panic, squinting at the computer monitor as he longed for the relative security and peace of prison. After his conviction for tax evasion, mundane prison routine had the odd effect of slowing his thought processes, which typically raced through infinite possibilities. Craving that safety and calmness wouldn't produce it, though.

His physicians and psychiatrists had strongly suggested medicine to treat his obsessions, compulsions, and paranoia. He'd refused, knowing that one day, the world would need every ounce of his unfettered brainpower.

Today is the day.

Who the hell were his captors, and how had they gained access to his proprietary data? They didn't have all of it, thank God, and much of what they had was encrypted. More sweat dripped into his eyes as he analyzed their latest stumbling block:

```
dsfcd;kafoAr,.idyeliwrknldJaKDlHSUXsgvn98
24NCPXOX63473166B643BE666F412C2EOx666436b
666f412c2e6979657777277bc44a4b444853dsfRx
yO66SdsE444853444276
```

Their isolation of this data stream indicated they were close to cracking his encryption code. Close, but they weren't there. It was only a matter of time before they'd see the clues. For now they wanted him to provide the key for hundreds of breakpoints such as the one he was studying.

Not in this fucking lifetime.

Pretending to be prison guards, yet not allowing him to know where they were taking him, had been leading indicators of a problem. The lab where they ordered him to work was exactly the type of place that made him feel safe and comfortable. It was too perfect, though. The tech was too state-of-the-art, the lighting at exactly his specified lumens, the temperature at precisely his preferred working temperature of sixty-two degrees. They'd copied his personal work environment at BY Laboratories, right down to the ergonomic keyboard he used with an integrated palm rest and a footrest under his desk at precisely his favored height.

Peripherally he was aware of other technicians and analysts working in the lab. From their sweat despite the cool temperature, hair-pulling frustration, pacing when they weren't typing, and furtive glances at him, he deduced that their frustration level matched his fear. If their extreme dedication to work wasn't odd enough, the six black-clad men with weapons, strategically positioned around the room, confirmed that this was no legitimate endeavor. There was one piece of good news, and for that he was elated. *My encryption program is working.* These men were running state of the art decryption programs and they hadn't broken through the bag of tricks he'd employed in protecting Shadow Technology.

A man approached and stood at his side. Richard glanced into the lead analyst's light brown eyes. The man pushed his horn-rimmed glasses up his nose. "You haven't typed anything in ten minutes."

"I have to think it through. This takes time," he lied. Richard knew the commands the characters prompted. What was taking so long was thinking through an alternate command that would prompt an invisible data purge, because his gut told him his captors weren't the government agents they claimed to be. For that reason, he wasn't giving them a damn thing. What he could destroy, he would.

"We need results," the analyst answered, with a glance to one of the gun-toting guards who stood at the doorway, "and we need them now."

Looking closer, Richard realized that moisture had seeped through the man's blue button-down shirt. His thin red hair was damp with sweat. The man was anxious, but trying hard to be cool on the exterior. "Who are you working for?"

"We've told you. We're with the National Security Agency. This is all a problem of your creation. You've created chaos. You must correct it."

I'm not falling for it. My programs made sense out of chaos.

The stakes were far higher than his mortality, and Richard's racing thoughts all collided at a dead end. *Help.* He needed it, badly. *This isn't paranoia.* These men were out to get him. Well, not him, but what he'd created. Shadow Technology and LID Technology. He needed help and, as much as he didn't want to involve her, there was only one person who could give it.

Alert Skye. The cataclysm scenario is in play.

"Maybe these two words will speed things up." The analyst stepped closer, bent, and said, "Skye and Spring," then stepped away.

The two people he'd protect with his life.

Richard's stomach rolled with sudden nausea. He resumed typing, narrowing his eyes as he read the monitor. *Yes.* That was enough to make things look good, but not enough to work. The analyst was absolutely correct. The way to ensure his cooperation was by threatening his daughters. By voicing their names, that's what the man had done.

I have no choice.

Richard almost choked on his fear for his daughters, typing commands that would, without his captors knowing, allow him to penetrate their network. He'd found the vulnerability in their system that would provide internet access hours ago. If he was in and out in a matter of seconds, he had a strong hope they wouldn't figure out he'd been there or see the message that he sent. He'd always known it would come to this, yet his hands trembled as he sent the message that would alert Skye.

Please God, help her.

Chapter One

13144141392311172208152620

The number stream, the one and only communication she'd received on the phone that was dedicated solely to transmission of such a message, jolted the last sleep-induced blur from Chloe's brain. Her hands shook as she mentally translated numbers to letters.

C-A-T-A-C-L-Y-S-M-N-O-W-R-U-N.

She gripped the phone tighter, checking her translation. Same result. It was the message she'd been hoping would never come. Maybe she'd made a mistake. Kicking aside the sheet and blanket, she turned on the lamp, opened the top drawer of the nightstand, pushed her revolver to the side, and pulled out a pen and paper. Drawing a deep breath, she started over, writing as she assigned letters to numbers.

Cataclysm. Now. Run.

Adrenaline surged through her veins, but as she stood, hope glimmered – maybe the message itself was a mistake. No. Not possible. A wrong-number text message would have made sense in a simple, uncomplicated life, rather than in her father's private code. As her father's daughter, her life was neither simple, nor her own. And despite her father's propensity for paranoia, the *cataclysm* part of his secret code galvanized her into action.

'Normal' wasn't part of her father's vocabulary. He wasn't normal, but he was her father. While a majority of the world now ridiculed him, Chloe didn't. Cataclysm wasn't supposed to happen. The word meant only one thing in her father's world, and she had instructions to follow. Without question. Well, maybe with questions. A train car full of questions, starting with how her father, who was imprisoned in a federal penitentiary, had managed to send her a text and why this particular message now. Yet she knew if he had a few minutes with a computer–any computer–he could do anything. Other questions bombarded her, but now was not the time to entertain them. Even with doubt, she'd follow the pre-arranged steps of his cataclysm scenario as though her life, and a whole lot more, depended on it.

Cataclysm. Now. Run.

Her father had taught her to act first, worry later. A simple idea, and one with value, although he had the luxury of living in grand schemes and high ideals.

He'd left her to contend with the real world, and to say it was a damn inconvenient day to have to run was an understatement.

She shredded the paper where she'd written his message, put the pieces in her mouth, almost gagging on the wad of pulp. With all that was inside of her, she knew that chewing and swallowing paper as a means of destroying the message was ridiculous. Yet she was committed by blood and loyalty to following her father's instructions, no matter how off-base, so follow them she did. She walked over to retrieve her personal ditch kit—cash, loose diamonds, gold medallions, and weapons—all packed in a backpack that was tucked in a locked trunk in her closet, under spare linens.

The location where cataclysm prompted her to run—a lake house on Firefly Island in Hickory Lake, near Nashville, Tennessee—had more supplies. For now, she just had to get there. Fast. She checked her backpack, put it by the bedroom door, and tried to calm herself by deep breathing. This first step of the cataclysm scenario—getting to the lake house within twenty-four hours and awaiting her father's next instruction— would be a no brainer if she were alone. But she wasn't alone.

Dear God, why today?

Living on the hope that the cataclysm scenario would never come, she had worked hard at creating the life that she and her younger sister, Colbie, were living. Today, of all days, was of supreme importance to Colbie, who even on an ordinary day couldn't just get in the car and run from one life to the next. Not without questions, not without coaxing, not without a story that would make sense in the world of Colbie-logic. She breathed deeply, then exhaled slowly.

Figure it out.

Realistically, with her sister, it would easily take a full twelve hours to get to Hickory Lake, and that was assuming everything went smoothly. She'd travel faster alone. She debated whether she should leave Colbie, go to the lake house, get the message, and return for her afterwards. Colbie would be fine for a few hours without her, as long as she felt comfortable in her surroundings, had people with her whom she loved and trusted, and had something to do that was time consuming and detailed. Chloe had built such a life for her sister in Covington, Louisiana, and maybe home would be the best place for Colbie today.

Chloe glanced at the clock. Five-thirty in the morning. The text had come in at five twenty-five. Breathe, she told herself. She had plenty of time. Allowing twelve hours for the drive with Colbie was acceptable. They shouldn't separate. In the cataclysm scenario, if they had to reach the end of the cataclysm road, they needed to be together. It was too risky to leave her in Covington.

Run. Now.

Allowing twelve hours, they'd be at the lake house in plenty of time to ready herself for the next set of instructions that should come in by five twenty-five the following morning, exactly twenty-four hours after receiving this morning's message.

Chloe deleted the coded text and took the phone apart, breaking it into as many pieces as she could. With the heel of one of the cowboy boots she planned to wear, she then smashed the pieces. Three toilet flushes later, the phone was gone.

She allowed herself a few minutes to shower. Hot water soothed her and helped her plan how the morning would unfold, once she awakened her sister. Colbie, of course, had no knowledge of the cataclysm scenario and wouldn't grasp what it meant, even if she was told every detail. With serious coaxing, Chloe would be able to get Colbie out of the house a few minutes earlier than normal. There was no way, though, that she'd be able to get Colbie on the road without stopping at their new bakery and coffee shop, Creative Confections, picking up the cake that Colbie had decorated the evening before, and delivering it to the customer. *Bingo.* She'd focus on the cake as a reason to hurry. Once they delivered the cake, they'd be able to run. She combed her wet hair and wound it into a twist, so that it would dry without wetting her sweater. No make-up. No time.

She slipped on the clothes that had been reserved for this day that was never supposed to happen, put on jewelry that she could use for barter later, if needed, and slipped into her sister's lamp-lit bedroom. The barrage of color that filled bowls on Colbie's oversized desk and apothecary jars on every bookshelf sent a chill through Chloe. Colbie's current project at home involved organizing marbles by swirl and color. Lots of them.

Please God. Not marbles. When she finally has her

meltdown, don't let her want marbles.

Candy, their eight-month old golden retriever, rested her head next to Colbie's head on the pillow. They were snuggled together, Colbie's body a larger crescent behind the long-legged, fluffy puppy. Her sister wore pink headphones as she slept, snoozing to the sounds of a rainforest. Colbie didn't stir at Chloe's entry, but the dog's big brown eyes opened, following her progress as she approached the bed. Before touching Colbie's shoulder, sadness threatened to choke her. Oh God. This had to stop. She couldn't let her sister see, or even sense, how afraid she was. Her sister would be worried. Colbie's worry led to anxiety, and anxiety led to meltdowns.

An anxiety-filled wake-up wasn't the way to start any day, much less this day. Not when so much depended on them getting where they were supposed to be. Chloe drew a deep breath, reminding herself she could start over and succeed again. She'd make their next life even better for her sister.

A half hour had elapsed since the message came through. Now she had twenty-three hours and thirty minutes to get to Firefly Island. Plenty of time, she assured herself, as long as she could get her sister going. As she touched Colbie's shoulder, her sister's blue eyes opened and she smiled her usual sweet, innocent, slightly-sleepy, morning smile.

Cataclysm. Now. Run.

"Today's going to be a fabulous day." Chloe forced calm and enthusiasm into her voice. "Why don't you shower? I'll put your clothes together and take Candy outside."

***

The sleek interior of Raven One, a Gulfstream 650 ER, with supple leather seats and polished wood accents, reminded Sebastian Connelly how much was on the line with his slim-ass hunch that Skye Barrows would lead him to her father. His hunch had better be right. Black Raven Private Security Contractors, his company, was at the top of its game. It had a long way to fall, and he was up to his ass in a problem that was becoming an uncontrollable downward spiral.

The tailspin had started four days earlier, when seven prisoners escaped from a low security satellite facility at a Federal Correctional Institution in Mississippi. Escaped on Black Raven's watch. His watch. Of the seven escapees, three remained at large. U.S. Marshals and Black Raven agents were closing in on one of them, and they had a decent lead on another. The one without leads–Richard Barrows–was Sebastian's problem. No one had a clue regarding the whereabouts of Barrows, the brilliant and paranoid computer genius, who should be sitting in the federal pen for tax evasion.

Should be, but wasn't, because there'd been a total failure of all systems at the prison. The systems failure hadn't been a simple electrical issue. There had been an electrical outage, and the security system that Black Raven was in the process of replacing had also failed. No one had detected anything going wrong while it happened. The end result had been an outage of every light, camera, lock, and security measure. They were damn lucky only seven prisoners had strolled out.

As the wheels touched the runway, Sebastian, alone in the passenger cabin, inserted a tiny audio transmitter and receiver into his ear, pressed a few buttons on his watchband that turned the earpiece into a phone and auto-dialed Ragno, Black Raven's senior data analyst. Unless Ragno's work was focused on a particular operation, she or someone on her team provided a steady stream of updates to Black Raven partners on sensitive operations. Phrases like *client safely delivered in Karachi* or *deposit made in Istanbul* were not uncommon to hear from Ragno or her team throughout a normal day. Today wasn't normal, though, and one hundred percent of Ragno's focus was on the prison break.

"Talk to me."

"Good morning," Ragno's tone was, as usual, clear, crisp, and calm. The woman was unflappable, non-alarmist, and always cool under pressure. She was Sebastian's conduit to the numerous agents who were working the prison break, his link to the rest of the world, and the point person for assimilating the massive amounts of information Black Raven's data analysts were gathering.

"Holt was just apprehended in Georgia, and we're getting more leads on Biondo," she said. Relief fluttered in Sebastian's belly. Holt, and one of the escapees who had already been apprehended, had been in the prison library with Barrows and Biondo when the blackout occurred. The other three prisoners had escaped from the prison laundry facility. "Holt is en route to the nearest federal prison for debriefing."

Five escapees down. Two to go. He might be able to save this clusterfuck after all. "Is Holt saying anything about Barrows or

Biondo?"

"No. So far he's saying he left with the others, before Barrows. He didn't think Barrows was going to leave. Didn't see Barrows or any of the others once he was outside the gate. Interrogation is continuing as we speak." She paused. "Did you manage to sleep while in flight?"

"No," he shut his iPad, slipped it into his backpack, and stood as the plane halted. "I've read through some of Barrows' interviews."

"Fascinating, right?"

"Yes," he said, slipping on his jacket. "Imagine if all of that brilliance could have been harnessed."

"Oh," she said, "I've been imagining."

At six-five, Sebastian could stand upright in the jet, but what he needed was a good, arms-over-head stretch, and that was impossible. "Get the senior agents for each team on the line for action reports."

"Back in five."

Sebastian slung his backpack over one shoulder and nodded to the two pilots, who stood at attention as he departed. "I'll call with a departure time. For now, plan on two hours."

He walked down the narrow stairs to the tarmac, breathing in fresh, crisp February air. Above the yellow and orange horizon, stars blinked in the clear, pre-dawn sky. He didn't bother breaking the connection with Ragno as she put together the conference call. He could hear her keyboard clicking and her soft breaths. While they worked the prison break, they'd keep an open line throughout the day and most of the night.

Sebastian walked to a black Range Rover that had pulled up to the private airport's landing strip. He usually enjoyed high-stakes hunts with elusive prey, but Barrows wasn't just elusive. He had disappeared, and Sebastian couldn't get a handle on where he might be. No one could.

Sebastian nodded to Pete St. Paul, the driver of the Range Rover, who had stepped out and opened the front passenger door for Sebastian. Pete was one of Black Raven's newer agents. "Good morning, sir."

"Morning." Sebastian dropped his backpack into the footwell of the passenger side, did an arms over head stretch before stepping into the SUV and extended his legs as he pushed the seat back as far as it could go. "Having fun yet?"

Pete's smile made it to his dark brown eyes. "I've done worse." He shut the door and came around to the driver's side.

Barrows. The tech-genius was famous for innovations that had revolutionized computer science and usage. At one time the man was regarded as one of the more brilliant minds of the computer age. He'd made a fortune off his inventions. But with his brilliance came passionate beliefs that were far-fetched and unsubstantiated. Before his conviction, implausible claims had outweighed the plausible. The same brain that had patented ingenious innovations in anti-viral software and spyware became a frequent target of late-night comedians for claiming that extra-terrestrial life had infiltrated the internet.

He'd been imprisoned one year earlier. Although he'd been paying taxes, he'd formulated a detailed personal tax code and, for years, had been paying in accordance with his own tax code. He not only formulated it, he published it, and encouraged others to use it. The running joke was that Barrows, with his considerable wealth and income, paid far more in taxes than required by the official tax code. Others, though, hundreds of thousands of Barrows' fans, paid less when following his formula. He had pleaded guilty and, because he had paid more in taxes than legally required, had been given a lenient sentence of two years.

Once in prison, Barrows' daughters, Skye and Spring, had seemingly disappeared. In truth, they'd done a world-class job of concealing their true identities and their connection to Barrows. They became Chloe and Colbie Stewart and lived in the small town of Covington, Louisiana, which was why Sebastian had flown there. His people were good at what they did and it still took them three full days post-prison break to find Skye and Spring. New identities—ones this good—cost big bucks, and only a few forgers were good enough to pull off such a seamless transition. Then again, they were the daughters of Richard Barrows, who could make computers do things others only dreamed about. Dad could have done it for them. Their fake names and assumed lives made Sebastian suspicious, but he didn't give a damn what they called themselves or where they lived. All he cared about was whether the daughters knew where their father was.

Where the hell was Barrows?

It was the question of the day, and he sure as hell hoped his hunch about the daughters would lead him to the answer. Pete had been in Covington, Louisiana, for almost twenty-four hours, assigned to in-field surveillance on Skye and Spring Barrows the minute that Black Raven had figured out their fake names and where they were.

"What do you have for me?"

"Their coffee shop is a ten-minute drive from here. Should I fill you in here," Pete said, "or on the way?"

"On the way."

Ragno's voice interrupted as Pete put the car in drive. "Conference call is ready."

The vehicle, from Black Raven's fleet, was equipped with customized telematics, internal and external cameras, a satellite navigation system, and tracking devices, all of which could be monitored at headquarters. The vehicle synced with his phone, as long as he activated the sync mechanism. He pressed a button, sending the call to the blue-tooth system, scanning the two-lane highway as Pete left the airport. Traffic was light. No one was behind them.

The agent whose team was with Holt said, "Good morning, sir. I just stepped into the transport. Can't talk. Check text."

Sebastian glanced at his watchband, and read the text as it scrolled through. *Holt has no info on Barrows. Didn't know Barrows had escaped. At this point, it looks like he's trying hard to tell the truth, because he's facing some big prison time. Truthfulness would help shave years. He just hasn't got anything. Will update if that changes.*

Another field agent said, "Morning, sir. I'm investigating a few leads on Biondo coming out of Jackson, Mississippi. At this point nothing is promising. It seems like the marshals were overly optimistic about how close we are to him, cause this lead isn't solid."

A deep breath didn't break the disappointment that came with his agent's words. Sebastian pushed the negative feeling aside. "Ragno. Have the analysts recheck everything we have on Biondo. Make no assumptions. Triple check any info coming from the marshals." He paused for a moment, glancing at the scenery as he thought through the best way to use Black Raven manpower. Evergreen pine trees lined the two-lane road leading away from the airport to the small town of Covington. The early morning sky was lighter blue now and, because Sebastian had grown up in South Louisiana, he knew the crisp, cool weather was the type that locals loved. It was a break from the usual humid dampness of the area. "Once Holt gets back to the prison, keep one agent with the marshal team processing him, but move our remaining agents to the search for Biondo."

He dropped the field agents, and kept Ragno on the line. To both Pete and Ragno, Sebastian said, "What will make his daughters tell me where their father is?"

"I'm not sure they can," Ragno said, "because I don't think they know."

Sebastian glanced at Pete, who nodded in agreement. Ragno said, "We've detected no contact between Barrows and his daughters."

"I've cloned their phones," Pete said, slowing as a truck carrying pine logs entered the roadway in front of them. "Well, all the phones we could find. Chloe, previously Skye, had one registered to her, Colbie, previously Spring, had another. There's one we haven't managed to tap."

"Yes," Ragno said. "Skye wears a small, old-fashioned flip phone tucked inside her jeans, in the belt area. I've detected it from images on the security system, which we've hacked. Motorola Razr, circa 2008."

Pete stopped at a red light. Sebastian glanced into the mirror that was on his sun visor. A blue Ford SUV was behind them. Two men were in it. "Pete. Have you seen that Explorer before?"

Pete glanced in the rearview mirror. "No."

"We're not monitoring the Razr," Ragno continued. "On the devices I've managed to hack, I've followed data transmissions and internet activity, which is limited to their business. Pete bugged their house and business. They haven't mentioned their father. Pete installed cameras at their house, one covering the downstairs, one covering the stairs and upstairs hallway. I've hacked into cameras at the coffee shop. Barrows isn't at either place. Everything seems normal so far."

"I don't think they even know their father's escaped," Pete told him, glancing at Sebastian as he stopped at a traffic light. "It hasn't been publicized. They haven't had contact with any source that's given them the information, because if they know, they haven't said a word about it."

Hell.

"However, it's...odd that Barrows hasn't contacted his daughters," Ragno said. "I don't think he'd go very long without contacting them. If not to get their help with his efforts to disappear, then to tell them he's all right. Before his imprisonment, they were a tight knit unit. Dad and his two girls. That's it. No other relatives. He'd call them and say he's fine," she paused, "unless, of course, he's not."

As Sebastian realized Ragno and Pete really had nothing solid for him, the dull thud of a headache pulsed behind his eyes. "So if we don't have any obvious link between the daughters and their father's escape efforts," he said, "give me details, something I can use to press their buttons and figure out where he might have gone."

"I sent a condensed version of my notes, coupled with Pete's observations, to you a few minutes ago," Ragno said. "There are pictures."

Sebastian reached into his backpack for his iPad and clicked on the file that Ragno had sent. "Got it."

She continued, "Skye and Spring Barrows changed identities shortly before Richard Barrows pleaded guilty. Most of her twenties Skye, who became Chloe—"

"Stick with their real names."

"Skye was an A-lister on the fast-track celebutante list."

Sebastian knew the type. Celebrity-debutantes. Black Raven had a few multi-billionaire clients with twenty-something-year-old children, who became famous simply by being attractive and living fast, hard, and mostly without direction as they partied, shopped, and blew through fortunes.

"Drugs?" He glanced through the windshield. Outbound traffic was getting heavier as they headed into Covington. They were about forty-five minutes from downtown New Orleans, and on this Monday in February, commuters were headed to work. A quick glance in the visor's mirror told him that the blue Explorer had disappeared. Good. As far as he could tell, no one was following them.

"Occasional marijuana reports. Social alcohol. Big parties, fast cars, yachts, high fashion," Ragno paused. "Skye ran through men. Lots of them—several well-known. She even dated Justin Timberlake. There are plenty of photos of the two of them together. "

On the iPad, Sebastian fast-gazed at paparazzi photos of Skye, who smiled at the camera like it was her best friend, while clubbing, bikini-tanning on yachts, and dining with other Alisters. Her smile was full and captivating and it was something she was rarely without. It set her apart from the others in the photos, because the current style for young heiresses in the fast lane was a perpetually bored, slightly annoyed, pouty look. Not Skye. She looked like she enjoyed the fun, and each time she was photographed in a group, more people looked at her than at the camera. He swiped backwards on the screen and started over, studying how she gave in to moments with reckless abandon, carrying everyone else along for the ride.

"Her partying pictures are all two years old or older. About a year before her father's conviction," Pete said, turning at a traffic light into the outskirts of the quaint town. "Skye had a serious car accident in the Florida Keys. She was driving and speeding. It was raining. She swerved to avoid a key deer. One passenger died. Her sister was injured. After that, she kept a relatively low profile. No more high-life partying pics, no reports of famous boyfriends. She and her sister disappeared from public view right before her father's conviction and imprisonment. Chloe and Colbie Stewart have established a new life here in Covington."

"And they've done a world class job of it," Sebastian muttered. "Do we know why they've gone to such extreme measures to conceal their identity?"

"No," Ragno answered, "other than to separate themselves from the Barrows name. Their father was constantly denigrated and mocked in the public eye before he went to prison. Or, maybe they're just as paranoid as he is."

As he scanned through the files, Sebastian's gaze rested on a photograph of a long-legged, sun-tanned blonde tiptoeing on the top deck of a Westport mega-yacht, arms arched high overhead, as she readied herself for a dive. The next photo was zoomed closer. A white string bikini bottom was Skye's only clothing. It was tied at the hips and only covered the barest essentials. Her small waist gently curved to full hips and a not-perfectly-flat tummy. Wet strands of platinum blond hair fell to her waist, partially concealing large breasts and pink nipples. "Wow."

Pete chuckled. "Yeah. That's two years ago, right before her car accident."

If she had any tan lines, Sebastian didn't see them. A flirty turn-up played at her lips, a gorgeous prelude to her stunning smile, and she was staring out, as though the only thing on her mind was the perfect dive, the sun, and the glistening, turquoise-blue water. A buff, dark-haired man in swim trunks reclined nearby, staring up at her with wide-eyed lust. Other suntanned women and men, all in skimpy bathing suits, were nearby, cheering her on.

"Did she dive?" Sebastian asked.

"Look at the next shots."

The photographer caught her in mid jump. The next shot showed a sloppy, legs-bent entry as her head hit the water. "Holy hell. She's not a diving pro, but she did it anyway."

"You're admiring her dive and not that body?" Pete asked.

Sebastian chuckled. "Her body's incredible, but beautiful, rich young women with perfect figures aren't rare. Moxie is. Hell." He swiped back to the prior photo. He'd been on Westport yachts before. Rich people who paid Black Raven for protection needed security on all kinds of toys. "The yacht's at least 150 feet. It was like she was diving off the roof of a three or four story building. She's either got balls of steel or," he paused, "she's really stupid."

"That assessment is overly simplistic for her," Ragno said.

"Unfortunately for the man in the photo who is drooling over her," Pete said, "balls are one thing she doesn't have. His wife divorced him after those pictures made the tabloids. A few weeks later, Skye had the car accident in the Keys."

Sebastian scanned reports of the car accident as Ragno continued, "As she and Spring were recovering from the accident, their father was indicted for the offense that led him to prison. In the year after the car accident, before disappearing into the life of Chloe Stewart, Skye kept a low profile. The remaining photographs, taken before she changed her ID, are tamer."

In the next photo, Richard Barrows and his two daughters were walking across a rooftop helipad to a waiting helicopter, the Manhattan skyline visible in the background. Pete glanced at the iPad, then back at the road. "There, Skye is looking at the camera. There's a strong resemblance between the sisters, except Spring has blue eyes, like her father, and looks, well," he shrugged. "Girlish, almost. Skinnier. Not as curvy. Younger than her age. Their hair is black now."

Skye had gray-green eyes, high cheekbones, and full lips. She was pretty. Gorgeous, even, with alluring planes and angles in her square jaw and high cheekbones. Her form-fitting slim skirt, wrap sweater, and high heels showcased a body too curvy for super-model status, but in the real world, it was hell-yes-perfect. Too bad she wasn't his type, and that had nothing to do with her status as Barrows' daughter, which made her doubly not his type, because Sebastian didn't mix work with anything but work.

Ragno said, "Medical records indicate Spring was tested multiple times for autism spectrum disorder and Asperger's syndrome. I can't find conclusive diagnoses, perhaps because none exist. She seems to defy explanation, even for experts. She has a mix of psychological problems, learning deficits, and savant-like qualities. In contrast, Skye is brilliant, yet she's turned her back on her brilliance by not pursuing the type of work for which her mind is suited."

"How brilliant?" Sebastian asked.

"Like don't let the bikini photo fool you. MIT at fifteen," Ragno said. "Graduated with honors at nineteen. Teachers and professors indicate she has her father's brilliance. Problems in school were due to boredom and inconsistent focus."

"Smarter than you?"

She chuckled. "I'd love to find out. Anyway, their mother died when Skye was thirteen, right as Barrows hit it big with his software. Eleven years separate the sisters. Skye just turned twenty-nine. Spring is eighteen. Spring's mental challenges make Skye the one to talk to."

"We're three minutes away now," Pete said, hitting the blinker and braking for a turn.

"They're in day three of opening week of Creative Confections, which in a recent interview, Skye, um, Chloe," Ragno said, placing emphasis on the letter C, "described as a cake and coffee cottage. Chic and cozy, specializing in confectionary decorative arts."

"What the hell does that mean?"

Ragno chuckled. "Spring is an icing artist, with a unique flair for color. Every cupcake and cake is a work of art. She should have a reality show. The cakes and cupcakes, decorated by Spring, are the centerpiece of the business for now. Eventually, Skye plans to offer celebration planning services."

"Wait," Sebastian groaned. "Chloe. Colbie. Covington. Creative. Confections. Cakes. Cupcakes. Chic. Cozy. Can there be one more goddamn word starting with C?"

"Cynical? Cranky?" Ragno gave a low laugh. "Actually, the c's could be tied to obsessive compulsive disorder, a diagnosis that is constant for Spring. I think the c's are clever, cute, and catchy."

"Spare me the humor." He eyed Covington's quaint downtown as they stopped at a traffic light. It wasn't where he'd have expected a celebutante party-girl like Skye to settle, but nothing about Barrows or his escape made sense yet. In the distance, brake lights of a lone car flashed as it turned off the street. Although the sun had risen, there were no pedestrians, not even a jogger. His eyes followed Pete's gesture down the road, about a half a mile away, to a corner property where a wide, tree-filled lawn was surrounded by a white picket fence.

Pete said, "There it is."

"None of this is making any damn sense. If Skye is so damn brilliant, why didn't she pick up the pieces of her father's business? What the hell is she doing running a coffee shop?"

"Great questions," Ragno said. "My intel isn't giving me answers. Yet."

A large Creative Confections sign, readable even at a distance, stood on the corner of the property. Nestled in the center of the lawn was a white wood cottage with cream trim, tall, glistening windows lit from within and adorned with open shutters, a wide porch that had seating areas with white wicker tables and chairs. In the porch's far corner there was a swing with cushions. "There's a paper trail for the business? Permits? Tax I.D. numbers for federal and state?"

"Yes," Ragno said. "Chloe and Colbie Stewart are owners of a legitimate business. Their identities are solid and even include social security numbers. I'm impressed."

Tall pine trees and oak trees with thick, meandering branches surrounded the cottage. Clear lights sparkled in trees. Wisps of smoke escaped from chimneys that were on either side of the cottage. It was February, it was chilly, and in charming coffee houses in Louisiana, fireplaces would, of course, be lit. Sebastian couldn't imagine a more inviting setting, and if quaint towns were your thing and long mornings with a hot cup of coffee and a good newspaper, book, or friendly chitchat was appealing, Creative Confections looked like the jackpot. Sebastian didn't typically like small towns and he couldn't remember the last time he'd sat down for a cup of coffee. The quiet town and the homey-looking cottage looked like a planet that was different than the hard-edged world in which he lived. "Is it open?"

"No, it opens at seven. In ten minutes," Pete said. "Want me to park down the street?"

"Are they there?"

"Yes," Ragno said. "Just arrived."

"They park in back, a small driveway with a couple of parking spaces," Pete added. "The driveway entrance is on the side street. It's narrow. Not intended for traffic or customers."

"Park in front," Sebastian said. "The party's over for Chloe and Colbie Stewart. Time for them to be Skye and Spring Barrows again." Even without the oddness of living under an assumed identity, Skye was running a retail business, selling the sort of items people still purchased with cash. "Weapons?"

Pete accelerated as the light changed. "She keeps a laser-sighted .38 Special Smith & Wesson Centennial in her nightstand."

Sebastian knew the model. The snub-nosed revolver was a perfect fit for a woman's hand.

To Pete, Sebastian said, "You were in her house yesterday, while she was at the coffee shop, and the gun was at the house?" Pete nodded. "So there might be other weapons," Sebastian said, thinking it made sense she'd carry one to work. He watched a golden-brown, four-legged blur dart from the coffee shop lawn and run, without pause, into the road and head directly in front of them. "Brake. Now. Brake!"

Chapter Two

Tires screeched as Pete made a sharp left turn, coming close to the dog but missing by an inch or two. There was a hiss as the left front tire hit a culvert.

"What happened?" Ragno asked. "Camera views didn't reveal why evasive moves were necessary."

Sebastian opened the door and jumped out. "Near miss with a dog. We're fine," he said as he ran for the animal. "Not so sure about the dog."

The golden blob ran to the opposite side of the street from where the Range Rover was perched, half on the sidewalk, half in the street. The dog tucked itself under a bench, in front of an art gallery. Big brown eyes followed Sebastian as the dog trembled from tail to snout. It looked like a young golden retriever, somewhere less than full grown, a much-purer-bred version of the pound-variety, yellow lab-ish dog Sebastian had as a child. As he paused a few feet from the scared animal, he heard a distant, feminine yell.

Pete, at his side, said, "She's their dog. Name's Candy."

"Great," Sebastian said.

"Candy, Caannnndddyyyy."

"Fucking great," Sebastian muttered. "Killing their dog is one way to earn cooperation."

"I didn't hit her. I'm certain of it. And that's Spring, running in our direction, screaming for her."

"I've got this. Park the car. Change the tire."

Sebastian crouched to the ground, held out his hand, and, with the dog's large eyes focused on him, said, "Hey, Candy. Sweet girl. Let me see if you're hurt. Come on, baby. Come to me." She pointed her snout in his direction and sniffed. "Come to me, Candy," he said, using a nice, play-with-dog voice. The dog crawled towards him, tentatively at first. When she was out from under the bench, she stood. After a fluff-inducing shake, she took one step on a big paw, and two more steps, both of which looked normal. After three steps she paused, gave a slow tail wag, and walked another step in his direction.

"Candy," Sebastian said, prompting a faster tail wag. As the dog inched closer, he picked her up. "Are you a bit of a drama queen?" She was solid, with strong muscles and thick fur. He probed at her legs and ribs. No yelps, no squirming, no pain, he thought, as her moist tongue bathed his left cheek with swipe-kisses and an over-sized paw batted his right cheek. He chuckled as he dodged her licks. "You sure are cute, you know that?"

"She's okay?" Ragno asked.

"Seems to be," he said, as he turned towards the coffee shop and realized why the owner hadn't made it to the dog's rescue. She'd fallen, facedown on the lawn.

As he crossed the street, he watched Spring attempt to stand. She sat instead, gripped her ankle, and yelled, "Candy. Cannndddyyyyy."

Skye was running from the porch, towards Spring, and an older man and a woman were coming out of the coffee shop, moving slower. The dog squirmed in his arms, but Sebastian kept a tight grip on her, not wanting to release her until he was sure Spring wasn't hurt and could handle what he guessed would be a lively reunion with thirty pounds of dog. Sebastian and Skye reached Spring at the same time.

Skye was prettier in person than in photographs. Black, free-flowing waves of hair added an exotic touch to high cheekbones and almond-shaped eyes that were the color of flagstone. The photographs hadn't captured the restlessness he saw in her gray-green eyes, as Skye's gaze travelled over the dog, Sebastian, and her sister. Nor had the pictures captured the deep, inner light of her eyes, as subtle as the warm glow of a gas lantern on a dark, foggy night. His mind flashed to the pictures of her almost naked body as she readied for the dive, and his gaze dipped to her bosom. He dragged his eyes up, mentally shaking off thoughts of her full, round breasts.

She narrowed her eyes as she looked at him, and he didn't blame her for looking at him as though he was odd, because he was staring, and *son of a bitch*, he couldn't stop.

What in the fucking hell is wrong with me?

Thankfully, Skye's attention turned to Spring, and she bent to help her sister stand.

"I'm sorry," Sebastian said, finally finding his voice. "We came close, but we didn't hit her. She seems to have gotten over the scare." To Spring, he said, "Are you hurt?"

Ragno had said mentally challenged. To Sebastian, with her large, denim-blue eyes, and long black hair that, like her sister's, hung loose and mid-way down her back, Spring just looked like a pretty teenager. The sweet look in her eyes made her seem young for her age. They were both tall, but Skye was taller. The top of Skye's head was almost shoulder height to him, which put her at about five feet eight.

Skye was all woman, sensual and vibrant, yet reserved. Spring was almost a mirror image, but girlish. They were dressed in matching cream-colored wrap sweaters and skinny jeans, off-white leather belts with large silver buckles, and off-white suede cowboy boots. Ragno had said that Skye wore a phone tucked inside her waistband. It wasn't there now. The wide leather belt hit right above her hipbones and accentuated her small waist. Spring's winter-white jeans had grass stains and a tear in one of the knees.

Skye's attention was also on her sister. In a soft, calm voice, one that could guide anyone through any hell, Skye said, "Colbie, take a few steps and test that ankle."

Spring didn't move. Instead, she gave Sebastian a shy smile and extended her arms outwards, for the dog. Sebastian glanced at Skye, uncertain whether to give the animal to the girl. In the photographs, Skye had been a beautiful blonde. Darker hair, though, made her stunning. The inky blackness of her hair, which hung loose and free to a few inches past her shoulders, contrasted with clear, ivory skin. Her cheeks were flushed. She seemed to be holding her breath, gauging her sister's reaction. Skye glanced at him and gave him a slow nod. Sebastian stepped forward.

"Are you sure you're not hurt? She's heavy. I could just put her on the ground."

"She's mine." There was that shy, wide-eyed smile, again, and this time it was accompanied with a firm headshake. "Of course I can handle her."

Not exactly a logical response, but Sebastian placed the wriggling dog into Spring's arms anyway. Spring giggled as the dog licked her face and, over Skye's shoulder, Sebastian watched the older couple retreat back into the coffee shop. When Skye leveled her gaze on Sebastian, he wished he could get that damn topless-bikini picture out of his mind. Her gaze was direct, but there was nothing forthcoming about it. Unlike in the partying shots he had looked at earlier, her eyes were guarded. Her full smile—the one that had been his focal point in the photographs—was absent, yet her lips naturally turned up at the corners, giving her face an inviting expression. "Thank you for returning Candy to us."

"He's a really nice guy, Chloe," Spring said, "He saved Candy."

"I know," Skye gave her sister a solid gaze. "Now you're fine, and so is Candy, so we can just go back inside and make our delivery, right?"

Spring shook her head. "I have to change. My jeans are ripped."

"How is your ankle?" Skye asked.

Spring took a tentative step. She gave her sister a thumbs up that was almost concealed by dog hair. "Doesn't hurt much."

Skye drew a deep breath. "Well, we have to hurry. We promised the bank that the cake would be there early."

"At nine," Spring said.

"I told you. They called and want it for eight."

"Well, they can't have it at eight. I need to double check my work."

"You did that last night," Skye said, with a trace of impatience that anyone less observant than Sebastian would have missed.

"It doesn't matter. It's my first really big cake here and it has to be perfect. You said I could double check each petal."

"Well," Skye glanced at her watch, "make it fast. Go inside now, don't let Candy run away from you, get changed, and do your double check."

Spring didn't listen to her sister. Instead, she turned to Sebastian, cocking her head to the side as she studied him. Skye sighed as she also refocused her attention on Sebastian. Something in that sigh of exasperation, in the way her eyes seemed just a little weary, made his stomach twist. He understood that feeling.

Whatever vulnerability caused her weariness to peek through her on-guard glance at him disappeared fast, though, as she held his eyes for a second longer, and said, "I heard the tires screech. I know that you guys," she glanced back at the SUV, where Pete was changing the tire, "did some crafty driving to avoid her. I apologize. I should have noticed she was outside."

"No apology is necessary."

"Yes. It is. Candy shouldn't be running in the street. We're training her, but," she shook her head, "obviously, we need to do a better job. Thank you," she said, as she took a step away from him.

"Wait. I need to-"

"We're testing morning muffins today, with samples for all of the customers." Spring, who was still holding onto the dog, interrupted him, "You should come in and try them."

"Colbie," Skye said, taking three steps further away from him, then pausing because her sister wasn't moving. "We have to go."

"And I also have to go," Sebastian said, "but-"

"Please, please come in," Spring said, interrupting him just as he was going to say that he didn't have time to linger, that he was there to talk about their father. Spring was happily oblivious to both her sister's frustration and his need to do something other than taste muffins. "You see, we're testing three different recipes, and you can help us. Carrot-walnut-cinnamon, banana-caramel-nut, and peanut-butter apple."

She was giving him such a wide-eyed, happy and hopeful look, he wasn't sure how to say no. Perhaps no wasn't what his answer should be. After all, he was there to talk. He shouldn't turn away from an opportunity to do so. Besides, he didn't think direct questions were going to give him what he needed with this one or her sister.

Spring continued, "The morning muffins have either buttercream icing or cream-cheese icing, and some have crumbles. We went a little lower in sugar than with our regular cupcakes, so they're healthier, but they still taste really good." She gave him a full smile. "At least we think so. If you'd like, you can try all of them and let us know which one you think is best. I know that you'll love at least one of them, and we want to know which is your favorite. Will you? Please?"

Despite the hard-edged impatience that snaked through his gut, Sebastian knew that *where the hell is your father'* was not the correct answer to the hopelessly sweet young woman. *Hell.* He wasn't here to make friends. He was there to manhandle information out of them, and he didn't have time to soft-shoe around it. At a minimum, he was going to let them know that their identity was no longer secret. But Spring's innocent blue-eyes made him pause long enough to wonder about the best way to deliver that information, because straightforward delivery wasn't going to work.

There weren't many things that made him hesitate when he knew that he was on the right track. Innocence, though, in any form, got to him, and even though she was a young woman, Spring's eyes were those of a child. Dammit. He had to talk to the older sister, and he had to do it alone.

When his eyes slid to Skye, he caught her in mid-breath of exasperation as she watched her sister. "Colbie. Go inside. Now."

Spring ignored her sister. To Sebastian, she said, "Aren't you coming in?"

Skye met his gaze, eyes as guarded as her sister's were guileless. She gave him a resigned glance and a half-smile that seemed more than a little forced. It absolutely wasn't the same smile that he'd seen in the pictures that Ragno had just given him. This woman was stressed out about something, and if it had anything to do with her father, he needed to find out. "My sister doesn't always turn on the charm so much to strangers. If you have time, come in and try the muffins."

Sebastian's business didn't require coffee and muffins, but Skye didn't wait for an answer. Instead, she took Candy out of her sister's arms, avoided a lick across the face as she gently placed the dog on the ground, and guided both the dog and her sister into the coffee house.

Aw hell. Fuck me to hell, Sebastian thought, as he followed them in the direction of their picture-perfect, white-on-creamy-white coffee house. He stepped on the porch, while Spring held open the door. Aromas of cinnamon, vanilla, and baked apple greeted him.

At the threshold he glanced back at the street. The Range Rover was on a jack, and Pete was unscrewing a lug nut. For a second, Sebastian wished that he were the one changing the tire. Trendy coffee houses normally seemed stuffy, overcrowded, and pretentious. Yet this one, painted in shades of white and cream, had high ceilings that gave it a spacious feel. Two seating areas, with tables and chairs, bordered a wide aisle that led to the counter. Overstuffed chairs faced large marble fireplaces that were on either side of the cottage. Ottomans and lamps made the place look homey and inviting.

"Sarah will get you anything that you'd like," Skye said, glancing at the trim gray-haired lady who'd been on the porch as he delivered the dog. Sarah was behind the counter, above which a large chalkboard hung. Neat, handwritten block letters provided a myriad of coffee offerings, all of which seemed too complicated for his taste. Skye turned to Spring and pointed to circular stairs in the back corner. "Better get cleaned up before the delivery."

"Sarah," Spring called out before disappearing up the stairs. "Give him one of each of the morning muffins. He's doing a taste test."

Sarah gave him a nod as he walked towards the counter. "Muffins," she said, with a pleasant smile, "and what kind of coffee?"

"Double shot of espresso with a splash of cream."

"Take a seat," she smiled. "I'll bring it to you."

Sebastian would rather stand. He wasn't there to socialize. Ask a few questions, get the necessary answers, and get the hell out of Mayberry. That had been the plan.

Instead he was stuck in an unfamiliar world, where gleaming glass cases displayed neat rows of muffins, decorated in a riot of color that made his eyes linger. An open kitchen with stainless steel appliances and large ovens was in the back of the counter. The man who had been on the porch with Sarah was there, pouring batter into pans. To the side of the kitchen was a hallway, a back door, and on the opposite side of the hallway, another room, with a large glass window that looked out on the coffee shop. He walked to the window. On a table sat a three-tier cake and what looked like clusters of turquoise-colored berries nestled in orange leaves. A vase of flowers stood—he presumed for inspiration—on the counter near the side of the cake. Sebastian wondered idly if the younger sister might be colorblind.

He made his way into one of the seating areas and sank into an overstuffed chair near the fireplace. It was angled so he had a view of the stairs and the business counter. He almost sighed, as it conformed to his body. Random chairs normally didn't fit his tall frame so well. He accepted the espresso from Sarah, along with a plate of still-warm muffins. "Thank you."

She smiled and pointed to one of the muffins. "My vote is for this one, the apple."

His appetite, like other basic necessities of life, had been nonexistent since July. Lack of an appetite didn't keep him from eating, though. Food was fuel, and he needed plenty of it to stay at his optimum weight, somewhere right above two hundred and ten. After July, he had learned to graze all day, even when he wasn't hungry. Now his mouth watered and his stomach grumbled, as he inhaled the aromas of baked goods and fresh coffee. He bit into the apple-peanut-butter muffin, tasting sweet bits of apple, salty nuttiness, and brown-sugar crumble. As he wondered how apples and peanuts could blend to taste so damn good, Ragno's voice grounded him. "Have you selected a favorite?"

He chuckled as he watched the sisters descend the stairs. Spring now wore a pair of blue jeans, but otherwise, her outfit remained the same.

Skye went behind the counter, while Spring went into the room with the cake. *Good*, he thought. With the sisters separated, he could talk to Skye without interruption. Before he could stand, three customers walked into the coffee shop and headed to the counter, where Skye had joined Sarah. Dammit. His opportunity to talk to her alone had, for the moment, disappeared.

"Ragno," he said, keeping his voice low as he watched Skye talk to the customers and waited for the customers to leave the counter. "Has there been any contact between the daughters and Barrows' lawyer?"

"None," Ragno said, "but she called Black Raven yesterday evening to see if we had managed to locate Skye and Spring."

Sebastian had been present at the interview of Jennifer Root, the lawyer for Barrows. They had interviewed her within the first twenty-four hours of her client's jailbreak, at her office. She had a reputation as a hard-ass lawyer, who'd made a name by pursuing, and winning, high-stakes copyright infringement actions on behalf of BY Technologies, Barrows' company. Root also had been Barrows' defense attorney, when he had pleaded guilty. She had called in criminal defense experts, but she'd taken the lead with the government in negotiations for the plea deal.

In the interview, Root had claimed to be unaware of Barrows' escape. News of the escape hadn't hit the airwaves, and the only way she would have figured it out was from someone with the government, Black Raven, or Barrows himself. She had seemed believable.

Root had assured the marshals and Sebastian she hadn't heard from her client since the conviction, but she did say she was worried about Barrows' daughters. Root couldn't—or wouldn't—tell them where the two women were. She professed to have no idea, shrugging off the secrecy as due to Barrows' paranoia. The interview had left Sebastian unsettled, for reasons he couldn't explain. He'd requested Ragno start a Black Raven-style profile on her, and Ragno's team of analysts was now on the task.

"Minero is holding for you," Ragno said, interrupting his thoughts just as Skye handed a cup of coffee to the last person in the line. He had to take the call. Anthony Minero was the lead U.S. Marshal in charge of the manhunt. So far, the marshals thought Sebastian's trip to Covington was a waste of time. That's why Sebastian didn't have a marshal with him. From Sebastian's perspective, the biggest mistake the marshals had made so far was not immediately grasping how difficult it was going to be to find Barrows. It was also why the marshals had dragged their heels on putting together a cyber-felon-manhunt team of FBI agents and marshals.

Despite what Minero thought, Sebastian's gut told him Barrows' daughters were worth pursuing, and that's why he was sitting in their coffee house eating muffins. There was one giant, nagging problem with trusting his gut, and Sebastian knew it. In the past year, his gut instincts hadn't always been accurate, and right now, even though he was following his instinctive hunch, he certainly wasn't on the fast train to an answer for the question of the day.

"Put him through."

"Holt's at the jail, not giving us a damn thing on Biondo or Barrows," Minero said. "We're getting more leads from other sources on Biondo. We have nothing on Barrows. Have you made contact with his daughters?"

"I just arrived."

"Anything?"

"Not yet," Sebastian answered. "Haven't managed to have that conversation."

"Media's getting close," Minero said. "A local paper called the warden a few minutes ago, seeking confirmation on a possible escape. We think a prison employee leaked the info to the media."

Rubbing the pain at his temples with his free hand, Sebastian muttered a curse. The press getting a hold of this clusterfuck would make retrieving the remaining two prisoners that much harder. It would also diminish the likelihood of Black Raven getting more government jobs. Worse, Black Raven would be painted as incompetent.

The other six prisoners hadn't been noteworthy. On the other hand, Barrows' escape was going to be front-page news for days. If Black Raven was publicly tagged for Barrows' escape, their reputation would be pulverized. His company was going to be ridiculed for letting the paranoid genius walk out of prison. And this was just one of his current problems, but he didn't allow himself to think of the other disaster he was facing.

Minero continued, "We might have twenty-four hours before news of the prison break becomes public, but I doubt if we have that long. A few senators are getting nervous."

No shit, Sebastian thought, keeping his earlier conversations with various senators to himself. He had no plans to share with the marshals the identities of the power holders in Washington who were friendly to Black Raven.

"They're thinking it might be wise to release official reports before the media distorts the story," Minero added. "Damage control. Earlier, rather than later. By tonight."

"Thanks for the heads up."

"I'm rethinking my strategy with the daughters. I'm sending a team to Covington. We need to talk to them."

"Not a problem," Sebastian said, biting back the impulse to say, *I told you they were important.* "Do what you need to do."

"Also, my cyber-team is attempting a forensic analysis of any chatter involving Barrows prior to his imprisonment," Minero informed him. "The problem is, his internet activity was encrypted in a manner that's challenging, to say the least. We're having problems breaking through. I know your people are a couple of steps ahead of us. If we were operating from integrated systems-"

"No." Sebastian interrupted, his eyes on Skye. She glanced in his direction, but turned when Sarah said something to her. Together, they focused on the espresso machine. "Not an option." No one accessed Black Raven's systems, just as no one without clearance ever walked into the company's Denver-based headquarters. Black Raven did not allow integration, from anyone, anytime. Period.

He and Minero had become acquainted for the first time four days ago in the immediate hours after the jailbreak. Black Raven's contract didn't provide for this contingency, a what-to-do-in-case-of-jailbreak plan. Because Minero was the head Deputy Marshal in charge, Sebastian guessed that, technically, Black Raven was working for Minero. He didn't care much about official lines of authority. His job was to get the prisoners back into custody, and that was also Minero's job. So far, Sebastian liked the guy. The Deputy Marshal had made fast, cool decisions with the considerable manpower that he had at his disposal.

Minero was a great tracker of escaped prisoners, and this wasn't the first federal prison break where he'd taken the lead. Federal inmates could be drug distributors, felons who possessed a weapon, a bank robber, an illegal immigrant with a laundry list of prior felonies, men who loved internet kiddie porn, wayward politicians, or fraud conspirators. There weren't many prisoners like Barrows, though, because the man was one of a kind. He was a computer genius, who, if given computer access, could manipulate security systems and walk the hell out. What had the man been doing before walking out of prison? Sitting at a goddamn computer with internet access, which the Bureau of Prisons, in their infinite lack of wisdom, had provided in the legal library, for fuck's sake.

"I'll send you one of our best men for your cyber-team," Sebastian offered. "He can liaise between my people and yours." *And let me know if you guys find anything that I don't.*

"I'll take him."

Sebastian didn't like the near-desperation that he heard in Minero's voice. Desperate men made bad decisions, and desperation was contagious. *Hell.* Minero's superiors were probably breathing down his neck, hard. He too had crappy repercussions if he didn't get the prisoners back where they belonged before their escape became a media circus. "Name's Zeus. He'll be knocking on their door in two hours."

"What kind of name is that?"

Sebastian chuckled. "A damn good one." It wasn't the man's name at all, but Minero didn't need to know that. Zeus was the anglo-style nickname Sebastian and other Black Raven agents had given to Jesus Hernandez. The name Zeus fit the large, quiet man, who had as much brain as his ample brawn. Sebastian regarded him as an intellectual powerhouse, a partner who provided solid, reliable advice. He was also a friend Sebastian trusted without question.

"How does Zeus know where to go? I haven't told you where they are," Minero said.

Ragno chuckled, but Minero couldn't hear her. Ragno muted her line when Sebastian had callers, unless the call was intended as a conference call. Unless he disconnected her, she was always there. It saved filling her in later.

"My people figured out your location around midnight, we're in your system, and we're following them," Sebastian said. "I figured Black Raven might benefit from your research. So far, your cyber-team is stumbling in the Dark Ages."

"Son of a bitch," Minero muttered. "I'll call you back in a few and let you know logistics on when my team will arrive in Covington."

"Before you go, have you made progress on unsealing the Barrows transcripts?" Sebastian asked, sinking further into the comfortable chair. Barrows had been thoroughly debriefed by the FBI in connection with his offense. Usually, sealed court documents weren't an obstacle for Black Raven. Barrows was a special case, though. None of his records were in the federal court's public access databases, and Ragno's team couldn't break into the sealed electronic records. It seemed that the government never wanted his rants to see the light of day and, four days post prison break, Sebastian was damn tired of asking for them.

"We should have access this morning. I secured clearance. Now we're just waiting on the word to travel through the chain of command," Minero said. "Not sure I understand why the transcripts are such a high priority for you."

Sebastian swallowed back his exasperation, as he listened to the same thing Minero had been saying for two days. The marshals had been reactionary throughout the entire manhunt. Reactionary wasn't how Black Raven operated. "We need to understand the man to know where he might be. To understand the man, we want to see what he had to say. About anything and everything."

He almost added that it wasn't rocket science, then thought better of it. Instead, he bit into the carrot-walnut-cinnamon muffin, softly chewing on carrot shreds and crunchy walnuts. Ragno was used to hearing him eat. He didn't care whether Minero heard him chewing. The muffin was too good not to eat.

"Court personnel informed me that there are thousands of pages," Minero said. "It seems like once Barrows had an audience of FBI agents and IRS investigators, he wouldn't shut the hell up."

"Volume isn't a problem for us."

"Well, good, because I don't have the manpower to make sense of his rants or to search thousands of pages for clues. The summary in the public record is enough for me. At one time, the man was brilliant. Damn shame he couldn't focus on something good. Also a damn shame he became obsessed with surveillance technology and its Fourth Amendment implications. What a waste."

Sebastian was actually looking forward to seeing the transcripts and, one day when he had time, if that ever happened, reading what the brilliant scientist had to say about the Fourth Amendment. The constitutional right protected by the amendment—freedom from unreasonable searches and seizures—was a concept that meant something far different in the digital age than when the country's forefathers drafted the amendment. In law school, he'd found Fourth Amendment jurisprudence fascinating, and he continued to study it.

Minero added, "Paranoia does strange things to brilliance."

Sebastian didn't need or want Minero's opinion. He wanted the data to form his own. "The transcripts are in electronic files, correct?"

"Yes."

"The minute they're released, send them to Ragno."

"Will do."

"We'll see how quickly we get those transcripts," Ragno said, her tone indicating she wasn't expecting great speed, as Minero ended the call. "We've been asking, and no one is giving. Senator McCollum's office called while you were on the line with Minero. He wants to talk to you ASAP."

Robert McCollum, the senior senator from Texas, was the Chairman of the Bureau of Prisons Committee, a joint committee comprised of various senators and representatives. The committee had handled the bidding process through which Black Raven had been hired for the multi-million dollar contract for upgrading security systems at multiple federal prisons.

Pete, who was also mic'd to Sebastian, said, "Two local cops are walking in."

"Thanks for the heads up. Ragno, call McCollum's office back," Sebastian said, glancing at his right hip and making sure his leather jacket was concealing his Glock. The two officers walked into the coffee shop. Early thirties. Fit. Uniform blues. Glocks holstered at their hips. Mace. Stun guns. Ray-Ban Aviator sunglasses were on, and weren't removed until they got to the counter. He didn't need to worry about them noticing him, because their eyes were only for Skye. He didn't blame them. If he were a local cop, she'd be on his radar every morning. She welcomed them with a slight smile, one that wasn't anything like the radiant smile in the photographs he'd seen earlier.

As two more people walked in behind them, her not-quite-full smile faltered. Not exactly what he'd expect of an owner of a brand new business. Interesting. He could tell she wasn't happy to see the line at the counter. He wasn't either. He hadn't flown across the fucking country so he could sit in a coffee shop, watch Skye Barrows pretend to be Chloe-the-barista, think about her in a topless bikini with her arms extended to a clear-blue sky, figure out nothing about where Barrows might be, and have telephone conversations that weren't bringing him any closer to an answer for the goddamn question of the day.

Ragno said, "Senator McCollum is on the line."

"Status?" McCollum asked. His curt question was a testament to the hard-ass truism that there was no need to say good morning when there was nothing good about it. Sebastian couldn't agree more.

"Same as eleven last night when I last spoke to you."

"Son of a bitch, Connelly. Find Barrows, get his ass back in jail, and do it ASAP. The others on the committee are pushing me to go public with the full circumstances of the jailbreak. I'm doing my best to keep the story under wraps, but it's getting harder."

"I'd appreciate a bit more time before this hits the media outlets," Sebastian said. "Front page news will only turn this into a circus."

"I'm trying. Embarrassment runs deep, though." McCollum didn't have to explain to Sebastian the reasons why, as the fuck-up had occurred under the largest outsourcing contract the Bureau of Prisons had ever executed for jail security. "I had a few allies on this outsourcing effort, but they're now forgetting they were in my corner. The ones who weren't in my corner from the beginning are gloating, chomping at the bit for a chance to throw egg in my face. It's an election year. I have stiff competition. I can't be tagged as the senator who allowed Richard Barrows to walk out of prison. I don't want this blemish on my career. I also can't afford to look like I'm covering up a story. I'm holding them off, but I don't know how much longer I can give you. Understand?"

"Got it," he said. He'd worked with McCollum before, on security missions for the man's oil interests and also on governmental matters. The man was a lifelong, powerful politician, but he'd always shot straight with Sebastian. "Thanks for the warning. Senator, minor issue. I know you made a call the other day on Barrows' debriefing transcripts."

"Two days ago."

"Can you make that call again? Seems like some clerk somewhere isn't getting the message."

"Goddamn bureaucracy. Will do." McCollum ended the call.

Sebastian appreciated the heads up on the media, because no matter how the story was made public, all fingers would point at Black Raven. Even fingers belonging to many of Black Raven's allies, like Senator McCollum. Until the jailbreak, Black Raven had held the lucrative contract to design and provide automated security systems at twenty federal prisons. No matter what happened, that contract was going to be yanked, and, depending on the political fall out, Black Raven could lose many other government contracts.

He watched Skye hand the cops their coffee. One of them looked at her, let his hand linger on hers as she passed the coffee to him, and then said, loud enough for Sebastian to hear, "Everything okay?"

She froze for a second, before her face transformed with the beautiful smile Sebastian had seen in the photographs. "Yes," she said, "fine. Just busy, and trying to get Spring to let go of her first cake. I'll see you guys tomorrow morning?"

He said, "Yes. Same time."

As soon as the cops turned away, her smile faded. She was faking that smile, and Sebastian wanted to know why. He also wondered what the hell was going on between Skye and the cop. He almost choked with that thought. Damn. Her attractiveness was fucking with his head and that was...weird. He never let attractive women get to him in that way and made it a practice not to be distracted by beauty while on the job.

He stood and approached the counter, as the local cops left. Chloe Stewart was about to become Skye Barrows, and, if she knew anything at all about where her father might be, Sebastian was going to make damn sure she told him what she knew.

Chapter Three

Cataclysm. Now. Run.

Skye now hoped to be out the door of the bakery at 7:45, which was fifteen minutes later than the departure time she had planned once she received the message, but given that their dog had almost gotten herself killed, a fifteen-minute deviation from the schedule wasn't too bad.

Candy was snoozing on the dog bed in the upstairs office, Spring was making sure her cake was perfect, and Skye had guessed that the tall man with the serious, steady gaze wasn't interested in coffee, muffins, or the ambiance of Creative Confections. The driver of the SUV hadn't come in, even though she could see through the glass panes of the front door that the tire was changed. Mr. Blue Eyes had eaten two of the three muffins that Sarah had given him and taken a bite out of the third. He talked low. His gaze took in his surroundings, the customers, and her. She couldn't make out what he was saying, and, although no cell phone was apparent, she guessed that he was on the phone, because he didn't seem like the crazy type who would talk to himself.

Suddenly, his eyes were on her. His square jaw was set, and as the policemen left, he approached the counter with a steady stride.

"I need to talk to you." His deep, rich voice was a fit for his large stature and broad shoulders.

Her heart skipped several beats as she absorbed his steady gaze and his somber, dead-serious tone.

No. Not today. She had to run.

When she glanced into his eyes, silently questioning why this man would need to talk to her, and wondering whether she misheard him, he smiled.

Skye had sworn off men two years earlier, just like she'd sworn off so many other things. At first, abstinence had been easy. Now it was damn hard, and she was finally going crazy from it, because this man's smile was charming and unexpected and made her aware of exactly how long she'd gone without sex.

Even though his face was lean, with slight hollows beneath his high cheekbones, when he smiled deeply, really deeply, dimples appeared in both cheeks. Full lips, with a slight turn-up that made the left side slightly higher than the right, riveted her attention. Clean-shaven, his skin was vibrant, with olive undertones. He lifted his right hand and pressed his right temple, for just a second. His dark brown hair, with a little blonde, was clipped short along the sides and longer on top. He arched an eyebrow as he gazed at her, as if his mere words should have galvanized her into action.

"We need to talk. Privately."

He had the kind of hairstyle that could be smoothed back and look sophisticated, but this morning he hadn't gone for the polished look. A few pieces fell over his forehead. He captured the wayward strands with his fingers and pushed them back as he returned her stare.

With his action, fear jolted her body. When he had lifted his arm to smooth his hair, his loose-fitting black leather jacket rose with it. After noticing that his close-fitting, simply tailored white button-down shirt revealed a broad chest and a tapered waist, her gaze screeched to a halt on the weapon that was holstered at his waist. Coinciding with his insistence that they talk privately, she realized that his preening was more about revealing the gun than an attempt to straighten his tousled hair.

He had inspired a deep ache for good sex, but that was something she was used to doing without. Danger was not something that she was interested in experiencing. She looked for a way to stall, forced a pleasant-yet-slightly-confused expression on her face, and said, "Excuse me?"

"You don't want to have this conversation out here," he said, as two yoga-clothed women made their way to the coffee counter. They waved at another woman, who had snared a seating area near the left fireplace. Skye nodded hello to the two friends, who, in day three of the business, like the cops who had just left, had become regulars. They didn't seem to notice her. Instead, they were focused on the tall man, whose attention was focused on her.

No shit. She didn't want to have a conversation with him anywhere. And she certainly didn't want to be alone with him.

Even in broad daylight. Every instinct screamed at her to grab her sister and run like hell.

"I didn't catch your name," Skye said, keeping her tone cool. They hadn't introduced themselves. She had wondered about his name after she had gotten Spring upstairs. If he had said it, she'd have remembered it. She remembered almost everything, even things she preferred to forget.

"Sebastian," he said. "Sebastian Connelly."

"I'm Chloe Stewart," she said, "and we can talk right here."

He frowned. He gave her a slight headshake. "Try again. This time with the name you were born with."

Now he had her attention. His words, coupled with the weapon that was holstered at his hip, jolted her heart as her world shattered.

Run.

Was this why her father had sent the warning? *Him?* This Sebastian Connelly? Who the hell was he, and what did he want? Was he the reason the cataclysm scenario was in play? No matter what it was, Skye knew instinctually she shouldn't hang around to find out. Oh God, she had to get away from there.

She drew a deep, deep breath. This couldn't be happening now. She needed fresh air, so she could think. But there was no time to step outside as the walls started to close in on her. She drew another deep breath and slowed her thoughts, pushing aside her blossoming claustrophobia before it choked her. She focused on the three simple words her father had drilled into her, the reason why she and Spring were in hiding.

Trust no one. No one.

Trust no one.

No one with the government. No one with law enforcement. No one from your past, and no one from your future.

Trust no one, and that included gorgeous men who carried runaway puppies across the street and were gentle and patient with Spring, when he was the type of guy who didn't seem like he had the time to pause. Maybe Mr. Blue Eyes was guessing. When in doubt, she had taught herself, say nothing. She stared into his eyes without flinching, wondering, *why him? Why now?*

"I'm here to talk about your father," he added, despite her silence, "and I need to do it now."

"My father died three years ago." Skye said the words that

she had practiced. The lie came easily, without thought.

Sebastian's eyes hardened. As the remnants of his charming smile disappeared, her father's words floated through time, and she could almost hear his voice, deep inside her brain.

Trust no one, and especially trust no one who knows you're my daughter.

"We both know that isn't true," Sebastian said, "and I don't have time for lies." He leaned over the display case until he was just inches from her. When he whispered, "Skye. Skye Barrows." His face was close enough that only she heard him. "You can talk to me in private right now or we can have this conversation in public right here."

His breath warmed her cheek, but his words sent chills down her spine. She hadn't heard her real name in over a year, and the fact that he was there within hours of activation of the cataclysm scenario couldn't be a coincidence.

Figure it out.

Her father's words, his voice, floated to her with the answer he'd given to every question she'd ever asked. Figure it out.

Her first instinct was to flee. She couldn't just charge out the back door, though, because she couldn't leave her sister behind. Her second instinct was to figure out exactly what he wanted and why. And if the answer wasn't good, which it probably wasn't, she was going to kill him. Then she was going to run like hell.

"Upstairs," Skye said, reaching under the register and into the cubby where she kept her purse. With a practiced, quick twist of her fingers, she unsnapped the interior compartment that hid her revolver, before grabbing the purse by the handles. She glanced into the icing room, saw that Spring was absorbed in adding yet more icing to the cake, and nodded to Sarah as an indication for her to take over.

Skye climbed the steps with Sebastian at her heels. Once at the top, she opened the door to the office with her right hand. Candy slipped past her and ran down the stairs. "After you," she said, dipping her left hand into her purse and gripping the revolver. As Connelly turned to her and folded his arms, she shut the door with her right hand.

Trust no one.

Especially not an armed man who knew that she was her father's daughter. With her left hand she tightened her grip on the revolver and let her purse fall to the floor. Raising her weapon, she used her middle finger to press the button on the grip that triggered the laser sight and aimed the red light between his eyes.

Breathe. Just breathe, she told herself, as she focused on the man, who had now become a target, because he was standing in the way of what she needed to do. She needed to run. "Raise your hands."

Sebastian eyed the weapon, jaw clenched. "Lower it."

She shook her head. "Not until I know who you are and what you want. Raise your hands."

Eyes flat and tense, he raised his hands to his shoulders, palms facing her. His eyes bounced from the gun to her eyes.

"Why are you here?"

"I told you. I'm looking for your father."

"Whom do you work for?"

"Black Raven Private Security Contractors. I'm working with the United States Marshals Service. We're looking for your father. Lower the damn gun."

"Show me identification," she said. Hell. She'd made a rookie mistake, because he couldn't show her I.D. with his hands in the air.

"In the top pocket of my jacket."

"I'm not falling for that," she said, knowing she shouldn't be the one to reach for his identification.

His eyes had moved away from the weapon. He was studying her hands, her stance, and her face. She used both hands to hold the revolver and aim, hoping that he didn't notice that her hands were shaking. The gun weighed just over fifteen ounces, but it felt heavier than it had in her practice sessions.

"Is this the first time you've ever pointed a gun at a person?"

"There's a first for everything. It will be the first time I kill someone, but keep talking, and I'll do it. Shut up and get your identification," Skye said, willing her hands to stop shaking. "And keep your hands slow and steady while you do it." *Oh dear God*, she thought. What if he had another gun in a shoulder holster? "D-Don't reach for your weapon."

Skye kept her eyes trained on Sebastian. He reached into the front of his jacket with his right hand. She drew a breath, as he pulled out a black leather case and held it out. In the instant that she let go of the revolver with her right hand to reach for the credentials, he moved with a lightning-blur of speed, simultaneously grabbing the weapon out of her hand, swipe-kicking her legs out from under her, and immobilizing her in a full-body bear-hug, from which she had no hope of breaking free. Down was the only direction she could go.

***

When Sebastian swiped at Skye's knees with his left leg, she'd have fallen, hard, except he caught her on the way down. He fell with her to the floor, cushioned the impact with his body, and rolled over her. Impulsiveness was something Sebastian admired, but impulsiveness mixed with a handgun was just plain stupid.

The fall had stunned the breath from her body and gave him a few seconds where she was still. He took advantage of it by using his body weight to smash her to the floor, as he unloaded her weapon and pushed the rounds and gun out of arm's reach. She smelled of vanilla and cinnamon, and the soft mounds of her breasts pressing against his chest felt damn near perfect. When her stunned stillness wore off, her wriggling movement made him realize the sooner he got off of her, the better off he'd be.

Fuck.

He should have just used his gun on her. The cold muzzle of his Glock pressed against her forehead would have proven to her that she shouldn't pull a weapon without planning to use it, especially when she was hesitant and standing in striking distance of a man who could so clearly overpower her. He didn't point his weapon at anyone, though, unless he intended to use it.

Skye gasped for air beneath him and tried to knee him in the balls, but his knees were on her thighs, and his shins were pressing into hers. He didn't give her the option of moving her legs. She tried to scratch at his eyes, but his elbows were pressing into her arms, pinning them down, while he covered her mouth with his right hand. He had at least eight inches of height on her and outweighed her by at least seventy pounds. He put every centimeter and most of his extra pounds to good use, thankful that he regarded his body as a weapon and treated it as such, and thankful that he was several months past July, when he had almost checked-out on life. He was leaner than ever, but damn glad that he was back to his fighting strength. His friend, Brandon Morrissey, whose ass he had kicked a week earlier in a Krav Maga fight, was six feet four. Sebastian could handle Skye

Barrows with minimal exertion.

When Skye almost stopped struggling, Sebastian took his hand off of her mouth. "Get off of me," she hissed.

"I'll let you go," he said, "if you promise to be calm."

Skye tried to head-butt him with her forehead. "I said, get off of me."

"Calm down first," he said.

Sparks flew from her eyes. "I'm calm."

"Like hell."

"You're hurting me."

"That's the point." He ground his right elbow into the soft skin of her arm, and pressed more of his body weight into her. *Hell.* She was no longer a woman who had pointed a gun at him, no longer a person with information he needed. She was nothing but a gorgeous, fiery woman, and dammit, he was on top of her. His body reacted to her full, lush breasts and good God, she was a perfect fit under him. He grit his teeth, as his dormant-since-July libido returned with a mind-numbing rush.

"You should have thought that you might get hurt before you pointed your gun at me," he gritted out, fighting to regain control of himself.

Skye wasn't his type, he reminded himself, though the reasons why suddenly weren't so important, because his body was reacting as though it had found the perfect match. One part of his brain, thank God, reminded him that he'd never been the kind of man who got turned on by manhandling a woman, who so clearly wasn't enjoying it.

Fuck me to hell.

"I'll scream."

"Don't care," he said, "and screaming will only guarantee that anyone who comes to your rescue will know exactly who you are. Dammit. I said that I wanted to talk to you. I'm not here to hurt you, at least I wasn't, until you pulled your weapon out."

"You," she gasped for air, "you made sure that I saw yours."

"What?"

"Downstairs."

"What the hell are you talking about?" He hadn't shown his weapon to her. At least not intentionally, but he was used to working in situations where weapons were worn to be seen as a warning to stay the fuck away. Compared to some of the firepower that he typically strapped on himself, the Glock that he wore on this day was innocuous.

Dammit.

He never thought that he'd feel more comfortable in Middle Eastern war zones than in the United States, but there he fucking was, a foreigner in his own country and unintentionally scaring a woman with a weapon, when he needed her cooperation.

"I can't breathe," she gasped, "really."

He could breathe, though, and it sucked, because he inhaled her light perfume, or maybe it was just vanilla from all of those damn muffins they were baking, and it didn't matter what the scent was. It lit him up like a sixteen-year-old virgin, because she was long-limbed and lean, yet soft where it mattered, and thanks to that photo he even knew what her goddamn nipples looked like.

He could feel her heart beating beneath him. If he really liked a woman, and that hadn't happened in a long time, Sebastian loved to feel a woman's pulse points, loved to focus on her heartbeats as he made love to her. There was no focusing on the pulse of this heart, though, because Skye's labored breathing reminded him that she wasn't enjoying the moment, and her heart wasn't just beating, it was racing. Tiny beads of perspiration dotted her forehead, right at her hairline. To the extent that she was breathing, it was shallow and labored. Either she was putting on a damn good act, or he'd done enough to scare the hell out of her.

He lifted himself into plank position, with his weight on his forearms and toes. He kept her pinned, but stopped trying to press the breath out of her. The new position brought Sebastian some mental relief and allowed her to draw a few deep breaths. Plus, the space between them meant that he didn't have to worry she'd feel his hard on. He was thrilled at his erection, because he hadn't had one since July.

He doubted she'd have the same reaction.

"Now that I have your attention, Miss Barrows, like I said, I'm a private security contractor. I'm working with marshals who are looking for your father. And just so we're crystal clear, I know without doubt you are Richard Barrows' daughter and he didn't die three years ago, so ditch the pretense. Now," he said, his eyes locked on her, his face just three inches away from hers as he studied her, "where's your father, and don't waste time with bullshit."

"As far as I know, prison," she said with a narrow-eyed glare. Yes. She was pissed. But her anger didn't mask her fear. Follow that scent, he told himself, of vanilla-spiced sweet perspiration and scared-to-death fear. "Dumb-ass. You're a private security contractor? What does that mean?"

"My company is Black Raven. We're investigating-"

"Well, you need to do a bit more investigating-"

"Don't play stupid," he said, admiring her ability to be cocky when he had the upper hand. "Where is he?"

She gave him a puzzled, worried stare. "He's been incarcerated for a year. He has another year on his term. You aren't much of a private investigator if you don't know that."

He gave her a slow headshake. He liked women with a stubborn streak, who wouldn't cower when life hit hardballs at them, but this game had to end. "His remaining year grew to seven when he decided to escape four days ago."

She gasped. Wide, searching gray-green eyes studied him. He detected more than a little fear and a bucket load of surprise and, in that instant, he knew that she didn't know about the escape. *Hell.*

"Please," she said, her voice barely a whisper. "Let me up. Please."

Sebastian used one hand to do a somewhat haphazard frisk of areas of her body that he hadn't pressed against and bent to lift the left leg of her jeans. He thought he'd detected something there, and he was right. He pulled a retractable knife out of a shin holster, and tucked it into his jacket pocket. He rolled off of her, snagged her revolver, and put the rounds and the weapon in his pocket with her knife. He extended a hand to her, and she let him pull her up off the floor. Once up, she immediately sat down, hard, on the small sofa facing her desk.

"You can't keep my weapons," Skye said, drawing a deep breath. She looked worried, but not desperate. He wanted her desperate, so desperate that she'd tell him anything she knew. If she knew anything.

"I'll return them to you," he paused, "when I decide to."

"Now," she said. "I need my weapons-"

"When I decide, Skye."

"You can't-"

"Try stopping me."

Anger flushed her cheeks. She gave him a steely-eyed glare. "My father never would have escaped."

Sebastian walked around and stood in front of the couch. He towered above her, arms folded. Her dark hair was tousled, and her wrap sweater had loosened, showing cleavage and upper mounds of full breasts, that were encased in a creamy, lacy bra. She swallowed as she noticed where he was gazing. She narrowed her eyes as she re-tied her sweater. He shrugged off her glare. "You don't have to take my word for it," he said. "Call the marshals who are working the manhunt. Ask for Deputy Marshal Minero. I'll give you the number."

He saw more fear in her eyes. "The marshals know where I am?"

He nodded. "I know, so they know. The marshals and I are working together, Skye. Your cover's blown."

Her gaze flashed to a wall-mounted monitor that showed camera views of the front door, the cash register area, Spring's room where she decorated cakes, and the rear parking pad. Spring was in the back room, just as she had been a few minutes earlier, absorbed in her cake. The other views looked like everything was normal in the coffee house, yet Skye's hands shook.

He watched her breathe in deep, and breathe in again, without exhaling in between. "What are you so afraid of?"

Skye looked away from the monitor. Her eyes focused on him. Her shoulders and chest rose with another deep breath. She stood, squared her shoulders, and smoothed her hair. It was a great attempt at composure, and she found some, because when she spoke, her words were smooth. "My father pleaded guilty. He wanted to serve his time, and get out as soon as he could," she shook her head, "but he would not have escaped." She added, with conviction. "There's absolutely no way he escaped."

"He could have easily wrecked the prison's security system without leaving a trace." The Black Raven system had only been in the testing phase, he reminded himself. Still, it had been blocked, and he had no idea how.

"He wouldn't have done that," she said, with a solid head shake.

Great, he thought, *Skye Barrows would need to be persuaded about every damn thing.* "Trust me. He did. I need you to tell me where he is, or where he might be."

"You're not a very good listener," she said. "I didn't even know he escaped. How could I know where he is? "

"I'm listening," he said, "But let me tell you a few things. One, the lengths to which you've gone to conceal your identity is a giant red flag. Your alias is damn good. So good I find it suspicious, and I'm wondering if your father also has an alias that he stepped into when he left prison. If he does, I'd bet my last dollar that you know what it is. Two, if your father self-surrenders, and I mean soon, there may be leniency. Every minute, every hour that he's out, his term of imprisonment is growing longer. So if you want your father to have freedom again in this lifetime, it's time to talk."

Her lips were pursed, her hands were shaking, and she was breathing deeply. She lifted her right hand to her upper chest, straddling her neck with her thumb and index finger, tapping at her collarbone with her index finger. *Good*, he thought, interpreting the tapping gesture as nervousness, and glad that he was getting through to her. "Three, aiding a felon on the run is a serious crime, one for which you will do time. Any knowledge you have. Anything at all. If he's contacted you. Where he might be going. Now's the time to cough it up."

When she saw that he was watching her collarbone tap, she dropped her hand and folded her arms. "I have nothing for you."

"I don't believe you."

She shrugged. "Do I look like I care what you believe?"

"Spare me the smart ass comments. In case you're not understanding your predicament, here's where I do you a favor and spell out your new reality. You really need to care what I think, because I'm the nice guy. Got it? Cooperate with us-"

"Us?" She shook her head and gave him an eyebrow-arched look of skepticism. "I only see you."

"I'm working with the marshals, but there's quite a few differences between the marshals and me. For one, the marshals wouldn't hesitate to arrest you for pulling out a weapon and pointing it at them. You're lucky you got that out of your system on me. I don't give a damn what you do. All I care about is finding your father and throwing his ass back in jail. Cooperate with me, and maybe, just maybe, the marshals won't detain you for hours, or days, or however long it takes to find your father. Don't lie to us, because if you do, your problems won't end when we find him. I'm doing you a favor by explaining your biggest nightmare, which is if you're withholding one goddamn shred of anything, you're going to be charged with aiding an escaped federal prisoner and your ass is going to be sitting in a jail cell for years to come. With you and your father both sitting in prison, there'll be no one to take care of your sister. That's what you do, isn't it? Take care of her?"

"Is that a threat, Mr. Private Investigator?" Skye's words were laced with narrow-eyed distaste. She tried to walk around him, in the direction of the door. "Because if it is, you can just go to hell. You have no authority over me, and since I haven't heard from my father in months, you're wasting your time asking me anything."

He stepped in front of her, blocking her access to the door. "Well, you do have to talk to me." *Gorgeous*, he thought, but she was working him as hard as he was working her. "I'm acting as an agent of the government in this instance and, by the way, I'm a private security contractor," he said, "not a private investigator."

"Wow. Big man, big threats. I'll let a real agent of the government ask the questions. If the marshals come, I'll talk to them."

"There's no if. They are coming," he said.

"Whatever. I'll see when they get here."

"Dammit. Stop acting like talking is a choice and don't 'whatever' me."

Ragno said, her voice filling his ear, "Minero's on the line."

Sebastian was so absorbed in arguing with Skye he'd almost forgotten that he was basically tethered to Ragno. Holding Skye's gaze, wishing she didn't look so damn good with her hair loose and wild and her cheeks flushed with pink, he said, "Put him through."

Skye said, "Who? Through to where?"

Sebastian pointed to his ear. "Phone call."

She lifted her hand and pushed at his shoulder. "Well, take your phone call in your car as you're driving away. Jerk."

Ragno, privy to the entire conversation, chuckled, and said efficiently, "Here's Minero."

He was tempted to stand his ground, to see if she'd try pushing him again. A push-fest with Skye, though, wasn't something that would end well for either of them. He'd only end up getting aroused again, and she'd be even less likely to talk. He'd be no closer to an answer to the question of the day, and he'd have a hard-on that might never go away, unless he did something about it.

Fuck.

Suddenly feeling like a frustrated adolescent whose hormones made him ineffective at everything, Sebastian walked to the only exit from the small office. Turning his back to the closed door, he kept his eye on Skye as he effectively blocked her departure. For the moment she was still, standing between the couch and the desk. At least she was far enough away that he couldn't be distracted by how damn good she smelled. Although her cheeks remained flushed and her eyes were still wide with fear, her gaze was introspective, as though she was thinking through options.

She has no option but to cooperate, but I'll let her figure that out.

He wondered how long it would take. Hours? A day? Two days? More? Damn. He hoped not. He didn't have luxury of time, nor the patience to wait her out. The sooner he had what he needed from her, the sooner he'd be out of her hair, and she'd be out of his.

"Tell me about Barrows' daughters," Minero said. "They know anything?"

Sebastian eyed Skye, who had walked closer to him and was now only an arm's length away.

"Nothing," Sebastian answered, wishing she had kept her distance. "Didn't even know that their father had escaped."

Skye's intense focus was all on him, as though she had collected her thoughts and come up with a plan. "Let me out of here."

He stayed in place, and met her icy glare with one of his own as Minero said, "I have two marshals on their way to you. They should be there in an hour and a half, two hours tops. Keep the daughters where they are."

He said, "Okay." He broke the connection with a discreet touch on his watchband. He added, as though the phone call was ongoing, "You may be wasting your time. I was just about to leave." Sebastian glanced at Skye as he lied. No point clueing her in that her day was going to get much, much worse when the marshals arrived. He had threatened her enough. Now he wanted to see what she did with his threats. It wasn't time to let the canary fly, however. He leaned firmly against the door, so that she couldn't open it, even though she tried to pull it open against his weight. He had one more thing to ask her, and he didn't want to do it downstairs, with other ears around.

She looked at him and said, "You're a giant jerk. Let me out of here."

He folded his arms. "What are you so afraid of?"

She glared at him, her cheeks flushed, her arms at her sides, and her hands balled into tight fists. "Let. Me. Out. Of. Here."

So. No answer. At least not yet.

He pressed a button on his watchband and called Pete. "Pete. Come into the coffee shop. Get a cup of coffee. To go. We're moving on. Marshals will arrive later today to talk to them."

His words were only a charade. Sebastian's company was founded on protection. As a protector, he was also an observer. An observer of people, surroundings, of every minute happening that could present risk. His early survival had depended on understanding his abusive father's difficult-to-read moods, and he had a rare aptitude for being in tune to undercurrents. In other circumstances, watching Skye would have been pure pleasure, with those luminous, flagstone-colored eyes, inky-dark long hair, curves that were perfectly accented by her wrap sweater, and snug, hip-hugging jeans, with the wide belt that called attention to the sexy space where her hips tapered up, to her tiny waist. This was work, though, not pleasure, and this was one hell of a fucked-up job. It didn't matter how gorgeous she was. Something was just plain goddamn wrong.

Skye wasn't glancing away from him, a look that he'd have taken to indicate deception, that she knew something about her father that she wasn't telling him. No. She wasn't lying when she said she didn't know where her father was. In Skye's gray-green eyes, he saw wide-eyed fear that she was working hard to conceal. Her cheeks were flushed. Her forehead glowed with dewy perspiration. She was afraid. Terrified, actually.

As he watched her draw a deep breath, he could smell the musky, sweet aroma of fear, and it seemed like more than just concern for her father's safety. Finally. He had a scent on something interesting, and it was her fear. Instinct told him to follow that trail. She had a blown cover, sizable assets at her disposal, and a tendency to be impulsive. If given the opportunity, she'd run and regroup. He was going to give her that opportunity.

Skye glanced into his eyes, folded her arms, and squared her shoulders. She was trying damn hard to look composed. Sebastian slowly stepped away from the door before opening it for her. "Go ahead."

She passed, making sure that she didn't touch him. "Asshole," she muttered under her breath.

You have no idea, lady.

Chapter Four

Run.

Skye frowned as she jogged down the stairs. Stopping by the coffee shop before getting on the road had been a mistake. A bad mistake. Was Connelly telling the truth about her father? There was no reason for him to lie. What purpose would that serve? And if it wasn't a lie, where was her father? A prison break was the last thing she'd have expected from him, a man already so paranoid that he didn't trust a living soul other than his daughters. And sometimes, Skye wasn't even sure about that. Because if her father had somehow pulled off a prison break, the first person he would've contacted was her.

Which he'd done.

C-A-T-A-C-L-Y-S-M-N-O-W-R-U-N.

Which she was trying like hell to do. All she had to do was get away from Connelly before the marshals showed up. Should be simple, but this was her life, and nothing was ever simple. She had to get her sister to hurry, without freaking her out, and walk away from their new lives with nothing but the clothes on their backs, a puppy, and a freaking cake that absolutely, positively had to be delivered, if Skye had any hope in hell of getting her sister out of town without a meltdown.

Please leave, she thought, as she felt him following her down the stairs like a tall, dark, annoying shadow. *Just get the hell out of my coffee shop and my life.*

Once downstairs, Skye joined Sarah behind the counter. If Sebastian was leaving, he wasn't going right away. Instead, his dark-haired partner entered the coffee house and talked to Sebastian for a few seconds.

Leave. Just go.

In a low voice, Sarah asked, "Chloe, is everything alright?"

Skye nodded as the two men approached the counter. The dark-haired guy gave her a slight smile and a nod. He introduced himself as Pete St. Paul, and ordered to go a cafe-au-lait and an apple peanut butter muffin. His words revealed a Southern accent and a nice-guy persona that working with Sebastian hadn't yet snuffed. *Probably a recent hire,* Skye thought. Sebastian ordered a double espresso, with a splash of cream. In contrast to Pete, Sebastian had no accent that made him seem nice. He was just deadly serious and studying her in a way that put her on edge.

Run.

She had to get the heck out of there, but she sure as hell didn't want him following her. How long did she have before the marshals got there? Could she believe what he'd told the person on the phone, or was that bullshit? For all she knew the marshals were parked around the corner, waiting for these two to leave, and for her and Spring to make a run for it.

God. She was as paranoid as her father. The apple didn't fall far from the tree. *Where the hell are you, Dad?*

When Pete tried to pay, Skye waved him away. "Thank you for helping with the dog." *Now take your pushy friend and go.*

Out of the corner of her eye she observed Sebastian swallow the cupful of espresso. As he placed the small to-go cup into the trash, Skye exhaled.

Please. Please leave. Go.

Sebastian didn't immediately follow Pete out the front door. Instead, he walked to the rear of the coffee house, to the icing room, where Skye could see Spring's three-tier cake spotlighted on the worktable that was positioned in the center of the plate-glass observation window. The window was designed to provide customers with a view of Spring as she worked on her confectionary masterpieces. Skye could see her sister at the sink, methodically washing and drying her decorating tools, and putting each in its place in the travel box that she always carried with her.

Treating the *Do Not Disturb* that hung on the glass door of the icing room as a suggestion, and one that he wasn't taking, Sebastian knocked on the door.

Spring turned, freezing before she even saw for certain who was at the door.

"No," Skye called across the room as he reached for the doorknob, a surge of panic running through her veins. "Don't open the door."

Skye closed the distance between the counter and the icing room as fast as she could, mentally bracing for Spring's yell as Sebastian opened the door. When Spring was absorbed in her work, she didn't like to be disturbed by anyone but her big sister, and, in the world that Skye had created, where most of Spring's odd rules were honored, the icing room was Spring's domain. Customers could stand at the glass window and watch Spring decorate cakes. She liked to have an audience, as long as strangers from the audience didn't talk to her. No one but Skye, though, could open the door of the icing room. It was one of Spring's many compulsions, one that Skye indulged. The path of least resistance worked best for her sister, and Skye considered anything or anyone who threatened the hard-won peace the enemy. Currently, Sebastian was arch-enemy number one.

Braced for hysteria, Skye barreled into the room, hard on his heels, almost colliding into his back. There was no screech from Spring, nor was there a high-pitched yell of terror, or any other resistance to Sebastian's uninvited presence. Spring was smiling at him.

Heart in her throat, with every pulse point in her body pounding, Skye stumbled to a stop.

Smiling. My God. Smiling.

Her sister was looking at Sebastian in that beautiful, wide-eyed innocent and welcoming way that Spring showed to only a few people.

In a nice-guy voice, one that was upbeat and light and far different than the flat tone that had just accused Skye of knowing where her father was, Sebastian said, "Well, I tried the muffins."

"Did you? Which one was your favorite? No. Don't tell me." Her sister shook her head as she dried her hands on a dishtowel. "Let me guess. I think." She narrowed her eyes, cocked her head to the side, and studied him. A lump formed in Skye's throat as she took in Spring's sweet, trusting innocence. It was beautiful, and, in this case, totally misplaced. Normally Spring, with her highly tuned sense of empathy, had an instinctively accurate read on people and their motives. Not this time, Skye thought, as her sister beamed a welcoming and beautiful smile at the asshole that had just threatened to throw her in jail. "No, I know. The apple-peanut-butter-caramel was your favorite."

"You're correct. Not that I didn't like the others. But I could eat fifty of those apple muffins." His back was to Skye. She couldn't see his face, but his voice was positively charming. *The bastard.* "How'd you know that would be my favorite?"

Spring shook her head, pursed her lips, and arched an eyebrow. "Sometimes I just know things about some people," she shrugged, "and I'm usually right."

Sebastian chuckled as he jerked his chin to the bank's cake. "Now that's a work of art."

Spring blushed. "Really? You're not just being nice, are you? I had a hard time with the colors. If you look at the real flowers in the vase, you'll see what I mean."

Sebastian moved closer to the cake, turning in Skye's direction as he did so. His eyes held Skye's eyes for a brief second. There wasn't a threat there. None at all. He looked different from the man who had delivered the bombshell news that her father had escaped. There was none of the impatience, none of the you-don't-understand cockiness that he had exhibited while upstairs in her office. There was just an honest, slightly pained empathy, as though he realized the bittersweetness presented by Spring, who was physically a teenager, but mentally a sweet girl, many years younger than her age. Skye reminded herself that he was the same asshole who had tackled her and threatened her with jail time while upstairs in her office, and now he was stalling, looking like he didn't have a care in the world, while her heart was pounding and she could barely breathe.

Leave. Please leave.

Spring had a talent for making intricate beauty out of sugar and dye, but her creations were unusual. Sebastian's eyes widened slightly as he bent to study the cake. He spent a few long seconds focusing on flowers in colors that didn't resemble anything close to the hues intended by mother nature. People couldn't get enough of Spring's unusual creations, but at first sight, they were jarring. Watching Sebastian study a dense cluster of chartreuse rose buds with orange leaves and purple stems, Skye braced herself for a what-the-fuck comment. Instead, he turned to look at Spring, with a gentle smile. "You're very, very good at what you do. It's all perfect."

Spring's eyes shone with delight. "Thank you soooooo much. The bank is having a party this afternoon, but we want to set it up early so that all the customers can see it. Maybe they'll place orders." Her guileless blue eyes focused on Skye. "Isn't that the plan? We were going to deliver it at nine, but they called and want it early. It's ready."

"I see that." Skye forced a smile, though her heart twisted. "It'll be the most beautiful cake they've ever seen. And once they taste it, we'll have more orders than we can handle."

Run.

There'd be no cake orders. At least none that they'd be there to fulfill. Maybe one day they'd return to Covington and Creative Confections, but not until her father was found and they were safe again, and that wouldn't happen until the cataclysm scenario ended.

Run. Trust no one.

Skye could adapt easily, but this was going to be hard on Spring. To say that her sister didn't handle change well was an understatement, and sudden change was the worst. She drew a deep breath. It was going to be one hell of a long day. And tomorrow? Skye's stomach twisted. Until she received the next set of instructions from her father, she couldn't think of tomorrow. She just had to have faith that once the cataclysm scenario, for better or worse, was over, she'd be able to make things right again for Spring. Faith in her abilities and courage to act.

Skye straightened her shoulders, gave Spring a nod, and said, "Why don't you let Sarah and Daniel know that we'll be leaving in just a minute. Daniel can help us get the boxes of pastries that the bank also ordered into the van."

On her way out of the icing room, Spring gave Sebastian a shy smile and a hopeful glance. "You'll be back soon, won't you?"

He nodded. "As soon as I can."

His smile faded as Spring shut the door. His deep dimples disappeared, as though they'd been a mirage. Blue eyes hardened as his gaze met Skye's eyes. *Goodbye, nice guy*, Skye thought, folding her arms, *hello, jerk.* "Weren't you leaving?"

"What? Not fast enough for you?"

"I'll give you fair warning," Skye told him, a steely edge to her voice. "Mess with my sister, and no U.S. Marshal will be able to protect your ass from me. I won't need a gun to hurt you, and I won't rest until I do."

He gave her a short nod, his gaze going over her head to the counter area beyond the window, where her sister was talking excitedly to Sarah. With a slight frown, his eyes returned to her. "Message received."

"How did you find us?"

He shrugged. "It's what we do. The only thing you need to know is no matter where you run, no matter what name you use, I'll find you again if I need to." His tone was flat, his words certain, and his eyes were like hard blue rocks. "On the other hand, once your father is back in custody, you and your sister will be free to enjoy your lives and be whoever in the hell you want to be. If living anonymously is so important to you, you have an interest in getting your father back in prison. Are you ready to talk to me?"

"When hell freezes over," she mumbled, not intending for him to hear, and added, "you pretentious, self-important prick."

He narrowed his eyes. "I have really good hearing, so when you feel the need to resort to childish name calling, don't waste effort on whispering."

As Sebastian turned to leave the small room, she said, "Wait. My revolver."

He turned to look at her, shaking is head as he did. "Like I said, you'll get your weapons back when I decide the time's right."

He left the small room, shutting the door as she said, "Cocky jerk."

He turned, through the window gave her a half-smile and an eyebrow arch that indicated he heard her, and then continued on his way out of the coffee house. When the front door closed behind him, she exhaled in relief.

***

"You have GPS on their van?" Sebastian slammed the door of the Range Rover.

Pete nodded, pointing to the screen on the dashboard. "Their GPS system is merged with ours. They're the blue dot. We're red."

"Drive away."

Pete looked at Sebastian expectantly as he put the car in drive. "Where to?"

He'd seen enough to know that she was scared and ready to run. "Far enough to make her think we're disappearing from her life. Not so far that we can't be on her in a matter of minutes. How far's their house?"

"A mile and a half."

"Let's go there for a minute," Sebastian said, pulling a pair of sunglasses out of his backpack. The northeast was expecting snow and in Denver, at headquarters, wintry precipitation had been falling steadily for the last twelve hours. But in the deep South, snow wasn't likely in any given winter, and on this February day the clear blue sky and warm sun seemed to take the chill out of the air. "Keep an eye on that GPS. She's going to run. I'm giving her a few minutes of freedom before we catch up and scare the truth out of her."

"Why let her run at all?"

Sebastian liked Pete. While many of Black Raven's agents had military or police backgrounds, Pete had neither. Brandon had recommended him, so Sebastian had personally facilitated the application process. Most of the skills their agents needed to operate effectively could be taught at their training facility, but some skills, like the deep-rooted instinct for danger possessed by exceptional agents, couldn't be taught. The thorough background checks and psychological testing that field agents went through had revealed that Pete had a rough past that rivaled Sebastian's own suck-ass years as a child and teenager. Pete, like Sebastian, was an observer. He was also tough, smart, didn't trust anyone, and in early training sessions had proven that he could adapt fast. He'd thrive in Black Raven.

Pete glanced at Sebastian, waiting on an answer.

"Right now, she's not desperate enough to talk. When she realizes there's no escape, she might change her mind. I'm giving hope, some slack on the rope, before reeling her in and taking away her option to split." And it was going to be damn ugly. He wasn't looking forward to being the one who put fear back in her eyes. Hell. He didn't want to be an ass in front of the younger sister either. He'd done a hell of a lot worse, certainly more brutal, in the name of work, but scaring the truth out of a beautiful woman while his body ached for her was a new one. Chalk it up to his post-July life. Everything was different now and, other than the fact that he was alive, most of it sucked.

"Ragno, any news?

"Barrows' debriefing transcripts just arrived," she told him, voice crisp. "We're diving into them now, hoping we can come up with a clearer vision of his theories, which may lead to something. Amazing how much he talked about Shadow and LID Technology, which is something I picked up on the interviews that we already had. Anyway, aside from Barrows, Holt still knows nothing. They're not any closer to Biondo, either."

"Give me something to push Skye's buttons."

"Aside from knocking her to the floor and lying on top of her?" Ragno asked. "Really, Sebastian."

"Give me a break." Yeah. He'd been breathing heavy. *Hell.* He tried not to think of how perfectly toned yet soft she'd felt, when he was on top of her. "She pulled a gun on me. I did exactly what I was supposed to do. I disarmed her. No one got hurt."

"Well, I suggest that you try reasoning instead of manhandling. She's truly her father's daughter, one of her MIT professors said. She's off-the-charts intelligent. After MIT, reports from therapists, which her father insisted that she see, indicate that she consciously chose to turn her back on the more cerebral world her father lived in for a more people-oriented lifestyle. It was an act of rebellion on her part, and explains the serious pursuit of partying and meaningless relationships with friends and lovers. From her therapy reports, it seems that everything she's done, she's done consciously. When you're dealing with her, don't forget how smart she is."

She might be smart, but that damn topless bikini photo sure as hell has a way of making people not think about her brains. He kept that thought to himself. He was a professional. Black Raven's workforce was mostly men, and most of them had more than a healthy dose of testosterone. He led by example, and one primary rule was that hormones were to be kept under control while on the job.

"While Skye was in college she wrote papers on elegance in computer algorithm design and provided theories on how to accomplish it," Ragno paused, "at seventeen. Can you believe that?"

Sebastian knew about algorithm design, but it was enough to let him know that there was a reason he had people like Ragno on his payroll. The vehicle slowed, and Pete indicated the house as Sebastian half-listened to Ragno continue on about algorithm design. The two-story Victorian-style house was painted a crisp white with mint green shutters. An oversized white porch swing with pillows that matched the trim of the house hung on a wide front porch. A bay window overlooked a yard with flowering azalea and camellia bushes. Skye seemed to have a knack at making places seem both chic and homey. Her front porch looked like a great place to hang out, to settle into the porch swing, read a newspaper, and sip coffee on a long, lazy morning. That the home could inspire such a thought in him, a man who never had long lazy mornings, meant Skye was skilled at decorating.

Slowing the Range Rover to a crawl, Pete nodded in the direction of a black SUV that was parked in front of the neighboring house. "Something's not right. Right before you walked out of the coffee house, that SUV and a black sedan passed in front," Pete said. "What are the odds of it passing there and being here?"

The scene took on a surreal clarity, the kind that came when Sebastian knew bad shit was about to go down. Some people with a sixth sense for danger felt a prickle at the back of their neck when warning instincts kicked in. He usually didn't feel that prickle. Instead, time slowed, his brain processed vision more clearly, touch receptors in his body became super-sensitized, and his sharp hearing became even more intense. Faint odors and aromas became overpowering. The neighborhood became too normal, as though 3-D photographed. When Sebastian got the feeling he was looking at a facade, that's when he knew trouble was about to happen. It had been that way since he was a kid.

The dull whump-thud, whump-thud of his heartbeat was an undeniable warning. He glanced at the dashboard and the GPS screen. Skye hadn't left the coffee house. Returning his attention to the SUV they were approaching, Sebastian absently noted the vehicle's make, model, and license plate. He observed a young mother wearing exercise clothes, pushing a stroller as she jogged away from them, about one block away. In the opposite direction, a gardener's truck was two blocks away, tailgate down, bags of mulch waiting to be placed. "What was it about the vehicles and the occupants that stood out?"

Pete shrugged. "There were two men in each car, which is a little different for this time of morning in this town. Covington doesn't seem like a ride-sharing kind of place, unless people are headed into the city, and the coffee shop isn't on the way to the commuter roads to New Orleans. Both cars braked in front of the coffee house. Neither stopped. All four men turned their heads, like they were looking at the coffee house. I looked at the plates. I committed them to memory. I'm positive that," he gestured with his chin, "is the SUV from the coffee house. When they kept going, I dismissed them. You got in the car two minutes after, so the SUV hasn't been here long."

"Minero said two men would arrive from the marshals' office in an hour or two," Sebastian told him, his eyes scanning the quiet street. A man wearing khakis walked across a yard, towards the truck with the mulch, and reached forward as he gripped one of the bags. The scene was suburban normal, devoid of obvious threat. "These guys aren't marshals. They're here too soon, there's two men too many, and the marshals would have just walked into the coffee house." He shifted in the seat, stretching his legs as much as he could as he glanced at the dashboard. Skye's blue dot was still at the coffee house.

"Ragno. There's a security system with video at the coffee house. Do we have access?"

"Yes, but I'm not there. Give me a minute."

They were slightly past Skye's house and almost parallel to the suspect SUV now. It was empty. Even though he had to assume the occupants were in the house, Skye's house revealed no life. Assuming that the SUV and black sedan together made up a surveillance team, as Pete's observations suggested, Sebastian didn't like that only half of the team was there. The other half of the team—the black sedan—wasn't at Skye's house and it wasn't anywhere in sight. Instead of racing, his pulse slowed when he had to focus, and now, his blood was crawling through his veins.

People here in the burbs never expected anything bad to happen in their idyllic worlds. Sebastian knew, though, that crap happened everywhere. Every neuron in his body warned him that the shit was about to hit the fan. Where? Didn't matter. He knew where he needed to be, with absolute certainty, because the blue dot still hadn't moved.

"Coffee house. Now!"

***

Run.

The minute Connelly left, she was galvanized into action, but ten minutes later, she was still doing anything, it seemed, but running. In her ideal plan, she and Spring would be able to leave in a minute flat. But nothing was as ideal as her plans, especially not with Spring, because her sister couldn't just be told to get moving. She'd have too many questions. So, delivering the cake was a good ploy, but getting the three-tier cake onto the floor-level platform in the rear of the van took precious time, even with Daniel's help. Daniel offered to follow her to the bank and help them with the delivery, but she assured him she could handle it.

The van was in the rear parking area, behind the coffee shop.

It was a small parking pad, with just enough room to turn a car around, an area that was intended for deliveries and a few parking spaces for employees. The long driveway that led to it was on a side street, and the parking area was not visible from the front of the coffee house. Adjoining businesses, a hairdresser and an art gallery, weren't opening until ten. No one was around. Once she and Spring checked on the cake, Daniel shut the door to the van.

Skye smiled at Spring, and said, "Let's take Candy with us."

Spring gave her a puzzled glance. "To deliver the cake to the bank?"

"Sure, why not?" Skye said. "She loves car rides, right?" *And because we're not returning here for a long time, if ever, and I know that you won't make it through the next few days without her.*

"I'll bring her favorite leash and a chew toy, okay?"

"Great idea. Go upstairs and get whatever you think she might want. Hurry or we'll be late for our first delivery."

Spring beamed. "Come in and help me carry."

Skye nodded. Spring didn't travel light. She never went anywhere without her thoroughly bedazzled backpack, which fit not only her travel tote of cake decorating tools but also her iPad and whatever other items were needed for her current obsessions. Skye followed her sister back inside. She glanced into the kitchen. Daniel gave Skye a smile before opening an oven and pulling out a fully-loaded baking sheet. She paused in the center of the large public space that had materialized from her dreams. The shop was momentarily empty, except for Sarah, who was behind the counter, organizing muffins in the pastry cases. There was a lull between the early customers and later-morning customers. The same lull had happened the last two mornings.

The place was so pretty and peaceful it brought tears to her eyes. For the last nine months, she had worked hard to make it perfect, a comfortable place where people would sit for a moment of peace. It was a beautiful gathering place, one where many special moments could be made. The white-on-creamy-white decor was her vision, providing the perfect backdrop to the shocking mix of colors that Spring used to decorate her confections. Spring would have continued to thrive here, and Skye would have loved being at the coffee shop, and in their home, which she had made equally special. She shook her head, willing away the urge to sob at losing it. Spring couldn't see her upset.

Sarah paused in her task of organizing the muffins. Kind brown eyes gave her a worried glance. "Is everything okay? You seem stressed."

Skye would have loved to confide in her. But Sarah and Daniel knew nothing of their real lives and one rule was that she was never to tell anyone the truth. So Sarah and Daniel only knew them as Chloe and Colbie Stewart, and the cataclysm scenario in which she was now mired made no sense in that world. "Just a little tired."

"Ready," Spring said, as she ran down the stairs.

Finally. Skye had plenty of cash on her, tucked into her belt. Her back-up revolver was in her backpack, which she had locked in the van. Yes. Ready.

Run.

She drew a deep breath, turned her back on the coffee shop, and followed Spring and Candy out the back door. As usual, Spring's rhinestone encrusted backpack, with its kaleidoscope of colors forming intricate flowers, was slung on one shoulder. Thank God for compulsions, Skye thought, shutting the door to the coffee shop behind her. Otherwise, she'd have to explain to Spring why she needed to take the backpack on what should have been a short, uneventful delivery.

Spring and Candy slipped into the passenger side of the van and shared the front passenger seat. As Skye walked around the back of the van to get to the driver's side, a black, four-door sedan pulled up, blocking the van's ability to back-up and exit. As soon as the car stopped, the driver and a front passenger stepped out before she could make it to the van's driver side door and safely inside. A not-quite-conscious thought wondered why the trunk of their car popped open, but Skye was more concerned about them, who they were, and why they were in the back of the coffee shop. She didn't have any scheduled deliveries, and customers usually went through the front. A sign that they'd driven by, and ignored, said 'service drive only.'

"Skye Barrows," the driver said. He was a large, dark-haired man. He walked towards her with a steady stride.

Skye's heart raced. She hadn't heard anyone say that name in over a year. Twice in one morning was twice too often. Her stomach twisted with the certainty that ten minutes had been too long to enact her plan to run.

"I'm U.S. Marshal Bill McClendon," he said, without showing credentials. In his face, she saw thin, unsmiling lips. Something in his expression told her not to waste time asking for identification. Even if he was a marshal, it didn't matter. "This is my partner, Dennis Snead. We have some questions for you about your father."

Run. Trust no one.

Dear God, I am trying.

Aviator sunglasses with mirrored lenses concealed his eyes. She saw her own reflection there and hated that she looked vulnerable, uncertain, and afraid. Snead, with sandy-blond hair and a receding hairline, had a smaller build. He stood next to McClendon. He wore the same kind of sunglasses as McClendon and the same somber expression.

"I'm sorry, but I don't have time to talk right now," she said, trying not to panic, "and I don't have any information about my father."

From inside the van, Spring shot her a questioning glance, as Candy gave a loud bark. Skye drew a deep breath. *Run.* But she didn't know how to escape from them. *Stall,* she thought. *Think.* "My sister and I are going on a delivery. We'll be back in fifteen minutes. Why don't you go in, get a cup of coffee, and I can talk to you when I return."

McClendon frowned, while Snead went around to the passenger side of the van.

Skye said, "Leave her alone. Please. We can talk now. Just let me get my sister situated inside the coffee shop."

Spring screeched, a loud, high-pitched, incomprehensible screech that signified that she'd been startled by someone she didn't know, and the person was too close to her body space. Loud barks from Candy accompanied the screeching. Skye would have run to Spring's side of the van, but McClendon gripped her forearm with a hand that felt like a steel clamp. She hadn't seen that McClendon had a weapon, or when he had unholstered it, but she felt cold metal against her temple and didn't have to look at it to know what it was.

McClendon said, "Get in the car. Now." He didn't mean her van, either, as he pulled her in the direction of his car, while she tried to pull her arm away. She locked her legs so that she wouldn't move with him. After a few seconds where he pulled at her but made no progress, his fingernails dug into her arms. "Stop resisting me, or your sister's dead."

With his threat, Skye stopped pulling away. She stumbled as he pulled and dragged her to his car, past the driver's side, and past the back seat, and *Oh God*, he was dragging her to the rear of the car. *Not the trunk*. She'd die if he put her in there.

Spring yelled, "Chloe. Gun. Chloe. Gun. Chloe. Gun."

Skye twisted to see Spring. All she could see, though, was the van, which blocked her view of Spring. She couldn't see her, but she could hear Spring's panicked screams, then sudden silence. *Oh God*. Another second of quiet went by. Her silence was worse than her screams. The man who had Spring yelled a string of garbled words. Skye saw Daniel run to the back door, take in the scene with wide eyes, and run straight for Spring, who had again started wailing in the high-pitched, panicked way that signified a meltdown. There was a quiet pop, and Daniel fell to the ground, between the back door and the van.

"No," Skye yelled. "No."

Candy barked, then growled. A canine yelp of pain turned Skye's blood cold. Skye looked for an opportunity to knock the gun out of McClendon's hand. Sebastian had made it seem easy when he did it to her, but she couldn't wriggle either arm out of McClendon's steel-armed grasp on her. He dragged her the last few feet, to where the trunk of the sedan was open and the interior was a huge, dark void. He punched her upper back, pushing her towards the trunk. Skye stumbled forward and down, but caught herself on the rim before falling in. There was no way she was going in there alive. Claustrophobia wouldn't let her. She wouldn't be able to breathe. She'd die once he shut it. No way.

Snead, red-faced, came around with Spring. He was half carrying her, half dragging her. Spring was limp, with blood dripping from her nose. The left side of her face was bright red. Skye kicked at McClendon's legs, trying to break away. Spring couldn't get away from Snead because he was pulling her by the hair, but she wasn't even trying.

Oh God. He had knocked her out.

"Fucking bitch bit the shit out of me," Snead said.

Sarah came to the back door.

"Help," Skye yelled, meaning go get help. Sarah gasped. Wide-eyed, she ran to Daniel.

As McClendon strong-armed her towards the trunk by pushing her lower back and her shoulders at the same time, Skye heard an engine. She heard car doors, but her attention was locked on Snead. He had thrown Spring into the trunk and, lifting his right arm, he pointed his weapon at Sarah.

Skye yelled, "No. Please no. We'll go with you."

From behind her, a deep, authoritative voice, yelled, "U.S. Marshals. Freeze."

Chapter Five

Sebastian and Pete arrived back at the coffee shop in two minutes. The street in front of the coffee house was empty.

Ragno said, "I'm in the security system. Camera on the back parking pad reveals a partial glimpse of two men, weapons drawn. Skye is struggling. I can't see Spring."

"The back," Sebastian said to Pete, slipping off his sunglasses, his hand on the door handle. "Block the drive."

"Partial glimpses aren't helpful. I can't manipulate the view," Ragno said, her tone calm. "Your eyes will be better than mine. I'll be on stand by. Let me know if you need anything."

Leaping out of the truck when he saw the black sedan, with every nerve in his body firing, Sebastian's mind was in calm assessment mode. Snap-fire assessment while acting under pressure was something he had learned and practiced since he was a kid. Fear was good. Panic was bad. Controlled fear fueled positive reactions in life-threatening situations. Panic was a brain drain and stupidity meant death.

Breathing deeply as he ran up the long driveway, he took in Skye, hair loose and wild, resisting as an armed man tried to one-arm push her into the trunk. Spring, head down, hair falling around her face, was limp and still, as an armed man dragged her and pushed her into the trunk. Both men held semi-automatic pistols with silencers. Always a way out, Sebastian reminded himself. Lethal force was the last option. He scanned the scene.

Find. The. Other. Options.

The baker was lying in a growing pool of blood near the back door. Sarah was frozen, two steps out of the door that led to the driveway, in mouth-opened shock. Assessment time, over. Lethal force was his only option. Sebastian's Glock was in his right hand, and he stopped at ten yards away, using his left hand to signal to Pete to hold steady. There was no way to have an easy or even moderately hard shot at these men, not when they were using the sisters as shields. Pete was good, but not sniper-quality good. Not yet. Sebastian almost had a shot at the asshole who had Spring. He didn't have a shot at the one who had Skye, because he was holding her too close. The situation snowballed straight to hell when the asshole who had Spring simultaneously one-armed the limp Spring into the trunk and lifted his arm to fire at Sarah.

"No," Skye yelled. "Please no. We'll go with you."

As he aimed, Sebastian yelled, "U.S. Marshals. Freeze."

Not correct, but now was not the time to worry about technicalities. He aimed his weapon about one inch above where the arm of the man's sunglasses met the frame, and fired as the man fired at the baker's wife. *Fuck me to hell.* He hadn't been fast enough, because the asshole managed to fire a shot before being hit with Sebastian's bullet. The loud report of his own weapon barely registered as he saw the blood and brain spray from both of them. Sarah fell in the instant before the would-be kidnapper dropped to the ground. Dead. One down. One to go.

Sebastian ran, shaving a few more yards off the distance between himself and the black sedan. The second man pulled Skye closer, shut the trunk on Spring, pressed the pistol against Skye's temple, and turned to face him. Skye was five feet eight inches of human shield, give or take an inch, and she wasn't taking being held at gunpoint lightly. She was writhing, struggling, biting, scratching and using some creative curses at the top of her lungs. He admired her determination to break free, but her efforts weren't helping him get a bead on the man holding onto her. The top of her head reached between the man's jaw and his upper lip. Her height compared to the kidnappers gave Sebastian only a few inches for a kill shot, and the inches were unsteady, because he was walking backwards and dragging her closer and closer to the rear passenger door.

Sebastian aimed at the kidnapper's forehead. He was holding Skye close with his left arm, pulling her in a bear hug around her neck so that her back was against his chest, edging step-by-backward-step to the side of the car. His right hand held his weapon and it was pressed into Skye's forehead, but that wasn't stopping her from trying to get away. The more Skye resisted with elbow jabs and shin kicks, the faster the guy moved, which made Sebastian's percentages for success suck.

"Skye," Sebastian said, his tone commanding. "Stop fucking *moving.*"

The kidnapper raised his voice. "Put your weapon down by the time I count to three or she's dead."

"If you want to stop me, point your weapon at me. Not her."

The man's weapon stayed trained on Skye. "One."

Time crawled as Sebastian absorbed the horror in Skye's eyes. She had no way of knowing that he wasn't going to miss. She was wide-eyed, and, finally, he thought, as he drew a deep breath, she was still, so still she appeared to be holding her breath. Four inches separated Skye from the point where Sebastian's bullet was going to enter the man's head, right in the middle of the forehead, just a hair above the metal bridge of his sunglasses. Big, meaty arms, had a chokehold on Skye, but because she now was still, with each backwards step, the space between Sebastian's target and Skye's head remained the same, give or take an inch.

Four inches was plenty of distance. Plenty. He was damn good at hitting targets. Any target, especially human assholes who held a gun to a woman's head and used her as a shield. When the man's lips parted for the next count, Sebastian fired. A hole appeared directly above the guy's right eyebrow, not quite at dead center between the eyes, but close enough.

Sebastian ran forward as the kidnapper slid against the car, releasing Skye as he fell. He kicked the guy's pistol away as he grabbed for her. She was pale and silent, her eyes focused on the man who lay at her feet, with his blood pooling underneath him. Sebastian tucked his own pistol back in its holster. She was too quiet. Too calm. She was standing under her own power, but slowly reached back, for the car, and leaned back against it as her legs started to buckle. Sebastian reached out, trying to steady her by grabbing her shoulders. The strong woman who had enough moxie to point a revolver at him, who had fought back with the full weight of his body on top of hers, who had resisted a burly thug with a gun pressed to her head, was trembling from her hands to her shoulders, and her legs wouldn't support her. Before she fell to the ground, he wrapped his right arm around her back, and his left arm lifted her up by tucking under her arm.

Skye smelled like vanilla-laced fear, her body was soft, and she trembled from deep inside, as though shivering in extreme cold. In her almost-passed-out state she was pliable and limp. As Sebastian held her upright, the hyper-kick that adrenaline from the gun battle had given to his senses wreaked havoc through his body, sensitizing every feeling, every smell. Sensitizing everything, dammit. Volumes of blood pumped into unintended places. *Son of a bitch.* Killing men normally didn't give him an erection, so he knew his arousal was all about her.

As he held Skye upright, Ragno said, "Saw a partial view of the action. Nice work. Talk to me, Sebastian. Can't see you now."

"Two kidnappers, dead." He watched Pete check for vitals on the baker and his wife. A headshake confirmed what he suspected. "Two collateral killings, compliments of the kidnappers. Pete. The trunk. We're getting Barrows' daughters out of here."

He mentally switched from Ragno to the woman who was leaning into him, her face buried in his chest. She was silent and so still he wondered whether she had fainted. Her full chest hit at the bottom of his ribcage, her nose was pressed into the hollow of his neck, and if she was breathing, he couldn't tell. But God, he could feel her heart beating. The pounding went straight through her chest, through the thin wrap sweater that she wore, and through his cotton shirt. "Hey. You're okay. Skye?"

She didn't respond.

"Breathe. Come on. Fight through it," Sebastian said. "You're going to be fine."

Pete popped open the trunk. Over Skye's shoulder, Sebastian saw Spring lying in the well, curled into a fetal position. Her eyes were open. She was quiet, but tears were flowing. Relief pulsed through him at the sign of life. A crimson smear of blood was on her cheek. More blood dripped from her nose. He set his jaw. *Fucking bastards. They deserved bullets through their brains.*

"Come on, Skye. Don't pass out. Spring needs help. We've got to get out of here."

Sebastian started to lift her, planning to carry her into the SUV. Then he could return to help Pete with the sister, but when her sister cried out, Skye stiffened. Spring sobbed again, louder, and Sebastian felt strength returning to Skye's limbs. When Spring cried a third time, a small, pathetic sound of fear and pain, Skye gasped for air. Gray-green eyes wide with fear searched his, as more strength returned to her legs and arms.

She drew another deep breath and nodded, "I'm ok." Her words were barely a whisper.

"That's a champ. You're doing fine," he said, relieved beyond words that she didn't break down and start crying. When strong women like Skye cried, they reminded him of his mother and he'd sell his soul to make the tears stop. No, he studied her as she drew a deep breath. Not the type to break down. Instead, she was pulling herself away from an almost-faint that was induced by shock and fear, all because of Spring's cry. He understood Skye's strong will to protect. His body, still pumping with adrenaline from split-second decisions that focused on the need to kill, was sizzling with, among other things that he didn't have time to think about, the need to get these women to safety. Now. He didn't let go of her. He wasn't certain she was ready to stand under her own power, because she was still leaning against him.

"I'm fine," she repeated, her voice stronger.

"You sure?"

She nodded. "Yes."

He loosened his arms, but kept them encircled around her, just in case he needed to catch her. She managed to hold up her own weight.

"See," she stood under her own power and turned to go towards the trunk, towards her sister. "I'm fine."

Letting her do her thing with her sister seemed to give her more equilibrium. Sebastian crouched beside her would-be kidnapper, as Skye stepped closer to the open trunk. "Take Spring and get in the SUV." Sebastian started looking through the man's pockets, where there was no phone, no ID, no wallet, not one goddamn clue as to who the men were.

"Not going with you," Skye told him as she moved past him. "Not now, not in this lifetime."

Sebastian watched her walk through, not around, the pool of blood and guts that blocked her path. He guessed that she didn't see the puddle of gunk or that her cream-suede boots became speckled with red blood and gray matter, because she was too focused on getting to her sister.

Not in this lifetime.

Feisty pep in suck-ass situations was something Sebastian normally found amusing, and he almost did now, except that two more of these assholes were going to show up at any second, and he didn't have time to argue with Skye about getting in the SUV. Though his aim was dead certain, he frowned as he glanced at the bodies of the baker and his wife. Sometimes, like this fucking time, really bad collateral damage happened.

Pete was kneeling on the ground on the other side of the trunk, searching through the other guy's pockets. He stood as Sebastian did. Pete said, "Nothing. Nothing in the car either."

"Ragno. Pete. Did we record the camera footage?" Sebastian

asked, walking to where Skye stood consoling Spring, who was still lying in the trunk.

Pete nodded as he scanned the area. "Yes, even if we weren't recording through our system, the cameras have a digital recording through an online application, so Ragno can access that."

"Ragno. Access the recording system. Keep a copy for us, then delete it from the application. Pete. Lock the front door. Put out the closed sign. The longer we can keep this from going public, the better."

"Ragno. Send a Cleaner here. Have him call me when he's en route." Cleaners were Black Raven agents who were trained to deal with fucked-up situations. Since most of their operations were international, only a few Cleaners were in the U.S., and all were now working on the prison break. "For now, hold onto the camera footage. Later, I'll get it to Minero. Skye, we have to go."

"Should I alert Minero?" Ragno asked.

"Yes, but I'll give him details. Tell him we interrupted a kidnapping, the sisters are safe, we're in transit, and I'll be calling in ten minutes." Sebastian glanced at Skye. Pale and unmoving, she had rested a soothing hand on Spring's shoulder, who still lay curled in the trunk. From where Spring lay, if she sat up even an inch, she'd have an unobstructed view of the carnage that was between the coffee house and the sedan. Skye's eyes were on Sarah, who had fallen sideways against Daniel. A bullet had blown away a chunk of her head. The baker lay face up, eyes open, with a round entry wound in his forehead. Thick, crimson-black blood pooled around them.

Skye's wide-eyed, stiller-than-still reaction told Sebastian she'd never seen this kind of death before, at least not in real life, in people who she knew and cared for. *Hell.*

"Hey," Sebastian said to Skye as he grabbed her arm, "we need to get moving. Pete." *Dammit.*

"I'm in the coffee house," Pete responded, through the mic, "locking it."

"We need to call for help!" Yanking her arm out of his grasp, she tore her eyes from the bodies to look at him. His heart twisted with the abject misery that he saw in her eyes. He fought the urge to scoop her in his arms again and shield her from the carnage.

"They're dead. No one can help-"

"Call the police." Her hair was wild and loose, blood splatter was on her sweater, and her eyes were wide, her gaze once again locked on Sarah and Daniel.

"We can't do that."

"Dial 9-1--"

"I'm it, Skye. I'm all the help that's coming," he said, "and," he softened his voice, because when she looked into his eyes, the raw pain there stole his breath, "They're gone. Stop looking at them. I need to get you and your sister the hell away from here. *Now*."

Spring whimpered and, thank God, the sound captured Skye's attention.

"Hey, honey, those bad guys are...gone," Skye's voice shook, "and we're going to get in the van. Can you sit up?"

Spring nodded, but didn't move.

"Not your van. My SUV."

She ignored him. Her attention was focused on Spring. "All right," Skye said, "so we're going to try to get you to sit up, but I need you to close your eyes and not open them until I tell you."

"Why?" Spring said.

"Move it, Skye. Now."

Spring, wide-eyed, said, "He called you Skye. Not Chloe."

Skye gave him a furious look, but her voice remained calm and comforting. "That's because he knows our real names. We can use our real names with him. Just trust me, honey. I need you to keep your eyes closed, and we need to go."

Holy fucking hell. At this rate, they were all going to die of old age before he got them to the SUV. Sebastian moved around Skye, using his body to push her out of the way. Spring was five feet six and, he guessed, weighed just about one hundred and twenty. With a bit of effort from his thighs, shoulders, and arms, Sebastian managed to get her out of the deep well of the trunk with a two-armed lift. Thank God he was back in shape. Spring groaned, opened her eyes wide with surprise, as he straightened with her. "Hey pretty girl," Sebastian said, "I'm helping you and your sister. You're safe."

Spring whimpered and pressed her face into his chest.

His heart twisted. Again. *God.* These two women were getting to him. "I know it hurts," Sebastian said. "We're going to get help for you."

Pete returned to the doorway. "I locked the front door and put up the closed sign."

Spring said, "Chloe?"

He paused when he heard Spring say Skye's fake name, even though Skye had just explained to her sister that he knew their real names. Spring really had no fucking clue what was happening. *Son of a bitch.* The learning curve on this one was going to be pretty goddamn steep. Sebastian turned so that Spring could see Skye. "See. She's fine."

"Put her in my van," Skye instructed, clearly used to giving orders that were followed. *Tough shit. So am I.*

Sebastian moved fast, turning again, so that Spring didn't have a chance to see the bodies. "Your sister's getting into the SUV with us," he gave Skye an over-the-shoulder, hard look, "and she's doing it now." He walked down the driveway, away from Skye, confident he had the one thing in the world that would make her follow him.

Within seconds, Skye was walking at his side. "I did not say we were going with you. You can't manhandle us into doing that, and you don't have authority to make us go with you. You're just a private investigator, not a U.S. Marshal."

"You see those two men?" He gestured with his chin, over his shoulder, to the corpses. "There are two more just like them at your house right now."

She shook her head. "You're just saying that."

"The only difference between them and the two at your house is that the two who are at your house are alive. They're going to show up here at any second. They won't be thrilled when they figure out that their friends are dead, and I don't feel like killing two more people today."

Skye shook her head, eyes wide. "You're lying."

Sebastian glared at her, but kept walking. "And why would I make up this crap?"

"Who are they?"

"Hell if I know, " he said. "I was hoping you had a clue."

"Me?"

Hell. She managed to look surprised, innocent, sexy, and angry all at the same goddamn time. "Well, we sure as hell don't have time to figure it out."

"They said they were marshals."

"So did I, and we both know that's not true."

Pete pulled the SUV up to where they were. He jumped out to open the rear passenger door. As Sebastian bent to place Spring into the seat, she whispered, "Candy."

Sebastian froze as her blue eyes drowned him in innocent, questioning light.

"Candy," Spring said loudly. "I need to get her." Tears flowed down her cheeks, smearing in the dried blood around her nose. Rocking, she gripped a clump of hair near her scalp and pulled. "We need Candy."

Fuck me to hell, Sebastian thought, as Skye turned to run for the van. *There is no time for this shit.* Human lives versus one dog life. Sebastian knew the relative weight of each, and he knew which one was more important when they had no time. Yet Spring's big, innocent eyes inspired a deep, searing hurt, one that was long repressed. He had learned just how much life could suck when, at fourteen years old, he'd watched the man who had fathered him kick his dog to death. This wasn't the day that Spring was going to learn how much it hurt to lose a dog, not if he could help it. He glanced at Pete. "Turn the SUV around. If the other guys come, leave."

"Wait. Should I stay to deal with local law enforcement, at least until our Cleaner or the marshals get here?"

"No," Sebastian said. He appreciated Pete's take-one-for-the team attitude, but he wasn't about to give up Pete for what promised to be a lengthy exercise in futility. "Local officials will detain you for God knows how long and they ultimately won't even have jurisdiction over this, because it will all be linked back to the prison break. I need you. We saved lives today. You did nothing wrong. You didn't even fire a weapon." He turned for the van. Over his shoulder, Sebastian said, "Get the hell away from here if you see the other guys. I'll worry about Skye.'"

Sebastian caught up with Skye, who had made it to the van, where the front seat was empty.

"Candy was here," Skye's eyes were bright with panic, "She barked for a while, then there was nothing."

To make the vehicle into a delivery van, the passenger seats had been removed. Now, the long cargo space was filled with smears of white, chartreuse, purple, and orange icing, and chunks of cake. Only a fraction of the cake remained standing on the almost floor-level platform where the sisters had placed it.

Skye gasped, and pointed at golden fur that was curled into a tight ball, tail between her legs, with her nose pointing in the corner.

Awww hell. Don't let her be dead. Sebastian opened the passenger door, stepped into the van, hunched down so that his head didn't hit the ceiling, and walk-crawled to the dog.

"Please let her be alive," Skye said, right behind him.

He touched fur that was sticky with globs of cake. She was warm and trembling. "Hey, Candy," a long snout turned to him. Big, sad brown eyes gazed into his. "Alive." She yelped when he put pressure on her right shoulder and neck, but fast-licked a warm trail across his cheek and nose as he lifted her. "From her licks, I think she'll make it." He stepped out of the van, the dog in his arms, looked at Skye, and said, "Come on."

Pete had the SUV running, and Spring opened the door as Sebastian approached with the dog. He placed the dog on Spring's lap, and said, "Push over." To Skye, who stood at his side, and who showed no sign of getting in the car, he said, "Get in."

She folded her arms with her feet firmly planted on the ground. "Where are you taking us?"

"Away from here. Somewhere safe."

"I understand," she nodded, her eyes fiery, "but my sister needs medical attention. She had a bad concussion two years ago. Doctors told me to be careful with future injuries, and that bastard hit her so hard I think she passed out. She needs a Doctor. An MRI. A CT scan. Now."

"Ragno. You hearing this?"

"Yes," she answered.

"Is it bullshit?"

"No. She was in Skye's car accident. Remember?"

"Head injury then?"

"Concussion," Ragno said.

Fuck. Fuck. Fuck.

"Hey," Skye snapped her fingers, her hand just a few inches from his face. "Listen to me. Not whoever is talking into your ear. Candy needs medical help as well."

"No need to snap. I can handle more than one conversation, which seems to be one more than you can handle, because you're not understanding any goddamn thing I'm telling you. There are two more, just like them, at your house. People pay me one hell of a lot of money to protect them. When I say something, I'm used to people damn well listening. For the seven hundredth time, get in the fucking SUV now." He didn't raise his voice. Didn't have to. The woman wasn't stupid and the problem wasn't her hearing.

Pete had turned and was looking at them, and Spring was wide-eyed and staring at Sebastian as though he'd grown three heads.

Skye's eyes flicked to Spring, then she focused on him. "Stop talking like that."

"Like what?" Sebastian asked. Yes, he was exasperated with her. But he wasn't yelling. He never yelled. He was using the exact voice he used when he was knee-deep in an operation. The kind of tone that everyone but Skye responded to by following the orders he issued.

"Like I have no option but to listen to you."

He paused, drew a deep breath, and wanted to punch something when he read resistance in her folded-arm stance and uncertainty in her eyes. "Exactly what are you not understanding about this?"

Pete, his tone agitated, said, "There really are two more of these men, and they'll be here any second. We've got to go now."

Skye drew a deep breath, and there was a moment of silence as Spring looked with wide-eyed fear at the two men. To Spring, Skye said, "Honey. It's going to be all right." To Sebastian, she said, "Speak nicely."

"Are you fucking kidding me? Armed men are on their way for you and your sister, I'm trying to save you, I even rescued the damn dog, and you're bothered by the tone of my goddamn fucking voice?"

"Noooooo. No. No. No. Noooooooo," Spring whispered, as quiet as Sebastian was yelling, her misery a match for Sebastian's anger. Spring looked straight ahead as she tore at her hair with both hands. "No. No. No. No. No. No."

"I'm not bothered one bit, dumb ass. She's bothered, and just in case you're not getting the picture here, everything I do is about her. So if you can't speak nicely," Skye's voice was low, her tone normal, as though she was talking about the weather on an uneventful mundane day, "we can't go with you-"

"Funny," he interrupted Skye, "but all the intel that I have on you didn't point to stupid and senseless, but I guess there's some things you just don't know until you're face to face."

"You're the one who's not understanding-"

"You have nowhere to run," Sebastian snarled, trying to persuade her to move. "Now. Get. The. Hell. In. The. SUV."

"No. No. No," each time Spring said the word, it became louder and faster, until the words rolled together, "NONONONONONONONO."

The incessant yelling was unlike anything he'd ever heard. Her constant stream of no's had a rhythmic quality, more like a drum beat than a human voice, more scared than angry. She was holding her ears, rocking forward and back. Skye pushed past him in an effort to get in the SUV, to her sister. "What the hell?"

"You've upset her." Skye pushed Spring and Candy over, slipped onto the seat, put her arms around her sister, and tried to stop her sister from pulling at her hair and scratching her own face. "She's having an anxiety attack, thanks to you," she mumbled, "asshole," under her breath.

Sebastian kicked the running board in exasperation, provoking another steely-eyed glare from Skye as his kick produced a loud thumping noise and another stream of no's from Spring. "Did you really just say that? Thanks to me? Asshole? When you mumble, I can hear you, so just go ahead and say it."

"Thanks to you, my sister is having an anxiety attack," Skye said, keeping her voice calm as she managed to wrap her arms around Spring, who was trying to wriggle free. The no's started to subside. "Now, when you speak, please use a nice voice." Sparks flew from Skye's eyes, but the tone of her voice suggested that they were having a nice, pleasant conversation. "If we go with you, will you take us to get medical help?"

"Yes," he snapped.

She glared at him. "Nice voice. Got it?"

He softened his tone, "Of course I'm taking her for medical help."

"Immediately?"

Even under duress she was bargaining? He bit back a smile of admiration and nodded. His smile disappeared when he realized Spring wasn't making eye contact with either of them and Skye looked as scared as he'd seen her look all day.

"Her meds are in my purse. In the van," she paused, drew a deep breath, and worked her hands around Spring's fists, which were now clenched around long strands of her own hair. "And we need our backpacks," she informed him, not removing her eyes, or her arms, from her sister. "We can't leave here without our backpacks; right, sweetheart? Come on, honey. You're fine. We're fine. There's no need to be scared. Breathe for me."

Some of his adrenaline-driven emotions faded as he watched Skye try to soothe Spring, but his irritation didn't ebb. "Why the hell didn't you," with Skye's glare, he softened his tone to one that was as nice as he could make it, "grab your things when you were just at the van, retrieving the damn do-" Another glare made him soften his tone even more. "Candy?"

"Because I hadn't decided to go with you," Skye said, trying to restrain her sister, who was once again fighting the contact. "Until now. If you're in such an all-fire hurry, do your thing, and let's go." Her tone was calm and sugar-sweet, but her eyes blazed sparks into his. "No one knew who we were before you figured it out, so I can only assume you're the one who led them to us. So hurry, and get us out of this mess that you created."

Chapter Six

Sebastian was at the van in a few seconds, grabbed a purse, two backpacks, and made sure he wasn't leaving anything behind, before running back to the Range Rover.

To Pete, over Spring's loud, steady sobs, Sebastian said, "Go. Now."

Jesus. *Clusterfuck?* Yes. Of epic proportions. A frosting-covered dog, one female who wouldn't stop sobbing so loud it resonated in his head, and another female who had figured out a way to blame him for the debacle, when she should have been thanking him for saving her ass. Four dead, two of whom were bystanders. His fault? Unlikely. Yet he sure as hell was going to figure out the how, the who, and the why. Raven One was an option for evacuation, but he didn't want to jeopardize Spring, if there was a possibility of brain trauma. New Orleans and doctors he knew were less than an hour away by car. Proximity made driving a better option than getting on Raven One and heading to headquarters, and given that they were already in the car, he decided it was best to just drive the whole way. "Head to New Orleans."

On a more minor level, he had Skye's purse, their two backpacks, one of which was decorated with about a million rhinestones in a riot of color, and his own backpack, all crowded into the space where his legs needed to stretch. Embrace the suck was a Black Raven mantra. It meant all kinds of things in his line of work. He could handle this, no matter how odd it was. While his gut told him he'd just gotten one step closer to an answer to the question of the day, a sinking feeling told him that if this was how he was going to find Richard Barrows, the ride ahead was going to be damn turbulent.

As Pete put the car in drive, Sebastian unholstered his Glock. Keeping the gun at his side, he glanced into the backseat. Smears of white cake, orange and turquoise icing, and blood marred the dog's fur and both sisters. Spring had her face buried in Candy's fur and her shoulders heaved with the force of her sobs. Skye wasn't looking at him, and, though her arms were around her sister, her attention wasn't focused on Spring, either. Rubbing her sister's narrow back, she looked out of the rear window and didn't return his gaze until Creative Confections was gone from view. Gone, he knew, from their lives for now and for the foreseeable future.

When her eyes finally met his, Skye's eyes had the fear of a trapped animal and the irritation of a woman who had lost control. "Hand me my purse." No longer pacifying, she now sounded defeated, worried, and not at all happy about her predicament. Her cheeks were flushed and her eyes were bright. If he hadn't seen so many photographs of her gorgeous smile, by looking at her now he'd have thought that she wasn't capable of such an expression. "My purse?" she said, this time her tone firm, with a question in it, as though she really thought he hadn't heard her the first time.

"Not yet," he said, his eyes returning to the road. No tail.

"I need her meds," she said through clenched teeth. The woman had a temper. What was fascinating was watching her win the struggle to control it. She drew a deep breath, tried to lower the window, and couldn't. "Please put a crack in the window."

She said please as though she meant it, without irritation or sarcasm. Pete glanced at Sebastian. Sebastian nodded, and Pete lowered Skye's window about an inch.

She lifted her face to the fresh air, breathed deeply, before refocusing on him. "Thank you. Her meds. You really should be helping me out on this," her voice was low and controlled and barely audible over her sister's cries. "If you want her to be quiet anytime soon."

In her neatly organized purse, Skye had another handgun, just like the one that she'd pulled on him earlier. He unloaded it and slipped it into his backpack. A cell phone was in a zippered pocket. He found a clear plastic bag with a zipper and prescription bottles. He studied the meds, recognizing most of the meds in Spring's name and knew the symptoms they treated—anxiety, attention deficit disorder, headaches, sleep aids. Birth control pills were in Skye's name. Great. That was one piece of information he didn't need to think about. He handed the medicine bag to Skye, who met his gaze with a glare at the invasion of privacy.

He took out Skye's cell phone and dialed Ragno's direct line. A glance in the visor mirror, positioned so he could see those in the backseat, as well as the road behind him, told him they weren't being followed. When Ragno answered, he said, "This is the one that you've been tracking, correct?"

"Yes," Ragno said. "That belongs to Skye. Can you even hear yourself think with that crying going on?"

"Barely." *And it isn't helping this damn headache.* He'd had a headache since July. When he had made a near-fatal mistake, while helping his best friend. While each day guaranteed a headache, severity was a crapshoot. He hoped that this one didn't become mind numbing, the kind of icepick through the brain pain that reminded him the doctors weren't finished with him. He shrugged off that concern. There was not one goddamn thing he could do about that problem, except remind himself to embrace the suck.

He searched the rhinestone-encrusted backpack, took out a phone that was tucked into a side compartment, and dialed Ragno again. She answered, "That one is for Spring. We've been tracking it. It's been ten minutes, Sebastian. Ready for me to get Minero on the line?"

To Ragno, he said, "Give me five more." To Skye, he said, "Where's your other phone?"

She stared at him without answering.

"Your other phone. Where is it?"

She stared straight into his eyes with an expression that was suddenly so blank it was almost laughable. He mentally added *piss-poor liar* to her long list of attributes, as she said, "I don't have another phone."

Pete glanced at Sebastian. He gave a slight 'no' headshake before refocusing his attention on the road.

Hell. She couldn't lie worth a damn, yet she had lived a fake life with the skill of a spymaster. She was a goddamn ball of contradictions. He sure as hell hoped that he didn't have to figure her out in order to find her father.

"We observed another phone. Tucked into your belt."

She gave him the same steady, blank look. "You're wrong."

"Ragno, she says you're wrong."

"Like that ever happens. It's a Motorola Razr."

"Keep it up," he said, turning into the backseat. A warning that lying to a federal investigator was going to give her jail time faded into the world of unsaid words, as he watched Skye extend her hand to Spring, with two small white pills in her palm. Still sobbing, face red and eyes swollen, Spring slapped her sister's hand away. The pills flew and landed somewhere, sight unseen. Skye didn't react to the slap by doing anything except drawing a deep, exasperated breath. Spring turned from her sister, sobbing louder as she bent to bury her face into the scruff of the shaking, whimpering dog's neck.

"It h-urts," Spring said, between sobs. "It really h-urts."

"I know it does, baby. I'm trying to help you. Please, please take your meds. They'll make you feel better," Skye said and fumbled with the pill bottle.

"N-No," Spring sobbed louder.

Don't look, he told himself, when Skye gave up with the pill bottle and glanced at him without bothering to conceal the raw desperation in her eyes. *Just don't fucking look at the pathetic mess of cake and blood-splattered women, and the dog that hasn't stopped shaking.*

He returned his attention to the front, and opened the backpack that wasn't covered in rhinestones, figuring that the plainer one was for Skye. He tried to ignore the sound of Spring crying with the reckless abandon of a child. He pulled out a family photograph, in a frame, of a much younger Skye with her mother and father. Spring was a baby, in her mother's arms. The mother looked like Skye-gorgeous, with long black hair, eyes that were so pretty they were the focal point in the picture, and a smile that lit up the world. So, he thought, the long blonde hair in the bikini photo had been straight out of the bottle. *Fuck.* Focus, Connelly. Figuring out her natural hair color sure as hell wasn't relevant to the problem of the day.

Inside the bag, there were two fabric pouches. The smaller one had handwritten letters to Skye from her mother. He unzipped the larger one, which filled most of the bag. *Well, well.* The pouch had cash, and plenty of it, bound together in clumps of five thousand dollars. A silver, metallic-zippered pouch contained a handful of gold medallions, and a small, black velvet pouch. Ten loose diamonds spilled from it, when he emptied it into his hand. Most were sizable, at least two carats. Some were larger.

The cash, gold, and diamonds spelled a run-like-there's-no-fucking-tomorrow bartering system. The woman was a regular Girl Scout—prepared, ready to act, and even taking irreplaceable family heirlooms with her. Was this a daily readiness, or had she gotten wind that someone was coming for her today? Who had she been anticipating?

Had Barrows somehow contacted his daughter and warned her there'd be a manhunt, and to split before her secret location was found? Because not only had Black Raven found the Barrows girls, those goons back there had found them just as quickly. His people were the best at what they did. And yet those guys had shown up at exactly the same time. There were four scenarios, none of which Sebastian liked. One, someone was as smart as his own people. Two, he'd been followed. Three, someone inside Black Raven was working for the other side. Four, the marshals had a breech.

He hadn't been followed. That ruled out one of the three scenarios. He said quietly, and with leashed fury. "Check for a mole."

"Already working on that scenario," Ragno said in his ear.

Pete cast him a worried, frowning glance. None of the scenarios was acceptable, and no stone would be left unturned until he had all the answers.

At least the crying was tapering off. Sebastian turned around. Skye rubbed Spring's shoulders and shot him a glacial look, as he showed her the glittering diamonds in the palm of his hand. "I'm approximating I've got about a half a million here. You were poised to run, even before I showed up. Who alerted you, or was it just a psychic flash?"

Cheeks flushed red, her hostile eyes held his. "It's all for you, if you let us go now."

Closing his hand, he chuckled. He had worked his way though law school as a cop, using every cent that he earned for rent, tuition, and books. Overtime work helped, but there still hadn't been enough money. He'd eaten red beans and rice, the cheapest, filling food he could find, for months on end. Even then, he had never considered taking a bribe. "Not in your lifetime, lady."

Spring had stopped sobbing. Her face remained buried in Candy's fur, but one eye was visible, and focused on Sebastian.

His eyes bounced from the younger sister to the older. In a benign tone, as though she was asking something as simple as whether he wanted a cup of coffee, Skye said, "I can get more, if that will help you decide."

Ragno gave a low whistle. Sebastian glanced at Pete, who gave him an arched-eyebrow look, then into the eyes of the woman who was trying to buy him off. "How much more?"

"Name your price," she glanced at Spring before her eyes leveled on his, "and use your nice voice."

***

"Two pieces of bad news," Blake Dunbar said as he entered the ninth-floor, spacious office.

"I don't pay you to deliver bad news," James Trask said, while thinking, *idiot*. Dunbar was Trask's top adviser on Project LID, and his job was simple. Acquire LID Technology. Make it work. LID was the encryption program that Barrows used for Shadow Technology. If they could access it, they'd have access to the data the U.S. government was collecting on citizens, countries, and the world.

Bad news was not a part of the equation.

Before Dunbar appeared, Trask had been studying a pulsing, light-driven wall of monitors. Since he didn't consider bad news as news, per se, he kept his focus on the display of seven continents, which revealed the global network of his holdings. Scrolling numbers measured economic activity. When his assets had reached the billion dollar mark, he'd stopped counting anything but millions. Before turning to Dunbar, he waited to see if one number in particular was going to pulse red or green in its next iteration. Red. The South American subsidiary was on his watch list for the week. Depending on what he found, heads would roll. Perhaps literally.

Trask was never going to be bored with acquiring wealth, but his most important project of the moment—Project LID—wasn't on the wall. It couldn't be measured by dollars. Project LID could only be accomplished by obtaining information from Barrows, who wasn't cooperating.

He turned to Dunbar, a tall, fit man in his early fifties, with the posture of a military man, and full head of black hair that he was particularly vain about. It didn't occur to him to offer Dunbar a seat. This wasn't a social call. Since Trask stood while working, he expected all who entered his office to do the same. He and Dunbar were almost eye to eye. Most of his work involved analyzing data and telling other people what to do, and those tasks could be accomplished on his feet. Sitting led to sloth. He also didn't tolerate uncontrolled emotions in business matters, and Dunbar's calm manner did nothing to reveal any measure of just how bad the news was.

Trask raised a brow when Dunbar remained mute. "Well?"

Dunbar glanced away before answering.

The quick action was almost imperceptible, but he knew that the hesitation and eye shift signified fear. His subordinates had good reason to be afraid to deliver bad news. It was a task that sometimes came with lethal results, and in his world, death wasn't easy, clean, or fast. The logical part of his brain, the gray matter that fueled the public face at the pinnacle of the world he created, did not become a demon with bad news. There were times, however, when something else thrived. The demonic part of his brain had nothing to do with logic. His demonic side was as drawn to bad news as a hungry infant was drawn to suckle at its mother's breast. Once internal fires stoked the dark side of his mind, his only release came through domination over human weakness. Torture was a game in which he excelled. He loved to touch flesh as he killed his prey.

Several carefully-selected executive assistants were well compensated to assist him in those moments where he allowed his dark side to rule. The end goal was to make sure that the mess he created could never be traced to him or anything having to do with him. Dunbar, one of those assistants, had stood, side-by-side with him, in some of his most depraved moments. Dunbar was wise to be afraid. The negative energy that Trask so carefully channeled as he navigated through an imperfect world had to be released, and when he gave himself license to release the molten, anger-driven energy, he amazed even himself at how much of a thrill he received. He readied himself for the news that made Dunbar hesitate.

"Barrows' daughters escaped," Dunbar said, "and, in our effort to secure them, two of our men were killed."

Trask savored the rocket-fueled surge of fury that came with the bad news. He channeled the energy to a place where it could be released later. He turned his back on Dunbar to face the wall of windows that gave him a panoramic view of Norfolk Naval Station. Preferring dimness to the stark brightness of the clear morning, he pressed a button and lowered the sun-filtering, see-through shades on the windows. Other than the red, green, and blue lights on the wall of monitors, there was no light in his office.

His gaze slid over the aircraft carriers, cruisers, and guided missile destroyers that were in port. Such physical displays of old-school power only made him feel more superior, because he understood something that others did not. Cyber-power was more important than military power. His gaze slid to the USS Harry S. Truman, an aircraft carrier that was home-ported in Norfolk. He would have a hell of a time stealing an aircraft carrier and getting away with it, but the U.S. government was assembling a treasure-trove of information in PRISM and other databases, and now that he had Richard Barrows, the treasure would be his. With access to the information, the possibilities of what he could do were infinite. He'd be able to hold the U.S. economy hostage.

If he chose.

His people obviously weren't grasping how important the daughters were to Project LID. He swallowed back his fury and forced himself to reflect only calm on the outside, as he gripped the binoculars and scanned the naval station. "There is no risk that this will get back to us, correct?"

"No. Fingerprints aren't in databases. There's no association on the corpses with our operations. Our other two men returned, did a site assessment, and disappeared before law enforcement arrived."

He focused on the navy's missile destroyers, methodically training his gaze from bow to stern, shifting his attention from ship to ship. It was his method of counting to ten for calmness. Sometimes it worked. He had known that Project LID would be an extraordinary challenge. He would succeed; it was just going to take time.

"How is it that you sent four men, trained in extraction techniques and military tactics, to secure two women, one of whom is mentally deficient and barely lives in the real world, and they failed?"

"We're gathering information," Dunbar said, trying to sound calm, but his voice had undertones of indecision and worry. With the sound of Dunbar's weakness, delicious fury grew. Trask focused on the gun turret of the USS Cole as he listened. "We believe Black Raven arrived on the scene and ambushed our men. Sebastian Connelly was on the premises, and we believe he secured the daughters."

His heartbeat quickened at Connelly's name, his senses as sharp as a great white shark detecting the first drop of fresh blood off an island of fat seals. He'd been working on extracting Barrows from prison for months. He'd known that Black Raven had secured the federal contracts for providing prison security systems; he just hadn't expected them to start at the prison where Barrows was being held. Once Black Raven focused on the facility where Barrows was imprisoned, he knew they needed to secure Barrows before the Black Raven security system was fully operational. His top advisers had admitted that breaking into a Black Raven security system would present challenges they might not be capable of overcoming.

Now that Trask had Barrows, he doubted that the marshals alone would have put the pieces together and presented a significant stumbling block to Project LID. Black Raven, though, was capable of being more than a stumbling block. Thankfully, he was smarter than Black Raven and the marshals combined.

Black Raven had, in the past, been a thorn in the side of some of his more sensitive operations. Connelly was the founder of the company, which had been in its infancy in 2001. It had grown exponentially after the September 11th attacks, and Connelly had expanded Black Raven by taking on partners who had private security contracting companies of their own, with varying specialties. The partners called themselves Ravens, and they recruited their agents from top talent in the military, local police forces, technology schools, and even, if rumors were true, street gangs. In overseas operations in particular, Black Raven was a formidable force.

His company regularly attempted to cherry-pick Black Raven agents for his internal security force, as did others with complex global security needs. In the last year, cherry-picking operations had been more successful than in years past. "The former Black Raven agents who now work for me?"

Dunbar nodded. "Yes?"

"Assemble them here. ASAP." He drew a deep breath. "Where are the daughters now?"

From behind him, as he focused his binoculars for a closer view of the gun turret on the USS Winston S. Churchill, Dunbar said, "With Connelly."

Jesus. When had the man become a moron? "You just said that. What is their location?"

"We're not sure."

As Dunbar's news fast-tracked from bad to worse, Trask channeled the negative energy to his dark side, while keeping his features calm, and willing his pulse to remain steady. He put the binoculars down on his desk and faced Dunbar in time to catch him pulling out a handkerchief and wiping his brow. The need to wipe sweat from the brow was a gesture that reminded him that no matter how good his people were, they were human, with weaknesses. He hated weakness of any kind. He looked Dunbar in the eye, gave him a reassuring nod, while debating whether to slice through the man's carotid or make it slow and painful, and said, "Okay, so we're having a few issues. We're smarter than these people, and that includes Connelly. We'll work through it."

Dunbar drew a deep breath and exhaled, his relief with the reassuring words palpable. *Fool.* As soon as he figured out what the hell was going on, and what the next step should be, Dunbar was going to die.

"Do we have access to Black Raven's communications?"

Dunbar shook his head. "Their system is impenetrable."

"Nothing is impenetrable."

"Black Raven's system is as good as ours. It might be better." The man's face was sweaty and flushed. "That's why we spend so much money and time trying to recruit their personnel."

"I've hired his agents and we still can't penetrate their system?"

"That's correct," Dunbar said, "the Black Raven agents we've managed to hire haven't been hacking or techno experts. For the most part, they're field agents."

He paused. Well, maybe Black Raven's system was impenetrable. He and his men had attempted to breach Black Raven's communications a year earlier. They had failed then and would fail again, unless they could recruit key technological players from Connelly and his Ravens. He made a mental note to make a more concerted effort on hiring a broader spectrum of Black Raven agents, as he shifted his focus to the task at hand.

"What do you propose?" He let Dunbar give himself his next assignment. By allowing his people to think for themselves, or letting them think that they were thinking for themselves, he empowered them. Empowered people tried harder.

"The marshals' communications systems and databases have operations that we can infiltrate. That is how we knew Connelly was involved and how we knew the location of Barrows' daughters. We're monitoring all of the marshals' communications that we can access," Dunbar informed him, stuffing his handkerchief in his pocket, looking relieved that he could deliver details. Like a puppy wagging its tail, some of his hangdog moroseness disappeared with his explanation.

Imbecile. As though monitoring the communications of the marshals was an achievement worthy of pride, when the average sixth grade nerd with an iPad should now be able to accomplish that. Yet he gave a nod of encouragement and a benign, calm smile, while hoping Dunbar's incompetence hadn't infected the other people who were working on Project LID.

Dunbar continued, "Unfortunately for Connelly, in this operation Black Raven has to communicate with the marshals. We'll learn from the marshals where Connelly and the daughters are. Once we know where they are, we'll have them."

"I want to be there for the intercept."

Dunbar frowned. "I'm not sure that is advisable."

"My project. My world." Even though Trask questioned Dunbar's capacity to provide advice, logic told him that his on-scene presence was not advisable. He didn't always follow logic, though. His most logic-defying moments had gotten him where he was today. "I'm not seeking advice. I'm telling you to make it happen."

"As you wish. That was just one piece of the bad news."

His spine tingled with Dunbar's momentary hesitation. "There's more?"

"Barrows knows we're lying."

With that bit of bad news, Trask's world stood still. "How do you know that?"

Blake handed him a piece of paper.

"*131441413923117208152620.*" He read the numbers twice. He glanced up with a frown. "What is this?"

"Our code cracking system indicates it is three words. *Cataclysm. Now. Run.* Barrows texted it at exactly five twenty five a.m. this morning. We learned the location of the phone at the same time we confirmed through our intercept of the marshals' communications where the daughters were. Barrows wouldn't have sent his daughter such a message unless he saw through our G-scenario."

Like molten lava, anger billowed through his veins. He breathed deeply and managed to keep his facial features calm, but barely. "Barrows had the capability of sending a text? From our system? Who allowed that to happen?"

Dunbar gave him a slow headshake. "No one."

"Bullshit. Who are you protecting? And know that they're going to die in the next ten minutes. It has to be someone's fault."

"No. It isn't. I told you from the beginning that providing Barrows access to computers was dangerous. He created the capability. Also, it appears that for the last two days, while he pretended to cooperate with us, all he was doing was attempting to destroy our data."

Now his heart was racing, but he merely said, "Time for Plan B."

Blake nodded. "I anticipated the switch. I implemented it before I came up here."

"In the meantime, let's give Connelly and the marshals something new to worry about."

"Is it time for the media to break the news of the prison break?"

"Soon. But first, let's give them one hell of a story. You have secured the information that we needed on Biondo, correct?"

"Absolutely."

"Kill the primary witness against him in his trial. Now. Alert officials. Let the media know that there's been a cover-up, the prison break happened four days ago, a killer is on the loose from the prison break, Barrows escaped, and no one in authority has any idea where he might be. Paint the marshals as incompetent, but lay all the blame on Black Raven. Turn up the heat with every piece of bad news you can find on Black Raven. Let Americans know that Black Raven is an unregulated army of vigilante, assault-weapon toting extremists who are operating in their backyards. Create what you can't find. You remember those crazy people with foil hats on their head, who kept vigil when Barrows was first imprisoned?"

Dunbar nodded.

"Use them. The media will pounce on that image."

Chapter Seven

Skye's request that Sebastian name his price gave him an answer to the question of how desperate she was. *Off-the-charts desperate.* Now he just had to figure out why, and soon. The intense fire that burned in her eyes revealed a resilience that told him that he was nowhere close to an answer.

He peeled his eyes from hers and glanced at her body, counting at least five places, including body cavities, where she might have more cash, diamonds, and gold stashed. He contemplated a strip search after they stepped out of the SUV, a task he'd done more times than he cared to count. Thinking about doing one on her, though, prompted an instant throb between his legs and his mind flashed to how he'd explore one particular body cavity of hers. Invasive strip search? Unlike any he'd done before? Hell yes. Long, slow, and hard. It would be pure pleasure.

Son of a bitch.

Now that his libido was awake, he needed sex, and that was just another problem to throw upon the shit-pile that he was shoveling through. He shifted in the front seat and dragged his eyes up, to her face, and away from her killer body. Her narrow-eyed, dagger-filled glance suggested to him that she knew exactly where his mind had wandered.

Fuck me to hell and back.

He could only hope. He wasn't touching her to search her. She could have billions on her. He didn't care. She wasn't getting away from him. No matter how hard she tried. "You're smart enough to understand the serious criminal penalties associated with an attempt to bribe a federal official, right?"

"You're not a federal official."

"No. That's why you're damn-"

"Nice," Skye interrupted, as Spring broke into a fresh batch of sobs. "Speak nicely, underst-"

"Damn lucky right now. I can pretend that this never happened. Try it on the marshals, though, and see how many years that gets you." Instead of arguing further, he faced the front of the SUV and returned his attention to Spring's backpack, where there was order and tidiness. Thankfully, there were no weapons and nothing that could be used for bribes. He pulled out a plastic case with about a hundred pointy silver things, a few white things, and metal discs with a silver handle. He'd seen similar tools in the icing room. They couldn't be considered a weapon, at least not much of one. She had a pack of wet wipes. He helped himself to one and wiped his hands before passing the pack into the back seat to Skye.

"There's blood on your hands," he said, "And it could be theirs."

The color faded from her face. As she gasped, Spring's sobs ramped up in volume. *Dammit.* Skye ripped open the pack of wipes and scrubbed her hands, before attending gently to her sister. He returned his attention to Spring's backpack. Until Spring quieted down, there was no point in trying to call Minero, because now that the sound was in his head, he could barely hear himself think. He saw an iPad and pink headphones, a zippered pouch with colored pencils, and a sketchpad.

He opened the sketchpad. Spring drew the cakes that she decorated with an architect's precision. He thumbed through the pages where the bank's cake, the one that was now smeared all over the sisters and Candy and even on him, had been painstakingly laid out. He could understand the design, because he'd seen the cake, but the words she used, in neat, block letters, made no sense. Columns of numbers were next to the words. He shut the pad, glanced into the back seat, and waved it in the air, wondering if her sketchpad would shut her up. She glanced at it and sobbed louder. Nestled into the bottom of her backpack, beneath a bag containing rawhides for the dog, he saw a large bag that contained what he guessed were two pounds of assorted jellybeans. Ah. Maybe candy would work. He doubted it, but maybe. He lifted the bag of candy, recognized the popular name brand, turned to look at Spring, and showed her what was in his hand. "May I?"

She sniffed as she lifted her face from the dog's neck. Her nose wasn't bent or crooked. It had stopped bleeding. There was dry blood caked around her upper lip, but when she rubbed her sleeve against her mouth, most of it disappeared. He hoped that her nose wasn't broken, and he took the fact that her eyes weren't black and there was only minimal bruising as good signs.

"May I?" he asked again, holding the bag of candy higher.

She shook her head. Between loud sobs she said, "No."

"Please? Jellybeans are my favorite." Not exactly true, but he certainly didn't mind them. His sweet tooth wasn't very discriminating. He loved sugar, in most forms. Her denim-blue eyes held his as she gave a loud sniff. They had about forty-five minutes to drive to New Orleans, and he had way more important things than jellybeans to worry about. However, getting Spring to stop crying so loudly that windows could break seemed as important as anything else. If nothing else, the quiet might alleviate his headache.

Between deep gulps of air, Spring asked, "Do you have a favorite flavor?"

"Cherry."

She frowned. "You can't have those."

"What about cinnamon?"

"No," she shook her head, and for the first time since the debacle in the driveway, he saw something less than misery in her eyes. "You can't have any of the rosy ones."

He chuckled. "Don't tell me you're only going to give me the black."

"Squid's usually for Candy, unless I'm mixing it with another flavor."

"What about popcorn?"

"No. No movies for you, and don't even ask for the sun."

"What can I have?"

"Daydreams. You can only have the daydreams."

What the hell? "What color is that?"

Spring gave him an intense stare, as though she couldn't understand what he was saying. "Chloe. Help him."

He glanced at Skye, whose irritated glance told him that helping him do anything wasn't high on her list of priorities. "Coconut. They're opaque white. Pure white. Not whitish yellow. And don't make a mistake, because she won't be happy," she said, in a nice voice, but with unamused eyes. "Now hand me her iPad and headphones."

"Three," Spring said. "Only take three. You see, I started with exactly forty-five of each color. I haven't eaten any of those yet, because I don't like them. So you'll really be helping me, because the numbers are off."

He didn't press for details on why that made sense. He reached into the bag and fished out three opaque white jellybeans before handing the bag to Spring. He popped one in his mouth, chewed slowly, and savored the coconut explosion. "You know," he said to Spring, "this could make me daydream. I think your name's right on target."

Spring rewarded him with a beautiful smile before focusing her attention on the bag. "It isn't my name, it's my father's-"

"Her iPad," Skye interrupted, with a snap of exasperation, "and earphones. Now."

"Use your nice voice," he said, glancing into her gorgeous, pissed-off eyes while he popped a second jellybean in his mouth. "And say please."

Skye's cheeks turned pinkish-red, matching some of the jellybeans of that hue. Spring was digging in the bag of candy, for the moment oblivious to her sister's tension. Skye gave him a smile that dripped with sarcastic sweetness. "Please."

Sebastian glanced at the iPad, went to the data settings, and coded it so that data streaming and communication was off. He installed a new security code, so that Skye couldn't undo his settings.

Ragno said, "It's been five minutes."

"Get Minero on the line," he answered.

Sebastian brushed Skye's hand with his fingertips as he handed her the tablet. Their eyes locked with the touch, and for a second, all he saw was fear. He didn't know the source of it, but he needed to figure out a way to make sure that she wasn't afraid of him. Irritation with him was fine. Fear was bad. With fear, she'd never tell him a goddamn thing that could be helpful in the search for her father. He glanced out of the SUV's rear windows as Pete changed lanes, accelerated, and passed a slower car. They weren't being tailed. "When I get on the phone with Minero, the marshal who is in charge of the jailbreak, I'm going to have a conversation that's going to be disturbing." He gave a quick, pointed glance to Spring. "Understand?"

Skye gave him a small nod as she put the earphones on Spring's ears and fooled with the iPad. She sighed in relief as Spring looked up, gave her a thumbs up, and returned her head to Skye's shoulder.

With Spring's attention focused elsewhere, he said, "It would be damn helpful if you'd tell me why you were living under an assumed name."

Her cheeks flushed pink as she held his gaze. "It was easier to be someone else than to be Richard Barrows' daughters."

"That's it?"

She gave him a blank expression and a nod. "Yes."

"I'm not buying it. Your alias was too good. Too elaborate."

She shrugged. "I'm Richard Barrows' daughter. I don't do halfway." She paused, her eyes bright. "Just an FYI. My father never would have escaped. Not voluntarily. Someone kidnapped him."

Doubtful, but possible. Anything was possible. "Who would go through that trouble?

"Isn't that your job to figure out?"

Fuck.

Yes, it was, and he wasn't going to be getting help from her anytime soon. Sebastian turned to face forward. No matter how fucked-up the situation had become, this was progress. At least he'd gotten there in time to thwart the kidnapping.

"Minero's on a conference call," Ragno said. "His office said he'll be available in a few minutes."

"Find Brandon," he said. Brandon was from New Orleans, and part of his legal practice involved crisis management for Black Raven. "While you're doing that, talk to me about Barrows and any of his work that could be relevant to his escape."

"As you know, Barrows has an enormous body of work involving computing innovations," Ragno said. "The backup for his theories, the data that he produced, has to be somewhere. There's just no way of knowing what could be relevant to his escape."

Her voice was low and controlled, but there was an undertone of excitement. Innovative ideas in computer and spyware technologies were a hobby of hers, so she loved the Barrows project. "Plus, there are interviews, some with credible tech magazines, but there's also hundreds of transcripts of late-night conspiracy theory-type radio shows. And there are the debriefing transcripts. Thousands of pages, where it seems he took the time to tell the government everything that he thought was wrong with every governmental program, every agency. We're only at the beginning of dissecting the transcripts, but check out the excerpt that I'm sending you now. With your fascination with the Fourth Amendment, you're going to love it."

He popped the last jellybean in his mouth, savoring the candy shell before chewing through to the soft inside. Save for the feel of Skye's eyes boring into the back of his head, the quiet that now filled the SUV made the ride relatively pleasant. He reached into his own backpack for his iPad. He switched it on and read through the text that Ragno sent.

> **FBI Interrogator:** *Mr. Barrows, I'm trying to focus on the tax evasion offense for which you're being prosecuted. I don't want speeches on civil liberties.*
>
> **Barrows:** *But it's the same theme. The government is taking good ideas and implementing them the wrong way.*
>
> **FBI Interrogator:** *And you have answers?*
>
> **Barrows:** *The government is collecting every e-mail, phone call, internet search, book download, and social media post. They're not only collecting, they're assimilating. I know, because I created the assimilation technology. They're shadowing people. These are shadows from which the average American cannot separate. The bottom line is that such action is a search that is contrary to the Fourth Amendment. I can't force the government to abide by the Fourth Amendment, but the data that's being collected needs to be protected.*
>
> **FBI Interrogator**: *And you have a proposal to do that?*
>
> **Barrows**: [Pause]. *What is your clearance level?*

Sebastian chuckled. "Did he explain his proposal to the interrogator?

"If he did, we don't see it. Yet," Ragno said, as her fingers ticked away on her keyboard. "We're only at the beginning. Fascinating, right? Check out this passage."

> **FBI Agent:** *After September 11, 2001, you were an advocate for mass data collection by the U.S. government as a method of preventing future terrorist attacks, am I correct?*
>
> **Barrows:** *Yes, but never to the extent the government is collecting information from U.S. citizens without their knowledge and without*

anything resembling probable cause. Any legitimate reading of the Fourth Amendment to the U.S. Constitution prohibits such action. I designed Shadow Technology as a tool for use after probable cause is established. Instead, the government is using it without probable cause, on law-abiding citizens. All day, every day, without probable cause.

"Some of what Barrows is saying here makes sense," Sebastian said, scanning the road as Pete stopped at a red light. They'd come to an area that was congested with strip malls. Drive-thru windows at fast food outlets were busy. Schools were already in session. Most cars had just one person, and that was the driver. Using the visor's mirror, he glanced at Skye, who used the mirror as well. Their eyes met and their gazes locked on each other. Her expression was blank, as though she had no interest in what he was saying to Ragno, yet her intense look told him otherwise. "We now know that the government's data collection efforts through PRISM are pervasive, and this debriefing occurred in 2012, right?"

"Correct."

"Barrows is talking about things that didn't come to light until more recently, with the whistle-blowing from employees at the National Security Agency." He looked for a reaction from Skye. None. Her face was impassive, yet her eyes were trained on his.

"Well, that's one way of looking at it," Ragno said, her tone dry. "The official way of looking at it, and I mean official way being from our sources at the NSA and the FBI, is that Barrows made lucky guesses that were the product of a paranoid mind. He talks about Shadow Technology, which I was looking into even before we received the transcripts-"

"Is Shadow Technology something he developed?" Sebastian noticed Skye lift her chin and smooth her hair as he asked the question, but otherwise, there was no reaction from her at his mention of Shadow Technology.

"In Barrows' mind," she said, "but in reality, the official line is it doesn't exist."

Black Raven spent a lot of time investigating security threats of all sorts, enough time that Sebastian knew official lines were often bullshit. "What's your unofficial line?"

"Well, we're still looking into it, given how often he refers to it, but we haven't managed to receive one confirmation that any such software was ever developed. Interspersed in all of those moments of prophetic brilliance are passages that analogize computer intelligence to extraterrestrial life. It is going to take some time to unravel this ball of yarn."

"Time is a luxury we don't have. Back away from the details. Are there any odd occurrences?"

"Yes. When the feds were collecting data on his tax evasion scheme, they secured search warrants for BY Laboratories, the company that Barrows and Zachary Young founded in the nineties. When the feds arrived there, about one month before Barrows pleaded guilty, everything was stripped. Barrows had infected everything with a virus. It seemed that he had destroyed his life's work. Young was no help, because by then, he was dead, and the timing could be considered an odd occurrence, because the feds were turning the heat on the company for the tax evasion scheme."

He felt a tap on his shoulder. He turned. Spring had her hand extended, reaching out to him. He reached for her hand, and she dropped three more coconut jellybeans into his hand with a smile that made him damn glad she hadn't been killed on that driveway. The world needed her brand of sweetness. "Thank you."

While Spring was disheveled, but smiling, big sis's expression indicated she'd have been glad if the jellybeans were poison. He popped a jellybean in his mouth, chewed it slowly while he looked at Skye, thoroughly enjoying irritating her before turning to the front of the car. To Ragno, he said, "I thought Barrows admitted that he was the architect behind the tax evasion crime."

"He did, but the company, of which Young was half owner, was on the line for millions upon millions of dollars for back taxes."

"Tell me the circumstances of Young's death."

"It fits in with the odd occurrence label. A plane crash. Private jet. Entire family. Wife, two daughters, one son. All died. No one could have survived," Ragno said. "The jet inexplicably crashed into the side of a mountain instead of gaining altitude as it should have."

"Cause?"

"Undetermined."

"Any foul play suspected?" He looked into the mirror where he met Skye's strong-willed gaze.

"None that we've uncovered."

"What else is odd?"

"Barrows claimed that he didn't have backup for any of his projects that were in development," Ragno said. "That's odd. Ridiculous, as a matter of fact. He also consistently talked about Shadow Technology and LID Technology as though these things existed and had been implemented by the government, as though he worked for years creating it, but there is absolutely no evidence that these things ever existed. What's odd is that in his ramblings, he consistently refers to data collection capabilities, and the timing of what he's saying—remember, his debriefing occurred in 2012—actually predates some of the revelations that were made by government whistle-blowers. So it looks like he had inside knowledge, and how would he have had that, if he hadn't actually been privy to the information?"

"So Barrows claims that he developed Shadow Technology, a state of the art spyware," Sebastian said, "which you've already determined does not exist, right?"

"Well, what we know is that the government says Shadow Technology doesn't exist. We're trying to find out if it was actually in the developmental stage. All I can tell you is that if Shadow Technology exists, Black Raven wants it. We want it bad."

"Why?" He watched a truck merge in front of them. He glanced into the visor's mirror, saw a woman in a ponytail driving an Escort and talking on a phone behind them. He caught Skye's glance, saw that her attention was still riveted on him. Despite her impassive expression, he wondered what answers she might have.

"According to the pieces and parts we're pulling together," he could hear Ragno typing as she continued talking, "Shadow Technology seamlessly ties together all data collection mechanisms. Look at it from the perspective of an individual. Say someone named Mark wakes up, using his cell phone alarm. That's a collection point in surveillance programs. He checks e-mail. That's a collection point. He finally opens yesterday's mail, sees three checks, and deposits them online. Another collection point, and Shadow Technology now has his bank account numbers and passwords. Mark reads USA Today on his tablet while he drinks his coffee. Another collection point, where the government even knows how long Mark spends on what articles. The telematics on Mark's fancy Mercedes traces his steps to his office, and so does the GPS mechanism in his phone. After he kisses his wife goodbye for the day, he detours to his girlfriend's house every Tuesday. The holder of Shadow Technology knows all of that, instantly. Once Mark arrives downtown, he's walking on a busy street with surveillance cameras. Those are also collection points."

"Right. I got it. We know the government collects everything, all the time. So what's new?"

"But the official line from the government is that they don't collect everything, while Barrows insists that they do, and Shadow Technology is more than a collection device," Ragno said. "Barrows claims that Shadow Technology ties all collection points together, assimilates the data, and presents a picture of what that person did that is relevant to search criteria. It turns raw data into knowledge, with just a few keyboard clicks. Say you want to know if Target X ever did anything relevant to Target Y. With just a few key words, through Shadow Technology, you can search the endless data that's been collected and find it. Say you want to know the private banking pass codes of every American who uses the internet to do their banking. Shadow Technology gives you that information on a silver platter. In the wrong hands, it could cripple the economy."

As he listened to Ragno, his heart beat slowed to a dull whump pulse and the day took on a surreal feel. When Black Raven created full-scale profiles on people and businesses, the type of profile that had led him to Skye and Spring, and the type that they were now producing on Jennifer Root, Barrows' lawyer, the profiles were the result of time consuming, in-depth data compilation and analysis. What wasn't available from public data, his technology agents discovered by hacking. Nothing was left untouched. Credit card transactions, banking data, telephone calls, real estate transactions, medical tests. All information was fair game and once it was acquired, it took time to assimilate the information into something useful. Assimilation required computing technology to analyze lifestyle patterns and make predictions regarding behaviors, but it also required human intelligence.

"Are you saying that Shadow Technology could produce one of our profiles in a fraction of the time that it takes your team to do the same thing?" he asked.

"That's exactly what I'm saying. According to Barrows, the Government collects everything, all the time. Shadow Technology instantly makes sense of it," she said and paused. "In contrast, once Black Raven identifies a target, we have to not only collect, we have to process."

"So Shadow Technology takes a surveillance state," he said, his skin crawling with the implications, "and makes it a super smart surveillance state." He looked into the visor's mirror and wondered how Skye managed to reveal nothing.

"A brilliant surveillance state," Ragno said. "It does what we do in days, in a matter of minutes."

He chuckled. "So Shadow Technology might make the cyber geniuses on your team, even you, obsolete?"

"Well, don't start cutting payroll yet. As far as I can tell, Shadow Technology, as Barrows described it, doesn't exist. Remember, the government claims they don't have it."

"What is LID Technology, the other program Barrows referred to?"

"According to Barrows, the LID is an encryption mechanism that protects the data assimilation results produced by Shadow Technology. However, as far as I can tell, in reality, Shadow Technology doesn't exist, and the LID doesn't exist. And based on the FBI reports, when they executed the search warrants for the BY Technologies lab, the virus that Barrows used destroyed everything, and he told officials he had no backup," Ragno said.

"Maybe that's what Barrows claimed," Sebastian said, "but surely law enforcement found some. Right?"

"No. Investigators did not find backup. Even if he was spouting about things that don't exist, like Shadow and LID Technology, he is still a brilliant man. How could the world's foremost pioneer in anti-viral technology not have backup? I don't believe that for one second. Neither does Zeus by the way. None of your technology agents do. We back everything up, Sebastian. We have backup for our backup. A man like Barrows would have even figured out a way to backup his dreams. There has to be backup somewhere. "

Sebastian glanced into the backseat. To Skye, he asked, "Do the terms Shadow and LID Technology mean anything to you?"

"No." She gave him a blank expression, one he couldn't decipher except to think it meant she was lying.

Hell.

"Where's your father's backup?"

It would have been more productive to ask the dead pirate Jean Lafitte where he had buried his trove of gold and jewels. She arched an eyebrow, gave him the same blank expression she'd been giving him, which he now equated to a broadcast beam of a lie, and a slow headshake. "I didn't pay attention to my father's business."

"Algorithms," he said, remembering an intel tidbit that Ragno had fed him earlier.

She shook her head. "Excuse me?"

"You wrote a paper on elegance in algorithm design when you were just a teenager, and you graduated from MIT when you were nineteen. All of your professors declared you to be as brilliant as your father."

She shrugged. "So?"

"So don't play stupid. Telling me that you didn't pay attention to your father's business is just plain stupid. I know you're not stupid. Don't play that card on me."

Her eyes flashed with irritation, but her clenched-jaw silence told him that she wasn't going to be giving up an answer. Even with dark smears of god-knew-what across her right cheek, and tangles in her long hair, her high cheekbones, full lips, and almond-shaped eyes made him want to get closer to her. *Dammit. He was fucked.* He tore his gaze away from the beautiful woman whose existence had, in the flash of a morning's sunrise, become the opposite of the idyllic coffee house world she had created out of thin air. As he faced the front of the car, Ragno said, "Brandon's holding for you."

They reached the Causeway, a 24-mile bridge spanning Lake Pontchartrain and leading to New Orleans. He and Brandon had grown up together in River's Bend, a small town thirty minutes south of New Orleans. They'd been friends since grade school, joined the New Orleans PD together, and gone to law school together. In July, Sebastian had almost gotten himself killed while helping Brandon save the life of the woman who had, in December, become his friend's wife. Brandon knew enough about Black Raven's predicament not to waste time with questions, when Sebastian relayed the fact that he needed a doctor who could look at both a dog and two Jane Does, fast.

Sebastian asked his friend, "Can you get Cavanaugh set up?"

"Yes," Brandon said, "but he's going to give you hell for not showing up yesterday."

"I cancelled the appointment in advance."

"That's not the point, and it wasn't just an appointment. It was pre-op for surgery, which you didn't even bother to tell me about. He had neurosurgeons lined up. You're supposed to be at Ochsner Medical Center now."

"It isn't happening tomorrow, or anytime soon."

"Cavanaugh is pissed. He says the surgery is essential. You could die without it."

And I could die with it. Or worse. "Whatever happened to doctor-patient confidentiality? He shouldn't have talked about my health with you."

"He did so in the context of asking me to tell you to make sure your affairs are in order. I *am* your lawyer."

Fuck me to hell. Cavanaugh's team of neurosurgeons had determined a few weeks earlier that scar tissue was growing in his brain, and the surgery to remedy the problem was going to be tricky. The longer Sebastian waited, the more the scar tissue grew, and the trickier the surgery would become. He had hoped to spare Brandon the worry.

"Until I talked to him," Brandon continued, "I hadn't realized how bad of a situation you're in."

"Don't worry about it. My affairs are in order, and you and Zeus know what to do if-" he let the words trail as he glanced at Pete, whose eyes, for a second, had drifted from the road to him. Pete refocused quickly on the road. He didn't have to look in the mirror to know that Skye was staring at him and listening to his every word. Ragno had listened as well, and her silence was deafening.

Beautiful. Fucking beautiful.

"Cavanaugh's overreacting. He's still the best choice for the moment. I can handle him." He'd have to. He didn't have any other doctors from whom he could secure immediate action in a private setting, and he knew Cavanaugh had the diagnostic tools and personnel that were necessary for a quick assessment. He not only practiced at Ochsner, the area's largest hospital, he ran a boutique hospital that catered to wealthy, private clients, the only one of its kind in the deep South. "Would you get him set up for me now? I've got to get on the phone with a marshal. We're dealing with a multiple-deaths-involved shoot out. Two were collateral damage, two were perps. I've got a Cleaner headed to the scene, but I need you or someone from your office there for damage control. Crisis management is big on this one. Avoid media contact. Steve Broussard would be good on this. He's savvy, street smart, and knows his way around competing law enforcement jurisdictions."

"Got it," Brandon said. "I'll assess, then decide. Where did this happen?"

"Covington. I don't have agents in the New Orleans area now. So on a more basic level, I need you to have someone get a change of clothes for me and two women. We'll only be with Cavanaugh as long as it takes him to get clearance to travel. Hopefully not more than a couple of hours. Ragno?"

"Yes."

"Alert Raven One's pilots that we'll be departing from the New Orleans Lakefront airport. Destination unknown. For now."

He glanced into the back seat, where Skye's eyes, though trained on him, were unreadable. "Sizes?"

"Four for Spring. She's allergic to synthetics. Only natural fibers, like wool and cotton. No rayon, or-"

"I know what synthetic means."

"Six for me-" Skye said.

Her voice trailed when he gave her a slow, appraising glance and a headshake. "I'd have thought an eight." Damn. The comment surprised him as much as it irritated her. He just couldn't resist an easy opportunity to get to her.

Her cheeks turned pink. "Six."

He shrugged. "If you insist. Shoe sizes?"

Skye glanced down to her feet. He'd watched her step through blood and guts. Her cream-suede boots didn't wear that well, and he now realized that she hadn't noticed. When she met his eyes again, all color had faded from her face.

Ragno said, "Jennifer Root called in and is insisting she needs to talk to you."

"About what?"

"She wants to know whether you've found Skye and Spring."

"Tell her no. I'll get back to her later."

"Will do," Ragno paused, "and now Minero is on the line."

"Give me a second," he said. "Skye? Shoe sizes?"

Pained eyes held his. "Eight for me. Spring's a seven and a half." She smoothed her hair back, squared her shoulders.

"Thank you."

He gave her a nod, relayed the information to Brandon, and then broke the connection. To Ragno, he said, "I want me, Minero, and you on the call. No one else. Snap the connection if you have any doubt regarding contamination from his end."

He waited, shut his eyes, and tried to tell himself that his headache wasn't so bad. Yes. He needed surgery. He had no time for that now. When Minero picked up, Sebastian opened his eyes, made sure that Spring had her earphones on, then leaned into the seat and shut his eyes again as he gave Minero details of what had transpired at Creative Confections. He ended with, "Ragno, who is on the line with us, will send you the recording from the coffee house's camera. I haven't looked at it, so I don't know what it captured. Now I'm getting medical assistance for Skye and Spring."

Minero said, "Where?"

"That's on a need-to-know basis."

"You don't have authority to act on your own."

"I'm not telling you where I'm taking them, because it's a safe place, but it isn't a safe house with restricted access, and I'm not sure where the leak came from."

"Whoa. What makes you think there's a leak?"

"Someone knew where they were at the same time that Black Raven did. What do you think? We need to figure out who the hell did this, but we need to be smart about it."

"Did the two coffee house workers who were killed have a relationship with Richard Barrows?"

Sebastian paused. "Ragno?"

"No. They were Covington locals," Ragno answered. "Skye hired them when she arrived there a year ago."

"As far as Black Raven knows," Sebastian said, "as of this morning, the only people who knew that Chloe and Colbie Stewart are actually Skye and Spring Barrows were with Black Raven or the U.S. Marshals Service." Sebastian drew a breath. "Barrows' daughters had great cover. It's entirely too coincidental to assume these thugs were able to find them on their own, or someone else broke their cover just as I did. So at this point, I can't rule out the possibility that the marshals may have a leak, and you can't either."

"What the hell makes you think that it comes from my side?"

"I know my systems and I know my people, Minero," Sebastian said. He did, but it didn't mean that he wouldn't explore whether he had a leak. Just in case. Minero didn't need to know that. "There's no leak on my side. I'm sure of it. One hundred percent sure. If you need details on how secure our system is, talk to Zeus, who'll be helping your cyber-team. My cyber-team doesn't need anyone's help. Understand?"

"Well, given that news of the prison break is about to hit the airwaves at any minute," Minero said, "and given what just happened with Barrows' daughters in Covington, it would be best if they are in official custody. Black Raven doesn't count in this scenario as official custody."

"Once we get an all-clear from the doctor," Sebastian turned and looked at Skye as he spoke, "I'll bring them to you. Come up with a safe house for them, unless you want me to."

"No. I can handle that."

"Fine," Sebastian shrugged, fighting back sudden unease as he tore his eyes away from Skye's wide, alarmed eyes.

She'd heard his side of the conversation, and knew that she was going to be handed off to the marshals. Her fear was palpable. *Why? Why was the prospect of talking to the authorities so frightening for her? What the hell was she hiding, and could it lead to her father?*

"And I mean-an-honest-to-God safe house. We need to figure out who was behind the kidnap attempt and until we do, close your circle. Make sure people who you use for this are on clean lines and that they're not talking-"

"Not my first rodeo, Connelly," Minero interrupted. "I don't need instructions from you. The U.S. Marshals Service has a bit more experience at this than Black Raven."

Sebastian let the comment drop without response. He didn't need to piss the guy off further, because Minero, technically, was in charge of this whole fucked-up situation. Domestic contracts came with a price, and that price was cooperating with the U.S. government and local authorities. It was a high price. That was why Black Raven, until recently, had focused on international operations in far-flung destinations. Keeping top personnel in place, though, meant they had to develop domestic work, because in every agent's life, there were times that the agents wanted to work close to home. For the last two years, Black Raven had focused on developing domestic work, the kind that would keep some of his work force on U.S. soil, but the effort had come with speed bumps.

Sebastian and Brandon's widely-publicized shoot-out in July, which involved the death of a Black Raven agent and an FBI agent on U.S. soil, had not helped the company's reputation or its push for domestic-work, and the prison-break disaster, coming just eight months later, wasn't going to help, either. It was also going to affect their international work, because it made Black Raven look incompetent. Good agents didn't want to wear the badge of an incompetent company, and they'd jump ship in the time it took an elephant to blink.

Black Raven's reputation was at stake, Black Raven depended upon its reputation, one hell of a lot of employees and their families depended on Black Raven, and even more clients depended upon the company. If he was honest with himself, it wasn't just his employees or his clients that he was worried about. Hell.

Without Black Raven, he'd have nothing, and losing the company that he'd built out of thin air would make him exactly what his father had predicted for him. A loser. He'd never been one in his life, and he didn't plan on getting acquainted with that status now. Once he found Barrows, dammit, this would all end. He glanced into the back seat, into slate-green eyes that mirrored his own desire to be out of this fucked-up mess. Once it was over, Skye and Spring could move on with their lives, and he could get on with his.

Chapter Eight

"Take off your mask," Barrows said, between uncontrollable bouts of shivering.

The mask was a custom-fit, lightweight silicone face. It distorted his features into a large forehead, uneven cheekbones, and a comical grimace, though no one ever seemed to recognize the humor. It was a technological marvel, a modern-day mood ring that changed colors with his body heat. His captives never saw him without it, so Barrows' request wasn't going to be met. Trask didn't answer his captives and he never responded to their demands. Not even to laugh at their ridiculous suggestions. He let them figure things out on their own. It gave him pleasure to watch them squirm as their new reality dawned. Rather than give Barrows an answer, he stood there, staring at the man.

Barrows was naked, clamped to a steel chair at his wrists, waist, and ankles, in a white-tiled room designed for easy cleaning of blood and guts. The chair and metal clamps that tied Barrows to the chair were designed to be temperature sensitive. As ice cold water rained on Barrows, the clamps and the chair exacerbated the chill. The room itself was a frigid forty degrees.

Tall, with a naturally lean build, Barrows was in good shape for a man in his fifties. His year in prison made him even leaner, and the soaking chill was sending full-body shudders through him. His lips were almost as blue as his eyes, which gave him a glance that was filled with defiance and loathing, despite the misery that was raining on his body. Between bouts of shivering, Barrows said, "I want to talk to the person who is in charge."

Silence was his answer.

"Who the hell are you?"

He answered that question, from the man who was widely regarded as the world's most brilliant mind, with silence. He never responded to their questions. With a wave of his hand, a signal to a handler who was watching through cameras, the rainfall of frigid water stopped. He approached Barrows and, with his bare index finger, he touched the man's ice-cold shoulder. He traced a line to the man's neck, and pressed the palm of both hands on Barrows' head. Barrows had been inside his headquarters ever since the prison break, but this was his first meeting with him.

Barrows' hair was wet. He bent closer to see into the man's eyes, where angry defiance remained. Barrows' brilliance came with a widely publicized price, and that price was paranoia. He'd have to work hard to come up with a scenario that Barrows hadn't already imagined or anticipated. This man believed in UFO's, after all. He folded his arms, stood a few feet away, gave the signal for the freezing rain, and as the water torture resumed, he waited for Barrows' next question. It didn't take long.

"How did you get my data?"

"So," he paused, "the data that I have is your data, and it is part of the code for the LID?"

Barrows became even paler. He was only inches away from the man, and in the silence that followed the question that he would never answer, he could hear Barrows' teeth chatter. "Who are you? How do you have this information?"

"You're a smart man. You should understand that this is my world, with my rules. Rule number one is that only one of us gets to ask questions. Why doesn't the data work?"

"You only have incomplete code," Barrows said. "What you have is useless."

He shook his head. "That's why I have you. You will complete the code."

"I can't complete it, even if I wanted to. I don't know it. I don't have it memorized. The data sets are too long for anyone to memorize."

"If you don't have it memorized, where is it? Where is it stored?"

"The full data set was destroyed when my lab was destroyed," Barrows said.

"You're too smart for that. Where's the backup?"

"There was no backup."

He believed that about as much as he believed in relying on luck for anything that mattered, which was not at all. Luck only happened to people who had the wherewithal to make things happen. "I have your daughters."

Barrows had a moment of wide-eyed fear, before snarling in

defiance and narrowing his eyes. "You're lying. You don't even know where they are."

"Chloe and Colbie Stewart. Creative Confections. Covington, Louisiana. You sent Chloe a text this morning. *Cataclysm. Now. Run.* Now that we know you sent a text from our system, we're analyzing every keystroke you've made. If you have sent any other messages, I will know. I have your daughters. I have you. Are you willing to cooperate?"

"Bring them to me."

He went to a wall and pressed a button. Hidden compartments opened, revealing gleaming stainless steel trays and tools of torture. His eyes rested on a tray containing custom-made steel rods, in lengths that varied from five inches to two inches, the diameter of each being slightly larger than a pinhead. The hammer that he was going to use could be purchased at any hardware store. The steel chair on which Barrows sat could be manipulated with a press of a button. He lifted Barrows' leg. Bodies were such wonderful things to touch, to torture. Every man could be broken, and Barrows, though a genius, was nothing but a man. He signaled the rain to stop.

For a middle-aged man, Barrows had nice feet. Not too hairy. A few callouses. His toes were straight, the nails were trim. He took his time placing the tip of a four-inch-long steel rod underneath the nail of the man's large left toe. He lifted the hammer and pounded the rod so that it speared into the soft flesh, under the toenail, through the cuticle, and into the toe. He got closer, watching the crimson blood seep around the metal, as he reached for another rod, it's diameter about that of a pinhead, and relished every howl from Barrows that came with each pound of the hammer. Ten rods later, two for each toe, he asked, "What is the code?"

The man was breathing heavy. His blue eyes were wide with panic, yet there was more than a bit of belligerence. "Fuck you."

He gave the wave that signaled for the water torture to begin. "This time, make it hot."

A voice asked, "How hot?"

"Blistering."

Before walking away, he lifted the hammer, and, because Barrows had work to do, he exercised slight restraint. He pounded the head down on Barrows' left kneecap, drawing delicious strength from the feel of steel hitting flesh and shattering bone. "I'll be back for that answer in one hour."

***

10:15 a.m., Monday

Cataclysm. Now. Run.

Almost five of her twenty-four hours had disappeared. Instead of traveling to the North, they had headed South. They'd moved in the wrong direction, away from Tennessee. Now they were trapped in a private hospital in Metairie, a congested suburb of New Orleans. Skye had listened to every word Sebastian had said in the car. As soon as they were done at the hospital, assuming they got clearance from the doctor, he'd hand them off to the marshals.

No way that was going to happen.

One way or another, she and Spring were escaping before he made the hand off. Pete didn't use it, but the hospital had a valet stand. If she needed to persuade the valet attendant to look the other way, she had money. She'd take a car. Lucky for her, Sebastian hadn't realized that the trendy-looking leather belts that she and Spring wore held hiding places for more currency, gold, and diamonds. He could have what had been her purse. It was a small fraction of what she carried to buy freedom.

Sebastian and Pete ushered them into a patient room that looked more like a hotel room than a hospital room, with hardwood floors and a seating area with a couch and two chairs. A wet bar held snacks and bottles of water. Two queen-size beds, spread with crisp linens and plumped pillows, looked inviting enough for Skye to want to fall on the closest one, face first. A man in a lab coat was talking to a nurse. Their conversation stopped as their eyes fell on their group. Skye felt as pathetic as she knew they looked—disheveled, blood-splattered, and sticky with turquoise, orange, and white icing.

To Sebastian, the doctor said, "You look like hell." He gave Candy, who was in Sebastian's arms, a pat on her head, which prompted a slow tail wag. The doctor was middle-aged and slightly balding, with kind brown eyes that rested on Skye and Spring.

Sebastian placed Candy on the bed nearest to the door. He half sat on it, half stood, keeping a reassuring hand on Candy's back.

If this was the 'look like hell' version, Skye wondered about a better one, because Sebastian's tough-guy-yet-charming handsomeness had been obvious from the moment that he had walked across the yard with Candy in his arms, and it hadn't faded, even though his white shirt was blood-smeared from carrying Spring, and maybe some of the icing with which Candy had been covered had rubbed onto his black leather jacket. In the well-lit room, Skye saw heaviness in his eyes, but they were still riveting, with thick lashes and clear blue irises. They belonged to a tall, lean, yet muscular man who felt like he was made of steel when he'd knocked her on the floor of her office and laid on top of her. She'd seen him in action on the driveway, and he was fast and agile. He also had steady aim. She'd seen his smile when he talked to Spring and the dimples and full lips were worth studying, but there was also nothing wrong with the hard set of his strong, square jaw, when he wasn't smiling. Which he usually wasn't when he looked at her, and he wasn't now.

Ignoring the doctor's comment, Sebastian glanced at Skye. "Mary and Jane Smith. This sweet thing," he gestured with his chin to the dog, "is Candy."

Spring, thankfully, was wearing her headphones and was quiet, eyes on the floor, as she leaned against Skye. If Spring had heard the off-the-cuff pretend names, there would have been questions.

The dark-haired nurse looked young, pretty, and fresh. After introducing himself to Skye, the doctor introduced the nurse, Rhonda, to Sebastian and to Skye. She wore a white uniform dress with a pearl-buttoned black sweater with lapel pins. One pin was the pink breast cancer swirl, another was a yellow ribbon, and a third was a cross. Rhonda wore her causes, and a woman with causes, someone who had to be introduced to Sebastian, might fall for a sob story.

Spring hadn't looked up since they entered the room, and the doctor's gaze was now riveted on her.

"I foiled a kidnapping of them," Sebastian explained. "Shots were fired at close range. Two innocent bystanders, friends of theirs, were killed. The younger one seemed unconscious after a hit in her face, and after awakening she had one hell of an anxiety attack."

The doctor's gaze moved to Sebastian, after he provided these details. "Head injuries are serious business," the doctor said, his eyes on Sebastian, "aren't they? They should be treated as such, right?"

The doctor's comment explained Sebastian's habitual fingers-to-the-temples gesture, which Skye had observed since he'd barged, unannounced, into their lives. He pressed at his temple on the right side of his head whenever he was still, as though soothing a throbbing headache. In the car, when he'd been on the phone, he had mentioned an appointment in the same context as an irritated question about doctor-patient confidentiality. *His affairs were in order.* Those comments, coupled with the doctor's 'look-like-hell' assessment and the pointed comment about head injuries, led to only one conclusion—a head injury that was still a problem.

Maybe her luck would turn, and he'd drop dead.

She felt a momentary pang of remorse. After all, he had rescued them and brought them to a hospital.

Well, maybe not drop dead.

Just something that would be temporarily immobilizing. Something less serious than death. Problem was, he looked way too healthy for any real illness, and his steely-and-irritated glance told her he was too angry to die anytime soon.

Sebastian's answer to the doctor was a slow nod and a terse, "That's why we're here."

He lifted Candy from the bed, placed her on the rug in the seating area, and removed the room's cordless phone from the cradle. He gave Skye a pointed look as he kept it in his hand. He walked to the doorway with the phone in his hand.

The doctor glanced at Skye, studying her and Spring. "Tell me what happened."

Skye recapped, ending with, "I'm not worried about me." *There is absolutely no time for that.* She drew a deep breath, smoothed Spring's hair, and said, "My sister has preexisting issues, which may make her answers to your questions seem odd. Developmentally challenged, generalized anxiety disorder, obsessive-compulsive disorder, and, she's socially awkward."

Skye fought back the lump in her throat when she thought of all the labels that had been placed upon Spring. She squared her shoulders, dug deep for strength, and continued, "She's mentally challenged, stemming, doctors believe, from oxygen deprivation at birth."

"The autism spectrum?"

Skye shook her head. "She was tested. Repeatedly. Nothing

conclusive."

Benjamin was quiet for a moment. "What is she listening to?"

"The encyclopedia," Skye said, "The reader's tone soothes her."

"Does she retain any of it?"

Skye nodded. "Reasoning and logic present problems, but her memory is phenomenal."

"How so?"

"She can remember words in a dictionary. In order. She has almost perfect recall for dialogue in movies. But at times, her short-term memory of real life events is nonexistent." Skye hesitated, and braced herself for the hard part. "She was in a bad car accident two years ago."

My fault.

Her father's voice came to her, with the message he had provided in the awful days and weeks after the accident. *People have accidents, Skye. Forgive yourself.* She straightened her shoulders and drew a deep breath. "She had a severe concussion, which could make her more susceptible now to a head injury, right?"

The doctor frowned. "It could."

"Mary," Sebastian said, from the doorway. She hadn't realized that he was still there, that he had listened, until he spoke her newest name. Her consultation with the doctor was none of his business, but a quick flare of anger quickly ebbed as empathy in his eyes reminded her of his strong, yet gentle, embrace as he kept her from falling in the driveway. How, as masculine muskiness had enveloped her, his hard chest had become a welcome wall of strength, while her thoughts spun with the residual need to get out of a dead man's clutches and the impossibly loud sound of gunfire.

Yet even as she found reassurance in his eyes, warning bells clanged. Reassurance wasn't something she should seek from Sebastian. Her father had taught her, *Trust no one. Especially anyone who knows you're my daughter.*

There was more than just reassurance. He was undeniably the most attractive man she'd ever met, and she'd been around many attractive men.

Unavailable.

If ever there was a man who fit that bill, Sebastian was it. Not in the sense of married, though he could be, or gay, which he didn't seem to be. No. He was unavailable in the sense of not interested, because no matter what expression graced those clear blue eyes, full lips, and square jaw, underneath it there was impatience. He was looking for her father, and she was a means to that end.

In years past, his restless, brooding seriousness would have been a challenge, but not now. Skye had spent serious time and effort overcoming her attraction to unavailable men. That self-destructive phase in her life was over. And she had to get the hell away from here and him. She had to get to Tennessee.

Run. Now.

"Pete will be here. I won't be far. You're safe," Sebastian said as he turned from the doorway and disappeared down the hallway.

Safe? *No.* Trapped.

Dear God. Precious minutes slipped away as they went from one examining room to the next, in the unnaturally quiet hospital. Technicians ran a CT scan, an MRI, and x-rays, while testing Spring's ability to pay attention, her balance, and her memory. Skye stayed with Spring, and they were never alone with Rhonda, her only hope for an escape. Pete shadowed them. Sebastian was nowhere to be seen.

After an hour and a half of tests, they returned to the hospital room to wait for the results. Two matching suitcases stood side by side at the foot of each bed. A small table was set with silverware and dome-covered dishes.

"Those suitcases are full of clothes and essentials for the two of you. Go ahead and eat. Grab a shower. Let me know if you need anything else," Pete said. "I'll be right outside."

Skye and Spring showered. After wrapping themselves in large towels, they bathed Candy. Someone had not only shopped, they had carefully folded the clothes and packed toiletries. There were slim black jeans, blue jeans, fresh and crisp white-cotton button down shirts, and wool cardigans. Panties and bras, in various sizes, flannel nightgowns, cotton turtlenecks, soft cardigans, leggings, and jean jackets. Thin socks and black leather ankle-boots, with solid one-inch, wood-stacked heels, were also tucked into one of the suitcases. The volume of clothes—a supply for more than just a day—made her heart beat faster.

Spring said, "These aren't our clothes."

"They're a present from Sebastian," Skye said. "They're nice, aren't they? And the boots are fabulous. Right?"

"I really like him," Spring said.

Don't get too attached. They both put on blue jeans. Skye wiped the off-white leather belts with a damp cloth, and they used those instead of the belts that had been purchased for them. It wasn't exactly a fashion statement she was proud of, but today wasn't the day to care about appearances. Spring chose a pastel yellow cardigan, Skye took a charcoal gray. The slip-on boots were snug, but the soft leather made them comfortable.

Skye went to the table, where assorted finger sandwiches, fruit, and chips sat on platters. The table was set for two. "Are you hungry? There are ham and turkey sandwiches."

Spring shook her head, "We need to get the cake to the bank."

Skye paused. She drew a deep breath. Memory loss was a symptom of a concussion. *Oh, God. Don't let her have a concussion. Please.* "Sarah took care of that for us. We can't leave yet. We need your test results."

A worry line bisected Spring's brow. She touched her nose, and winced. "Who were they?"

Skye hesitated. "What do you remember?" Obviously, not everything, and Skye didn't know whether to be grateful or worried.

"A man hit me. Everything turned dark. The next thing I remember is Sebastian was carrying me. You and Sebastian yelled at each other." She paused, and more worry filtered into her clear blue eyes as she shook her head. "We were in the car. I gave Sebastian jellybeans. I don't remember anything else."

"Don't worry about what you don't remember."

"Who was the man?"

Skye shook her head. "I don't know."

"What did he want?"

"I don't know," Skye said, careful to keep her voice calm, her mood upbeat, as she wondered how in the hell they were going to get away.

Fear filtered into Spring's eyes. "Was it about Dad?"

Of course it was. "I don't know."

"How did he find us? Did I make a mistake?" Spring's eyes welled with tears.

Spring had never understood why they were hiding. She just understood that they were hiding. "Oh, honey. Don't cry. You didn't make a mistake. I don't know how the man who hit you found us, but I'm going to figure that out, and no one will ever find us again."

"You know that I'll never tell anyone anything about Dad," Spring paused, "I really, really won't."

Thank God. "And if anyone ever asks you anything about Dad, what are you going to say?"

"I'll say I don't know. Or I don't remember. Or," she paused as she gave Skye a sly, quiet smile, "I'll tell them about the Pyrenees." She lifted her ear buds and waved them at Skye. "I'm on the P's. The Pyrenees."

Skye seized upon the distraction. "Would you like to go hiking there this summer?"

"No."

Even on ordinary days, Spring didn't like to travel. It upset her routine, and that had been one of the problems with being Richard Barrows' daughter. Their mother had been the family's anchor. After she died, when Skye was thirteen and Spring was two, homes had just been houses, and the addresses always changed. With the guilt-induced clarity that came after the car accident, Skye had been working on changing that for Spring and, until Sebastian had appeared at the coffee house, she'd succeeded.

Spring frowned, "I'm really, really tired. Can we go home now?"

"Soon. But not now."

"We're going home when we leave, aren't we?"

Skye drew a deep breath. "Not right away."

Fat tears spilled from Spring's eyes.

"Honey, please don't cry," Skye said, struggling to keep her voice calm. "We're returning there just as soon as we can, but we have to make sure the man who hit you is gone."

"If we can't go home, can we go to Firefly Island?"

"Yes. I'll take you there, once we're sure you are fine. But don't tell anyone that's where we're going," she said, gripping Spring's hands. "Not Sebastian, not anyone. Remember, the lake house is our secret. Only me, you, and Dad know about the lake house or Firefly Island, and it has to stay that way. Understand?"

Spring gave her a wide-eyed nod and a sniff.

"Now I need to talk to the doctors." She got Spring situated on the couch with a plate of sandwiches, a soda, and earphones on with her iPad playing the P's. Candy, her fur damp, snoozed in a bed of towels on the floor, near the couch. Skye paced for a few minutes. When she saw that Spring's gaze was following her, with a worry line bisecting her brow, she sat down just before the nurse and doctor entered the room. She stood as they did.

"I've ruled out bruising on the brain or bleeding," the doctor said.

Skye exhaled with relief, but there was still concern in his eyes. "Does that rule out a concussion?"

He frowned. "Not entirely. Her lack of memory could be a symptom of concussion, as is extreme anxiety, which she exhibited. However," he paused, "both memory loss and anxiety are somewhat normal for her, right?"

"Yes."

"Because there's a possibility that she suffered a concussion, for now, she needs rest, and I've told Sebastian I'm not releasing her for another few hours. I'll conduct more tests at five. Assuming all goes well, you can be on your way. Even then, there's to be only mild exertion, lots of naps. For the next twenty-four hours, wake her every couple of hours. If it's difficult to wake her, or she complains of a headache, if she's nauseated or vomiting, if she's sensitive to light or noise, if she can't balance, if she sleeps too much, if she's more emotional than normal," he paused, "anything unusual, bring her back to me, or to an emergency room. Don't hesitate."

Skye drew a deep breath. This complicated her plan of running, but it was better than learning that Spring had traumatic brain injury. "Her nose?"

"There's a hairline fracture in the bridge of her nose, which should heal on its own. She stopped bleeding, so we don't need to pack it. Rhonda will give you supplies for if she starts bleeding again." He paused, "Candy's x-rays showed no signs of a fracture in her shoulder or neck. She's just sore."

He left, as Rhonda opened a supply cabinet.

Finally.

Chapter Nine

Two thirty p.m., Monday

"It's all a lie. The kidnapping. Everything you've been told about why we're here," Skye said. "We need your help."

Rhonda turned, a pack of gauze in her hands, an uncertain look in her eyes. "Excuse me?"

"We were trying to escape from Sebastian. We're married. My sister lives with us," she paused, "Last night I caught him going into her room." Rhonda's eyes widened. Her face became pale. "When I confronted him, he beat me. He knows where to hit so that his fists don't leave marks. Normally he's not in a rage," she shuddered, "but this morning he was. This is the first time that he took it out on her more than me. I can't let this go on. I have to leave. I need your help."

"Why didn't you tell this to Doctor Cavanaugh?"

"They're friends. Don't you see?" She stepped closer to Rhonda, who had put the supplies down and was still, intent on Skye's every word. Spring, headphones on, wasn't listening. "The doctor isn't going to help us get away from him. This morning I was trying to leave. He figured it out. He attacked me, my sister tried to defend me, and that's when he punched her. Candy got in the middle of it, and he kicked her." She couldn't cry on cue, but she could make her voice break. "He, he l-loves us. There's always remorse after one of our fights. That's why he brought us here. Please." Skye dropped her voice to the lowest of whispers. "I don't care what he does to me. But he's hurt her, for God's sake. I just need your help to get out of here. I have a place to go. I have cash. I just need to get away from him, and I need your help to do it."

"I'm not sure what I can do," Rhonda said. "Besides, Doctor Cavanaugh just advised you to stay here a few more hours."

"We can't stay. Create a distraction." Skye grabbed the other woman's arm, and said urgently, "just get Pete away from the door for a minute, and we'll get away. Now is my only chance to do something I've needed to do for years. Now. We have to leave now."

Worried brown eyes held hers. Skye saw concern, but also skepticism. "Have you tried the police?"

"They're no help. They file a domestic disturbance report and that's it. Like a piece of paper does anything. It only makes him madder. We have to get away from him," Skye paused, glanced at the clock. 2:30. Dear God. Time was racing by. She had to run. "And I need to do it now."

"Pete's not going to just leave," Rhonda said. "He looks like he's pretty good at what he does, and right now, that's protecting you and your sister."

"Not protecting. Guarding us so that we don't run away," Skye said. "With your help, a fire alarm, something, I'll make it work. Please."

"Didn't they drive you here?" Rhonda asked. "How are you, your sister, and the dog going to leave?"

She guessed that Rhonda wouldn't appreciate the idea of stealing a car from the valet stand, so she didn't share it. "We're on a busy street, with stores and businesses. Plenty of places to disappear. Please. Don't you understand? I'm not afraid of what's out there." She waved her arm in an all-encompassing signal of the world beyond the hospital. "I'm afraid of him."

"I'm sorry. There are rules. I'm supposed to report all cases of domestic abuse to the authorities, but first, I'm supposed to report it to the doctor in charge of your care. As much as I want to help you, I can't just let you run away. "

Well, Rhonda wasn't quite the gullible and naive bleeding heart she had hoped for. It was time for economic incentive, and this better work, because if it didn't, and Rhonda reported this story to the doctor, she knew one man who was going to be furious. She thought of a way to make an offer of cash and diamonds seem like something less than a flat-out bribe. Skye drew a deep breath, "I'll pay you if you give me your car keys. I have cash and diamonds."

Rhonda was wide-eyed and silent.

It was time for show and tell. Skye undid her belt. The outside of it was a solid band of leather. The inside of it, the part that pressed against her jeans, was fabric with three zippered compartments. She undid one zipper, and pulled out the contents—a stack of bills and a small, black-velvet pouch. She placed the stack of bills in Rhonda's hand before opening one of the small pouches and letting the contents spill into her palm. Six high-quality diamonds, of various shapes and sizes, glittered in the well-lit hospital room. Rhonda's eyes were drawn to the fiery diamonds.

"That's five thousand dollars. These diamonds are worth over one hundred thousand dollars. They're all for you, if you walk back in the room with your car keys, then create a distraction. Pull the fire alarm and ask Pete for help in assessing the emergency. It can be as simple as that."

Rhonda tore her eyes from the diamonds and focused on Skye. "My keys are in my locker."

Skye returned the diamonds to the pouch and tucked the pouch into the pocket of her jeans. "Keep the cash. Bring your keys to me, agree to create a distraction, and the diamonds are yours."

Rhonda tucked the cash into the pocket of her dress. "I'll be right back."

"Hurry." Skye slipped the belt onto her jeans and buckled it.

As Rhonda left the room, Pete glanced in. He held Skye's eyes for a second, before shutting the door. Skye drew a deep breath in relief as her eyes rested on Spring and Candy.

Please let this work. Dear God. It has to work.

As 2:30 became 2:50, she couldn't sit. Staying still for too long required too much effort. Daytime television didn't hold her attention. She paced. In the gap between the door and the floor, she could see the dark shadows of Pete's feet.

Where was Rhonda?

The door to the hospital room finally opened a half hour after Rhonda left. Skye's heart plummeted as Sebastian opened the door, instead of the nurse. He'd changed into a pair of jeans and crisp white cotton, long-sleeved shirt. His hair was damp. The fresh scent of soap followed him into the room. Maybe he had accomplished tasks other than showering and changing out of his bloodstained clothes, but if he had, none of the tasks had lightened the serious look in his eyes, or softened the hard-as-stone set to his jaw.

He glanced towards the couch, where Spring still slept, wearing her earphones. Candy's eyes followed Sebastian, but other than a lazy tail wag, she didn't move from Spring's side, evidently having decided somewhere during the morning that

Sebastian was not anyone to worry about. He shut the door behind him, barely making a sound but infecting the room with his brooding, angry-at-the-world presence.

He walked to where Skye stood. She backed up, until the wall prevented her from going any further. He kept coming at her, invading her personal space as his eyes drowned her with cobalt sparks, stopping only when he was so close that she could feel his heat and sense the power in his large body. He pinned her to the wall with a solid palm press to her chest, with his fingers on the soft flesh of her neck, as she pressed her palms against his chest and tried to push him away.

"I'm sexually abusing your sister and beat the two of you? Really?" With his free hand, the one that wasn't within an inch of shutting down her windpipe, he reached to her waist and unbuckled her belt. She hammer-fisted at his chest and struggled to break free. It was like pounding on a tree trunk. He didn't even flinch, and she was punching as hard as she could. All he did was press his fingers into her neck, cutting off her air, while his other hand worked her belt out of her pants loops. His gaze held hers with a hard expression. "The sooner you decide to cooperate, the better off you'll be."

Candy started barking and Spring sat up on the couch, awakening just as he released her and stepped away with the belt in his hands.

"Chloe?" Spring said, eyes wide with concern as they bounced from Skye to Sebastian.

There was his smile again, which he only seemed capable of giving to Spring. "Everything's ok. Your sister and I just need to have a serious conversation." He glanced back at Skye, pointed to the door of the room, and although he was still smiling, with deep, apostrophe-shaped dimples, the light of his smile didn't make it to his eyes when he looked at her. "In the hallway. Unless you want to be the one to explain all of this to her, right here, right now."

Skye drew a deep breath. "I'll be outside the door; ok, honey?"

Spring nodded, wide-eyed and uncertain.

As they stepped into the hallway, Pete stepped to the side, giving them space. "Your bullshit story just wasted twenty minutes of my time, because I had to explain more things to Doctor Cavanaugh. You see, medical professionals have to take all kinds of crazy people seriously, and that means even you. Look," he said, as his eyes suddenly weren't angry or frustrated. He was calm, and his tone was matter of fact. He was within touching distance of her, but his arms were folded.

"If you run from the marshals' interrogation, all you're going to do is make them take you seriously, when this morning you weren't even a blip on their radar. Just tell them what you've told me. Tell the marshals that you don't know where your father is. Tell them you don't know who those kidnappers were, that you don't know why anyone would want to kidnap you. That's your story, right?" He arched an eyebrow and was silent as he waited for her response.

"Yes, and it's not a story. It's the truth."

He studied her face, his lips pressed together in a thin line of disapproval. "You lie worse than you fight. When you lie, you put this flat expression on your face, when normally your thoughts are transparent. In different circumstances, it would be amusing. Problem is, the fact that you're rotten at both fighting and lying doesn't keep you from throwing crappy punches and lying as much as you breathe. What the hell has you so afraid?"

"More men like this morning," she said, not lying at all.

His gaze was both sharp and skeptical. "If you don't know who they are, or why they were sent, why are you so sure that there are more men like them?"

"My father's skill set is a highly-coveted commodity," she said, heart pounding with the force of what she was saying, because it was the truth. "Don't you get that? Someone has him, and now they want us."

Sebastian arched an eyebrow and gave her a slow headshake. "Most people, including the authorities, believe that your father's claims are the product of a deranged mind."

"That's what the uninformed believe," she said, her cheeks burning with the need to defend her father. "But they turn on their computers and use software that he designed, without even thinking about how his brilliant mind made the innovations that they now rely upon for things that we take for granted in every day life. Anti-viral software. Encryption technology. Data storage. It's easy to forget that someone is a genius, when there are articles in tabloids that were planted by men who tried to discredit him. His claims are dead-on accurate."

And, she thought, in certain circles, upper-echelon circles

that were only entered by those with the highest of clearances, her father had created a firestorm by creating technology that would allow integration of the world's most sensitive databases and assimilation of the information in those databases at the speed of light. Now that the cataclysm scenario was in play, the end goal for her, if her father gave her the signal, was to go straight to the top.

And straight to the top does not mean spilling her father's secrets to a private investigator.

"Tell me how, Skye. Just tell me how something he designed or was working on could be a reason for him to escape from prison. Something real. Not the bullshit he fed the world. He never worked with the government. He claimed to have created Shadow Technology, technology that allows super-assimilation of data collection, but the government says it doesn't exist. Give me something solid to go on, because in case you haven't figured this out—no one has a clue as to where your father is."

His eyes were hard, yet his tone, as it had been whenever he had spoken to her, was low, controlled, and compelling. The man was a master at using his voice to get others to listen to him. "Tell me what is so important that he would escape prison now. Because there's one certainty that I can give you—he will be found, and his prison term will be extended. Hell, they might just throw away the key."

She couldn't. The cataclysm scenario was in play, and if she told Sebastian anything about what that entailed, she'd never be able to break away from him. Everything having to do with cataclysm was top secret. "He didn't escape. Someone kidnapped him. There are people in the world—countries, even—who value his capabilities-"

"Do you hear how freaking preposterous that sounds? Kidnapped from a federal prison? How and by whom? Escaping is almost impossible, and," he paused, "based on what? You think the Chinese sent a band of computer experts to kidnap your father? In case you haven't gotten the memo, he's been thoroughly discredited. He's a criminal, who is ranting and raving about things that don't exist or even make sense."

Inwardly, she flinched. Skye hated that the world ridiculed her father, and evidently, Sebastian was no different. Outwardly, she didn't let him see anything other than cool and calm. She could play his game. "You sound like all the other small-minded, ignorant people, who can't understand the importance of my father's work. Trust me. Someone kidnapped him, and if they get me and my sister, he'll do whatever they want him to do. He can change the world, or terrorize it, with carefully orchestrated keystrokes."

"And he can send me to a rendezvous with a UFO, right?"

Sebastian's comment cut deep and told her that there'd be no persuading him. "I can't help you find my father, because I have no idea where he is. Just let us disappear. Please."

"I can't do that." A pulse was visible, pumping at his temple. His eyes traced her cheekbones and hovered on her lips before finding her eyes again.

"Please let us leave," she said, "Whoever sent those men won't stop trying, and, if this morning doesn't make you pause, I'm going to spell it out for you." She jabbed a finger into his chest. "You can't keep us safe."

He looked at where her finger was pressing into his chest, arched an eyebrow, and chuckled, as he refocused his attention on her eyes.

She had to fight to keep herself from reaching down, slipping off the half boot, and pounding the wooden heel into his thick head. She'd do it, if she thought she could get away with it. There was no way, though. He was too fast. "I don't care how good of a private investigator you are. You're not good enough."

"I'm not sure what your idea of safe is," he frowned, "but in my world, this morning was pretty damn successful. You weren't kidnapped, you're not dead, and the bad guys are."

"You live in one screwy world-"

"No, I live in the real one. Not the pretend world of pretty coffee shops and cakes with weird-as-shit icing."

She drew a deep breath. "Are you always this much of a pig-headed jerk?"

"Always. Especially when someone is questioning my capabilities. Pretty soon you'll be with the marshals. They're experts at protecting people and they're damn good at what they do. Under the circumstances, you need to talk to them, you'll be safe with them, and once I get you to them, you'll never have to see me again."

"Dumping us on the marshals sounds like a brilliant move on your part. In the SUV, on the way here, you accused them of having a leak. That doesn't sound so safe to me," she paused, realized that she wasn't above begging, and went for it. "Please.

Just let us leave."

"The marshals know how to close the circle on people with knowledge of a safe house. My job is to find your father. That's it. Now finding your father includes getting you and your sister safely to the marshals, and I'm not about to screw that up by letting you disappear, no matter how many times you say please." He reached into his pants pocket, pulled out an old-fashioned flip phone, and handed it to her. It felt like gold in her hands. "If you don't want to listen to me, listen to your lawyer. She's called three senators on the Bureau of Prisons Committee, who have in turn leaned on the marshals, who are now insisting that she talk to you." He touched a button on his watchband. "Ragno. Put Root through now. Give the conversation two minutes, max."

The phone's ring sent shivers through her. "Aunt Jen?"

"Skye," Jen answered. Skye almost sobbed when she heard the familiar voice. "Thank God. Are you and Spring okay?"

Jen had been her mother and father's best friend and, until she and Spring had changed identities, had been a constant, steadying presence in their world. After her mother's death, Jen had been like a surrogate mother to both girls. Given her father's absent-minded preoccupation with work, his typical, convoluted thought processes, and his paranoia, Jen had often been the only well-grounded, steadying force in their chaotic life.

Breaking contact with Jen had been one of the most difficult things that she'd done when she became Chloe Stewart. Her father had insisted it was necessary. Skye had no idea what Jen knew—if anything—regarding the cataclysm scenario.

"Yes," she said, bringing her up to speed on Spring's condition. Without pausing for a breath, she said, "What's happening to Dad?"

"I don't know. It looks like he just walked out of prison. With six others. There was a glitch in the security system, electricity went out, and they left," she said. "As far as I can tell, no one has any idea where he is."

Skye glanced at Sebastian. "Would you please tell this private investigator to let me leave? He has no authority to hold me against my—"

"Private investigator?"

"Yes. He's acting like he's got authority to detain—"

"Connelly's not just a private investigator. His company is

elite, with worldwide presence. Fortune 500 companies hire him. Government officials hire Black Raven, and, in this matter, he's got the authority of the marshals behind him. Connelly is taking you to a safe house. You have to go, and you need to cooperate with the marshals when you get there. Tell them everything you know."

"Dad never would have escaped. He wanted to serve his time and get out of there."

"I know and if someone kidnapped him, the marshals and Connelly will figure that out as well. You're not safe on your own. Do you understand? Cooperate with Connelly and the marshals. Connelly is the best at what he does. You'll be safe."

As she broke the connection, Sebastian plucked the phone out of her hand. "When we walk back in the room, ask your sister to take off her belt, and hand it to me."

She thought about telling him no.

A hard, blue-eyed glance told her he easily read her mind. "I'll do it myself, if you won't."

She couldn't do that to Spring. They returned to the room, Skye plastered an easy, calm expression onto her face, and persuaded Spring to hand her the belt. When she did, Skye passed it to Sebastian.

"I'm sorry," Sebastian said. He was a large, powerhouse of a man, with broad shoulders and long, muscular limbs, but he knew how to make his body less intimidating. He bent to one knee so he was eye level with Spring, who now had Candy on the couch and who was holding onto the dog for dear life. He touched her shoulder with his right hand, a touch that looked reassuring and gentle. "I'll keep this safe for you. We need to make sure that everything you and your sister wear is new, OK?"

That made no damn sense without more of an explanation, but Spring fell for his easy, good-looking brand of sincerity. She gave him a nod and a half smile, and said, "Can we go home now?"

Skye thought his smile faltered, but, if it did, it was only a passing thing. "Not right away. I need to take you and your sister somewhere else first. There are men who need to ask your sister some questions. You two will be safe there for a couple of nights." Skye's heart pounded. *No way. No. Not going to happen.* "Is that ok with you?"

"You'll be with us?"

He glanced at Skye. Dear God, the man had the most expressive eyes she'd ever seen, and now he wasn't being a jerk or a hard-ass or anything but a nice guy, who Spring had managed to capture with her sweetness. Without a word, his eyes said he hated to disappoint Spring and he also wasn't enjoying lying to her. "I'll stay as long as I can. Once your sister talks to those men, and once we're sure that you two will be safe, you and your sister can go home."

He stood. Nice guy gone, replaced with cool, matter-of-fact efficiency. "Cavanaugh says if all goes well, we'll be leaving around six. You and Spring will be at the safe house at least until we find your father, debrief him, and figure out who the kidnappers were. At this point, I have no idea how long that could take. Assume you'll be there at least a few nights and days. Put together a list of things you guys need and hand it to Pete. We'll make sure the things are there."

As he opened the door to step out, she said, "You said you were just a private investigator."

"No. You said that," he gave her a half smile, "right after you called me a dumb ass. Labels don't mean much in my world. Results matter more. Besides," he shrugged, "I am a private investigator."

When the door was almost shut, she mumbled, "And you're way, way too cocky."

He opened the door, leaning into the room. "Yeah," he said, his eyes serious, "Just cocky enough to keep you alive, Miss Barrows."

Chapter Ten

By nine p.m., they were a forty-minute drive from Atlanta and the private airport, where they had landed in Raven One. He'd sent the jet and crew away. He and Pete would drive to Jackson, once the sisters were in the safe house. At night, he estimated that the drive would take less than three hours, since they were already heading West, in the direction of Jackson, Mississippi. Sebastian was fielding phone calls, talking to Ragno, and assessing the sprawling neighborhood where 211 Orchid Street—the safe house—was located. Pete was driving an SUV that the Black Raven logistics division had sent to meet them. The sisters and the dog were in the back seat. At her request, he'd given Skye a couple of inches of a crack in her window.

The neighborhood resembled Anywhere, U.S.A. The village-style shopping and residential area had manicured green spaces. Some homes were townhouse-style, others were single-family homes, with five-story condominium buildings strategically placed throughout the neighborhood. The floor level of each taller building had coffee shops, restaurants, dry cleaners, and other businesses. The neighborhood was well-lit and filled with both pedestrians and vehicles. Nobody would notice or care what went on inside the safe house.

A vague sense of unease made Sebastian's vision super-sharp, his senses heightened. Everything looked right. Adults. Kids. Traffic congestion. The safe house was a red-brick, two-story, single-family home with drawn drapes, an attached garage, and a driveway of pale pink pavers. It looked normal. "Drive around for ten minutes."

Pete glanced his way, his eyes serious, then guided the vehicle past their destination. Safe-house deliveries were just part of the job of a private security contractor, something he and his agents had done more times than he could count. Before July, when the head injury had temporarily sidelined him from high intensity international work, he had frequently handled high-profile deliveries in war zones as a way of staying in touch with fieldwork and his agents. This was just a transport. Safely deposit the client to the delivery point and move on. Sniper fire and improvised explosive devices were typical concerns in the Middle East. These concerns didn't seem relevant in this generic neighborhood.

After this morning's kidnapping attempt, though, Sebastian was on guard. He and Pete weren't alone. Two Black Raven agents were inside with two marshals. He'd noticed a tail vehicle, about a half-mile away, with two more Black Raven agents. They were following, but not obviously. He doubted that Skye had noticed them.

When his eyes weren't trained on his iPad and information that Ragno sent to him, or scanning the neighborhood, he kept an eye on their passengers by glancing into the passenger sun visor mirror, which he'd angled so it was trained on Skye. Child security locks were engaged on the windows and doors. Spring leaned against Skye, her head on her sister's shoulder, dozing on and off. His eyes locked on big sis's serious eyes, which, in the incandescent glow from streetlights, matched her smoky-gray sweater.

She was alert, and, for the most part, watching him watching her. Wary. Scared. Fidgety. Irritated as hell, too. What got to him more than the anxious, trapped look she had when her sibling dozed, was the calm mask Skye managed to wear when Spring was awake. He admired the effort she made for her sister. He didn't doubt Skye was listening to every word he said as he talked on the phone, but there was nothing to be done about that.

Damn. It would have been easier to fight gravity than the pull of Skye's eyes.

Over the course of the day, watching her had become a thing. She was decisive, even when her plan wasn't well-thought-out. *Bribing the nurse?* Brilliant, but stupid. Another contradictory move on her part. It was never going to work. Not in Cavanaugh's hospital. Cavanaugh had laughed, and so had Sebastian. Sebastian had only acted pissed with Skye. Over the course of his career, he'd had all kinds of clients. He never felt an emotional pull with the people who were in his protection, no matter how beautiful. Work was work. That's all it was.

It was also hard to remember impartiality when Spring handed him three coconut-flavored jellybeans. She'd done that five times since leaving the hospital. Each time he'd asked for red, but she said 'no', with the prettiest, sweetest damn smile that had ever accompanied the word. Even more fun than interacting with Spring had been watching Skye get more and more irritated with the game he played with her sister.

What the hell was wrong with him?

Games for him normally involved guns and physical combat. Not jellybeans and innocent smiles. He blamed his weakness for Skye and Spring on his July head injury. Nothing had been the same since. He'd awakened from the two-week coma feeling...different. Everything that had once been right was wrong, and he'd yet to shake the changes. The constant headaches he could live with. The suck ass feeling that everything was wrong had to go. It was more than general dissatisfaction. More than a depression. His entire life felt off course, when before it was perfect.

Today was just another day when he didn't feel right, and his inability to stop thinking about Skye's high cheekbones, or the bare-breasted bikini shot he'd gotten a glimpse of more than twelve hours earlier, or the absolute wonder of innocence that was Spring, was now another problem on the shit-pile. Thankfully, this one was going away soon. Once he had them deposited in the safe house, he'd leave them in the rearview mirror.

Pete had driven a circuitous route for fifteen minutes without incident, but Sebastian still felt a persistent sense of something not quite right.

"We're good?" Pete asked quietly.

"Yeah. Go back." They couldn't drive around all night because he had a 'feeling'. He reached into his backpack, pulled out a power bar that he had no appetite for, opened the wrapping, and bit into the nuts and raisins. He'd eaten a sandwich on the plane and some pretzels, but that had been a couple of hours ago. Instinct told him the night was going to be long, and he needed fuel. He had places to go and other things to do, and the sisters needed to be settled. He needed to end his babysitting duties and keep looking for good old Daddy.

"Skye," he met her misty eyes in the mirror. Immediately alert, she held his gaze. "We're almost there. Follow my directions and don't try anything stupid. Let these people do their job, which is protecting you guys. Understand?"

She nodded.

The lack of a smart retort caught his attention. He turned to glance into the back seat and took in the calm, serene expression on her face. He didn't believe for one goddamn second that she had any intention of listening to any instructions he gave.

During the day, he'd lost track of the number of times she'd glanced at her watch. It was too often to be a nervous tick. She had demonstrated a tendency to lie, fight, and try to run, so he had to consider her a wild card in a delivery that was otherwise under control.

He'd learned all kinds of things in life and on the job. One guiding principle was that the demons within a person were sometimes as much of a security risk as the external forces the person was worried about. Black Raven could protect people from external sources. It was a damn hard job to protect people from the demons within, and sometimes it just couldn't be done.

Fear was Skye's demon and she had made it perfectly clear that she wasn't revealing to him the source. Perhaps she was as crazy as her father. He didn't give a damn. He was just a few minutes from being rid of her. Lucky for him, the sweet, blue-eyed baggage that was Spring was keeping the impulsive-chameleon that was Skye in check.

Everything else related to the prison break had spiraled into the basement of hell. Right before they left the hospital at 6 p.m., Sebastian had learned from Minero that the search for Biondo had uncovered a murder victim in Jackson, Mississippi. Unfortunately, the victim wasn't Biondo himself. He'd heard from his agents that local media was clamoring for news, and national media outlets were arriving in Jackson. A press conference was scheduled for 9:30. Reports of the prison break were going to be plastered across the nightly news. Black Raven wasn't likely to be given a spot at the podium, but, in case pigs flew, Sebastian sent a Raven media specialist there. The only likely thing his company could do was watch as fingers were pointed at them.

They were one house away from the safe house when Ragno said in his ear, "Minero's calling in."

"Pete. Do another loop around the neighborhood." Pete accelerated. "Put him through."

Minero had detoured to Jackson, and there was no telling when he'd be at the safe house. Two marshals—Philip Manckie and John Stamfield—were at the house with his agents. Sebastian had communicated with both teams on the premises. Once the sisters were safe inside, he'd head to Jackson.

"Where the hell are you?" Over the course of the day, Minero's tone had become increasingly irritated. Whatever coolness the man had possessed in the beginning of the prison break was now gone. "You said you'd be at the safe house at 7."

"Standard operation for safe house deliveries. I don't know how marshals do it, but Black Raven doesn't accurately give arrival time."

"Not even to the agents who are in charge of the safe house? What kind of fucked up world do you operate in? Manckie and Stamfield have been waiting for you for two hours."

"What the hell else are they supposed to be doing? Safe houses are all about waiting, for crapsake."

Pete turned off of Orchid and onto Wisteria Street. Jesus. All the streets looked alike.

"Not the point," Minero said, voice testy.

Instead of asking the marshal, '*What the fuck was the point?*' Sebastian exercised restraint. "What's the news from Jackson?"

"The murder victim was a witness in Biondo's trial."

"Fuck me," Sebastian muttered, as he focused on what he knew about Vincent Biondo. Convicted of tax evasion, wire fraud, and money laundering. Biondo had been the brains behind an illegal gambling ring that had operated out of Jackson, Mississippi, for years. Co-conspirators had testified against Biondo in exchange for lenient sentences. Biondo had a twelve-year sentence and had served seven. "Biondo was convicted of economic crimes. Not violent offenses."

"I know," Minero said. "He was considered low risk for violent offenses, but his organization was tied to violent offenders."

As Pete turned back onto Orchid Street, Sebastian eyed a security camera on the entrance of a coffee shop, half a mile from the safe house. "Any evidence indicating that Biondo was the killer?"

"His prints are all over the place. Biondo developed a mean streak while in prison. He killed this guy by slicing his carotid. Left a note. A warning to the other witnesses. Written in this guy's blood. Now I'm spreading resources and managing protection efforts. I have to assume that if Biondo went after one of his witnesses, he's going to go after the others. Including today's murder victim, eight witnesses provided significant testimony against Biondo. I'm sending agents to Jackson, New

Orleans, Tampa, and points in between."

With Biondo a bigger threat, fewer agents would be focused on Barrows and his girls, who had now dropped a notch on Minero's priority list. Sebastian flashed back to the cold, calculating manner of the kidnapping he had foiled. Low priority status for Skye and Spring bugged the hell out of him. "The timing of the Biondo kill isn't relevant only to Biondo's escape. It's relevant to whatever else has happened since the escape."

"What do you mean?" Minero asked.

"Biondo's been out for four days, and you just found the victim."

"That's right," Minero said. "The murder happened sometime after twelve. That's when the victim was last seen."

"Why do you think it took Biondo four days to kill the guy?" Sebastian asked, as Pete stopped at a stop sign.

"Hell if I know," Minero answered, "but it's logical that it would. After all, Biondo had to get to Jackson, acquire a weapon, and strategize."

"Right. But it happened today, after the kidnappers didn't get Barrows' daughters."

"What's your point?"

"The fact that the killing has made you focus more on Biondo and not Barrows could be damn convenient to someone."

"Well it might be convenient to someone, but for now, that's reality. When are you arriving in Jackson?"

"Heading there as soon as the sisters are safely inside."

"Good," Minero said. "Because your agents don't always grasp the fact that I'm at the top of this hierarchy."

"My people answer to me."

"Yeah, but you answer to me," Minero snapped.

Fuck. "Nothing in my contract spelled that out." That much was true, because the contract hadn't contemplated such a colossal fuck-up. "I'm working with you, and so are my agents."

No response.

Ragno said, "He hung up on you. Maturity level? I'd say questionable."

"Great." He drew a deep breath and shrugged off his frustration. Pete had driven in a one-mile loop. They were three blocks away from the safe house. He gave Pete a signal with his index finger and a nod. "It's a go. Ragno. Put me through to the inside."

"Here you go."

In a second, the phone clicked. "Agent Lewis."

"We're about 200 yards from the driveway."

"Great," there was a long pause. "We're ready."

With those three words, Sebastian's heart slowed to a whump thud. The man's tone was normal, but that was not the correct response.

"Sorry. Bad connection," Sebastian kept his tone calm, but he was momentarily in disbelief that even this wasn't going to go well. "Did you say ready?"

"Yes."

Sebastian didn't breathe as he waited for the rest of the words, but they didn't come.

Agent Lewis continued, "Marshal Manckie and I will meet you in the garage."

Black Raven agents had internal protocols for safe house deliveries. There were customized, pre-arranged words that the agents on the inside were supposed to use, regardless of the collateral authorities who were on the job. The all-clear signal for this delivery from his agents was supposed to be *"We're ready for the sisters. We even have the damn jellybeans."*

Skye's list of necessities had been enormous, and, from what Sebastian guessed, geared to keep her sister busy. The woman didn't stop at toothpaste and a toothbrush. Her list included organic foods, baking pans that were a certain brand, flour, cake mixes, extracts, five pounds of assorted jellybeans, two hundred three-inch clear glass stackable bowls, and that was just the beginning. Ragno had informed him that it had taken two agents hours to acquire the goods, and they'd had fun doing it. Best assignment ever, they'd reported back.

Sebastian had worked with Agent Lewis before. The man was experienced and competent. His failure to say the correct words meant something wasn't right. The lines of the house became straighter, while the night became darker, and his heartbeat drowned out all extraneous noise. Sebastian said, "Approaching now. Give me twenty seconds before opening the garage door." He touched his watchband, muting the connection to Agent Lewis.

"Ragno, you caught that?"

"Yes. The absence of code words is the first indication from Lewis that anything's wrong."

"I'm going in."

"I'll direct your tail team to split up. One will be on your heels and in the house in three minutes. Driver will stay in the vehicle behind Pete."

To Pete, he said, "Let me out. Keep going until I give you an all-clear signal. If I don't say," he opened the door of the SUV, "'*It's time to walk the dog*,' do not return. After three minutes, if you do not hear from me, drive out of this neighborhood. Ragno will give you instructions."

He glanced in the back seat before stepping out. Spring, barely awake, looked confused. Skye was focused on him, a worried expression in her eyes. "What's wrong?"

He said, "Nothing you need to worry about. Listen to Pete and you won't be in danger." He shut the door to the SUV and stepped onto the driveway. The night air was cold. The neighborhood suddenly seemed quieter than before. As Pete pulled away, his last glimpse of Skye made him pause. Dammit. She was worried, but not afraid, and she was thinking. He hadn't been worried she would try something in the car, not with him and Pete in the front seat and child locks engaged on the rear windows and doors. But with only Pete in the front seat, and with him focused both on driving and communications with Sebastian and Ragno, Skye could present a problem. As the automatic door of the two-car garage at 211 Orchid Street started a slow rise, he said, "Pete. Be sure to watch the backseat."

"Yes, sir."

"Ragno, activate the vehicle's internal cameras and keep an eye on her."

"Done."

The lines of the house became straighter and the interior of the garage seemed unnaturally bright. Sebastian's breath slowed as he walked up the driveway and into the garage. His heart pulsed hard and effectively, and blood pumped through his veins in slow motion as his mind and body anticipated danger. There was a blue-black SUV in the garage on his left. The garage was otherwise empty. Two doors led into the garage, one from the house, and another from the back yard. The house door opened as Sebastian entered the garage.

A tall, muscular man with close-cropped brown hair, who

looked to be in is early thirties, stepped into the garage in the empty parking area. "U.S. Marshal Philip Manckie," he said in a booming voice. "You're over two fucking hours late. Where are the guests?"

Far from you, asshole.

None of this was right, and the fucking wrongness confirmed his suspicion that his agents on the inside were in trouble. If things had been running smoothly, his agents would have met him at the door with Manckie. Plus, Manckie should have proffered his credentials. It was a simple act, but consistent with basic protocol. After introducing himself, Sebastian said, "I'd like to do a walk-through before the delivery."

Manckie arched an eyebrow. He pressed a button that was on the wall, and the garage door slid down, sealing them inside. "Sure."

He'd bet his life that they had a car and men on Pete and the sisters. He'd rather go it alone than risk losing them, so the two Black Raven agents who were outside needed to stay there. "Ragno. All good here. Keep my back-up outside for now."

"Got it." As always, she knew exactly what he meant, even with his instructions abbreviated. "Keep talking," she said. None of the cool left her voice. "Tell me what you can, as you can. I'm trying to get a read from our agents who are in the house."

As the garage door shut, the man who called himself Manckie lunged in his direction just as Sebastian pulled his Glock out of his holster. Sebastian was ready. He crouched, jumped to the left, and dodged the man's frontal assault, but the man managed to smack the Glock out of his hand. It clattered on the garage floor, out of grabbing range.

Fuck.

No need to panic.

He loved his Glock, but his body was just as lethal of a weapon. They were centered in the empty parking space of the garage, with room to move. He turned to face 'Manckie,' positioning himself with knees bent, arms up, and leaning forward. The fact that the man was fighting with his fists and not a gun told Sebastian this man wanted him alive, as bait. Sebastian wanted the man who was impersonating U.S. Marshal Manckie alive, but not necessarily well—he needed information, and that wouldn't be forthcoming from a corpse.

His left side was closest to the man. He used his left arm to deflect fake-Manckie's blows while counter-striking with his right arm, all the while creeping closer and closer to his weapon. Just in case he needed it. The man's chest was solid. His punches were rapid-fire fast. He landed a glancing blow on Sebastian's chin. Sebastian had dodged most of the force, but the man's power was still enough to make him see stars.

Son of a bitch.

A busted jaw was going to feel nice with the headache that never went away. He shook off the pain, dodged another blow, and repositioned himself into a low crouch.

"Stop fighting now and you won't be dead like your agents," fake-Manckie said, gathering his breath and eyeing Sebastian's position. "They cried like girls when they begged for their lives."

Sebastian didn't waste time on a retort. *Cried like girls?* That fucking comment reduced fake-Manckie's time on earth. Information would have to come from another source.

Sebastian sprang into a low forward lunge, every inch of his body and force targeting the man's knees. He could hold his own in standing hand-to-hand combat, even with men like fake-Manckie, who were as large as he was, but he fought best when his opponents were on the ground. He hit the man's knees with his left shoulder and drove forward. The momentum knocked the man off his feet and flat on his back. Sebastian's fast lunge and the force of the fall onto the hard concrete momentarily stunned the man. He placed one knee on Manckie's chest, below the rib cage, and directed his body weight into the man's lungs. His other knee was on the ground, with the toe of his shoes digging down onto the concrete for leverage.

His position had the benefit of putting Sebastian within a few inches of his Glock. He thought about grabbing it with his right hand and ending Manckie's life the easy way. *No. Too good for him.* Just as Manckie's shock wore off, and the man started to struggle to get up, Sebastian held Manckie's head in both of his hands, his fingertips and nails pressing hard past hair and into the man's flesh. Brown eyes glanced into his. Sebastian saw sudden, wide-eyed fear.

"Yeah," Sebastian said, knowing that the man who had just taunted him with news that his agents had begged for their lives would do the same if given the opportunity. "Now who's brave?"

Two more men appeared in the doorway and ran in his direction as he pounded fake-Manckie's head against the concrete floor. He finished by twisting the man's large head with all of his force. Neck bones and cartilage snapped, just as another man landed on his back with enough body weight to knock him off his knees. He was chest-to-chest with now dead fake-Manckie, and sandwiched into him. The man who was on him should have started punching. His first mistake was that he didn't. The momentary pause gave Sebastian enough time to catch his breath and watch as another man approached from the doorway of the house, a gleaming knife in hand.

"There were three. Now two," Sebastian said.

"Good," Ragno said. "Keep working. Our agents on the inside aren't answering."

Sebastian drew a deep breath as he used his arms and feet to lift himself, along with the man who was on his back and punching his ribcage, off of now-dead fake-Manckie. Attaining plank position wasn't easy but once he was in it he had the upper hand. Almost. There was one problem, and that problem was still carrying a glistening knife with a six-inch blade. It would have been easy to get rid of the man on his back, if it weren't for the guy with the knife. He had to do something though, so he defaulted into the surest thing he knew, even though it would leave him momentarily exposed to knife man.

He lifted up and rolled to the right. The man who had been on his back was now underneath him. He head-butted the man's forehead with the back of his head, as he grabbed his Glock off of the floor. His action prompted punching, scratching, and clawing, but Sebastian didn't stay close to the man for the abuse. He leapt to his feet, and, as soon as he steadied himself, he landed four fast kicks into the guy's ribcage, then backed away from him. He had his right hand on his Glock, just as knife man lunged and landed a slashing blow on his right bicep. The blade ripped through the leather jacket, his shirt sleeve, left a trail of fire along his skin, and royally pissed him off, giving him the fuel that he needed to embrace the suck and to get power from the pain.

With his left hand he two-finger jabbed into knife-man's eyes. He shoved the man aside before he had an opportunity to land another slicing blow. Knife-man's hands were at his eyes, and the other man was on his knees, getting up. As they readied themselves for their next moves, Sebastian lifted his Glock and fired at knife man's forehead.

"Now one. He's my keeper."

The final man had a weapon at his hip, and reached for it.

Sebastian aimed for damage, not death. He pointed his Glock at the man's right kneecap and fired. As the man jolted and yelled in pain, he fired another shot into the man's left kneecap.

The man fell to his side, clutching at his knees, and howling. He didn't resist as Sebastian pulled his gun out of its holster. Sebastian undid his belt, kicked the injured man in the side until he turned so that he was on his stomach. He used his belt to bind the man's wrists. A zip tie would have been better, but he was strong enough to manhandle the leather belt into a suitable restraint, especially with the man's knees in such bad shape. The man couldn't walk, and now he couldn't use his hands. No longer a worry.

"Ragno," he said, as he checked the bodies for weapons. Three guns between them and knife man had a backup knife. "Call in Cleaners. More agents. I also want one of our interrogators on the scene. Someone highly skilled. We need medics. Let the marshals know what is happening here."

"Will do."

He went into the house and through a clean laundry room, pausing as odors of urine, stale sweat, and blood reached him. Blood splattered the walls and floors of what had once been a mostly white kitchen with gleaming stainless steel appliances. In the corner of the room, a table and chairs were pushed to the side, and three men lay on the floor. Two were face down. One was face up. Pieces of their heads had been blown away. He had no doubt they were dead, even without touching them.

"Ragno," he said, lifting his wrist and turning it so that the dial of the watch faced the room, and touched the button that turned on the video camera. "Rough footage coming. Three men dead. Two I don't recognize." He moved closer. "Presumably the men who aren't wearing the Black Raven logo are Philip Manckie and John Stamfield, the marshals who were in charge of the safe house."

He didn't waste time looking for identification. Ragno could confirm their identities with the marshals through the video footage, or the next group of Black Raven agents and marshals who'd arrive on the scene would figure it out. He bent to one knee, to the man who was face down. The man's shirtsleeve had the black bird logo that symbolized Black Raven. He turned the man's face to him. A bullet had entered the man's forehead and exited the back. His face was still intact.

"That's Paul Deal," Ragno said. "Two years in Black Raven. Formerly a marine. Just returned from a lengthy Black Raven stint in Iraq. When he's stateside he lives in Omaha. Near his mother and father. Not married. No children. Thank God." She paused. He could hear her breathing as she struggled for composure. He gave her a second, as he fought to control his temper. Blinding anger wouldn't be good for anyone at the moment. Sebastian didn't recognize Paul Deal, but that didn't make his death any easier. He also had never met the two marshals who had been killed, but he was equally irate at their deaths.

"You ok?" he asked.

"Yes."

He gently let go of his agent's head, stood, and glanced around the kitchen. "Agent Lewis isn't here."

Sebastian turned away from the three dead men, and walked through the kitchen. He found him after going through a large living room, down a short hallway, and inside a door.

"Holy shit," he said. For a moment he froze. He'd seen death in all forms, but the blood bath that confronted him was a shocking display of violence and depravity.

"Sebastian. Wrist up," Ragno said. "Keep the camera rolling."

He didn't realize he'd dropped his arm to the side, or that he'd turned off the camera. "Brace yourself."

"Is he alive?"

"Don't know. Naked. Spread-eagle tied to a bed. Castrated," Sebastian seethed with anger as he restarted the video footage for Ragno and approached the bed. Something crunched beneath his foot, "Oh fuck," he paused, looked down, and was relieved that he had only stepped on a discarded finger. He was thrilled beyond words that he'd killed knife-man, but wishing the man's death hadn't been so clean, efficient, and painless. "Face up. Every finger on his left hand severed. Three on his right hand. Hundreds of thin slashes all over his body. *Fuck.* Whoever did this was having fun. Sheets are dripping with blood. Neck's got a thick gash. Wait. He's still bleeding." Sebastian lifted the man's still-warm wrist. He glanced at the gash where he thought he'd seen blood pumping out. His eyes had played tricks on him. Maybe. "There's no pulse, but I think he's just bled out. Send this footage to forensics and get them here. Call Zeus. ASAP. We need his brains on this. This is more important than him babysitting the marshals."

"Will do," Ragno said, "Now we know why Agent Lewis kept talking to us as though everything was fine. He was tortured into it. Wait." Her pause lasted only a few seconds, which he used to make sure the camera recorded everything in the room. "Get in a vehicle. Move fast. There's a situation outside. It's escalating. *Go. Go. Go!*"

Chapter Eleven

Relief flooded through Skye as Pete drove away from the safe house.

Finally.

"What's happening?" Spring asked. "Why aren't we going with Sebastian? I thought he was bringing us there."

"He's going in to make sure it's safe," Skye said.

She turned to her left and watched Sebastian walk into the brightly lit garage of 211 Orchid Street, the house she never planned to enter. If she did, they were doomed. Once she and Spring were inside, she wouldn't have the opportunity to get away from the combined force of marshals and Black Raven agents. And get away she must, because she needed to get to the lake house on Firefly Island in just eight hours. She might not have the fighting capabilities, weapons, or skills of these men, but she sure as hell had the ability to disappear and never be found again. If only she could get away from their immediate grasp.

Her eyes met Pete's eyes in the rearview mirror, which he had adjusted so that he could see her. Sebastian's younger, quieter sidekick was an obstacle, but he was shorter, lighter, and seemed like less of a hard-ass. He broke eye contact with her as he stopped at a stop sign, then slowly drove away.

She faced forward, her eyes caught Pete's again, and she tried to appear nonchalant as she worked her left boot off with the toe of her right boot. Throughout the ride from the airport, she had visualized how she was going to use her boots—her only weapon—on the men in the front seat. Kicking wouldn't work. Their heads were partially blocked from her by the front seat headrests. Besides, by the time she had lifted her legs and raised them into a kicking position, they'd have noticed. Using one of the boots as a club could work, but first she had to ease the boot off her foot, and it was hard to do with only her other foot for leverage, because her heel was...stuck. She pressed her toes harder against the stubborn boot. Not one centimeter of movement. *Hell.* She was going to have to bend down and use both hands.

As she bent forward, Pete glanced in the mirror at her. "Everything alright?"

She nodded and straightened in the seat. When he refocused on driving, she started working at the boot again with her foot, and tried not to grimace with the effort. "What's going on?" she asked, keeping her voice normal. "Why are you driving away?"

"Just giving time for a routine site check," Pete answered as he drove further away from the house. "Making sure everything's safe."

"Seems like that would have been figured out earlier, since you guys have been calling it a 'safe' house all day."

No way. There was nothing routine about what was happening. Throughout the day, she'd grown accustomed to Sebastian's low monotone voice, even while saying words that signified tension. Throughout the high-intensity day he had seemed calmer and calmer as he dealt with adversity, until a few seconds before stepping out of the car.

He'd suddenly sat erect, with tension emanating from him. In the visor's mirror, she'd only been able to see his lower face. His lips were pressed in a thin slit. And since Spring was a master at picking up nuances from people—especially her sister—she was also aware the very second that things changed, and she had sat up, her eyes focused on Sebastian. Skye had forced herself to mentally block his tension, telling herself that none of his problems were hers. Her problem was getting away, and his tension and subsequent absence from the Range Rover spelled nothing but a lucky break for her, no matter what it spelled for him.

It was a lucky break she needed to capitalize upon. As Pete turned out of the residential section of the neighborhood and onto a street that had four lanes of traffic, Skye glanced at her watch. Two minutes had gone by since Sebastian had entered the garage. How much longer for him to check the house, talk to the marshals and his agents, and call Pete back? One more minute? Two? Dammit. She had to act now.

Without Sebastian in the SUV, the interior was darker, because the light from his iPad wasn't on. There was also an odd silence. They'd driven to the jet from the hospital, he had sat across from her on the jet, and they'd been in the Range Rover for almost an hour. He was a large man, but he wasn't loud. Yet there was a constant hum of energy around him, whether it was finger clicks on the keyboard he used with his tablet or the low voice he used in phone conversations. He stretched, he shifted his long legs, and he often touched the fingers of his right hand to his right temple and dropped his hand when he realized what he was doing. Without Sebastian there, without his serious eyes on her and Spring, she felt less...safe, as though whatever was going to happen wasn't going to end in her favor. Odd, because he was who she needed to run from. *Away.*

She had to get away, and Sebastian's absence gave her a small window of opportunity that she better not blow. This might be her last chance to make a run for it.

Finally. Her heel was almost free. She pressed harder against the back of the boot with the toes of her right foot. She just needed one more little bit of give, and precious seconds ticked away as she worked towards that goal. There. With a profound surge of relief, her heel slipped out of the damn boot. She used both feet to lift the boot into her lap.

"All good," Pete said, talking to someone who was mic'd to him, his eyes trained, for a second, on the rearview mirror and the traffic that was behind their SUV.

"What are you doing?" Spring asked, her gaze on the boot that now rested on Skye's lap.

"Don't worry, honey," she said, focusing on Pete and waiting for an opportunity to strike. "Everything's fine." He was a quarter mile from the next stoplight. Curbing impulsiveness wasn't a strength of hers, but as she gripped the boot, she took a deep breath. Her father's words of wisdom resonated in her mind.

Figure it out.

She came up with a plan. She'd hit him on the temple like she meant it. Grab Spring's arm and encourage Candy to follow. Run like hell. At the stoplight, a strip mall had a three-story Barnes & Noble, a Starbucks, and a two-story Cheesecake Factory. The parking lot was crammed with cars. Two women and a dog could easily get lost in plain sight there, but the light didn't turn yellow. He drove right through it.

Pete sat up, erect. "Where are our men on the inside?"

Here we go. More news that wasn't good. At least not from

Black Raven's perspective. Great from her perspective, because maybe if the news became terrible, maybe, just maybe, Pete would stop glancing at her in the rearview mirror every other second.

The busy four-lane street seemed to have every chain store she'd ever seen. She had used the stores as landmarks on the way into the neighborhood, and they ticked by as Pete drove faster. Applebee's. Chick Fil-A. Kohl's. Bed, Bath & Beyond. None of the locations seemed as prime as the huge strip mall they'd just passed. Maybe it was a better option to keep the SUV, once she immobilized Pete. Sweat dripped down the back of her neck. Her heart pounded as she tried to think through another plan, one that didn't involve having the luck of getting a red light.

"Spring," she whispered. "Push over a bit. You're crowding me."

Spring pushed Candy to the right and wriggled a bit to the right. Her sister's left side was still practically touching Skye, but at least now Skye could cock her arm back and have a good aim at Pete.

Figure it out.

If thinking through a scenario had ever been important in her life, now was the time. Okay. She could do this. She'd pound the wooden heel into his head, once to startle him, another time to knock him out, dive into the front seat, open his door, and kick him out of the SUV. His pistol, which he wore in a holster at his hip, wasn't going to be an issue because he was going to be disabled by the boot. She'd get it from him if she could, but the more important goal was to get him out of the Range Rover. Pound his head, figure out a way to open his door, kick him out.

Pound, dive, open his door, kick him out of the car.

She was going to be a one-woman army, so effective he was going to be glad to get out of the car. She gripped the boot, tight, in her right hand.

Was it going to work?

It had to, because she was only minutes away from being trapped, with no way out and no way to fulfill her father's vital instructions.

Cataclysm. Run. Now.

Those three words meant all kinds of things. One thing it did not mean was getting stuck in the custody of marshals and Black Raven agents.

Right when she was about to do it, caution bells clanged in her mind. What if the impact of the boot with his head made him jam his foot on the accelerator? Hell. Now that would be a problem. Her goal was to take control of the car and get as far away as possible. Not to get killed in a runaway car. She needed a red light.

Don't think. Just do.

"I'm taking off my boots too," Spring said.

So much for subterfuge. "No, honey," Skye said, her tone calm and not reflecting the roiling, panic-driven need to succeed that was now fueling her rapid heart beat. "We'll be back at the house in just a minute and we'll be getting out."

Pete glanced in the rearview mirror, met Skye's eyes, then his eyes drifted past Skye, and around the area. "I'm about five miles away," he said to someone. "Detecting no signs of trouble. How's Sebastian doing in there?"

The four-lane highway was getting more congested with traffic, as they passed Whole Foods Co., another landmark that she'd noted on the way into the neighborhood. In about a half a mile, if Pete stayed on this street, they'd come to a large shopping mall with a Neiman Marcus and a Nordstrom's. There was going to be a series of traffic lights at the mall, before they'd get on the interstate. She was running out of time.

Jesus Christ, please let us catch a red light.

They approached a traffic signal.

It turned yellow.

She gripped the boot, getting ready. "Spring," she whispered, "I need you to be quiet."

"Why?" Spring asked in a whisper that, thank God, matched Skye's whisper.

Pete sped up and went through the light.

Hell.

She wiped sweat off her brow, before it dripped into her eyes. "Just trust me, okay? Quiet, okay?"

Spring nodded, her eyes concerned and wide, but thankfully, her mouth stayed shut.

Pound, dive, open his door, kick him out of the car.

Buffalo Wild Wings was on the far corner of the mall, and they were almost at the series of traffic lights on which she was banking. The first one was green. The second one turned yellow.

She gripped the boot, and as the Range Rover rolled to a stop behind a car that had stopped as the light turned from yellow to red, Skye cocked her hand back and pushed herself forward, using her legs and feet and every ounce of strength she had. Spring started screaming, as Skye made her move. With Spring's high intensity yell, Pete turned and ducked in the second before the boot heel made contact with his head. She missed, and without hitting the mark that would have stopped her forward momentum, she flew over the seat in an uncoordinated, arms extended heap.

As she was flying face-first into the front dashboard, a large SUV pulled alongside the left side of them, in the left lane. Another SUV pulled alongside of them, on the shoulder of the highway. She righted herself and sat sideways, with her back to the passenger side door. In the split second pause, as she was about to start kicking at Pete, she froze, while Spring screamed and Candy started barking.

The SUV that had pulled next to them had a window lowered and an assault rifle pointed in the car. Because she was facing sideways and in position to kick Pete, the business end of the assault weapon was pointed directly at her.

A car was in front of them. Another behind them. There was nowhere for Pete to go.

Pete turned to her and yelled, "Down."

No encouragement was needed.

But instead of worrying about herself, she sat up in the seat and yelled, "Spring. Get on the floor. Now. Get down-"

She would have kept yelling instructions, and would have climbed over the seat to protect Spring, but Pete tackled her as glass shattered and bullets started whizzing through the car. "Not me. Protect Spring. Now. Spring. Get down. Now."

He pushed her further into the foot well. Car horns blared, Candy barked, and Spring, who had been screaming ever since Skye had cocked her arm back and started her lunge for Pete's head, was suddenly quiet.

There was a pause in the bullets, and then another barrage.

Bullets cut the air, coming from left and right. Then there was silence.

"Spring?" Skye yelled, trying to push Pete off of her.

Spring started screaming, shrill and loud, "No. No. No. NoNoNo." It was the best sound Skye had ever heard in her life.

Skye wriggled out from underneath Pete, who was heavier than he looked and deadly still, as she managed to push him up and off of her into a face-down position on the front seat. The SUV was edging forward, because he'd taken his foot off the brake when he dove on top of her. His left shoulder was riddled with bullet holes and blood was pouring out of him and onto her. He was so still he had to be dead.

Don't think about that. Don't think that he died saving you. Just don't think about it.

Think about Spring's no's and Candy's barks.

She tried to focus on what she could hear, the signs of life that provided her a reason to get moving. She lifted herself onto the seat, shaking safety glass off. She glanced into the back seat, where Spring was crouched low, with Candy, on the floorboard. "We're okay, honey. We're going to be okay."

She saw no blood on Spring or Candy. Just wide-eyed fear and howling and screaming, which became background noise for the drumroll of the three words that had filled her head ever since receiving her father's text.

Cataclysm. Run. Now.

No shit.

"Spring. Please, honey. Stay down." She had no idea whether her words registered with Spring and no time to figure it out.

Cataclysm. Run. Now.

The light was green.

Finally I have the opportunity.

The car that had been in front of them was nowhere in sight and they'd rolled into the middle of the busy intersection, so other drivers who approached the bottleneck of cars, unaware of what had just happened, honked impatiently. Whatever lull might have been caused by the explosive gunfire was ending, as cars pulled to the side, and people stepped out. No one was running to help them, though. She didn't blame them. A shoot-out on a busy road outside of a mall wasn't quite what one expected when finishing up shopping for the evening. Thank God anyone who was nearby was startled into momentary inaction, hesitant to run towards the epicenter of the mayhem.

The SUV on the left side of them was still there, as was the SUV on the right side. Impossible to distinguish good guys from bad from looking at them. All she knew was that they'd been aiming at each other, and both sides had met their mark, because in each car dead or dying men were slumped in their seats.

Not her problem.

"Spring, honey," she said, "we're fine. Just stay down. Why don't you try to make Candy feel better?"

The gunfire had ceased, she had a car, and a clear path to the next message from her father. If she stayed there too long, more bad guys were coming and soon the police would be there. Surely someone had called the police. She had to get away from there, now.

Pete hadn't had time to unholster the Glock that he wore on his right hip. She reached for it, unsnapped the holster, and took the weapon as she shifted to the driver's seat. She shook off more safety glass, realized that some had fallen down her sweater, and didn't bother with it. Jagged edges and small cuts were the least of her worries. She sat on top of Pete's calves because she didn't have time to move him from his face down position, jammed her foot onto the accelerator, and drove the hell away.

Two minutes of freedom were pure bliss, even with Spring freaking out, Candy howling, Pete's blood dripping off of her face, and driving as she sat on the legs of a man who was as still as death. She sped through the busy shopping area, and breathed easier when the signal for the interstate on-ramp was one traffic light away.

Interstate 20.

Skye had no idea if it would lead to Nashville and she didn't have time to figure that out with the Range Rover's complex navigation system. All she knew was that she needed distance between herself and the shoot-out, and the interstate seemed like the best available option. As soon as she had distance, she'd figure out what to do about getting a car that wasn't riddled with bullet holes and one that didn't carry a dead body.

The traffic signal gods didn't cooperate. Her final traffic light turned yellow and the wimp-ass driver in front of her stopped, even before the light flashed red. As she glanced over her right shoulder and weighed the possibility of an end around, Pete groaned.

Oh, dear God, *no.* Maybe she was mistaken. Impossible to tell, really, with Spring's chant-like scream of nos and Candy's barking filling the SUV.

"Uuuhhh." He tried to move his right hand to touch his left shoulder.

A car horn blew, alerting her to get back in her own lane and stop at the light, which was now red.

He was alive. Not dead. *Hell.* Pete needed medical help. *Now.* It was one thing to flee with a dead man. It was another thing to run for her life and be the reason why someone who was dying actually died. She tried to ease her butt off his leg, but since he wasn't moving, and she had to sit behind the wheel, it was an uncomfortable stalemate. She felt bad for him. Shot up, clearly in pain, and having a hundred and twenty-seven pound woman sitting on his leg as he bled to death.

Cataclysm. Run. Now.

Oh dear God. Cataclysm was bigger than one man. Any attempt to secure medical help for Pete was going to end her run for freedom and her ability to follow her father's instructions. If the shoot-out a few minutes earlier didn't underscore the urgency, Skye didn't know what did. The light turned green, the car in front of her accelerated and turned towards the on ramp. She hesitated before pressing on the accelerator.

The car behind her blew the horn.

Oh, dear God. What the hell was she supposed to do?

A police car, sirens blaring, sped in front of her, and screeched to a halt. Another one did the same. Four SUV's, black and with tinted windows, sandwiched her sides and a patrol car blocked her rear. She followed directions that were shouted at her through loudspeakers and stepped out of the car, hands in the air, as Pete's Glock fell at her feet. Two troopers had guns trained on her.

"There's a man injured in this car," she said. "He needs medical help. Now."

"Step away from the car and keep your hands high."

She didn't know where the voice came from. All she knew was that she needed to listen because she was in a shifting sea of confusion, and weapons were aimed at her. She stepped away from the vehicle and raised her hands, trying to figure out how to tell the officers she was innocent. Guns didn't need to be pointed at her. She glanced into the rear window. So far, Spring was still down, but now she was quiet, which meant she was gathering her breath either for more screaming or for movement.

"I'm not the one who was shooting," Skye yelled in an attempt to be heard, as more cars, sirens blaring, screeched to a halt. "I was trying to get away from the shooters." Not exactly true, but how could they know otherwise? "A man is dying. You're wasting time."

Another SUV sped onto the scene. Brakes screeched as it halted. Sebastian jumped out of the driver's side. *Thank God.* His eyes were on her as he approached a state trooper, who stood twenty feet away, and started talking to him.

The rear door of the SUV opened, first an inch, then another. She was more than an arm's length away, so she couldn't shut it. "Spring, stay in the car," she yelled, as more officers lifted their weapons.

Oh, dear God, *no.*

Her breath caught in her throat, as the door to the SUV opened another inch. Her instinct was to throw herself against the door, so that Spring stayed in and out of aim of the weapons. When she lowered her arms just an inch, readying herself to act, someone yelled, "Don't move."

She froze.

Her eyes bounced from the door to Sebastian. He was still talking to the officer, seemingly calm and not worried that she had enough firepower pointed at her to incinerate her to ashes. "Do something, goddammit."

As the officer who Sebastian was speaking to yelled to the other men, "Stand down," Spring leapt out of the car and into her arms. Weapons were lowered, and Candy followed, jumping up and pawing at her legs.

Sebastian walked to her and said, in a voice that sounded calm, controlled, and somehow exactly like what she needed to hear, "Are either of you injured?"

She pressed her hands along Spring's arms, legs, chest, and back, not trusting her eyes alone. "No. I don't think so."

"Skye," he said, his uncharacteristically gentle tone as he said her name immediately halting her frantic examination of Spring. His eyes were serious and concerned. "There's blood all over you. Were you shot?"

She shook her head. "It's Pete's blood."

His eyes hardened. "Stay here. Don't walk one step away."

He walked around to the passenger side of the SUV. Through the windows of the vehicle, she watched him bend towards Pete, as three ambulances arrived on the scene and joined what had become a parking lot for state troopers, squad cars, and dark SUV's. Sirens blared, people were talking to each other and on radios. Spring had her hands over her ears and her face buried in Skye's chest. At least for now, Spring was quiet, though her unusual quiet bothered Skye. As paramedics surrounded Pete, Sebastian stepped back to allow the medical personnel access. Skye watched him pause, as he stared at Pete, and the medical personnel who were frantically trying to help him. His face was grim and his eyes concerned. He glanced in her direction as he waved away a paramedic and walked towards her. Two men wearing jackets with oversized logos of a profile of a bird and the words Black Raven, walked in step with him.

"Let's go," he said, pointing in the direction of a Range Rover that screeched to a halt on the outer perimeter of the scene.

"Where?" she said, feet firm on the ground, arms tight around Spring.

"No time for discussion."

"I'm not going unless I know where."

His eyes sparked with anger and frustration. For the first time since he had arrived on the scene, she noticed details. He still wore the leather jacket that he'd been in all day. There was a slash in the right sleeve, where his bicep was, but the gap in the leather wasn't large enough for her to see underneath the slash. Fat drops of liquid were dripping from his hand. Blood. Her eyes bounced back to his face. There was a scrape on his check and a bruise on his jaw.

"Here are your choices," he said. Voice calm, but terse, indicating he didn't give a damn whether she liked her options. "One, I can handcuff you and throw you in the car. Two, you can fucking walk to the vehicle and get in."

Two police officers and three agents wearing the Black Raven logo on their jackets surrounded them.

He didn't wait for an answer. To one of his agents, he said, "Get all of their things," He glanced angrily at her feet. "Don't forget her boot. Put it all in the SUV." His eyes found hers. "Walk."

Cataclysm. Run. Now.

Oh, dear God.

It was 10:00. She wasn't giving up, but she didn't know how the hell she was going to make it to Firefly Island in Tennessee in just seven and a half hours if she couldn't get away from the trap she was in. She stared into his eyes as she stood her ground. Beneath his anger and impatience, the raw depth of pain and frustration that she saw there told her that he wasn't any happier about the current situation than she was, and it prompted her to move.

She guided Spring to the SUV. Candy followed.

The driver stepped out of the SUV and left the door open, standing erect as he nodded at Sebastian. "Sir."

Sebastian nodded. "The SUV that I used to get here might belong to the perps," Sebastian said. "It was in the garage, and it isn't a Black Raven vehicle. I was going to hotwire it, but keys were in it." Sebastian pointed towards the cluster of three police cars that had first arrived on the scene and the SUV that was behind it. "Keys are in the ignition. Start an assessment. Report in with Ragno. She's putting together the forensics team now for the site at the marshals' safe house and the scene on the road at the mall. We're working with local authorities and marshals on this, so be mindful of that. Don't trust anybody. Don't tell the marshals a goddamn thing. Local authorities either."

"Yes, sir." His agent paused. "Are you planning on driving yourself to the next site?"

"Yes."

"Pardon me, sir, but how bad is that arm?"

"Not so bad that I can't drive. I don't want to waste the manpower that we have here with a driver for me. State troopers are giving me an escort, until the agents who are on the road now can meet up with us."

"Would you at least let me do a field bandage?"

Sebastian shook his head. "No time. Get the first aid kit from the back." To Skye, he said, "Get Spring situated in the back. I need you in front."

Skye coaxed Spring into the back seat, opened her backpack, and with shaking hands, she handed Spring her tablet and colored pencils. Spring shook her head. She tried Spring's iPad and earphones. Spring wouldn't put the earphones on her head, but she held onto them. Skye dug in Spring's backpack for a rawhide for Candy and handed it to her, as the agent approached Sebastian with the first aid kit. Sebastian took it and placed it on the center console in the front seat. "Go. You have work to do."

The agent nodded. "Yes, sir."

He turned and left, as Spring eased her headphones on her head and buried her face in Candy's fur. Before getting in the car, Sebastian eased the jacket off with a grimace. She gasped. His shirtsleeve was soaked with dark red blood. Most of the right arm of it had been slashed through. He unbuttoned the sleeves, unbuttoned the shirt, and shrugged his left arm out of it, gingerly slipping it off his right arm. The man was obviously in pain, clenching his jaw and grimacing as the fabric fell away, yet he kept talking to people who were mic'd to him, giving orders, discussing logistics of how they were going to get to safety, as calm as she'd ever heard him.

Taut muscles rippled across his lean abdomen, chest, shoulders, and arms. He had the perfect amount of curly, golden brown chest hair. At any other moment, she'd have paused to admire the sculpted specimen of maleness, but the tendrils of red blood that oozed from a six-inch gash in his right arm, from firm tricep to midway across his generous bicep, stole her attention. The cut bisected a tattoo of a lone black raven. It was the same stark, sleek, and powerful profile of the bird that she'd seen on his agents' clothing. A crimson river poured from the inside of the raven and ran down his arm.

"How can you drive when you're bleeding like that?"

"I'm not," he said, opening a bottle of alcohol, drawing a breath as he poured it onto the gash. He clenched his jaw, shook his head, then ripped open a pack of gauze with his teeth. Letting the paper-wrapping fall to the ground, he used the gauze to dry his arm. "Get in. While I drive, you're going to make the bleeding stop."

Chapter Twelve

Sebastian waited for the troopers to box them in. They were using four vehicles, two troopers in each, with enough firepower to deter even the most determined kidnappers. It was going to make driving tricky, but he wasn't taking chances. Someone wanted the Barrows girls badly. Whoever they were, Sebastian wasn't going to fuck up again and give them another shot. He was hedging every goddamn bet from here on out.

As he put the car in drive, he glanced at Skye to see how she was holding up, just as she lowered her window two inches. It was the third time that day he'd noticed her need for fresh air. He wondered about the depth of her claustrophobic streak and made a mental note to ask Ragno about it.

"Too much cold air for you?" Skye asked, studying his bare chest as she pulled on rubber gloves from the first aid kit.

The car thermometer read thirty-four. He reached for the heater and turned it up. "No." He drove onto the interstate on-ramp, with their escorts surrounding them. "Ragno. Departing now. ETA forty minutes to the airport, total of ninety minutes driving time to Last Resort."

Last Resort was the nearest of Black Raven's training facilities, and one of the largest. It was also the closest significant installation where he felt comfortable bringing Skye and Spring, given what he'd seen at the safe house.

"Last Resort is a two-hour drive from your present location," Ragno pointed out. "With the stop at the airport, you're looking at more like two and a half hours."

"Not tonight." He planned to drive as fast as he could.

Using the Georgia state troopers as protection and guidance through traffic, he was going straight to the airport, where Raven One had landed when they'd been dropped off an hour or so earlier. For diversion, he'd drive into a private hangar, one that Ragno was now securing. There they were going to pretend to board Raven Four, a jet that was now en route from an airport that was closer to Last Resort. Raven Four would depart to parts unknown. The flight plan would not be made public. There'd be enough agents there and enough Black Raven vehicles to create a plausible scenario where he, Skye, and Spring had boarded the jet and left Georgia. The state troopers who were now privy to knowing that Skye and Spring Barrows were in the custody of Black Raven would think they had left the state on Raven Four. In reality, once the jet was in the air, he and the sisters were going to proceed to Last Resort in one of the Range Rovers, in a convoy. No one outside of Black Raven was going to know where they were.

"Lock down protocol is activated at Last Resort," Ragno said. "Interior and perimeter are secure."

"Update on the news conference."

"The good news is that it's over," Ragno said, her tone clipped. "Better news is that it ended before there was any tie-in between the prison break, the action at the safe house, and the shoot-out that just happened on the highway outside of the mall. We have a few hours before media's going to connect the dots. Bad news is that the world now knows that Barrows is out, that no one can find him, and that Biondo, an escapee, killed a man. As expected, fingers pointed at Black Raven, and now the talking heads are running with the theme of how private security contractors are nothing better than armed, unregulated militia. The politicians who opposed the outsourcing of prison security are calling for congressional hearings."

Beautiful, he thought, *fucking beautiful*. He adjusted his speed to accommodate the four state trooper vehicles, who at the moment weren't going above seventy-five. "How's Pete?"

"Alive. Holding his own in the emergency room. Nothing more for you until that arm is bandaged. Tell Skye you need a tourniquet first, butterfly bandages second, and then a pressure bandage."

The SUVs cameras were on, and Ragno was watching everything, as usual. Skye had been pressing gauze onto his arm in an effort to force the bleeding to stop. "Tourniquet," he told her, "and make it tight. Right below my shoulder."

He glanced in the rearview mirror, where Spring was watching her sister's first aid efforts. Tear streaks stained Spring's face, her hair was half in, half out of her braid, but her headphones were on and, thank God, she was quiet. Ignoring all of them, the dog was gnawing on an oversized rawhide, as though her life depended on each bite.

He glanced back at the road, as the lead trooper turned on his siren and picked up the speed to eighty. Atlanta's interstate system was busy, even after ten on a Monday evening. To maintain a speed of eighty, they needed sirens. Fine with him.

"Now what?" Skye asked, attention riveted to the wound.

With the tourniquet in place, he said, "Pinch the edges together and close the cut with butterfly strips."

He felt her fingers on his arm, pressing.

"You need stitches," she said.

"There's a needle and thread in the kit." He glanced at her. Her eyes were wide, studying his face, and she was frozen in place, her fingers on his arm as she leaned towards him.

She shook her head. "I don't even sew on buttons."

He chuckled as he focused on the road. They were moving steadily now and doing an average speed of eighty.

"Really," she said. "I have no clue how to do stitches on cloth, much less a human! You should have had a paramedic do this."

His lips twitched at her vehemence and the worry in her eyes. "I was joking."

"Not funny."

"The cut isn't as bad as all of the blood is making it seem. I take medicine that makes me bleed."

"For your headaches?"

He nodded and kept his eyes glued to the road. His headaches weren't a state secret, but he didn't like that she, or anybody, was aware of them. He wondered what else she'd learned about him in this interminably long day. He shook off the worry. Headaches were now a fact of his life, and, for better or worse, at least for the near future, so was Skye. Some of the pills that he was now taking for his headaches would be damn good right now, because his head felt like it was going to explode. He couldn't medicate while driving, and not when he was responsible for the two of them, but he sure as hell looked forward to a double dose of the medication smorgasbord when they got to Last Resort and were in capable hands.

"As long as you have your arm bent like that, I can't get the wound to close."

He'd been holding his arm at his chest, elbow bent, with his hand on his lap. He unflexed his arm and stretched. His hand had nowhere to go but in her lap, palm down. His tricep was up, his bicep was down, and the wound was positioned so that she could look straight down at it. When she did, her breasts pressed into his arm. On any other day, the position would have been a good thing. Her firm, yet soft, thighs inspired an urge to stroke her legs.

She shifted in her seat, and he frowned. *Damn.* All he had to do was touch her and he became hard, even with a headache, a gash in his arm, casualties among Black Raven agents, and more shit raining on him than he had ever imagined possible. His libido was back, and it didn't give a damn about everything that was going wrong in the world.

He tried to focus on driving and maintaining a safe distance between their SUV and the lead trooper. Out of the corner of his eye he saw her open another pack of gauze and throw the wrapping at her feet. He bit back a smile of admiration at her willingness to dive into a bloody first-aid project. She shifted in the seat, which caused her breasts to press tighter against his arm, and now his hand was between her thighs. With soft touches, she dried his arm one more time. The combination of her strong touch, delicate fingers, and breasts that were pressed against his arm sent sparks from his arm straight to his dick, igniting even more of a fire.

Hell. He groaned, not quite under his breath.

She cast a worried look in his direction. "You sure you're not lightheaded? You're going eighty. I'd hate for you to pass out."

"Nope. Feeling fine." He glanced at the speedometer. Eighty-five, with his dick rock-hard, and no relief for that in sight. He resigned himself to unrequited arousal as she held the gauze against his arm with her left hand, gripped a pack of butterfly strips in her right and tore it open with her teeth. She drew a deep breath as she pinched the edges of the wound together and applied adhesive strips across it. She used a light, but firm, touch.

The fact that she didn't know what to do told him that she wasn't highly skilled with first-aid, yet her touch was confident. He liked people who weren't afraid of doing things that were out of their usual orbit, and Skye certainly fit that bill. When she had eight bandages in place, crisscrossed into not-so-neat x's, she paused and studied the wound. "Hey, this is working. It stopped bleeding. Now what?"

"Gauze. Wrap it around the whole arm. After, tape it. Make it tight."

She ripped open another pack of gauze. "You're probably going to have a scar running through the tattoo."

"Not the biggest problem of the day, and it won't be my first scar." He glanced at her and saw her studying his exposed skin. All the lights were on in the car, and there was no hiding the collection of battle scars on his shoulders and chest that he'd gathered over the years.

"I'm through." She patted down the tape that she had wrapped around his bicep. "I think it's holding."

Ragno said, "It looks great, Sebastian. Elevate your arm and have her remove the tourniquet."

He chuckled. Ragno didn't have to say *Get your hand out of her lap*, but he knew she was thinking it.

"What's funny?" Skye asked.

"Nothing." He lifted his arm so that it was resting on her headrest behind her head. "Now undo the tourniquet."

As Skye turned in the seat to untie the rubber strip, she asked, "What happened at the safe house?"

"Same thing that happened on the road."

"It was supposed to be a *safe* house," she said. "What happened to the men who were there, making sure that it was safe?"

He glanced in the rearview mirror. Spring was looking at his arm. "Is she listening?"

"Not with her earphones on, but use your nice voice." Skye gave him a slight half smile, though her eyes looked more worried than happy. "Keep it low and try not to look stressed. She's a master at nonverbal clues."

"I was ambushed," he said, focusing on the road. "Three bad guys. The two marshals were dead, as were my two men."

"I'm sorry that you lost your men."

"Thank you," he said, keeping his gaze directly ahead, focusing on the taillights of the lead state trooper. He didn't want to see sympathy in her eyes. Her voice was packed with enough of it.

The path of feelings, for him, was a slippery slope into a dark house of horrors, a place where he never willingly went. With the two agents who had gotten killed on the road at the mall, the body count for Black Raven due to the prison break was four. If Pete didn't make it, it would be five. In his business he'd learned to develop a thick shell of hard-ass emotional armor, and the sympathy in Skye's voice prompted him to call upon that overly-developed skill.

The hardest part about the head injury he had suffered in July was that there were holes in his carefully cultivated emotion-shielding armor, and until he fully recovered from the head injury, he had to deal with feelings that zapped at him from out of the blue.

Nightmares for Sebastian, even before the head injury, were never what could go wrong with a job, or whether he was going to get himself in a situation where he'd die. No. His nightmares were made up of feelings, of horror, fear, and incompetence. Of failing to help some innocent person who needed his help, and it didn't take a rocket scientist to pinpoint the cause of why he'd prefer to be a callous son of a bitch than anything else. He was never going to be more than a few steps removed from the kid who had watched his father abuse his mother, physically and mentally. Before he had learned to turn off empathy as easily as turning off a light with a flick of a switch, he'd felt his mother's pain that came with every hit, and the misery that fueled her many, many tears.

"What went wrong?" Skye asked, her voice calling him back to the present. *Thank God.* Even today was better than reliving the memories of his childhood and the feeling of helplessness that came from being caught in the web that bound his mother and father.

"We're not sure."

"Is that all you're going to say? What happened to those men? To you?"

He exhaled and focused on the road, as he thought about what to tell her, because he now knew her well enough to know she wasn't going to let the question drop. Black Raven had lost men before. What they did was dangerous, and this wasn't the first day in company history with multiple casualties. Yet one death was one too many, and four deaths in one day was a disaster.

Aside from the human tragedy of the individual deaths, four deaths on American soil, with American media circling the waters of the prison break like sharks at a chum fest, was going to be a PR nightmare. Congressional hearings? *Holy fuck.* The fact that Black Raven routinely cherry-picked the military's top talent by offering huge paychecks was going to be aired publicly, and he wondered what kind of regulations would be enacted to prevent his hiring practices in the future.

The only way out was to find the remaining two prisoners, get their asses back in jail, and conduct serious damage control while they did it. Just as it had been when the suck-ass day had started, finding Richard Barrows was priority number one for him. At least with Biondo there was a trail to follow. Barrows? All he had was mystery men who were hell-bent on seizing the man's daughters.

As he wondered what the hell to tell Skye, and still came up with no words, Ragno interrupted his thoughts by saying, "Within minutes of your appearance at Creative Confections, everything in her life went to hell. If you expect her to open up to you and help us find her father, you need to at least give the impression that you're being open and honest. Tell her something. Now."

Ragno was correct. As usual. "Whoever's after you has a diabolical mean streak. You might think that you're running from me, or the authorities, or whatever you think you're running from, but all you're doing is running to them, cause there's no way you can avoid them." Eyes back on the road, he told himself, because her eyes had a magnetic pull—of not just fear, but defiance—that was dangerous. "Black Raven cars are loaded with cameras. Before the gunfire erupted you were trying to bash Pete's head in with your shoe." Clever move on her part, but given the shit-storm that had happened immediately after, he didn't dwell on the cleverness. "I know you were driving away from the scene, and I hate to think that you were doing that, regardless of whether Pete is getting medical help."

"I didn't say to pick a fight with her," Ragno said. "What the hell is wrong with you?"

"Whoa," Skye said. "Hold it for just one sec-"

"Nice voice," he said, as he glanced into the rearview mirror and saw Spring sitting up, erect, her eyes wide and focused on her sister.

Skye turned to glance at her sister and offered her a reassuring smile, as she flashed her an index-finger-meeting-thumb OK signal. She said, "I'm OK," before glancing again at Sebastian. "You're damn right I was leaving." Her tone was soothing and sweet, even though her words were razor-edged and to-the-point. "By now it shouldn't be a news flash to you that I want to get away. At first I thought Pete was dead, so whether he needed medical help wasn't really an issue, and you can't blame me for not wanting to stick around there. Who's to say more men weren't arriving within seconds?"

Well, maybe she had a valid excuse for running. Given the events of the day, her fear that the bad guys were winning and would continue to pursue her was realistic. If she truly had thought that Pete was dead, there'd have been no reason to pause to get him medical help. "If you succeed in running from me, all you're doing is guaranteeing a run-in with men who are taking orders from someone with a sadistic mean streak."

"Sadistic? What do you mean?"

"There's an iPad in the glove compartment," Ragno told him, exasperation evident in her voice. "You could show her the video footage that you took while in the safe house, because she's not taking your word for anything."

He paused as he considered Ragno's suggestion. Not a good idea. He'd have a hard enough time getting the images of Agent Lewis's tortured body out of his mind, and he'd seen death in all shapes and forms. Those images, once seen, couldn't be unseen. He didn't want to do that to Skye.

"Mutilation," he said. "Fingers gone. Castration."

She gasped.

He glanced at her. For a second, their eyes locked. She'd gotten through their suck-ass day fine, without a breakdown or tears, thank God, but he'd made the right call not showing her the video. In her eyes there were already shitloads of worry and fear and stress. She didn't need to see real life images of the depth of human depravity.

He dragged his eyes back to the road, as four black Range Rovers joined the convoy. Each SUV had two Black Raven agents in it. He breathed easier, knowing that eight of his own agents were now with him. Two of the state troopers peeled away. They now had five escort cars. "You're safe now, Skye. I'll make sure of it."

She gave him a glance that said she wasn't so sure. He didn't argue. Instead, he said, "Ragno, talk to me. Any clue yet as to what went wrong with the safe house?"

"None. Marshals are doing internal checks for leaks. They're moving at a slug's pace. There's too many drags on their attention right now—Biondo, Biondo's witnesses, Barrows, media, and now the safe house. Minero's deteriorated to reactionary mode. I'm not expecting much help from that direction."

"Profile Minero. Find out if there is any way he is the leak."

"I'm already on that."

"Have you found Jennifer Root?" The lawyer had been the only outside contact that Skye had been allowed during the day, and Root had been told that Skye was going to the marshals' safe house. When the safe house delivery went bad he had directed Ragno to track down Root.

"No. It's like she...disappeared. There's no telecommunication trace. One of her vehicles is parked at her office, another at her home. Agents are in her condo. She's not there. They're searching for clues as to her whereabouts. So far, nothing. It's a little trickier to break into her law office. Stay tuned on that."

To Skye, he said, "Tell me more about Jennifer Root."

"Why?"

"She knew you were going to the safe house, which became a disaster." Atlanta was behind them, and the interstate traffic had lightened. They were going a steady eighty-five. He tapped the car into cruise control, then stretched his legs. "Maybe there's a link."

"You think Jen is one of the bad guys? No. There's absolutely no way."

"I'm not saying she was involved. We have to pursue every possible lead. Because she contacted you today, she's one."

"Well." As she shifted in her seat, ends of her hair that had fallen out of her ponytail tickled his arm, which was still elevated on her headrest. "You really have nothing."

"Thank you for that assessment." He glanced at her. Though her tone was more than a little cocky and argumentative, her eyes met his with a glance that was filled with worry and fear. He glanced into the rearview mirror, saw that Spring's eyes were closed, and said, "Tell me about her. You called her Aunt Jen earlier today. Are you related?"

"Not by blood. By closeness. She was my mother's best friend in college, she introduced my mom to my father, she was at every birthday party, every graduation, and she was with us," she paused, "when mom died."

Her tone changed when she said those last words. He paused, hoping like hell she wouldn't start crying. Through reading medical reports, he knew that her mother's death was a life-changing event for her, one that had prompted her to develop protective emotional armor that kept her detached from others. Later psychologists had concluded that her defense mechanism wasn't working in her favor, but Sebastian was thankful for it, because one quick glance into dry eyes revealed that his strong woman wouldn't disappoint him.

As soon as he thought that, he almost choked. Skye was strong. No denying that. But she wasn't his, and he didn't know what in fucking hell had inspired such a thought. He normally didn't claim women as 'his', especially not women he was charged with protecting. *Back to the task*, he told himself. *Finding Richard Barrows, which for the moment was reduced to driving, and figuring out what Skye knew about Jennifer Root. Fuck. Skye was right. He had nothing to go on.* "I know she never married. Any significant relationships you know of?"

"Only that she was best friends with my mom and dad. She worked long, hard hours. We were her surrogate family. As far as I know, she was always my father's lawyer. When my father and Zachary Young founded BY Laboratories in the nineties, she became corporate counsel, and when the company fell apart, she oversaw the team that handled Dad's criminal defense."

Something wasn't right about the picture that Skye was painting. "With all that trust and closeness, she didn't know where you and Spring were until today?"

"When federal agents started pursuing my father, and after Zachary died, he stopped trusting anyone. During the plea negotiations, Dad even stopped trusting Jen," she paused.

"Why?"

"I'm not sure. After Zachary died, my father became even more paranoid than normal. All he told me was that he wanted Spring and me to have a clean break for a while, until things settled down. He told me not to contact Jen. I listened. Until today, when you handed me that phone, I hadn't talked to her since I started living under the name of Chloe Stewart. Jen knew we were disappearing, but we didn't tell her where we were going or who we were becoming."

There had to be more. "Your father's been in jail for just about eleven months, and she's visited him four times. Records indicate that they met each time for an hour," Sebastian said, repeating some of the intel that Ragno had provided earlier in the day. "Your father didn't have to sit down and talk with her."

"So?"

"It doesn't sound like your father felt the need for a clean break from Root for himself, but rather only for you and Spring. Your father was in jail for tax fraud and evasion. His company was destroyed. I understand that he wanted you and Spring to be free from the media that hounded you guys before he went to jail, but to sever all contact from someone who was like a second mother to the two of you? Why would he want that?"

She drew a deep breath. "My father is brilliant enough to pioneer innovations in computer virus detection and design technology for micro-chip brain implants, yet he wore foil-lined hats when he went outside. Even that had a twist, though." Her voice was hesitant. "He only did it when atmospheric pressure was at a certain level. The reality is that every time he came up with a brilliant innovation, he became paranoid about what the innovation could do in the wrong hands. He's a genius, but his thought processes aren't always logical."

Ragno said, "That's a candid assessment."

"I need more of an answer," Sebastian said, to both Ragno and Skye. "What was happening that made your father think that you needed a clean break from Root? There had to be something."

"It wasn't just Aunt Jen. It was the world, and that included Jen."

"Why?"

He glanced at Skye, who gave him a blank expression and a shrug, indicating that she wasn't giving more of an answer. Whether it was because she didn't have one, or she just wasn't telling it, he had no idea. "What made you listen to him when he told you to change your names and disappear?"

Instead of an answer, she gave him silence, a frown, a bit of fear, before forcing her features into a blank look.

As he focused again on the road, Ragno said, "In connection with debriefing interviews conducted in the tax fraud case, Barrows told investigators that he believed Young's plane crash wasn't an accident. He also told investigators Young's family was murdered along with him. Intentionally."

"Any basis in fact?"

"No," Ragno said, "but it could explain Barrows' paranoia regarding his daughters' safety. It could also explain Skye's concerns, and why she's so desperate to get away."

"Yes," Sebastian said, "but Skye was running before I showed up, before she knew her father had escaped. She's not saying why."

"It would be easier if you just put Ragno on speaker," Skye said tartly. "I could join in, instead of sitting here listening to your side of the conversation while you and Ragno talk about me."

He glanced at her. "Would you tell us anything helpful?"

She shot him an irritated look.

Right. That's what I thought. 'Fuck no, buddy'. Sebastian shifted in the seat, stretching his legs, making himself as comfortable as he could for the remainder of the drive. "Ragno, construct a profile of Zachary Young in the year before his death."

"Young's plane crash was two years ago. You want a profile of events that took place up to three years ago?"

"Yes. Everything." He was digging deep, he knew. But whether a man who had died two years prior to Barrows' escape could have possibly done something that would help him find Barrows now was an interesting question. He wasn't simply grasping at straws. He was clutching at thin air, and he was throwing a hell of a lot of manpower into the effort. Didn't matter. What he'd known from the beginning, and what the interminably long day confirmed, was that it was going to take something more than a bloodhound to find Richard Barrows.

"Well, from the data we've already gathered in constructing the profile on Jennifer Root, we know one thing. Phone records, cell phone and office, establish that in the six months before he died, Root talked to Zachary Young more than she talked to Richard Barrows," Ragno said.

"That's interesting," Sebastian said. "Might be meaningless, though. Young was the businessman behind the operation. Barrows was the creative genius. It makes sense the businessman would have communicated with the lawyer."

"Well, the communications were at odd times, too. Not just business hours. Lawyers work 24/7 though, so it may not mean anything. The profile is harder to come by than normal, because most of her communications were encrypted, so we have to break the code."

"Also compile a project list for BY Laboratories in the two years prior to Barrows' incarceration. I've read enough of the debriefing transcripts to know he consistently referred to Shadow Technology-"

"We've worked on that. Like I told you earlier, our government sources indicate that no type of Shadow Technology created by Barrows is in use in any government databases and especially not in sensitive ones like PRISM."

"Well, keep digging."

"FYI. All of our data analysts are working practically around the clock now. Aside from the prison break, some Middle East projects are requiring attention. Short breaks are only for catnaps, food, and hygiene. " Her tone was matter-of-fact. She wasn't complaining. She was just stating facts that Sebastian needed to know. "My department is operating past peak capacity."

"Remind me in an after-action-report. It's time to up manpower," he said. In the information age, his company needed the ability to secure massive volumes of data and process it. Taxing their resources wasn't acceptable. "Can't do anything about it now, except add to the work list. Here's another project. Compile a list of parties who were interested in BY Laboratory's products. Barrows was the brains behind the operation, but Young managed to get Barrows' ideas sold. I want the profile of Young to be business and personal. I want to know who Young was dealing with and what the hell he was trying to sell. As far as prospective purchases of BY Laboratories products, do an assessment of the interested parties and any possible correlations with the safe house crime scene and anything else that happened today." He paused. "How's Pete?"

"Holding his own. In surgery."

"Good. Play the press conference for me. Interrupt if there's new news."

Chapter Thirteen

Shattering Barrows' kneecap and hammering steel pins underneath his toenails was entertaining, but the injuries didn't produce the desired result. Barrows had a high threshold for pain, but even he had his breaking point. Finally, he'd passed out from the pain, and when he regained consciousness all he could do was mumble incoherently for hours after the morning's interrogation session. The wounds required treatment.

'Treatment' was code in Trask's world for readying the victim for the next round of torture. They had to feel well enough to fear what was going to happen to them. Without fear, there was no hope of cooperation. In Barrows' case, there had to be another round, because Barrows wouldn't deliver the fucking code. Couldn't. Barrows had spent two days destroying data, and now he couldn't put it back together.

Dunbar stood at Trask's side in his office, their attention focused on monitors showing treatment room B, anticipating the reunion of Barrows and Jennifer Root. The safe-house operation had become a disaster, compliments of Sebastian Connelly. One day, hopefully soon, he was going to cut off Connelly's dick and shove it down the man's throat.

He'd have to wait for that thrill. For now, all he had was Jennifer Root to exert pressure on Barrows. Root wasn't a sure shot like Skye and Spring would be, but it could work.

The monitors in Trask's private office revealed the treatment room that was on the floor beneath them. Bright, florescent light illuminated the treatment room. White linens covered Root's ass and her legs, leaving her back exposed. Eyes closed, she lay face down on a pillow. Her shoulder length, chestnut brown hair covered half her face. Root was attractive for a middle-aged woman, but her dark brown eyes typically gave away the fact that there wasn't anything soft or feminine about her. Trask knew and appreciated her, because she was like him. She was a barracuda of a lawyer, who'd rather eat her young for breakfast than have a glass of wine with friends. Chardonnay? Not something she drank. Like Trask, she preferred to sip the heady elixir that came with squeezing the resistance out of anyone that dared to challenge her.

Trask's intel on Root had told him that in the rare moments when she wasn't working, she exercised and pampered herself with massages and spa visits. Because so much of her life had been spent in offices and courtrooms and not in the sun, her skin, particularly the soft skin of her back, was smooth and creamy. There had been no massage for Root this afternoon. The space between her shoulders and her waist was crisscrossed with bleeding cuts and purplish-black bruises. Glistening ointment covered her wounds. In the white expanse of the treatment room, with light bouncing off white tiles and stainless steel, Root's wounds and her dark hair were the only splash of color.

The camera revealed an assistant in light-green medical scrubs as he wheeled Barrows into the examining room, then promptly left.

Trask lifted his cell phone and dialed the audio-visual room. "Give me a close-up on Barrows."

As the camera panned in, Barrows' eyes revealed the fatigue and misery that came with being a broken man. He wore a loosely-tied hospital gown. His face and arms were blistered with burns from the sizzling water that had rained on him in the earlier interrogation session. His shattered knee was bandaged, but not repaired. Despite his own sorry condition, Barrows gasped as he looked at his lawyer and best friend. He tried to stand, but instead he fell back awkwardly, grimacing in pain. He hadn't yet mastered the art of walking with only one operable knee.

Multi-angle cameras, concealed in lighting hardware and invisible to the occupants of the exam room, caught the drama perfectly as it played out on the monitors in Trask's office. He'd wanted to give them a few minutes together, alone, thinking that the surprise reunion, and her wounds, might prompt Barrows into revealing something useful.

Trask watched the monitors for several irritatingly long minutes as Barrows tried to breathe through his pain and collect himself. Finally, Barrows wheeled himself to Root's bedside and gently touched her shoulder. "Jennifer."

Root opened her eyes. She whimpered. Her eyes widened when she saw Barrows. She attempted to sit up, but collapsed onto the bed. Finally, she struggled up on an elbow, moaning as she did. She dragged the top sheet up, covering her breasts and most of her body. For a few long minutes, her eyes had the unfocused look of someone whose awareness hadn't caught up with the fact that she was awake. She stared at Barrows and shook her head in confusion.

Trask stepped closer to the monitors, riveted by the interaction between his two captives.

"Oh, dear God," she said. Her gaze became sharper as she took a quick visual survey of the room. She squinted against the bright lights, as she looked at Barrows sitting beside her. Her focused gaze revealed that her brain was, as usual, firing with no-nonsense, analytical thoughts. "We're in hell."

Trask glanced at Dunbar and chuckled. He'd orchestrated the reunion of Root and the client who had made her well known and wealthy. He hadn't expected Root to be overly effusive in concern for Barrows, but her lack of immediate concern for the physical condition of her client was downright comical.

Eyes back on the monitor, he folded his arms and watched the drama.

"He says he has Skye and Spring," Barrows whispered, as if he knew someone was listening.

Into his phone, Trask said, "Increase volume. Make focus on the close-up on Barrows sharper."

He held his breath as he waited for the adjustment on focus. Nice. He could see each fluid-filled blister on the man's high cheekbones, and the stark terror in his rheumy blue eyes.

"Is it true?" Barrows' voice broke off as he choked in panic.

"I don't know if he has them now, but he sure as hell came close this morning. He sent kidnappers after them. His attempt was foiled with not a second to spare. Last I heard the marshals had established a safe house, and they were taking them there. Dammit, but this hurts," she said, wincing as she turned to her side and sat up in the bed, wrapping the sheet around herself to cover her nudity, before sitting all the way up and easing herself off of the bed. She groaned when she was fully upright. "Son of a fucking bitch, this hurts." She lifted his chin with the crook of his finger, and said, "What the hell did he do to you?"

Barrows shook his head. "You don't want to know."

"We've got to get out of here," she said, her tone quiet but confident, her determination visible in the steady gaze she shared with him.

"Shhhh," Barrows said, eyes wide, glancing up, around, and

at the walls. "They're listening."

Jennifer's eyes blazed. "Good. I hope the fucking bastard who is doing this to us is listening. He'll realize that we're smarter than him." She broke eye contact with Barrows and glanced around the room. "I need clothes."

"What happened this morning?" Barrows asked.

"Aren't you listening? The monster who has us attempted to kidnap your daughters." She walked around the room, pulling open cabinet doors and slamming them shut when they didn't have what she was looking for. "A private security contractor who was hired to do prison security, and who now is trying like hell to find you, happened to be on the scene. Lucky for all of us, he's tough, tenacious, and, by all accounts, brilliant. Sebastian Connelly. Black Raven. He prevented the kidnapping, took Skye and Spring to a hospital to make sure they were okay, and they were heading to a marshals' safe house. I don't know if they made it there, because these bastards kidnapped me. I was in my office. Three men entered."

She opened the final cabinet in the room, where there were neatly folded linens and clothes. Rummaging through the stacks of linens, wincing in pain with each move that she made, she continued, "They gave me something. Chloroform. I don't know. I passed out. Woke up in a room down the hall, where a man in a mask whipped me." She glanced at Barrows. "He whipped me as he asked me questions about your work. I don't know what the hell all of this is about. But whatever it is," she sneered at him, "it's your fault and once again, I'm having to think a way through a mess that you've created. I can do a lot with my legal expertise," she turned her attention back to the clothes, "but the technological aspects are a little over my head. It's time for you to step up to the plate."

He stiffened. "Hospital? Jesus. How badly were my girls hurt?" Barrows demanded, not addressing the bulk of Root's concerns, his paternal instincts blinding him to personal peril.

Trask chuckled. The video monitors and audio mics were catching every nuance of the interaction between Barrows and Root, revealing that they were almost as narcissistic as he was.

Root shook her head. "As far as I know, not anywhere as bad as what the bastard's done to us. It would be damn nice right now if you were more concerned about our immediate survival." She yanked down a few stacks of folded clothes and found a pair of drawstring pants and a hospital gown.

She glanced at Barrows. "Shut your eyes." She dropped the sheet, exposing her naked body, seemingly unconcerned about the strong possibility that they were on camera. She pulled on the drawstring pants and hospital gown, which she tied in front, wincing as the gown touched her wounds.

"I talked to Skye while they were being examined at a hospital. She and Spring were scared but physically fine." Root gathered her hair off her face with both hands, winced, then dropped her arms, face pale. "Just having that conversation required me to pull every string I've ever managed to collect, Richard." She drew a deep breath and shot him a furious look. "I told you from the beginning not to cut me off from them."

"Don't you understand that I had no choice," Barrows said, his expression pleading with her for understanding, as he wheeled himself over to her and continued. "You know that. The only thing in the world that would get me to do what these people want would be threats to my girls. I did everything in my power to keep them from being used in that way." He shook his head. "I didn't want you in the position of being their protector. It's too much responsibility." He paused. "Who has us?"

"I don't think this madman is a who. I think he's a what," Root said, "and the answer is fucking obvious. He's a rich, powerful, sadistic psychopathic freak."

Trask glanced at Dunbar, who was sponging perspiration off of his brow. Root's description of him was accurate. He loved it, but Dunbar was holding his breath, awaiting his reaction. "She doesn't mince words, does she?"

Dunbar's dark hair and dark eyes made his face seem even paler as the color drained away. "No."

"Don't look so afraid," he said to his assistant, turning back to the monitor as he added, "I know exactly what I am."

"And he's got my data," Richard said, his desperation and despair apparent in every word. "He's got it. For the last few days I've done nothing but stare at the programs that he's running, analyzing the code, and wondering how he got it. It had to be Young, but why would Young give it to him?"

"Don't worry about that now. Focus on how we're going to get the hell out of here."

"For the first couple of days, they tried to make me believe that they were with the government, that there was some sort of emergency. I fell for it. Until I ran the programs. I was hours into testing and realized that he had an incomplete set of code. He's got 92.6% of the LID," Barrows eyes were wide. He dropped his head to his hands, his temples meeting his palms, and rested his forehead on his palm. "I let him know there's more. Dear God," he lifted his head to meet Root's gaze. "I let him know he had an incomplete set of code. I should have told him what he had was meaningless."

Root got on her knees, gently touched his hands, and said, "Richard, look at me."

He slowly lifted his head.

Root's dark eyes were steady, her gaze strong. Even through the camera, Trask could feel her strength. "You have to give him what he wants."

Trask held his breath, anticipating whether Barrows would now agree.

Barrows shook his head. "I can't do that."

"Hell," Trask said, anger pulsing through his veins. "Still resisting."

"He will eventually kill us," she told Barrows, voice merciless. "He told me to tell you that. I believe him, and so should you."

"I'm sorry. My life is expendable. Shadow Technology and LID Technology is not. I'm sorry-"

"Well, my life is not expendable!" She snapped, grimacing in pain as she walked stiffly to the bed and sat on it, easing her butt to the mattress. "If we don't get out of here, they will kill us, and I suspect not before testing our pain threshold further. I can't handle another whipping like that, Richard. I absolutely cannot! The girls are safe—for now. But who knows whether they'll be safe in a day? An hour? You have to make sure they're secure, and to do that, we have to get the hell out of wherever we're being held. You have to give the man what he wants. Are you listening? Just give it to him. We'll get out of here and you'll figure out a way to undo whatever damage he causes."

"I'm sorry," Barrows said, hanging his head and shaking it, resisting yet physically looking like he had the spine of a goddamn beaten puppy. "There's a limit to what I can do, and I can't do that. I'm sorry."

In the room filled with monitors and other surveillance equipment, Trask glanced at Dunbar. "It's time for more persuasion."

Dunbar nodded and made a phone call. Trask would have

walked away from the monitors, but he realized that Root hadn't given up.

"Stop apologizing," Root snapped as she stood up and started pacing in an eight-foot line, directly in front of Barrows' wheelchair. "I've negotiated with the best. I know how to assess relative strengths and weaknesses. Right now, our strength is that we—you—have something that he wants. We need to give this man what he wants, and it certainly isn't you saying you're sorry. Let's figure out a way to give it to him where he has to keep us alive. What we have has value to him only if it is operational. That's his problem. God knows how long he's had your data, but he needed you to tell him that he had an incomplete data set? Don't you see?"

Barrows stared absently at her, his head turning slightly as she walked, following each step. "See what?"

"Come on, Richard, would you please use some of your magnificent brainpower and think. He needs your knowledge to make LID Technology work, so that he can access Shadow Technology and break into PRISM and the databases that integrate with PRISM. That's our ace. His people aren't smart enough to manipulate the programs or diagnose problems. Even if you give him the data, he'll need to keep you alive to run the systems."

Jennifer Root was making perfect sense. Trask just wished Barrows would see it that way.

All color drained from Richard's eyes. "No. I'd rather die."

Root stopped pacing. She stood directly in front of Barrows, as the door opened and four men wearing white jumpsuits and white masks walked into the room. "You bastard. He's going to kill me before he kills you."

Root said it like she believed it, and the reality was she was right. As Trask's fingers itched in anticipation of a kill, Barrows and Root locked eyes.

"Richard," she said, backing away from the two men who walked towards her. "Listen to me. It is only a matter of time before he has Skye and Spring." She ran from the men. When they caught up to her, she slapped at their hands and punched at them to get away. "He won't stop trying."

A few minutes later, mask in place, Trask walked into the examining room as his men strapped Barrows to his wheelchair. His aides had restrained Root by strapping her to an examining chair. The aides had left her clothes on, but in her attempt to break free her robe had come untied. Her left breast was exposed. It was full and, because she wasn't a young woman, the gentle curve of it slightly sagged.

Still tantalizing, though, with a light pink nipple that complimented her easy-to-bruise, creamy-white skin. The arms of the chair were wide enough for her hands to be splayed out, palm down. Each finger of her right hand was separately tied to the table with zip ties that were locked so tight they were cutting her skin.

"Richard. Please listen to me." Her eyes were focused with horror on his mask, but her words were for Barrows. The woman had balls. She wasn't going to panic. "He knows that you told Skye to run. It is only a matter of time before he finds them. You do not want this man to have your daughters. Don't you understand that cooperating is inevitable?"

Barrows averted his eyes from her.

Trask went to a drawer, selected a knife, and went to Root. He bent to examine her hand, smelling the sweet smell of fear that was now rising from her body, enjoying the fast pace of her breaths. "You think about which finger is your least favorite, as I tell Richard a few things." He turned to Barrows, a blistered and broken man in a wheelchair. He walked closer, took the man's chin in the cup of his hand, and gently lifted his face. Barrows' blue eyes were wide with fear, and he wasn't even fighting his restraints. Nor was Barrows fighting his touch. More than fear, he saw resignation, and that bothered him.

He gentled his tone, realizing that the brilliant Richard Barrows was no different than any other man. He needed empowering. "I want something that you can give me. You have the power here. You have my word that if you give me the code, I will never harm your daughters. I'm close to them. I know who is protecting them. You need to understand me, so nod a bit, okay?" Dear God, the man had no spine. "The lives of your daughters will depend on your understanding exactly what I'm saying."

Barrows nodded.

"Sebastian Connelly and Black Raven are good, but they're not perfect. They have delivered your daughters to a safe house that I control. Nod if you understand that."

Barrows, wide-eyed and sweating profusely, nodded. He

returned to Jennifer, but his words for Barrows as he lifted the knife to her hand. "Even if your daughters would somehow manage to escape, there's a big problem. While the U.S. government would be fascinated to know the drama that is unfolding with their technological intelligence, the secrecy that they demanded for the project is now working against them. No one knows what is happening, so no one with the government is offering your daughters the type of assistance they would really need to protect them from me, the kind of assistance that would keep them off the grid for years to come. For them to disappear again, they need to rely upon their own devices, and I know all of that. I know all assets that are in their current, past, and next names. I know that you had carefully crafted backup plans for them, with alternate identities."

"There is no way you know their next identities."

"Bridgette and Brandy Tillman." As he rattled off the names, Barrows slumped further in the chair. "The only thing that I don't know, is where, in the goddamn universe you created, with bank deposit boxes in every major city, with more houses than an abacus can count, with storage units and safety deposit boxes that number in the thousands, what I don't know, is where you may have hidden the backup for the LID. Jennifer," he said to her, but his eyes were focused on Richard, "have you decided which finger?"

"Please, Richard," she screamed, as he pushed the sharp point of the knife into her index finger. Minimal blood, maximum pain. It would get worse, much worse. Slicing the skin was easy. Goose-bump thrills ran down his spine as he scraped the tip of his knife through flesh and weaved it into her knuckle. He smelled the flood of urine that escaped from her body as she howled with pain. "Richard! Tell him what he wants," she panted, screaming in pain as he pivoted the blade down and pressed hard, into the knuckle. "Tell him what he wants."

"There's backup that includes the code that you don't have," Barrows yelled over Jennifer's screams.

"Yes?" The metal had cut through the edge of delicate bone, but he hadn't started sawing at it. He leaned on the knife, the metal grinding deeper, as she shook her head and screamed as loudly as she could. His eyes locked on Barrows' eyes. "Well," he said, having to yell so that Barrows could hear him over Jennifer's howls of pain, "where's the backup?"

Chapter Fourteen

11:45 p.m., Monday

They'd left their intermediate stop, a private airport, ten minutes earlier, and on the dark hilly roads they now travelled she was losing her sense of direction. The 5:45 a.m. message from her father would be critical. Getting to the message depended upon Skye finding her way back to the interstate. If there were road signs, though, she didn't see them. Plenty of trees stood tall at the edge of the road—mostly skinny pine trees, with other foliage in the mix. There was another left turn, and a right. With no streetlights, the night was inky dark. Two Black Raven vehicles led the way. The state troopers had departed once they pulled into the hangar. Two other Black Raven vehicles were in back.

Once inside the hangar, Sebastian had stepped out of the Range Rover, stretched, and gestured to her to climb into the back seat with Spring and Candy. He got into the front passenger seat, and an agent, who called him sir and so far had not uttered another word, had slipped into the driver's seat. Sebastian hadn't stopped working for one minute. He was either listening intently or talking to Ragno. He'd had a few conversations with someone named Zeus. If his arm hurt, he didn't show it. She doubted he'd show if he was tired, hungry, bleeding to death, or horny. The man was a robot.

Focusing on the sequence of turns that they'd made since exiting the interstate —two right, one left, another right, one left, one right, another left— helped Skye block out the bare-chested man. Hell on earth was what he was, because his good looks were an irresistible lure, from his penetrating, blue eyes, to his golden-brown, wavy hair. His broad, muscular shoulders, and taut abdomen that was ripped with muscles would make a sculptor itch for a mallet, chisel, and a fresh block of stone. All of that exposed skin and muscles, just inches from her, made her acutely aware of how long she'd gone without sex.

In her partying days in the fast lane, she'd had plenty of it.

She'd had so much of it that she'd started taking it for granted. For years, Dr. Morris, one in a long line of therapists that her father insisted she see, had insisted that her sexual escapades were self-destructive. Dr. Morris had theorized that she was stuck in a pattern of being attracted to unavailable men, as a way of protecting herself from serious emotional attachments. Her grief over her mother's death was the root of her problems.

It was an interesting theory, but it didn't make her stop doing anything she usually did. She continued partying, until three things happened in the space of three months: she'd become aware of her father's legal problems, the tabloid press had published a bare-breasted photo of her readying herself for a dive off a yacht while she was on a date with a famous, and very married, movie producer, and she'd gotten into the car accident in the Keys. The three occurrences rattled her so much she decided to slow down, which meant giving up the pursuit of men and sex. She had a lot to think about, and men complicated life. So she gave them up. Abstinence had been easy.

For a while.

As of this morning, easy was officially over. Easy had ended when Sebastian had walked across the street with Candy in his arms. Even though she didn't like one thing that had happened since he showed up, he had awakened a deep-rooted awareness of her need for good sex.

Focus on turns. Not on the fact that any soap he had used in his last shower had worn off and now, the fresh, powerful woodsy fragrance that his body emitted—reminding her of a long ago hike through a redwood forest—was pure him. If she'd had any doubt in her life about the powerful pull of pheromones, sitting in the SUV with him dispelled it. Without even glancing at her or touching her, his presence was inspiring a steady pulse of desire, between her legs and deep within.

Two right, one left, another right, one left, one right —

He glanced back at her, frowned, and continued his telephone conversation.

"What?" he asked, talking not to her, but on his communication system.

He shifted in the seat, as though his tall, long-limbed body craved movement, and there just wasn't enough room for him in the SUV.

Dear God, would he just stop moving and shut up?

"Is he crazy?" Sebastian asked. "See if you can get Minero on the line. I'll tell him exactly what I think of that idea."

She needed to forget that he existed, because now she wasn't certain if a left followed the last right that they'd taken, and she usually didn't forgot things like that. Sequences were like codes, and she remembered most codes she had ever created or learned. But if he wasn't talking, he was listening, and even when listening, a soft-spoken comment to Ragno was only going to be a few breaths away, and she found herself waiting for his next comments, caring about hearing the rich timbre of his low voice as much as what he was saying. Except when he was talking to Skye, he defaulted to a low, steady voice. When he talked to Skye, tightly-controlled irritation seemed to be his default, as though he knew she was concealing something from him.

She didn't blame him for being irritated with her.

After all, he was dead right.

Spring had finally nodded off, her head resting on Skye's shoulder. Candy was snoozing, her head in her sister's lap, the chewed-to-death, soggy rawhide half in her mouth, like a loose cigar, as she slept.

Two right, one left, another right, one left, one right, one left.

Maybe.

"Well, when you do get Minero on the line, tell him no. He's not interviewing Skye tonight. She's had enough for one day. And he's never interviewing Spring. Dispel that notion now. You can give him reasons why, but he should have the medical reports that we provided on the sisters, shouldn't he? You provided that this morning, before the attempted kidnapping, right?"

As Sebastian paused, Skye asked, "What medical reports?"

He shot her a glance. "Anything my people managed to get."

His eyes back on the road, he asked, "Did Minero even read the material that we sent? No. Don't bother answering. Tell him he's not interviewing Spring. Not on my watch. She's off limits. There's no option on that."

Profound gratitude flowed through Skye at the dead-on protectiveness she heard in his voice, but the gratitude was mixed with hopeless exasperation. He was a hard man to dislike, yet he represented an insurmountable stumbling block in the most important task she had ever tried to accomplish. "Do you know everything about us?"

"Only what others know," he said, serious eyes on her, "and reduced to writing that is stored in databases." He refocused his eyes forward, his attention refocused on the phone caller. "Schedule the interview between Skye and Minero for 8 a.m. We set it up. Secure lines. You know the drill. Schedule a chopper lift for me after the interview, which shouldn't take long. Skye and Spring will stay at Last Resort two nights, then we move them to an isolated safe house, one not associated with any Black Raven assets. I'll head to headquarters in the morning, after the interview, and run things from there."

The convoy finally turned off the two-lane highway onto a one-lane, black top road. About one hundred yards into the woods, they stopped at a tall brick wall that faded away in the darkness. An iron gate with pointy metal spears opened as the first SUV approached it.

Jesus Christ.

They were entering a guarded fortress. She'd be trapped on the inside as much as others were unable to enter.

Cataclysm. Run. Now.

When she finally caught up to her father—and there had to be a time when she would, because if she imagined otherwise she'd break down, and if she broke down Spring would freak out—she was going to give him one hell of a mouthful for coming up with this impossible task.

Act first, worry later? Get to the lake house as fast as you can? Take care of your sister. Keep her safe. Take charge if the worse happens, if cataclysm happens. You can do this, Skye. Figure it out.

All wonderful ideas for an idealist, one who'd never actually been in the cross hairs of an assault weapon, one who never had to get around a man as tenacious as Sebastian Connelly.

At a guard station, two men and one woman wearing Black Raven logo jackets stood ramrod straight, arms at their sides, with serious expressions on their faces as Sebastian drove past. They wore assault rifles on their chests and pistols strapped to their thighs.

"We've made it. You can breathe easier. Nothing will happen to you here."

Breathe easier? Right. She was suffocating, because she was trapped. Once through the guard station, Skye only saw dark woods. She lowered her window a few more inches. The extra-fresh air, though cool and crisp and scented with the sweet essence of pine, helped her fight the encroaching panic-driven anxiety attack. "Where's here?"

"Last Resort. A training facility."

A big training facility. After a mile of a drive on a wooded street, two of the guide SUVs turned left. The other two turned right with them. They reached a clearing with a large two-story house that looked like a country French chateaux, with symmetrical, arched windows, a double front door, and tall potted plants. All three SUVs stopped in the bricked courtyard that was flooded with light, where there were four other SUVs.

A dozen men and women were outside, standing at attention. Pistols were strapped to their thighs. They wore cargo pants, and light windbreakers. All eyes were on Sebastian, yet he was oblivious to the attention. The driver put the car in park. As one agent opened the door for him, Sebastian glanced into the backseat and said, "This will be home for you and Spring tonight and tomorrow. After that, we'll move you. We'll keep moving you, until we figure out where your father is, and who is after you." He paused. "Until your father is back in prison, and you and Spring are safe."

"Wait just a second," she thought, feeling a glimmer of hope. "You've brought us to a safe house run by trainees?"

He glanced at the line of men and women. "Those are instructors. If it makes you feel better, we train both new and existing agents here. New ones only get here if they're coming in skilled."

"How skilled?" Hope came with the thought that maybe, just maybe, 'skilled' for Black Raven recruits meant training as security guards at Wal-Mart.

"Training with Special Forces. Seals. Marines."

Hope faded. "Why is it called Last Resort?"

"Due to the difficulty of the projects for which they're receiving training. A lot of our clients have run-of-the-mill security problems, but some come to Black Raven with lives that are royally fucked-up. That percentage requires top talent and creativity. We're their Last Resort." He gave her a serious look as he stepped out of the SUV. "When we came up with a name, Last Resort sounded one hell of a lot better than Lost Causes."

The house only looked like a gracious country-French chateaux on the outside. In reality, it was a well-guarded fortress.

The first floor wasn't a house at all. It was a workspace, with concrete floors, stainless steel desks, and sleek metal light fixtures. Along three sides of the first floor, there were offices with glass walls, so operations on the wide-open center floor were visible. The center of the first floor had computer equipment, monitors, and a dozen or so work stations. The instructors who had stood guard as they pulled into the driveway entered the building, presumably resuming their work positions. After being in darkness for hours, the bright light of the workspace was blinding.

The second floor, which they accessed by climbing sleek, stainless steel stairs and entering thick doors, was different. High ceilings, creamy-white walls, and coffee-colored wood floors filled a living room with soothing light and natural-colored linen furniture. Sebastian directed them down a hallway on the right, where there were two bedrooms and an adjoining bathroom. He nodded to a female agent, who entered the living quarters with them. She had blonde short hair and big, almond-shaped brown eyes. He introduced her as Dr. Claudia Schilling and left the doctor with them before disappearing down a hallway on the left.

That was an hour ago. She hadn't seen him since, and the doctor had examined Spring, then introduced them to Agent Reiss, the agent in charge of the house and their needs—from cooking for them to walking Candy. Agent Reiss had a Superman tattoo on one substantial bicep, a Black Raven tattoo on the other, an easy smile, big green eyes, and short-cropped, auburn hair. Freckles made him seem young, and the Superman tattoo made him just plain adorable. When Reiss returned from walking Candy, the doctor left them.

By 2:00 a.m., they'd had showers, and Spring had eaten a turkey sandwich. Skye had tried to eat, but couldn't. Despite not having had a bite of food all day, her stomach was a tight ball of nerves and disappointment at failing to fulfill her father's simple instructions.

She'd blown the deadline.

She couldn't get to Tennessee by 5:45 in the morning, but she had to get there as fast as she could. *Had. To.*

Candy had downed a bowl of kibbles like it was her last supper, and Reiss had walked her again. He had pointed to a phone on the bedside table and told her to call, if Candy needed a walk during the night. The phone was an inside line to central operations, downstairs.

As soon as she was sure that Spring was asleep, with her earphones on and the audio dictionary on Q, Skye sat on the edge of Spring's bed, and set the alarm on her watch for 4 a.m., because Dr. Cavanaugh had said to wake Spring every two hours. Claudia had also pointed to the phone, and told Skye that if anything seemed off, at any time, to pick up the phone and request her.

She glanced at the other queen-size bed that was in the room, and, although the crisp white linens looked inviting, getting in the bed would be pointless. She needed fresh air so she could calm herself and try to think of what she should do next. She needed help, and there was only one person she trusted enough to ask for assistance. Problem was, she had no phone and she didn't know if a phone would help her, because Jen was now on Sebastian's suspect list and, according to Sebastian, missing.

Her heart pounded as she realized she had no hope. No one to call. No hope for help. Like Sebastian had snapped earlier, when they'd been in the driveway and she had wanted medical help for Daniel and Sarah, there was no help. He was all the help that was coming. Dear God. If he was it, there was really no way out.

Fresh air.

She needed, at the very least, fresh air, because she couldn't breathe.

She tried a window in Spring's bedroom. It didn't open, even with the locks unlocked. She went into the adjoining bathroom, where there were no windows. Candy followed her, as though sensing her tension and trying to soothe it. The adjoining bedroom had two windows. They didn't open either.

She went down the hallway to the living room. While agents had accompanied them into the second floor living space, it was now empty and quiet. Light linen drapes covered large plate-glass windows. The windows didn't open, and as she stared out one of them, she paused. The other windows had looked out on darkness, and so did these. The bright, soft lights of the living room were reflected too cleanly.

As she got closer, she realized the windows were fake. She'd been thrown off because it was dark outside, but closer inspection told her that the windows didn't look out on anything but a wall. Outside air was only a remote hope.

No.

Please. Not one more thing could go wrong today. All she wanted was an open window and a breath of fresh, sweet air.

The kitchen was on one side of the living room and, when facing the kitchen, to the left of it, there was a dining area with a sisal area rug and a long, rectangular dining table. The table was rustic, made of wide, distressed planks of wood, with the side closest to the kitchen having a backless bench instead of chairs. Behind the table, there was a row of six tall, narrow windows that were covered in white linen shades. She ran there, yanked on a cord to lift one of the shades, and tried to push up the window as she realized she was staring at a reflection not only of herself, but also of Sebastian. He had suddenly appeared and was standing just a foot or so behind her.

She spun around. Barefoot, he wore jeans and an untucked white t-shirt with a Black Raven logo on the left side of his chest. "None of the windows will open," he said, "Actually, they're not even windows. They're just there to make the place seem like a house."

His hair was damp and there was a fresh bandage on his arm. Clean skin glistened, but he hadn't been able to wash away the bruise on his jaw or the serious look in his eyes that revealed just how crappy the day had been for him, too. Even the soapy-fresh scent that emanated from him was cloying. Overpowering. She preferred his natural woodsy smell, but now, even that would be too much. Anything but fresh, outside air was going to be too much.

"I need fresh air."

"There's plenty of it in here," his eyes searched hers, "The filtration system is sophisticated. Where's Spring?"

"Sleeping."

"Good. Doctor Schilling said everything seems to be okay with her. You agree?"

Skye glanced at her watch. "Yes. I'll wake her at four to check." He was only an arms length from her, studying her. His eyes were probing and serious and concerned, as though he knew that she was at the end of her freaking rope. The very end. He was right.

"By morning the agents will have gathered everything that was on the grocery list that you gave me for the marshals' safe house. It should all be here by the time Spring awakens," he said. "I'm also going to be leaving, right after your interview with the marshals. I assume you won't give the marshals any more than you've given me?"

She didn't bother answering. She had more immediate things to worry about than an eight a.m. conference call. *Like trying to breathe and squelching the panic attack that is bubbling up from my toes.*

"After I leave, Dr. Schilling and Agent Reiss will be your main contacts, while you and Spring are here, but any of the agents can help you with anything. If you change your mind about talking-"

She stared at him as his words trailed off. *Leave,* she thought. *Please leave now.* She needed to concentrate on breathing and not panicking, and with him standing there she was having a hard time focusing on either objective. He gave her a few seconds of arched-eyebrow silence.

"That's what I figured," he frowned. "You know, anything would be helpful at this point. We've got information overload, and none of it is adding up to helpful knowledge. It's just me and you now."

"Meaning?"

"I'm not mic'd. Ragno's sleeping for an hour or so. It occurred to me that part of the problem with you talking might have been the broadcast system I was using. Do you want to talk, my ears only?"

No. Stunning as it was to look at, she wasn't falling for his blue-eyed brand of sincerity. If cataclysm was in play, it meant that she had to go straight to the top, and last she checked, the person at the top of the hierarchy was not a private security contractor named Sebastian Connelly.

"Well, if you change your mind after I leave in the morning, any of my agents can find me in just a few minutes, if there's anything you want to tell me. You'll be safe with us, until we can figure this out. Is there anything else you might need? Anything that wasn't on that list?"

"Outside air. I need," she paused, giving into weakness, and worse, letting him see her beg. "I need to know that I can get out. I feel trapped."

He touched her shoulder. His light touch carried reassurance and strength. She could have fallen into his arms, because she felt like she was spinning out of control, and he was nothing if not a solid pillar of strength. But while his touch was giving, his eyes were hard. Security and reassurance were just his job, and he was doing his job well. Instead of getting closer to him, she reached down to pat the scruff of Candy's neck, trying to find comfort there.

"You're not trapped," he said, as his hand fell away from her shoulder. "You're in a safe house, and when I say safe house, I mean it. You're here for protection, and we take that seriously. The house isn't only bullet-proof, it's air-sealed. Chemical agents in the ventilation system? Infiltration from the air? Helicopter invasion? We have weapons on site that will blow airborne invaders out of the sky. Fire flush out?" He shook his head. "Not going to happen. Run through a list of possible ways those sadistic fuckers could get to you, and make you step one foot out of here, and you'll find that we've covered every contingency. After all that happened to you today," he paused, "yesterday now, I'd think you'd be thrilled to be here. You've got to be exhausted. I'm surprised you're not already asleep."

She crossed the kitchen, went to the water bowl that had been set out for Candy, lifted it, and turned to the sink to fill it with water. Once it was full, she knelt on the ground with it, carefully setting it on the flagstone floor of the kitchen. She didn't really care whether the water spilled, but she cared whether he was going to see that tears were filling her eyes. She turned from his matter-of-fact reality and closer to Candy and the soft, warm, canine comfort that she offered through the soulful brown eyes that were focused on her, as though the dog sensed her distress.

"But you don't understand," she managed to say without her voice breaking, "I'm claustrophobic. If I don't have fresh air-"

"I do understand," he interrupted. "I know that about you and I've watched you all day. You haven't once gotten in a car without lowering a window. You crave fresh air. Claustrophobia sucks, and, your actions, and the medical records that we've accessed, tell me that you've got a dose of it," he shook his head. "You were trapped in the car after your accident in the Keys, and it took them hours to cut you out of it. So you probably have a bit of post-traumatic stress on top of it. I'm sorry, Skye, but there are no windows here to open. You're in a safe place. Spring's here, and she's safe."

"I have to go for a walk," she said, still on her knees, holding her breath, and trying like hell not to allow tears to spill. Anger seeped into her misery at his reminder that they had hacked into her medical records. Candy whimpered and gave a soft lick on her cheek, trying to make her feel better.

The canine empathy was Skye's undoing. She sat down hard on the flagstone floor, not caring that he was watching. She'd been brave all day, but that was due, primarily, to wanting to keep Spring calm. Now, all the feelings she had repressed sizzled through her, reducing her to a heap of anger and fatigue and misery.

"Please. I just need to," she pulled Candy close, and buried her head deep into Candy's fur, barely managing to keep tears at bay. "I just need to go outside." She never cried and she certainly didn't want to do it in front of him. "I need to be outdoors."

Sebastian was silent. She wished like hell he had walked away and she simply hadn't heard his footsteps because he was barefoot. She looked up. No. Not one tiny bit of luck was headed her way. He stood just a few inches from her, towering over her, and there wasn't any sympathy in his frown and hard gaze.

"I wish I had something better to tell you, but from my perspective, you just lived through the beginning, cause we have no idea where your father might be, or who these men are. You thought today sucked? You think this place is a nightmare, because it doesn't have windows you can open?"

He shook his head. "Sweetheart, your nightmare has just started. Unless you can help me figure a way out of this mess, unless you start telling me everything you know about your father and his business, unless you tell me where you're so hell-bent on running to, and why, this isn't ending. Help your father and yourself by talking to me, because otherwise, welcome to lather, rinse, repeat, and get ready for the same fucked-up shit tomorrow."

With his harsh words, anger won over pathetic tears. Driven by fury-filled adrenaline, she shot off the floor with her hands clenched into fists. Without hesitation she started punching his chest. "How." Left jab. "Dare." Right jab. "You!"

Each punch into his hard ribcage only brought the desire for another hit. He didn't try to stop her. She didn't care about anything, except right, left, right. She tried to imagine her fists going through his dense chest. He didn't flinch, nor did he try to keep her from pummeling him. With his jaw clenched, concerned eyes looked at her. Skye kept going until her knuckles hurt, until her arms were tired, until she wasn't an arm's length from him but much, much closer. Her hits became less of a flat-knuckled punch and more of a hammer-fisted, soft futile blow.

She didn't stop, until his arms were around her and he had pulled her so close there was barely room for her to move. His arms around her brought warm, reassuring comfort. Deep, deep gulps of air were only the prelude to harsh sobs, as she finally broke down and cried, without reservation, into the comforting cocoon between his arms and his chest. "I," she gasped for air and sobbed harder, "never," she managed to say, "cry. N-never."

"I know that about you, too. It's okay," he said. "You're okay."

She slipped one arm over his shoulder and the right one around his waist. She held onto him for dear life, as she pressed her face against his chest and cried. Time stopped. Or maybe it raced. She didn't really know or care.

"Let it go. You're okay," he mumbled, his lips touching the crown of her head.

After long, long minutes of uncontrollable sobs, her tears slowed to shaky breaths and annoying sniffs. She could inhale again, because in his arms, being stuck inside a fake house with no windows felt tolerable. With his strong arms holding her close, the weight of her father's world seemed bearable.

As her misery dissipated, her body came up with a spark of an idea that had nothing to do with going outside and getting a breath of fresh air. Evidently, his body was thinking along the same lines, because there was now something between them that unmistakably spelled desire. She had no intention of letting Sebastian release her, and by the size of his erection, obvious through his jeans as it pressed into her belly, she'd bet that he didn't want to let her go either.

"Better?" he asked, breath almost as ragged as her own as she turned her face up and gazed into his serious eyes. His cheeks were flushed, his lips drawn together. The only motion was their breathing.

She nodded. "Don't let me go."

He didn't let her go, but his arms loosened. He shook his head. "Bad idea. Really bad."

"I bet you've had worse," she said. "Please hold me." She hated to beg, but she'd been begging him all day to let her leave. What she was begging for now seemed minor in comparison, and the fact that she was pleading for it from him showed her just how upside down her world had become.

"Problem is, I don't just want to hold you."

She pressed her hips closer to his, almost panting as she felt the rock-solid shape of his penis against the soft flesh of her belly. He tightened his arms on her and drew a deep breath. "Not a newsflash. And if you think I'm only asking you to hold me," she whispered, "I need to do a better job of communicating."

"I never do this on the job." But he gripped her hips with his big hands and pulled her closer. "Never." He bent to kiss her neck and moaned as his lips found soft skin. "Ever. Not once."

"Once with me won't count," she said, shivering as he pressed a trail of moist, warm kisses along her jawbone.

He lifted his face, and arched an eyebrow, as serious eyes held hers. "That's a refreshing view. You sure?"

"More than sure. Frankly," she said, "sex doesn't count for anything." *Because men leave. It's what they do. If not physically, emotionally.* Her fear of getting close to anyone wasn't just focused on men. No one could be counted on to stay. And if they didn't leave on their own accord, she'd be happy to lead them to the door. If she had no expectations, she couldn't be hurt. Sebastian didn't need to hear her explanation. He just needed to know her goal. "Just release. And God, I want that now. We can act like it never happened."

"Even more refreshing," he whispered into her ear. "Where the hell have you been all of my life?"

Taking her hand, he pulled her out of the kitchen, down the hallway, and into the room he was using. Soft white linens and oversized furniture in neutral tones filled the room. Two bedside lamps were the only light. He lifted her, carried her to the king-size bed, and laid her on her back. Before she was situated, he unpeeled her leggings from her hips and yanked them past her knees, her ankles, and off. He tugged her turtleneck up and over her head, and unhooked her bra. Moving fast, too fast, without even pausing to look at her, he unbuttoned his jeans and pushed them to mid thigh. His urgent moves took only seconds, all designed for releasing his huge penis and getting it where he wanted it to be.

She'd barely decided to go forward, and he was ready to fuck her. There wasn't another word for this. Surely he wasn't just going to do it like this. But he was, as he parted her legs with his knees, without a kiss, or any kind of foreplay, he gripped her hips, tilted them up to meet him, and stroked his way deep into her.

He groaned with pleasure as she gasped. He had moved too fast, and he was a large man in every way. It had been two years since she had sex, but the discomfort wasn't due to lack of exercising all the parts that needed to make good sex happen. It didn't matter how long it had been. She'd had enough sex to know this wasn't good sex. Actually, it was bad sex.

The. Worst. Sex. Ever.

No one ever manhandled her like this. At least not without warning and a grant of permission, and they usually made sure there was lubrication. She mumbled, "Don't you know what foreplay's for?"

He was so tall, that to look into her eyes, he had to angle his head down. He chuckled, but she didn't see the humor. Great. The worst day of her life just took another crappy turn for the bad. She drew a deep breath. Foolish, but because he was so good-looking, she had assumed he'd be good in bed. Totally foolish, and there wasn't anything to be done about it, because she had asked for it. She'd forgotten to specify that she wanted good sex.

She shifted her hips at the same time she pushed against his chest. "I've changed m-"

'My mind' faded into the world of unsaid words, as her hip shift caused sparks of desire to race up her spine. While her mind was offended that he seemed to be the type of guy who only cared about his own pleasure in bed, her body suddenly demanded that she wait it out.

Given the urgency with which he had moved, she figured she'd only have to endure a few more seconds of him. But he didn't move. He didn't thrust, didn't do anything, except look into her eyes. He lifted his chest off of her, let his gaze travel down her body to where they were joined. Holding himself slightly above her as he filled her, he touched every part of her body with nothing but his eyes. Her discomfort eased, and once that happened, once her inner walls relaxed, she realized that his erection was getting bigger, pulsing as he lengthened inside of her. The sensation stole her breath. He shifted his weight so that his chest rested on one side of her, his abdomen lay across hers, and his legs were between hers. He pressed gentle kisses along her cheekbones and her jawbone.

When she turned her face to meet his lips, he looked into her eyes. For a moment, he was absolutely still.

He glanced at her mouth, but he didn't touch her lips with his.

His eyes bounced back to hers. Something flashed there as he held her gaze. Maybe it was pain. A distant memory. Whatever the thought was, it was real, and it wasn't good.

She lifted her face closer to his, touching her lips to his, craving a kiss and ready to take it even if he wasn't ready to give it.

She only managed to graze his lips, because as their mouths touched, he shifted his head, bending to kiss her neck instead.

Flat-out rejection.

For a second, even with him pulsing inside of her, she felt vulnerable and more miserably alone than she'd ever been in her life. This—whatever they were doing, whether it was sex or just plain fucking—wasn't about tenderness or any kind of intimacy. For this man, intercourse was less intimate than a mouth kiss. For this man, sex really didn't count for anything.

Understood. Shake it off, she told herself, as she pushed her weak side away.

Enjoy the moment, she told herself, and maybe she'd get some release. It was the only thing she had requested of him, the only thing she should expect. Focusing on the feel of his gentle kisses on the soft skin right below her ear and jaw, she lifted her hips, adjusting to him. So. Much. Better. As he traced lazy circles around her nipples with his fingertip, she shivered with anticipation of movement. When he bent his head to her breast, lightning fast tingles ran through her. Shock at his fast, hard entry became a distant memory. She knew that he could feel the tension slipping away, because he lifted his head, and gave her a slow, sultry, proud-of-himself smile.

"Feels okay?"

"Can't you tell?" she asked, her voice deepening with desire, as her pelvic muscles flexed around him.

He didn't move his hips. He bent his head, opened his mouth on her left nipple, and swirled his tongue around it, tracing moist circles until her flesh hardened. She gripped his head, holding him to her breast. As she moaned, he nibbled at her peak, biting her almost to the point of pain, but somehow making the hard edges of his teeth bring so much pleasure she could only gasp. He sucked where he'd bitten, tonguing away the small discomfort.

She gripped his t-shirt and pulled it up. He helped get it over the bandage on his arm. His smooth chest, with just a bit of tight, curly hair, rippled with muscles that ran across his ribcage, his abdomen was flat and hard, and just on the inside of both of his hips the muscles formed a v, pointing downward to his groin. She traced the muscles with her fingers down, to where he entered her, and spread her legs more, welcoming him.

Her channel was now moist and slick, her breasts were tender and sending sparks through her body, and, as she lowered her hands to run them along the curve of his tight butt, he gave her a sultry-eyed smile. She wanted to move her hips. No. She needed to move her hips, because the need for release was building. His hips had pinned hers so that she couldn't move, and he wasn't moving. "Please," she said. "Thrust. Or something. Now."

He gave her a lazy, teasing headshake before bending his head and resuming his exploration, with his tongue and his lips, of the curves of each breast and the points of each hard, raised nipple. While his fast entry had taken her by surprise, now his languid pace was killing her. She reached around to the base of his penis and stroked him there, trying to induce him to get moving. When that didn't work, she touched herself, applying pressure to her clitoris, helping the process along. The men she'd been with before certainly didn't need a guide map to that anatomical wonder.

Instead of following her lead, he pulled her hand away from between her legs, then imprisoned her hands in one of his big ones, pinning them over her head.

She drew a deep breath and waited for him to rub her where her own finger had been, hoping he'd gotten the hint.

He looked into her eyes, arched an eyebrow, and gave her a slight headshake. He'd gotten the hint. He just wasn't taking it.

"Touch me," she said, craving the instant orgasm that would come with one fingertip in just the right place. Hell, if he couldn't figure it out, she'd show him.

He shook his head, giving her a slow smile as he pressed his hips against hers, capturing her hips in absolute stillness. Like he had all the time in the world and planned on taking it. She wondered whether he had come and she just didn't know it. He couldn't have this much willpower. That thought faded as he finally started rocking his hips against hers, grinding deeper and deeper into her without pulling out.

"Please. Touch me."

"Right now, I'd consider that cheating. Besides, I am touching you." He stopped grinding. Long, hard thrusts were followed by gentle, deep pulses. He watched her reaction, looking for what felt good, as waves of pressure built from deep within her and her legs fell even further apart. He gripped her hands tighter, as though reading her mind, knowing she was dying to use her hands on him, on her, on any part of their joined anatomy. He took his sweet time, moving slowly in and out of her, and, with each hard, deep thrust, he ground his pelvis into her, giving her the touch that she had begged for. She clenched her jaw, trying not to scream with pleasure. Soft whimpers and moans escaped. She thrashed her head from side to side and he kept thrusting, watching her, studying her expression as her climax came, and kept coming, and it finally stole her breath with a scream of relief as it went.

When she was through, and gasping for air, he pulled out, all the way. He used his fingers to part her folds, guided his fully erect penis there, pressing it hard against her clitoris. "Is this what you wanted me to touch?"

She couldn't answer, because she had stopped breathing. He didn't need words. Her body talked for her, her hips arching into him as he slid his shaft along the soft groove. She looked down, mesmerized, as he created a channel for himself through her soft folds. His penis was slick and wet with her moisture, and the slide of his hard shaft made a different kind of spark explode. She lifted her hips, longing to run her fingers over the smooth, silken head. Touching, though, wasn't something he planned to allow, because he kept her hands imprisoned. Her need for release built again. She pushed her hips up, losing control and grinding herself into him. He kept sliding through her valley of moist, sensitive flesh until she whimpered, "Yes. Yes. Yes," over and over and over. Finally, her words faded and she could only whisper, "Coming. I'm coming."

"I know," he said, as he let go of her hands. He knelt, lifting her legs so that her calves rested on his shoulders and her ankles were crossed behind his neck. Intense eyes watched her reaction as he pulled her hips closer. She felt two of his fingers penetrating her and massaging inside of her. Electric shocks exploded when he scraped about three inches in, using the tips of his fingers to massage where he had scraped, pressing hard.

"Oh, God," she moaned. He'd found her G-spot, which wasn't

something most men took the time to search for. Thank God Spring had fallen asleep with her headphones on, because now even her whimpers were loud. Once he found it, and once her moans reached a new high, he stopped before she climaxed. It didn't matter. She doubted she had the energy to come again.

He slipped his fingers out of her, and traced lazy, glistening circles around her nipples. "Ready?"

"For what?" As he dipped his head to her breasts to lick where his fingers had been, she realized how silly her question was as she glanced into his eyes. The raw hunger in his gaze told her he was just beginning. A sheen of sweat covered his chest, accentuating the power in his muscles. His chest and shoulder muscles rippled, as though poised and ready to pounce.

He gave her a half-smile as he knelt between her legs. "Release. That's what you wanted, right?"

She nodded.

"And to answer your earlier question. Yes. I know what foreplay's for."

She gave him a doubtful look.

Before she could say anything, he said, "Everything until now has been foreplay."

She could think of no retort, because the serious, focused look on his face stole her breath. He was breathing hard, readying himself, and he'd made sure that she was ready too, because two intense orgasms had left her pliable, dripping with moisture, and compliant as a rag doll, one that he could use at will. There had been a reason why he had searched for her G-spot, because she'd watched this man all day. Every action of his was deliberate. *Thank God.*

Without warning, and moving fast, he moved to the side, turned her face down on the mattress, lifting her hips high so that she was on her knees. Big hands, one gripping each hip, supported most of her weight. She only had time to plant the palms of her hands on the mattress before he entered her from behind, using one powerful stroke. Her body had no trouble accepting him this time. Buried deep, he didn't move. In a matter of minutes she'd gone from hating his style to loving it. Shockingly fast, then slow. She reverse-arched into him, relishing the complete fullness that came with having him buried inside of her.

"You okay?"

"God, yes."

He pulled slowly out, inch by delicious inch, before entering her again. He repeated the action, moving a tiny bit faster each time. Her weight was barely on her knees. She'd thought the position had been for his viewing pleasure, but the sparks that sizzled with each of his moves made her realize that at the angle he was holding her, as he guided her hips when he thrust, his penis scraped her G-spot with each thrust in, each pull out. After savoring and going slow, he changed speeds, suddenly pounding against her without pause. His breath became deeper and raspier. Deep, intense waves of pleasure rippled through her body, from her toes to her ears, and everywhere in between, and still he kept going, bucking into her at full strength. He had a powerhouse of a muscular body, and he was using all of his strength on her. She came, again, and again, each mini-orgasm fueled by the primal force with which he was using her, building her release to points where she'd never been before.

When she was seeing stars, he stopped. His grip on her hips tightened until his fingers were digging into her flesh. His clench-hold on her should have hurt, but it didn't. He held onto her hips as though he owned them, and ground her against him so that he was buried to the hilt, his groans becoming deeper, his breaths harsher, as his release built. She felt his spasms deep inside of her, felt a flood of warmth come from him, felt each pulse of his orgasm, and peaked again with him, her screams joining his harsh moans.

When they were through, when nothing but harsh intakes of breath were escaping from both of them, he bent over her back, gently scooped her into his arms and fell with her onto the bed, turning her so that she lay across his chest. Wrapped in his big arms, she was absorbing the warmth from his large body, without enough energy to move even a toe. Her cheek was pressed into his chest, which rose and fell with each of his ragged breaths. After a few seconds where she could do nothing but breathe, she glanced up at him, gave him a smile as his half-opened eyes locked on hers, and whispered, "Best. Sex. Ever."

A fatigued, but full, smile revealed dimples. His eyes started to close, as he mumbled. "Been waiting all day for that."

"What?" she whispered, not understanding through the fog in her brain and fatigue in her body.

"That smile," he said, as he dropped his head on the pillow and shut his eyes.

Chapter Fifteen

Strobe lights and beeps emanated from his watchband, which Sebastian had left on the bedside table. 7:15 a.m., wake up. Unless there was a crisis. Shaking off deep, dreamless sleep, the strobe's flash confirmed what he instantly knew. The bed beside him was empty. On her way out, Skye must have turned off the lamps. The room was pitch dark. He had no idea when she'd slipped from his arms and left the room. He'd fallen into a headache-med induced, fatigue-driven, post-coital hard sleep, as she had snuggled into his chest, given him her gorgeous smile, and whispered her approval. The intervals between the alarms would grow shorter, if he didn't respond to Ragno's good morning call, but for now he had a two-minute pause. He needed it.

He'd broken any number of rules by having sex with Skye— Black Raven rules as well as overarching, self-imposed ethical rules. Pushing Skye to the breaking point had been his intent, and that's why his comments in the kitchen had been unrelenting, but when she'd finally broken down, instead of trying to get information from her, he'd done something different.

Yet another fuck-up on his part.

As he inhaled a deep breath of exasperation, the aroma of almonds and vanilla distracted him. Someone was baking, but that wasn't unusual. When he was on Black Raven premises, agents cooked for him. What was unusual was that it smelled so good. He savored the aroma, shut his eyes, realized it was the same scent that had greeted him at Creative Confections, and groaned. He chose not to chastise himself—at least for a few minutes—for losing rational thought and acting on lust.

Best sex ever?

Glad she thought so. When he had time to think, without Ragno's alarm distracting him, maybe he'd remember another woman who he enjoyed being with as much. Right now, none in his memory bank compared. Demanding, yet complaint. Sarcastic, even in bed.

Don't you know what foreplay's for?

He chuckled. Off-the-charts responsive. Eyes-open as she watched him, beautiful when she came, arching into him even when he did her from behind. The memory of her body moving with him, her legs winding around him, the sound of her moans and her soft cries, faded when he remembered what she said while they were in the kitchen. He'd barely thought about it. Instead of listening to the words, he had focused only on two facts. One, she was offering sex. Two, he needed it.

Once with me won't count.

His good-morning-wanting-more erection had him wondering how many more times with Skye wouldn't count. Yet a part of his brain—the part that had somehow awakened after the hand-grenade slammed him into coma-land in July—made him wonder why. He'd never come face-to-face with a female version of himself, a female who thought of sex as nothing but release. Women either craved emotional attachment or they expected compensation. He'd learned that cash was easier to give, yet even frequent visits to the same high-priced woman could result in emotion-driven expectations on her part.

Why? Why was Skye as fucked up as he was in the intimacy department?

He sat up, suddenly remembering some of the things he'd learned about her in the last few days, things his brain had conveniently forgotten about when all of his blood had rushed to his dick. *Hell.* She was lying.

He'd acted on her vulnerabilities. He should have known better. He did know better. He was just an asshole.

Forget about it, he told himself, as Ragno's alarm sounded, lights flashed, and the pause between each annoying beep became shorter. Problem was, now that he had crossed the line of never mixing sex with work, he didn't want to stop. He was used to the feast or famine approach to sex, and right now his body was telling him it was ready for an all-he-could-eat feast. He could go weeks without it, get his fill in one well-planned weekend, and go about his business. Waking up with a hard-on just hours after sex, wanting more, and having no plan to get it was foreign to him.

Thank God he was leaving Last Resort after Minero's call. Soon, he'd be a few hundred miles from her and able to focus on more important things than satisfying his newly awakened, insatiable libido. He reached for the night table, grabbed the damn watchband as the strobes and beeps started again, and hooked on the earpiece.

"Morning."

"Good morning, though the grumpy sound of your voice pairs a question mark with that statement," Ragno said, her voice, as always, fresh and unflappable. "How's that headache?"

"Gone."

"Your arm?"

He'd forgotten about it. He sat up, flicked on the bedside lamp, and glanced at his bicep. The bandage was bloodstained. He'd put too much strain on his arms for the stitches. He shrugged. Definitely worth it. "I'll live. You know, Ragno, I'm not the only one with health concerns here. Weren't you supposed to have a doctor's appointment this week?"

"Yes. I cancelled it. Too busy."

"That's what you've said for the last few weeks."

"My problem isn't life threatening," she retorted. "Your head injury is."

"You haven't been outside in-"

"I have too."

"The rooftop terrace of our building doesn't count."

"Drop it. I'm fine. I can go anywhere I want to," Ragno said. "There just isn't a need for me to be anywhere but here."

Her tense tone told him to let it drop. He made a mental note to bring it up again with her in a few days. Hopefully then, the current crisis would be over and he'd be able to persuade her to seek help. "All right. I'm dropping it, but not forgetting it. You slept okay?"

"For a few hours," she responded, "like a baby."

"Pete?" He stood, walked to the bathroom, and turned on the water in the shower.

"Doing well. In ICU and stable."

"How is the interrogation going on the man I left alive at the safe house?"

"Brace yourself. You're not going to like the report."

He looked at himself in the mirror as he drew a deep breath, inhaling the steam from the shower, thinking that he needed to put on some muscle mass. "Tell me."

"Marshals got there at the same time as our interrogator.

They took custody. He's been in surgery for the last six hours. Doctors are busily repairing the kneecaps that you blew out," she said, "thanks to the never-ending dollars of American taxpayers. No telling when we'll be able to talk to him."

He groaned. "Next time I say we need to expand domestic operations, remind me of this." In the Middle East, Black Raven would have given the man just enough medical attention so that he'd be able to talk. They wouldn't have coddled him with a comfortable bed, corrective surgery, and good drugs. "With a little persuasion, he could have been a wealth of information."

"Aside from the Geneva Convention and its requirement that injured enemy combatants receive humane treatment, have you forgotten that you're operating on domestic soil? The techniques you've grown used to in other countries won't work here. You're in the land of the United States Constitution. On top of about a million other laws, the Eighth Amendment's prohibition against cruel and unusual punishment forbids the type of persuasion you're talking about. Here," her tone was low and sarcasm was high, "I believe they call what you're talking about torture."

"What would the average American call castrating a man while he's alive? Fuck it. Don't answer that. A few questions wouldn't have killed the man," he said, stifling his thoughts about fighting fire with fire. "What else do I need to know before I get in the shower?"

"Biggest news of the morning is that Minero's assistant is missing. She was last seen on her way to pick up lunch yesterday afternoon, after she did the organizational work on the safe house."

"Well, I'm guessing that's how they found the safe house." He stripped off the bandage. More than a few of the stitches were popped and where the thread had burst, the edges of his skin were separated. His Raven tattoo was marred through the midsection with a wound that was unevenly caked with dried blood. Fuck. He hated the symbolism. He knew the wound was supposed to be kept dry, but at this point, given the sorry state of the stitches, he didn't think a bit of water would hurt it. "Find Doctor Schilling. I need her to lay eyes on this cut after I get out of the shower."

"Will do," she said. "Interview with Skye is still on at eight. Exactly thirty-seven minutes from now."

"Make sure lines are secure. No video."

"Minero's insisting on it."

"Fuck him," Sebastian said. "It's too dangerous. Tell him video calls are easier to trace, a fact he should know. The profile you're doing on Minero. Is it turning up anything?"

"Nothing yet."

"Have you found Root?"

"No. She's now become a missing person, officially."

"Give me a few minutes," he said, placing the watch and ear bud on the granite counter. The devices were waterproof, but he typically spared Ragno the sounds of his morning rituals.

We can act like it never happened.

Skye's words, not his. Perfect, he thought, as he swished shampoo through his hair. But not. He'd taken advantage of her vulnerable situation, the breaking point to which he had pushed her.

He had to apologize. Before July, he might not have. Inexplicably, now he felt the need to do so, and he didn't know whether it was because of her or because after his near-death experience, he just felt different.

He'd apologize, and then he was going to act like it never happened.

Ten minutes later, he was pulling on Black Raven-issue cargo khakis that he'd found stocked in the bedroom closet, as Doctor Schilling knocked on his bedroom door. He turned, showing her the arm, even before she stepped across the threshold. "I made a mess of it."

Large brown eyes gave him an exasperated, questioning glance. She glanced past him and looked at the bed. The comforter was crumpled on the ground and the top sheet was twisted. Pillows, at odd angles, were not where one normally rested their head. She didn't ask how he managed to wreck her work.

Her job was to fix it.

"I'll call for the stitch kit. I brought bandages with me, but didn't think you'd manage to pop most of the stitches I put in as you slept. You're sitting still for the conference call at eight?"

He nodded.

"I'll redo the stitches then. Let's step into the bathroom and get it cleaned before I put on another bandage." As they stood at the sink, and she poured alcohol on the wound, she said, "Mr.

Connelly, may I speak about a medical issue unrelated to this wound?"

He knew from the deadly serious, concerned look in her eyes where this was going. Not wanting to hear it, but knowing that he needed to, he said, "Go ahead."

She drew a deep breath. "You really should submit to the care of your neurosurgeon. Today. If not today, tomorrow."

He fought the urge to groan. "Ragno's working in the background?"

Doctor Schilling nodded as she dried the wound and taped a gauze bandage over it. "And Zeus, and Brandon Morrissey. In this circumstance, they should. Your medical staff needs to be advised of your current status, just in case. The situation is urgent."

"Whoa," he said, pulling on a polo shirt from the extra-clothes closet. "No one has said that I'm in imminent danger of dropping dead."

"No, but that danger will become likely if you wait too long for the surgery. How long is too long? A week? Two weeks? A month? If you're expecting that kind of exactness from your physicians, your expectations are unreasonable," she shook her head, "and that shouldn't be your focus. To put it bluntly, your focus needs to be getting on the table, having the surgery, and getting back on your feet."

"Do you know the odds of me surviving the surgery?"

She held his gaze. "Well, it comes with more risk than an appendectomy-"

"Based on what the doctors have told me, I'm guesstimating fifty-fifty."

She frowned, but didn't say that he was wrong. "Your risk of surviving decreases with each day you wait."

Unlike the bloodstained clothes he'd worn the day before, the shoes that he'd had on, black-leather tie-ups with semi-hard soles, were fine. He found a pair of socks in the well-stocked closet. He wished that she'd disappear, but she didn't take the cue. He sat on the bed, slipping on the socks and said, as much as to himself as to her, "Dying doesn't bother me."

She held his gaze for a second, then gave a slight nod. "So why are you waiting?"

"What bothers me is leaving a mess for others to deal with," he said, tying the shoes, "and right now, Black Raven is in one hell of a mess."

"Black Raven is full of talent. We'll weather the storm fine." She drew a deep breath. "You may not weather this head injury fine, if you keep procrastinating. The headaches you're now experiencing will not go away without the surgery. The scar tissue needs to be removed."

He stood, found his belt in the pile of clothes that he'd left on the floor of the closet, and slipped it through the belt loops of the khakis. "I don't have a headache now."

"You took meds when you arrived. I watched you as I stitched. It was quite a cocktail. Those meds haven't worn off. Once they do, your head will be pounding again."

"Good to know," he said. "Now you can drop it."

She nodded. "Yes, sir." She gave him a slight smile. "I'm pulling for you, sir."

Nothing the doctor said before made him worry, because none of it was news. Her last statement, though, made his insides clench. Pulling for him? Like he was a goddamn underdog. He was fucked. Death? His own? Not a worry. Really. Considering how many times he'd faced death and escaped, he figured he was living on borrowed time and had been for years. Agent Lewis had been castrated while alive, and Sebastian had seen worse. Dying while under anesthesia sounded like a cakewalk in comparison.

Being an invalid? It was another risk of the surgery. Doctors called it neurological deficits. He could deal with minor issues. Larger issues? He had that base covered. He needed to make sure, once again, that Brandon and Zeus were on board. It was a lot to ask friends to assist in suicide, if he couldn't do it himself, but he damn well was going to make sure they weren't going to falter before he submitted to the surgery.

She continued, "Ragno's also told us to make sure you eat some protein." She gave him a full smile, finding humor in Ragno's mothering. "And Agent Reiss is waiting for you in the kitchen. Spring said she'd wait for you to have breakfast. Cable News is getting ready to feature a segment on the risks associated with giving private security contractors too much power. Plus, there's something unusual that I want you to see."

"What?"

"Spring. In the kitchen. It was difficult for Skye to awaken her at four." Now he knew the answer to when Skye had slipped out of the room. Sometime before four. Not much before. At least he didn't think so, but really, he'd lost track of the length of time they'd been at it. "Skye called me, concerned, thinking the difficulty in waking Spring could be related to the injuries she suffered in the kidnapping."

"Is she okay?"

Doctor Schilling nodded, "Yes. Actually, I'm more worried about Skye than Spring. Skye looks to me like she'd barely holding herself together. Spring's extraordinarily task-oriented, and as long as she has control of her tasks, I think she'll be fine. Once Spring shook off the drowsiness, she was wide awake and alert. She started having anxiety, which Skye informed me was normal. Before I administered any kind of med, Skye had her snapped out of it. Their supplies had arrived, and Skye guided her in that direction. Now Spring is calm. I've been monitoring her ever since, and she's fine. She's hyper-focusing on organizing colors. At first she couldn't handle an interruption, but now she's even talking to me as she does it."

Sebastian replaced his earpiece and strapped the watchband on as the doctor finished with the temporary bandage. He pressed the button for Ragno's connection, as he thought two things: Skye hadn't slept at all, and, although he didn't have time to wonder about medical curiosities such as hyper-focusing, he was relieved that Spring was okay.

As he entered the living area, his eyes slid over the large screen television. It was tuned to the weather report. Volume was muted. Agent Reiss stood at Black Raven-style attention, hands at his side, back erect, eyes on him. He released him with, "Good morning," but Sebastian's attention wasn't focused on Reiss.

Skye was pulling a pan of golden-brown cupcakes out of the oven. Her hair was pulled into a ponytail and loosely braided. She wore jeans that hugged her long legs, a deliciously snug pink cardigan, with white-pearl buttons, and socks. The pink sweater was a shade darker than pastel and almost the exact shade of her nipples. That thought confirmed for him how much of an asshole he was, because all he really wanted to do, at that moment, was unbutton her sweater and close his mouth on her breasts.

I am, admittedly, a total dick.

Dragging his eyes off of the swell of her breasts, he looked at her face. No make-up covered her natural beauty. She glanced at him and gave him the same calm and reserved look she'd given him the day before, when he had first met her. Underneath her cool reserve, there was a bit of stress in her eyes, but he had to look close for it. Her eyes shifted to the pan of muffins, her glance at him a mere passing thing, as though nothing had happened between them, as though her world hadn't fallen apart in the last twenty-four hours. As though there was no attraction between them, as though she wasn't exhausted and frightened.

Damn.

She was good.

Not good enough to fool him, though. He'd escorted enough people through war zones to spot the signs, when someone who was typically smart and brave was drawing upon immense strength and trying like hell not to show that they were afraid. Closer examination told him her eyes weren't quite as quick as they'd been the day before. When they returned to his, they held his gaze for a long second. Her eyes were shiny with fatigue and more than a little redness, as though she'd been rubbing them. She drew a deep breath, the same kind of breath she'd taken when she had figured out the windows wouldn't open. It was the sort of breath someone took when fighting through anxiety.

She said, "Good morning," as she turned to place the pan on a wire rack. Her hands were shaking. More than imperceptibly. She was just as close to her breaking point as she'd been the night before. Maybe closer.

Next to the wire rack, a prior batch of muffins stood in neat rows on the white-granite counter. She'd been up and at this for a while, being everything Spring needed her to be—brave, on-the-surface calm, and even baking muffins—when what she needed was a long night of sleep.

What Doctor Schilling had been focused on, and was once against focused on, was Spring, who wasn't paying attention to them. Spring stood at the long dining table with Candy lying on the rug, under the table. The dog's eyes were focused on him. Spring's headphones were on. Her back was to the room.

The two hundred three-inch, clear glass, stackable bowls that had been on Skye's list for the safe house were in neat rows on the right side of the table, spaced with precision in twenty rows of ten. The bowls weren't touching, but were separated all around by not more than a quarter of an inch. Bags of assorted jellybeans were on the far right, along with ten larger glass bowls. Tiny tubs of pigment sat next to the jellybean bags. Icing, in different shades of yellow, orange, and red, was in the larger bowls. Spring, dressed in black leggings and a light blue turtleneck, with her hair back in a loose braid that matched her sister's braid, was sorting the jellybeans by color into bowls. She focused on the icing, dropping tiny spoonfuls into bowls. Each time she added to the bowls, she used a colored pencil to write on the tablet that he'd pulled from her backpack the day before.

"Sir," Agent Reiss said, at the stove. "Eggs, ham, and toast?"

He looked at Reiss and shook his head. "Coffee first. Small splash of cream."

He was half listening to Ragno who was giving him a run-down of the negative news reports that Black Raven had received during the night and her expectations of what the news show was going to reveal. He couldn't tear his eyes off of Spring and her project. After Reiss handed him a mug of steaming coffee, he walked closer to the table.

"Not too close," Skye said. "She needs space." He stopped dead at mid step, even before she added, "Please."

Yesterday, he'd have stepped closer just to irritate Skye. Today, he listened. Potentially provoking Spring into an anxiety attack wasn't something he wanted to do again, and Skye didn't need more irritation.

At first, the array of colors seemed chaotic. But as he sipped his coffee and studied the table and its contents, he realized that the only color-chaos was in the bags of jellybeans that weren't yet sorted. The larger bowls contained icing in different shades of red, yellow, and orange, and only jellybeans in those shades had made it to the smaller bowls. In the grid of two hundred bowls, the spacing of bowls with jellybeans seemed random, and there was icing in some of the bowls in between.

Spring turned to him, slipped her earphones off, and gave him the same sweet smile she'd given him the day before. "Hey, Sebastian. I've got something for you," she said, pointing in the direction of the kitchen counter, where one lonely bowl, full of opaque white jellybeans, had been banished.

He chuckled.

"I sorted out the daydreams first. But remember, only three at a time. Or groups of three. Never more than three groups of three."

He glanced into her clear blue eyes and wondered how the hell such a simple gesture could make him feel so damn happy. "But I want the cinnamon ones."

"No," she said, her eyes twinkling. "Sorry. You can't have fire." She shook her head. "But why fire? Yesterday you said blossom was your favorite."

"Well," he chuckled, because he hadn't remembered which red flavor he had claimed as his favorite. He was dead certain, though, that he hadn't used the words blossom or fire to describe any of the jellybeans. "Well, can I have those?"

"No. I told you no rosy ones. Especially not blossom or fire. Blossom is the brightest. See?" She pointed to a small bowl on the table that contained the brightest red jellybeans. "I need them both for my color palette."

He nodded to the table. "What are you doing there?"

Before she could answer, Skye said, "Spring, don't you want to eat breakfast now?"

Spring's attention went from Sebastian, to Skye. A bit of her smile faltered as she stared into her sister's eyes. Without answering Skye, she glanced at Sebastian. "Are you eating now?"

"There's only one correct answer," Skye said, eyes on him, and now she wasn't trying to hide her exasperation.

He was unused to his dining habits meaning anything to anyone, but he remembered that Schilling had said Spring was waiting for him to eat. "Yes," he said to Spring, but holding Skye's gaze with his own, "I'm starving." He turned back to Spring, and said, "Let's eat together."

She clapped her hands. "Yay. I was waiting on you. I like my eggs scrambled, but not too hard. How do you like yours?"

"Exactly like that, and plenty of them," he said, nodding to Agent Reiss, who started cracking eggs into a bowl. Focusing on Spring, he said, "That's quite a project."

"Well, I'm going to do icing flowers on the cupcakes, you see?" She handed him the sketchpad, as she described the types of flowers she planned to put on the cupcakes.

As he listened to her, he glanced at the flower drawings and saw arrows from each petal to words. He spotted blossom, fire, sun, and other words that he supposed were descriptive of certain colors in Spring-speak, but in the real world they needed interpretation. Next to each word there were numbers. It was more fun to look at the light in her eyes than to try to make sense of the gibberish in the sketchpad, so he focused on her. "The numbers correlate to colors?"

She nodded. "But it's way more complicated than that. You see, the numbers correlate to letters in the words that describe the colors, and we have our own words for colors. So you need to know a lot of information before the numbers can mean anything to you. We worked on it for years-"

"Spring," Skye said, "Sebastian isn't interested in the details."

Spring's eyes widened as she glanced at her sister. She refocused her attention on him with a frown. "Are you just being nice?"

"No," he said, giving Skye a hard look for hurting her sister's feelings. Big sis was correct, but he didn't want to burst Spring's bubble. "I really am interested. You said we worked on it for years. Who? You and Skye?"

"Sometimes Skye. Mostly Dad though. And this is just one of the color palettes Dad and I developed. In this palette, the fireball palette, the icing matches the jellybeans, so the flowers will be super bright. I used ocean and forest for the first batch."

"What colors are those?"

Spring paused and gave him a questioning look. "Guess."

He paused. "Ocean's blue, forest is green?"

"See, I knew you were smart. The main branch of each color family is usually easy, but the shades get way trickier. Anyway, I didn't like the colors. So I had to start over. I thought I'd just use the different shades of red and pink-"

"So you do know that this," he picked up a red jellybean, "is actually red."

"Of course I do. I just call it something different. Anyway, I didn't like the shades of reds and pinks, so I saved all of the icing, and now I'm starting again with shades of cardinal, sun, and rosy."

He glanced at the table, looked at the shades of yellow, orange, and red, and said, "Wait. Which word describes yellow?"

"Cardinal."

"Cardinals aren't yellow."

She clapped her hand and laughed. "Of course they aren't. If secret codes were easy to figure out, it wouldn't be any fun, would it?" He finally understood why the holly cake was turquoise and orange. In Spring's world, with her color-code game, those oddball colors were simply an interpretation of the orange-red berries and deep green leaves. "Anyway," Spring continued, "the jellybeans are just markers for the palette. We take the color of the jellybeans, translate it to a word, and then translate the words to numbers. The numbers are the code, and we go back and forth with numbers and words. The jellybeans won't actually be on the cupcakes. The petals will be all different colors and tiny, so there will be lots of color on each cupcake, but not too much icing." She paused for deep breath. "The cupcakes are pineapple almond and they'll have butter cream icing. All full of almond and vanilla flavorings, and deep inside of each we insert one little squeeze of buttery, sugary, crushed pineapple."

"Spring, you need to clear at least part of the table so that we can eat," Skye said. "There's enough space on the counter for the bowls. Why don't we just remove the larger bowls from the table? That way we can sit at one end. I'll help you."

Skye approached the table, but before touching anything, she paused and glanced at Spring.

Damn, Sebastian thought. *Skye is asking for permission.* He caught Doctor Shilling's eyes. She met his for a brief moment, before refocusing her attention on Spring. The doctor was standing about five feet from the dining area, studying everything that was happening.

With both hands extended, Skye reached for two large bowls, hesitating slightly before touching it. When Spring met her eyes and gave her sister an almost imperceptible nod, Skye picked up the two bowls.

The subtleties were lost on Agent Reiss, who walked up to the table, and reached for two bowls before Skye, Sebastian, or Doctor Schilling could say anything. Sebastian moved fast, grabbing Reiss by the shoulder and pulling him back, but not before Candy stood and snarled at him, as Spring screamed, "NOOOOOOO. NoNoNo. Don't touch, don't touch. Don't touch. Don't touch. Don't touch."

Holy crap, Sebastian thought. "Reiss. Back further away."

"Spring," Skye said, grabbing her sister and holding her in a bear hug. "He's not going to touch."

Agent Reiss stepped into the adjoining living room. Sebastian joined him and Schilling there, giving Skye and Spring space. As Spring's 'no's' devolved into a long, loud, one-word string, he glanced at Doctor Schilling. "I saw this yesterday. Skye says this kind of anxiety attack is typical."

Agent Reiss looked like he wanted to run away. "I'm sorry. I was trying to help."

Doctor Shilling explained, "There's an order to everything she does. She's got her own protocol."

"You should have observed that. We don't just watch. We assess." Sebastian said, automatically slipping into instructor mode. "If you don't understand, ask questions."

"She looks so normal," Reiss said, "I forgot that she's," he paused, struggling for words, "different."

Sebastian's eyes met Skye's. She was across the large room, but the flash of pain he saw there indicated that she heard the agent's assessment.

"And that is a mistake you're not going to make again," Sebastian said, assessing Reiss, gauging the depth of concern he saw in the young agent's green eyes, and deciding there was enough. "Correct?"

"You are correct," Reiss said. "Sir."

"Doctor Schilling," Sebastian said. "While the sisters are in our care, Spring is your charge. Your one and only job from here on out is Spring; do you understand? Do everything in your power to make sure an incident like that does not happen again. Manage her world and all who enter it."

"Yes, sir."

"Now that Agent Reiss realizes the gravity of the situation," Sebastian said, his eyes returning to Skye, who was comforting Spring and trying to quiet her as she broke into a fresh string of no's. "Reiss will be your backup. Unless Spring doesn't want him near her. If that's the case, you're to find a replacement for Reiss, someone both sisters find acceptable."

"No, NONONONO," silence. "No." More silence. "I want to go home. To the bakery. I want Daniel and Sarah."

The pain in Skye's eyes, for a fleeting second, was palpable. "I told you we can't go back there for a few days."

Spring dropped her voice to a whisper and said, "I want to go to the lake house and I want to go there now."

Chapter Sixteen

If his hearing hadn't been so sharp, he wouldn't have heard it, and if he'd been able to tear his attention from the sisters, he'd have missed Skye's expression when Spring said 'lake house.'

Her gray-green eyes flashed to Sebastian. Color drained from her face. She froze, as though Spring had tossed a ball in the air, and Skye was watching to see whether it would hit him. It did—smack dab in the freaking forehead and reignited his belief that Skye knew something that could help him find their father.

Whatever was at the lake house, he needed to know. Maybe it was nothing, but maybe, just maybe, that's where Barrows had stored the backup that federal agents had never managed to find. He could ask Skye, but the more direct route was to send an agent there and figure it out on his own. "Ragno. Figure out which of the Barrows' family assets would be considered a lake house."

"Will do," Ragno said.

Louder, Spring said, "Please, Skye. Please. Can we go to the lake house now? Please? Pleeeeeeaaaaassssseeeee?"

The desperation that he saw in Skye's eyes ice-picked through his heart. He wanted to help her placate Spring, but had no idea how. Well, he had an idea, because Skye had done that for her sister. He'd plucked them out of that world the day before. He couldn't make their lives return to the picture perfect world of Creative Confections, if he couldn't find their father.

"In a few days, yes," Skye said. He watched her draw a deep breath, put her hand on Spring's shoulder, and rest her forehead on her sister's forehead. "But we can't go today."

"Sebastian," Ragno said, "the report is starting."

"We have so much to do here," Skye continued, "There's more than a hundred agents here, and tonight they're going to have your cupcakes for dessert. If you're going to make them look perfect, you need to get started now."

Spring sniffed, looked at the cupcakes, and gave her sister a nod. "We need to bake more."

"Can I help do that?" Doctor Schilling asked.

Skye glanced at her, "Do you have time?"

"Of course. I'd love to bake cupcakes," she said, "and I'd love to watch Spring decorate them." Schilling focused on Spring, and said, "Do you mind if I help?"

As Spring gave the doctor a small nod of approval, pulled her earphones on, and returned her attention to the bowls of icing, some of Sebastian's tension eased. Skye needed relief, or at least a few minutes of quiet sleep, and Spring's acceptance of Schilling was going to make that easier.

He reached for the remote, and turned up the television volume, as Reiss handed him a plate that was loaded with scrambled eggs and a fork. Evidently, the young agent had learned his habits and knew he didn't normally sit to eat. Not while on the job, and he was always on the job.

As he took the plate from Reiss, he glanced at Skye. "Would it be better if I sat with you and Spring?"

Skye gave him a quick headshake. "No. We'll eat later. Thank you."

"Anything else?" Reiss asked.

Sebastian shook his head, eating the eggs as he stood, his attention focused on the television as he watched five talking heads, presumably experts on private security contracting firms, being introduced by the anchor. The show flashed to an aerial view of buildings that were identified as Federal Correctional Institution-Mississippi.

A male reporter was standing outside the prison. "Two prisoners remain at large. Details, at this time, are still coming in. What we do know is that seven prisoners escaped four days ago. Two remain at large. Vincent Biondo and Richard Barrows." Details followed about Biondo and the suspicion that, after he escaped, he killed one of the witnesses in his prosecution.

Skye joined Sebastian in the living room, standing close, facing the TV just as he was, her arms folded, her attention on the screen. She stood so close to him he could almost feel her body warmth.

A fresh wave of vanilla and almond aroma enveloped him, and his body responded with a flood of desire. Goddammit. He forced himself to stop thinking about sex with Skye, and to start thinking about her reaction to what the reporters were saying about her father. He gave her a sideways glance. Nothing there, except intense worry, both for what was on the screen and whether her sister was paying attention. He followed her eyes to a backward glance at Spring, who was focused on the table and, thankfully, not the television.

He ate the last bite of eggs. "Have you eaten?"

She shook her head. "Not hungry."

Maybe she'd have an appetite later, after Minero's interview. He made a mental note to tell Schilling he hadn't seen Skye eat in the twenty-four hours that they'd been together. He doubted Spring could hear the television over whatever was playing on her earphones, but as Agent Reiss took away his empty plate, he lowered the volume a bit, Skye's eyes falling on him as he did so.

"Thank you," she whispered.

He had the irrational desire to tell her it was going to be all right, but the truth was, until he found her father and returned him to prison, he didn't know how the hell anything could possibly be right.

She broke their eye contact first, as the reporter continued, "Richard Barrows is the more notorious of the escapees. He needs no introduction on this news network. Conspiracy theorists across the country are rejoicing at his escape. A rally is ongoing at the site of the former BY Laboratories."

The video flashed to a scene of demonstrators in a parking lot, a large, empty slab for a building behind them. "The demonstrators are wearing baseball caps that are lined and covered with foil, a symbol that is universally associated with Barrows and his theory that technology can read brain waves."

As the camera focused on a man with a foil-lined baseball cap, holding a sign that said, '#RichardBarrows' and '#RichardBarrowsfreeforever,' the reporter continued, "Yes, theories abound. Hashtag Richard Barrows and variations of it are now trending on social media outlets. One theory is that he was rescued by extraterrestrial life. Another is that the government staged his escape so that he can continue working on high-security data and protection efforts. Government officials are emphasizing that Barrows never worked on government contracts, and that his claims of excessive government surveillance are incorrect. In the nine o'clock hour we're dedicating a segment exclusively to Barrows, the man, his work, and his claims—credible and incredible."

Sebastian glanced at Skye. "You ever wear a cap like that?"

Her cheeks flushed an absolutely riveting shade of pink, matching the color of her sweater, which made him think, again, about her nipples. *Damn.* His one-track mind kept dragging him back to her breasts. It was only with willpower that he focused on her eyes, which revealed fear and anxiety and something else that was more troubling.

Hurt.

Dammit.

He wished he could take back the tease, but his words were out there, effectively delivering the same ridicule that was in the voice of the reporter. Without saying anything, she refocused on the television, her absolute silence in response to his jest more effective at making him feeling like an asshole that any words she could have said.

"I'm sure she took that well," Ragno said, sarcasm flag flying high in her tone. "Now say you're sorry."

He almost followed Ragno's instruction, but he had a much bigger thing to apologize for, and he didn't want to dilute the effectiveness of that doozie. Instead of following Ragno's advice, he clamped his mouth shut and focused on the television.

A headshot of Root appeared on the screen. The reporter continued, "And there may be more to the story of Barrows' escape. A missing person's report has been filed on Jennifer Root, the attorney who represented Barrows." He paused. "So far, no connection has been established between Barrows' escape and Root's disappearance. This show's focus is on private security contracting firms, how they operate, and why they're given free rein. Frankly, the show's focus is on how they're able to create such a mess."

Skye glanced at him and gave him a slight smile, which didn't come close to making it to her eyes. "Seems like they're taking pot shots at what's near and dear to both of us this morning. Nice to not be alone for once."

"Ragno," Sebastian ripped his eyes from Skye as he refocused on the television screen. "We better already know everything they're going to say."

The camera flashed back to the prison where Barrows had been imprisoned. "Earlier this year, the Bureau of Prisons Committee, headed by Senator Robert McCollum, hired Black Raven Private Security Contractors to take over security at twenty federal prisons. This is the first contract of its kind, and there's already been a glitch. A big glitch. We've tried to contact the committee members, including Senator McCollum himself. So far, no one has agreed to an interview. Peter," the reporter said, referring to the anchor in the studio. "Tell us what we know about Black Raven."

The camera cut to a young, good-looking male anchor in the studio. "Black Raven is fifteen years old. Sebastian Connelly founded it. For a short time, he was a New Orleans police officer. He studied to become a lawyer as he ascended the ranks in the NOPD. Upon graduating from law school, he quit the police force and started Black Raven, providing bodyguard, security, and investigative services. His work was mostly local, and his company was small, with fewer than fifty employees, until September 11, 2001."

The anchor looked into the camera with steady, practiced sincerity. "From Black Raven's inception the company specialized in providing security services to oil companies, relationships Connelly developed due to his proximity to the oil fields of the Gulf of Mexico. Those oil companies have international holdings, and after September 11, 2001, the oil companies needed heightened security in the Middle East, which became the Wild West for men like Connelly. He struck gold by becoming a major player there."

With a photograph of Sebastian appearing over his left shoulder, the studio anchor continued. "Connelly is smart, charismatic, skilled, and ruthless. He's widely regarded as an expert at threat assessment and personal security. Black Raven is an exclusive outfit, providing security services to executives, celebrities, and wealthy people across the globe, and not just on-site protection and transport. Black Raven isn't simply a bodyguard service. Their services include high-stakes protection, technology-driven investigations, design and installation of digital security systems, and off-site monitoring. The Bureau of Prisons was using them for security system installation. The prison break occurred during the conversion from the BOP security system to the Black Raven system."

Skye glanced at Sebastian, "So your system wasn't in place?"

"No," he frowned, "We had about one day remaining on the installation."

She held his gaze. "If it wasn't your system that failed, why are you taking this so personally?"

"When Black Raven is on the premises, we're accountable.

Which means I'm accountable."

The reporter continued, "And now to our panel of experts."

As the reporter introduced the five talking heads, each was pictured on the screen. Two were actually on Black Raven's payroll, a fact that wasn't obvious from public records. He recognized the other two and knew their backstory. The fifth so-called expert, introduced as Clint Whittaker, was an unknown. As the show progressed, Whittaker was the most vocal and the most argumentative.

One of the 'experts' who was actually on Black Raven's payroll said, "Like most private security contracting firms, Black Raven's methods are, at times, unconventional. But they fill gaps left by governmentally-sanctioned law enforcement forces."

Another of 'his' experts nodded in agreement and said, "In these unconventional times, security firms need to use nonconventional methods."

One of the less-friendly experts said, "Yes, but focus on this prison break. By all accounts, Black Raven botched the job."

"Not true," a friendlier expert said. "Black Raven was hired precisely to prevent this type of situation. Their security system wasn't yet online. This isn't their fault."

"My sources indicate that Black Raven was on the premises when the prison break occurred. More important than that is what happened after," Whittaker said, his loud, indignant voice breaking into the conversation, "which proves Black Raven's manhunt capabilities are questionable, at best."

Sebastian's blood started a slow simmer as the verbal war continued. "Because they've been unable to find Biondo, a witness on Biondo's prosecution has been killed. Yesterday there was a shoot-out in an Atlanta suburb, on a busy street. Preliminary reports suggest that it is related to the prison break. Connelly himself was on site after the shoot-out. If local or federal officials had been involved, perhaps the scene would have been contained better. Black Raven agents are not opposed to using lethal force-"

"Lethal force is sometimes necessary, and there's a deputizing clause in Black Raven's contracts that spells out that they have authority to use any type of force possessed by the contracting individual or governmental agency-"

"Even local officials use lethal force-"

One of the not-so-friendly experts managed to talk above the others. "But private security firms like Black Raven do so without regard to public safety. They're not trained in public safety. They're trained in protecting their clients at all cost, and there's a big difference."

Whittaker nodded with enthusiasm, almost yelling, "Call a spade a spade. Essentially, Black Raven is a band of unregulated hired guns. Many have been trained on taxpayer dollars, before Connelly wins them over with big salaries. U.S. citizens spend millions of dollars training special forces. Outfits like Black Raven cherry-pick the best, by offering lucrative paychecks and perks that go with high-living lifestyles. Action needs to be taken, and it needs to be taken now. Aside from the drain on our military and our tax dollars, these private security contractors are highly skilled, and they're using their skills without any oversight except the pocket books of the people who hire them. They've got to be stopped. At the very least, it is time for regulation. The public cannot afford to be unaware of this issue. It is a matter of public safety. Black Raven makes millions of dollar a year off of government contracts. The prison security outsourcing contract is just the tip of the iceberg."

"How much?" The reporter asked.

Whittaker said, "That's a great question. I'm researching it now. My estimate tells me in the last fiscal year the number exceeded two hundred million."

The fucking asshole was way underestimating the number. Sebastian doubted that mistake would be continued for much longer. He muttered, "Ragno. Profile Whittaker. Figure out who is paying him." He paused, his blood slowing as a hunch developed. "And cross-reference him, and any of his contacts, to anything that's turning up in the profiles that you're pulling together on Jennifer Root, Zachary Young, and BY Laboratories. Only serious money buys that kind of hatred and I want to know who is funding him."

"We're cross-referencing everything in this case," Ragno said. "Problem is, these massive data searches take time. Especially since Young and BY Laboratories used encryption technology for most of their communications. Also, I'd imagine that any company that is paying Whittaker isn't using their real name."

"You can handle it," Sebastian said.

"Of course I can," she said.

Debates on the pros and cons of private security contracting firms weren't new, yet he couldn't stop watching this one. Until now, the hot-button debate hadn't been on the radar of the average American. With the popular twenty-four hour news network seizing upon the story and dedicating so much time to it, Sebastian knew he was slipping into a new era.

Ready or not.

Whittaker said, "Connelly was implicated in a vigilante-style shoot-out last July, which resulted in the death of an FBI agent and a suspected kidnapper."

"Suspected?" One of the Black Raven-friendly experts chimed in. "There was nothing suspected about it. The man had killed one woman, maimed another, and he was in the process of murdering a third, while extorting millions of dollars from her family. You need to get your facts straight."

"It was an uncontrolled shoot-out on domestic soil, complete with hand grenades. I have the facts," Whittaker yelled. "This was in the backyard of Americans. And last night's shoot-out was outside of a shopping mall. Hundreds of rounds were fired from assault weapons. Four men died. As we sit here, the scene remains under investigation. So right now, headline news involves not only a prison break, but also questions regarding the company the government hired to keep the public safe from prisoners. Vigilante groups such as Black Raven are unregulated hired guns, and often, like now, they create havoc."

"Vigilante group?" Sebastian said. "Vigilante? Great. That's just fucking great."

One of his experts chimed in, "You're forgetting that they do a lot of good. Remember the oil summit last March? If private security firms hadn't been providing protection there, the summit would have been a disaster, and the ramifications would have put the region in turmoil. To be blunt, turmoil there would have had impact on our prices at the pump."

Ragno said, "Time for the conference call with Minero. After that you'll have a helicopter transport to Raven One."

As soon as he heard the words oil summit, he braced himself for the footage that was coming. "Give me about forty-five minutes after the conference call ends before I leave."

"I'll make the arrangements," Ragno said. "If wheels are up at nine-thirty, you'll be here and situated by eleven. The firestorm in the media has all of your partners wanting to talk to you. Insisting on talking to you, as a matter of fact. Several Ravens are here."

"What's Zeus's status?"

"He's still managing safe house forensics and dealing with local authorities on the shoot-out outside of the mall."

"Has he found anything useful?"

"No. You would have heard," Ragno paused. "Should I arrange a meeting of the partners this afternoon?"

"Let's talk about that when I'm leaving Last Resort."

Sebastian turned to Skye, whose eyes were glued to the televised image of him, captured on video as the oil summit became a bloodbath. He had hoisted his rifle of choice, a black M4 Carbine, and switched it to fully automatic. The camera captured him shooting to kill anyone who crossed his path, while he shielded his client. Beautiful. Fucking beautiful. It was a great recruiting tool, but not anything the average American needed to see while they had their morning coffee.

The report flashed to a studio anchor announcing breaking news at the sentencing of international terrorist, Stonefish. The screen flashed to an image of a crowded city street, cars parked haphazardly, some with police signals flashing, and a burned out, multi-story building, with flames and smoke shooting from two floors. According to the anchor, Stonefish was missing and presumed dead, as were two of the judges of the international tribunal.

"Ragno, you see this?"

"Yes," she answered. "Let's count it as a lucky break. We weren't working security on any aspect of that tribunal, and now the media has something in addition to the prison break to focus on."

"If this is luck, I'm screwed," he said, "but I'll take what I can get." He turned to Skye, whose eyes were on him. In her expression he saw fear, worry, and questions. He sure as hell wished he had answers. "It's time for you to talk to the marshals."

Just leaving one room and going to another took time. Skye patiently spoke to Spring, before talking to Doctor Schilling. He heard Skye ask, "You're okay to stay with her?"

Schilling nodded. "Of course. Until we find your father and return him to prison, you're under our care. While you're under the care of Black Raven, you and she are in my charge. Whether that means administering medical care or helping with cupcakes," she shrugged, "it's no different."

A measure of relief filtered into Skye eyes. Her gaze encompassed both Sebastian and Schilling. "Thank you," Skye said, "When Spring is ready to start putting the icing on the cupcakes, she might need help. She'll ask if she does. Please don't try to help, if she doesn't ask for it."

Schilling gave Sebastian a smile that matched the light in her brown eyes. "Looks like I picked the lucky straw for the day. I get to bake cupcakes. I'll call another doctor. He'll be there in a few minutes to stitch your arm."

Sebastian guided Skye down the hall, past the open door to the room where he'd slept, to a conference room. He glanced at the bed and would have given his soul to be back in it with her, without the distractions of the day crashing around him like lava erupting from a volcano.

Hell.

Even with the firestorm he faced, the few inches separating them as they walked down the hallway weren't enough. His body craved hers, like a starving man craved food, even as he tried to force his attention to the task at hand. Keeping her safe. Keeping her sister safe. Finding her damned father, who was the root of this particular problem.

The room had a table, six chairs, a wall of monitors, and built-in speakers. It had one fake window and lots of bright light from recessed lighting. They were alone, but as long as he had a live connection with Ragno, she was present, even though not physically there. Ragno's presence was a good thing. Considering that he could barely keep his hands off Skye, being truly alone with her would be dangerous.

Mentally, he could pretend they never had sex. Physically, he had no hope of accomplishing that lofty goal.

He pulled out a chair for her, clenching his jaw as his fingers brushed the sleeve of her soft cardigan. As she sat, the end of her loose braid ran down his forearm like a caress. Or a taunt, dammit. As sparks shot up his arm, he wondered if she felt the same physical attraction. If she did, she was better at masking her desire.

He sat down next to her and moved his chair closer to the table, glad that it hid his arousal. "We'll be live in a minute. It isn't video. Only voice. The rooms full of speakers, so you can talk normally, and he'll hear you. I can't tell you what to say. Remember, you're talking to federal officials." He paused, glancing into her eyes. His legal training was deeply ingrained. At interrogations such as these, he always warned his clients of the manipulative capabilities of law enforcement officials. "I'm a lawyer," he explained, "but I'm not your lawyer, and I'm not giving you legal advice; do you understand that?"

She nodded, as there was a knock on the door. An agent who Sebastian recognized as a physician walked into the room. He was middle-aged and balding. It wasn't the perfect time to get stiches, but it was the only time that he planned to sit still that morning, before departing for headquarters. Sebastian stripped off his shirt, as the doctor laid a tray of scissors, bandages, surgical thread, and cleansing solution on the table and snapped on gloves.

He watched Skye's eyes drift from the wound, to his chest, and to his shoulders. A pink flush formed on her cheeks, as her eyes found his. The flush was barely there, but still noticeable. *Ahhh.* She wasn't immune to the pull that existed between them. Good to know it wasn't a one-way street. Why that mattered, when he'd be far away from her in just a matter of hours, he had no idea. It just did.

The doctor started working on his arm, pouring alcohol on the wound and swabbing at it. When he felt the first prick of the needle and the pull of thread, he drew a deep breath, thought about a couple of things that would hurt more, and blocked out the feeling of what the doctor was doing. With his arm to the side, and his face turned to Skye, he continued. "The last thing I want you to do is give Minero information that you haven't provided me. That being said, I need to tell you that you're not a suspect here, but keeping information from them is a crime. These guys are good at drawing information from people. Their questions are probing, their pauses are deliberate, and they want to know more than you ever want to tell them."

She straightened her back and pushed up the sleeves of her cardigan, her eyes serious. "I understand that. I only have to answer the questions that he asks, right?"

She was a smart woman. He locked eyes on her, detected more than a bit of the willpower he'd been battling since he'd introduced himself, and nodded. Minero didn't stand a chance. "That's right. Don't volunteer information." As the doctor tugged more loops of thread through his arm, Sebastian said, "Ragno, put the call through."

Sebastian was an outsider on this one. Minero took charge, and Sebastian didn't try to intervene. Minero began the call with only a slight haughtiness in his voice, but with a huge assumption, evident in his tone, that Skye somehow knew something about her father's whereabouts. There was also thinly veiled disdain for Barrows and his work, which not surprisingly put Skye's back up. Her entire posture changed, but her tone was polite and even as she professed to know nothing helpful, or where her father may be running, or who might be interested in her father.

Minero's tone became accusatory. Sebastian almost chuckled as Minero hung himself by making the same mistakes that Sebastian himself had made with Skye, the mistake he'd continued this morning when he had mocked the news show's images of the followers of Richard Barrows who wore foil-lined caps. The doctor finished with the stitches and began bandaging his arm.

"Mr. Minero, if you aren't going to take the time to understand my father's work," Skye said, her cheeks flushed red, but her voice calm. "The importance of it, and what it could mean to someone, and who that person might be, you will never find him."

With that pronouncement, Sebastian's heart pounded.

An answer had been staring at him, the minute he realized the lengths to which Skye had gone to make sure no one found her and her sister. It had just taken him approximately twenty-four hours in her company to realize that answer. The light bulb moment hit him like a train.

Holy hell.

As he listened to Minero's steady stream of questions, and Skye's indignant answers of 'No,' 'I don't know,' and 'I can't answer that," goose bumps prickled up and down his arms, on the back of his neck, and crawled down his back. He nodded goodbye to the doctor. When Minero ended the call with frustration and a big zero in intel-gained, Sebastian realized that it was time for something different than bullheaded doubt and thinly disguised ridicule. Skye wasn't just playing along with her father's delusions.

She was an integral part of them.

There was a reason that ridicule and disdain of her father

was a nonstarter. She believed her father's claims, claims that he'd spent the last few days investigating and, unfortunately, disproving.

Is she just as crazy as her father?

His stomach twisted. He normally stayed away from women who didn't have a firm grasp on reality, but he'd done something far different with her. Exactly what he had to do to figure out the depth of Skye's delusions, and whether unraveling her thoughts and theories would lead to Barrows, Sebastian had no idea. He also didn't have time to go there. Delusional conspiracy theories weren't something he was prepared to chase.

He'd apologize to her for what he'd done the night before, then he'd leave Last Resort.

As the phone call with Minero ended, he said to Ragno, "Give me some time on my own."

"Wait. I've got your answer regarding potential properties that can be considered a lake house. There are two. One in Florida and another in Seattle."

"Send agents to both properties. ASAP. Figure out if there's anything at either property that can be useful to finding Barrows."

"Maybe Barrows is at one of the houses, sitting on a pier, fishing."

He chuckled. "Let's keep those positive thoughts going." He focused his attention on Skye, took the earphone out of his ear and put the device in his pocket. He turned off the watch's receiver and transmission switches. As she backed her chair away from the table, he asked, "Still craving outside air? I need to make a quick stop, then we can go for a walk."

Chapter Seventeen

Figure it out.

The words were more than a faint thought, more than a memory of her father's voice. They were loud, as though he stood next to her, yelling in exasperation. Now that the phone call with the Marshal was over, she couldn't keep her exhaustion at bay, nor did she have the energy to sort through the racing thoughts that were turning her brain to mush. She knew what he'd be telling her.

Figure it out.

She couldn't figure her way out of this one. She was trapped. Stuck somewhere she shouldn't be, when she should be figuring out the next step in the cataclysm scenario. Either it was on, or it was off, and she was overdue on Firefly Island to figure it out. If her father had sent her another message, it was there. At the lake house. Waiting for her. If cataclysm was still in play, she needed to be acting on it. Not baking cupcakes, pretending for Spring's benefit that the only thing that mattered was that the agents holding them hostage had a pretty dessert to go with their dinner.

Cataclysm. Run. Now.

Instead of running anywhere, Skye had grabbed a jean jacket from her room before she stopped in the kitchen to tell Spring where she was going. Upon seeing the leash in Skye's hand, Candy had danced around her feet, either with excitement or a very full bladder.

Cool February air enveloped her as she and Sebastian stepped outside. The sky was partly cloudy. For the moment, the sun was hidden. Three black Range Rovers were in the concrete courtyard, all pulled to one side. Six agents were in the courtyard. Two agents were close to the front door, two were further out, and two were positioned on the far edges. All stood at attention as she and Sebastian stepped outside.

The only thing that mattered to Skye was that she was breathing fresh air. She relished the freshness, taking deep, cleansing breaths. On either side of the courtyard, the property was dense with pine trees. Their tangy fragrance tickled her nostrils. She inhaled, exhaled, and drew in another long breath, as she slipped on her jean jacket.

"Warm enough?" he asked. As she buttoned the jacket, his eyes scanned her arms, her chest, traveling up her neck, to her face, and finally, meeting her gaze. His gaze was just as intense as the look he'd given her the night before, when she'd been naked, underneath him, and his eyes had travelled her body, as though he was memorizing every detail. In the soft lamplight of his bedroom, the look had been sensual. In the daylight, the look was raw and hungry and, having experienced exactly what he was capable of delivering, a warm flush burned her cheeks as she met his gaze.

Yes, she thought, *if he requested a do-over, the answer would be yes.* Anytime, anywhere, and it didn't much matter what was going wrong in her life, because he'd made her forget her sorry situation with just a touch.

"I could find you a heavier jacket," he said. "We keep plenty of extras here. Temperature's dropping. Forecasters are calling for a winter storm."

He wore a short-sleeved polo shirt and no jacket and didn't seem bothered by the cold. After the phone call, he'd slipped into his bedroom and had come out with his gun, which was holstered on his belt. She pulled the ponytail holder out of her hair, shook loose the braid, and slipped the skinny elastic band on her wrist. He watched her hair fall around her shoulders, before his eyes rested on hers.

She said, "I'm warm enough."

"There's a trail." He pointed to a path, that was to the right of the safe house. "It's a short trek along a small lake. Sound good?"

She nodded and headed in the direction he pointed. She didn't care where they walked. She only cared that they were outside, and she could breathe. Maybe outside air would clear her brain.

Figure it out.

There was no way out, but there had to be a point to the walk. Everything Sebastian did had a point, and aside from his capability for mind-blowing sex, she didn't really like any of his points. But she wanted to be outside so badly she didn't care about his motives. Sebastian took Candy's leash, her tail was wagging, and she high-stepped in stride with Sebastian, as though she'd been trained to walk with him. The man had a way with females, even wayward puppies, who couldn't walk in a straight line when anyone else had her on a leash. Skye had offered Spring the opportunity for the walk, but her sister was content in the kitchen, smoothing the first layer of icing onto cupcakes. Doctor Schilling was baking another batch. One Black Raven agent walked about ten yards in front of Skye and Sebastian, two agents followed behind. Far enough away to be out of earshot, close enough to offer protection if needed. If the other three who had been in the courtyard were anywhere around, she didn't see them.

"I'm sorry about last night," he said quietly, getting to the point the minute they stepped onto the trail.

Oh, dear God, please don't let him talk about what we did.

Actually having a conversation after the fact wasn't something she was used to, particularly after she told a man that they could act like it never happened. The path was covered with a light frost, that had settled on the ground overnight. The thin layer of frozen moisture crunched underfoot as she continued along the path, but he stopped walking.

He shot her an inquiring, far too penetrating glance. "Skye?"

She could feel his eyes on the back of her head, burning into her. She walked fast, putting distance between herself and him.

"Did you hear me?" He caught up to her, walking in stride with her on the narrow trail, bending to dodge a branch.

"No apology is necessary."

"I took advantage of you," he said, "and I never should have done that."

She stopped walking, cringing on the inside as she turned to him and stared into blue eyes that had the depth of oceans, with an expression as sincere and focused as any that had been directed at her in years.

"Please," she said, unable to cavalierly come up with any words to brush off such honesty. "Please don't apologize." *Just be a jerk. Don't make me actually like you. Please. It's too hard to resist you when you're charming. And if I don't resist, I'll just get hurt.*

"I was an ass," he continued. "I never take advantage of

women in desperate situations, and I did that last night. I apologize. You deserved better."

She shook off the urge to say thank you. Not one of the men she'd ever been with before had told her that she deserved anything more than what they'd dished out. She shook her head, immediately correcting herself with wisdom she'd fought hard to attain. What she had let them dish out. Men had only treated her as a one-night, one-week, or one-month pastime, because that is exactly how she had always allowed herself to be treated.

Toughen up, she told herself. So he was sorry. Big deal. So he was telling her that she deserved something more. So he was saying something that no one else had ever told her before.

So what? So nothing.

"I enjoyed it. Very much, as a matter of fact. I said it wouldn't count for anything. It was sex," she shrugged, "between two consenting adults. I said we could act like it never happened, and I meant it. It's better that way, don't you think?"

"I know too much about you," his eyes held hers. "Things you haven't told me. Things I've learned from my cyber group-"

"Hackers," she corrected him.

He nodded, with a shrug. "You know the type of information that's out there. Medical records, school records, no one lives totally off the cyber grid. My people know more about you than they should, and so do I. Unless you've changed one hell of a lot in the last few years, since you saw your last psychologist, your tough-girl, casual-sex lines are bullshit, and we both know it."

She kept walking. He walked beside her as the path approached a lake, where swirls of mist floated up from the clear water and evaporated into the fresh, clean air. They continued along the path, with the lake on the right, woods on their left.

He continued, "It's all a defense mechanism for a woman who experienced heart-wrenching grief in losing her mother at a vulnerable age." As he said words that sounded exactly like what her counselors had told her over the years, anger bubbled up from her gut. She stopped walking and turned to him. He stopped walking as well, and continued, "You're a mature woman, who has an ingrained defense mechanism, borne from being a lonely teenager, who missed her mother, whose death inspired a fear of loving anyone for fear of losing them, either through death or abandonment."

Her embarrassment and anger mixed into a toxic cocktail

inside her. She slapped him. Hard.

He didn't try to stop her. He glanced at the agent who had been walking in front and who was closest to them. The man turned to them and took a step closer. Sebastian gave him a slight no headshake, then his eyes returned and locked on hers.

"You bastard." She'd never slapped anyone in her life. Her handprint formed a faint red outline on his face, while her palm stung from the contact. She didn't regret doing it. She only wished it made her feel better. "You have no right to know so much about me. Are you now going to tell me I should grow the hell up?"

"Hell no. I'd never be so judgmental. And you're absolutely correct. That's why I'm apologizing. I knew better, and I conveniently forgot what I know. I agree," he said with a curt nod as her handprint reached its peak before fading. "I deserved that slap."

"That psychologist was an idiot, anyway."

He gave her an eyebrow arch and a slow headshake. "You lost your mother when you were thirteen and she left you with a two year-old sister. Your father, on good days, had to be distracted and absent-minded. I had a childhood that was beyond shitty, but I didn't have to assume responsibility for a child with special needs. I only had myself and my mother to worry about. I can't imagine what you went through."

"My childhood ended years ago. I don't need your sympathy or your pity."

He frowned. Sparks of anger filtered through his eyes. "This isn't about your goddamn childhood. It's about now. If your dad's fathering was anything like the convoluted, mind-puzzling rants and speeches that he's delivered to the rest of the world, it's amazing that you're capable of living normally, yet you do more than that. Yesterday I wondered why someone with your brilliance turned your back on your father's business, or anything else your MIT degree had you trained for, and opened a coffee shop."

She saw an understanding in his eyes, and knew he didn't need an answer. Damn him.

"Though I don't have intel that confirms this, I'm guessing that you saw what your father's brilliance has done to him and you didn't want to be like him, did you?"

She shrugged, not wanting to acknowledge the reason why

she didn't follow her father's footsteps quite so starkly. "I wouldn't put it that way. I'd say I decided to be productive in a different way."

"Well, I'd say you excel. Creative Confections was beautiful, and you created it out of thin air. It was perfect for Spring, until all of this happened. Last night I pushed you to the breaking point on purpose, because I was trying to get information from you, but I gave in to this...*thing*...that I obviously can't control when I'm with you. I never lose control. But there's something about you that pushes my body into sexual overdrive, and I did it, even when I knew your words were bullshit."

The only thing she paid attention to was the very first sentence. *He'd pushed her to the breaking point on purpose.* "So you were fucking me..." she cringed with the harshness of the words, becoming even angrier when he didn't flinch. "...you fucked me on the outside chance I'd talk to you in some post-coital, confidence sharing? Was it all an attempt to manipulate me into giving you information, one that you might have screwed up by falling asleep the minute you came?"

"You weren't exactly complaining," he said, jaw clenched in frustration. "Hell. I'm not trying to argue with you. I wasn't manipulating you by having sex with you. I did it because I wanted it." He paused. "I wanted you more than I've ever wanted anything. I've tried to tell myself it's because I've gone a few months without sex, but it's not just that. Hell, I've gone without sex for longer stretches before, and haven't lost control. There's something about you. Something about your eyes," he paused, "your voice, your body. The way you're so wonderful with your sister. The way you're cocky, the way you try like hell to be a tough girl, the way you jump into action without a plan. Even the way you lie like shit, with a straight-faced, big-eyed broadcast that a doozie is coming. Dammit." He drew a deep breath, shook his head, and said, "Forget it. I don't know why the hell I want you. Maybe I just do. If we had the chance, I'd do it again right now. Chalk it up to proximity and sudden horniness. Hell. I knew better last night, and I certainly know better now. I crossed a line that I never cross. I'm sorry."

Please shut up.

She didn't want to like him. Instead of focusing on the nice words that he said, instead of acknowledging the sincerity with which he delivered the apology, the way he was complimenting her and telling her how attracted he was to her, she focused on his earlier words. *He'd pushed her to the breaking point on purpose.* "Is this apology just another psychological game?"

His cheeks flushed. He frowned, then started walking again. The agent who was in the lead had moved a wayward tree limb out of their way and was holding it as they passed. "No games. No manipulation. Maybe yesterday that was an option, but not now." He drew a deep breath, touched his fingers to his temple, shook his head, mumbled "hell," and dropped his hand. The gesture was quick, but it was enough to tell her that his headache was back.

"I stand by the rule that if you're apologizing to someone, they need to know exactly what you're apologizing for. I can't say much more than that. I'm sorry," he said. "Because my people are busy looking at every record that's ever been written and recorded about you, your family, and you're father's work, I knew better. Take it or leave it. The apology stands on its own. Regardless of the shit-pile of problems that I have, or the ones you have, I'm not playing a psychological game."

No answer required, she told herself. She stepped over another branch, glanced to her right, out over the lake, and tried to tell herself that he was still the asshole she'd originally thought him to be. The clouds had drifted and faded. There was more blue sky, and the edge of the sun was visible.

"If you're not already thinking that you should be talking to me," he said, "I'm not going to try to change your mind. Before I leave, though, you need to know that we've learned your next identity. You don't even have that security. Your cover's blown out of this universe. When this is over for your father, when he's safely back in jail, your only option for the moment will be to be Skye Barrows, because if we've found it, you have to assume someone else has it, too."

Her heart started pounding. "You're bullshitting." Stupid comment, she knew, because she'd already figured out he wasn't a bullshitter.

He shook his head. "Bridgette and Brandy Tillman."

She stopped walking. With his words, yet another door slammed shut. *Oh, dear God. Trapped. Now, and forever.* Because her father's revolutionary technological innovations were always going to be in demand. There would always be someone to run from. Always. She drew a deep breath, shaking off the panic.

Figure it out.

She'd have to come up with a new identity. It would mean transferring funds in an untraceable manner, securing documentation, and creating yet another cyber-footprint.

Doing that without her father's help was daunting, but she'd figure out how to create new identities. She could afford good help. Acting on her father's instructions, fulfilling her obligation under the cataclysm scenario, and keeping Spring safe while she did it, was something entirely different. All she could figure out was that she needed help, and she needed it now.

"Frankly," he continued, "I've figured out the problem with you, and we're at the end of a dead end street."

She shook her head. "What does that mean?"

"You believe your father's claims, while my people have spent the last few days disproving the bulk of what he's said. Even if you started talking right now, even if you started spinning theories as to why those men are after you, I'm not sure I'd listen. I don't have time for it. I'll find him, one way or another. When I do, he'll go back to jail. I'm just no longer looking to you for any kind of an answer."

She stood still, her back to the lake, her attention focused on him.

Trust no one who knows you're my daughter.

No one, and that meant not to trust this man who carried wayward puppies across a street, who played jellybean games with Spring, who apologized after having sex that he felt he shouldn't have. She shouldn't trust him, even though he took a hard slap on the face without flinching, nodded, and said that he deserved it. He desired her, due to things no one else had ever even noticed about her, yet that wasn't a reason to trust him, because she was to trust no one.

Figure it out.

She heard it before she saw it. There was a distant whirr of an airborne engine, which became louder. Undulating air, chopped by blades, circulated around her as a black helicopter skimmed the treetops overhead, in the direction of the house.

He glanced at the helicopter as he handed her Candy's leash. "Continue on the path. My agents will walk closer to you. I'll be gone when you return to the house. You and Spring will have Black Raven protection until we find your father, but unless you ask to see me, or talk to me, you won't."

He turned and walked back towards the house that really wasn't a house at all, retracing his steps. When he was five steps away from her she wondered whether she was making a mistake. When he was ten steps away, she had the same feeling that she'd had the night before, when he had stepped out of the SUV and walked into the safe house. His absence was immediately noticeable, and knowing he was walking away and leaving Last Resort made the void created by his absence worse. As he moved even further from where she stood, as he passed the two agents who had been walking behind them, she suddenly felt alone. Alone had always been bad, but she had coped.

Now, with the weight of the cataclysm scenario crashing around her, with both Jen and her father missing, without the safety net that Daniel and Sarah had provided, and with someone chasing after her and Spring, being alone was intolerable. Without Sebastian next to her, without his serious eyes on her, she felt less safe.

The night before, when he had stepped out of the SUV to go to the safe house, she'd had the premonition that whatever was going to happen without him in the SUV was going to be bad. She felt the same thing now. Shivering, she rubbed her arms, suddenly feeling colder, even though the sun was now fully visible.

"Wait." The word was lost in the sound of the helicopter engine. Before he disappeared from the clearing, she hurried towards him. "Sebastian. Wait."

He stopped walking away, turning as she caught up to him. Candy bounced around their feet. His eyes were hard, his stance only momentarily on pause. The man who had just apologized to her for what had happened between them was physically there, but his apologetic demeanor was gone. It was back to business for him, and he didn't have time to waste. If her needs were only about herself, if she wasn't so desperate, she'd have said never mind, because he was giving her a hard glance that suggested, *what now?*

He pointed to his ear, mouthed, the words, 'I'm wired,' then, 'Ragno's listening.'

"I'll tell you what I know if you promise that no matter what happens, if anything happens to me, Spring will be safe. I have a will. There are detailed instructions. All of it is in Jen's office. Jen is—was—her legal guardian, in the event that something happened to me."

He frowned. "I thought Root didn't know where you were."

"She didn't, but I had a plan in place so that Jen would be contacted if necessary."

"Lying time is over Skye. Everything you say from here on out needs to make sense. Understand?"

Irritation flared, but given her steadfast refusal to talk for the last twenty-four plus hours, he had the right to feel the need to lay different ground rules. "Yes."

"What was the plan? You unexpectedly drop dead," he said, his eyes as hard as his blunt words and his tone. "There's no link between Chloe and Colbie Stewart and your father or Root. How was Root going to know?"

"Daniel and Sarah. They didn't know who we really were, but they both knew there were instructions to follow in the event of an emergency, and those instructions spelled everything out."

He nodded. "Go on."

She drew a deep breath, relieved. "Without Daniel and Sarah, and now that Jen is missing, I need a backup. With things so uncertain, I need to make sure that Spring will be safe, that those instructions are followed, that someone will take care of her. She needs a legal guardian, and more. She needs someone as caring as Doctor Schilling. Does your company do that kind of protection?"

He gave her a curt nod. "Yes. We adapt services to client's needs. But before I agree to let you hire my company, you have to tell me everything you know."

"I will, but I need to make sure Spring is protected."

His lips lifted in a slight smile, which faded as quickly as it started. "Always bargaining, aren't you?"

She held his gaze. "Well?"

He frowned. "We're expensive."

"I have the financial wherewithal to pay for this, and trusts are established in the event of my death."

"We'll need a roadmap to find them."

"They're in different names." She tried to keep some of the desperation out of her voice, but when she talked about Spring, it was difficult. "I need to make sure someone other than me knows what to do. That someone else is responsible for her if I can't act, that someone looks out for her while my father is imprisoned, or," she drew a deep breath, "or worse. I need to know Spring will be safe and cared for. My back-up systems have fallen apart since yesterday morning. I can't function without knowing there's a safety net for Spring, if something happens to me."

He nodded. "Done. Ragno, you heard that?"

He paused.

"Good. You can tell her." He lifted the earpiece from his ear, stepped closer to Skye, and held it against her right ear. He was just inches from her. She longed for the comfort of his arms around her. He wasn't offering that kind of comfort, though, so she took what he gave her. She lifted her fingers to cup his hand that held the earpiece. He inhaled at her touch. For a fleeting second, the moment became more about her fingers on his, her smaller hand on his larger one, and how she almost couldn't fight the urge to throw herself against him, than it was about the phone call. The look in his eyes, tense and serious, told her he felt the same way.

"Skye, I'll memorialize that as a verbal request for hiring Black Raven. We'll memorialize it in writing later."

Skye drew a deep breath, as she realized that the person on the other end of the line, Sebastian's partner on the job, was a woman. Ragno's tone was that of a confident female—clear, crisp, efficient, intelligent, and full of authority. That he had so much trust in a female was yet another reason to like him. *Hell.*

"You can establish the parameters as we proceed. Spring's needs may be a little different than the usual type of services we provide," Ragno said. "But we adapt. Black Raven can handle this, no matter what happens to your father, or to you. You have Sebastian's word, and you now have mine. Sebastian isn't always adept at knowing what someone needs to hear."

Skye almost chuckled. Ragno hadn't been privy to the heartfelt apology that Sebastian had just delivered. She wasn't giving the man enough credit. Ragno continued, "What Sebastian meant when he said 'done,' was that hiring Black Raven means you and Spring never need to be alone again. We're the best safety net money can buy, and you have the assets to cover it. We can work out details later. Do you understand?"

"Yes," she said, her knees almost buckling with relief, as Sebastian reclaimed the earpiece. "Thank you," she whispered, intending it both for Sebastian and Ragno.

He nodded, still standing close to her. "Now, tell me more."

She drew a deep, courage-gathering breath, and said, "I don't know who is after us, but I know why."

"Ragno, can you hear this?" He nodded. To Skye, he said, "Go on."

She glanced around the clearing. The three agents were on the perimeter, spaced equally apart, backs to them. The sun was shining in full now. Sebastian's eyes were on her. Waiting. She had no choice. With one more deep breath of the fragrant, pine-laden air, she said, "It has to do with Shadow Technology."

He frowned. He gave her a slight headshake. "It doesn't exist."

"Yes," she said. "It does."

"Look. It's damn hard to make sense of anything your father's said in the last five years or so. There are thousands upon thousands of pages of his writings and even more thousands of pages of debriefings, that were conducted in connection with his offense. Your father consistently talked about Shadow Technology, as though it was something that he created, but in reality, Shadow Technology doesn't exist. Plus, it's hard to believe anything that he said, because he also consistently talked about UFO's, brain-wave scanners, and things that are total bullshit. You heard the disdain in this morning's news report, you heard it from me yesterday, and you heard it from Minero. I'm trying hard to find a thread of logic, but my people are telling me that Shadow Technology doesn't exist, and my people would know if it did."

"It exists," she said, emphatically. "The government's denying it, but my father developed the technology for the National Security Agency. They're using it now."

His frown deepened.

I'm finally talking to him, and he doesn't believe me.

"The government admits that PRISM exists," she grasped for something that he would agree with. "There are other data collection programs that they're now admitting to using, and even some programs that aren't public knowledge. It's public knowledge that they're building warehouses in Utah to store and process the volumes of cyber data they're collecting, but what isn't so well known is how the government is processing the information that's being stored in the Utah Data Center. Officially, the mission of the Utah Data Center is unclassified." Skye drew a deep breath. "But unofficially, my father's Shadow Technology is an integration and assimilation program that the government is using there and elsewhere to tie together data collection efforts of various agencies."

"Skye. There's no evidence that Shadow Technology exists." She watched him clench his jaw, and shut his eyes for a second as he pressed his index finger and his middle finger on his forehead. He gave his temple a slow, hard-pressured swipe.

Not twenty-four hours earlier, when she had first learned of his head injury, she had wished that he'd drop dead. Now, she thought, *please, God, let him be all right*, and said, "How bad is that headache?"

He opened his eyes, stared at her for a second, with an expression that she couldn't read, and said, "Not as bad as it's going to get." He gave her a slight smile. "But I can handle it. The only guarantee I have today is that the headache will not be my biggest problem." His expression turned serious again. "Ragno, don't worry about it." Eyes on Skye, he said, "Please tell me you have more than this."

"When the September eleventh attacks happened, my father became obsessed with the fact that our security agencies had the raw intel that could have warned us of the attacks. The government had clues. We also-"

He held up a finger, and stepped closer to her. "Ragno, are you hearing this?" To Skye, he nodded. "Speak up."

"My father believed that the government had an opportunity to kill Osama bin Laden and the government would have done so, if it had accurately read the clues in advance of the attacks. It drove my father, to distraction. He believed that such important intelligence gathering and assessment didn't need to be subject to human error, so he designed the integration and assimilation program that he called Shadow Technology. Before he was charged with tax evasion, he'd spent five years working with the NSA, adapting it to their various data collection efforts, which, as you know, grew exponentially in that time frame."

A breeze rustled the pines. He ran his fingers through his hair, pushing back the pieces that had fallen over his forehead, and nodded. "You're talking from 2008 to 2013?"

"Roughly."

"There's a big problem with that," he said, his eyes flashing with impatience that matched his curt tone. "The NSA denies that your father ever worked with them."

"You're taking their word for that? They deny everything.

Even as they were building warehouses in Utah to store the data they're collecting through PRISM, they denied the existence of PRISM, until their own employee leaked documents that proved that it existed."

"Well," he said, his tone more pensive than curt, "you're right about that."

She continued, "Something changed in that five-year period. You see, as he worked with the NSA, my father was able to observe what they were really doing with the technology he created. They weren't using Shadow Technology as he intended. They're not just collecting data on known suspects or persons of interest. They're collecting everything, all the time, on all of us. You at least know that, don't you?"

He nodded, and she felt a small measure of relief.

She continued, "The pervasiveness of government intrusion into the daily life of law-abiding, average Americans horrified my father. But there was an even bigger problem that kept him up at night, and he was determined to find a resolution for it."

He shut his eyes, drew a deep breath, and shook his head. "Because that's what paranoid conspiracy theorists like your father do. They come up with bigger and bigger problems, each scenario more outlandish than the last. When people like your father wake up in the middle of the night, why the hell can't they have a bowl of ice cream and fall back asleep like a normal person?"

She didn't fault him for his irritation, but she had to press on. "He was worried that the government didn't have adequate systems in place to protect what they collected, so he developed encryption technology that would protect Shadow Technology."

"He called it the LID," he said. "We know all of this. He claims it is the most effective encryption technology ever invented." Sebastian shrugged. "There's one giant problem with this. My people are telling me that it doesn't exist. Shadow Technology doesn't exist and neither does LID Technology." He gestured with his chin in the direction of the house. "Let's start walking."

"You're wrong. Both exist," she said, her heart pounding as she struggled to keep up with his long-legged stride. "The LID not only exists, it is in place. Everywhere there's Shadow Technology, the LID is protecting the intelligence that it produces. Whether the information is relevant to defense, weapons, finances, transportation, whatever. The LID protects it. Where the LID is in place, the U.S. government's systems are impenetrable." She drew a deep breath. "Your hackers are good, right? "

He nodded.

"Can they break into any aspect of PRISM?"

He didn't bother to answer.

"I'll take that as a no, and the reason is because the LID is protecting it. Look. Even if I can't persuade you, in terms of finding my father, does it matter whether Shadow and LID technologies exist?"

"What do you mean?"

She walked beside him, trying to think of something that would make her points seem logical, because if he didn't believe the premise of the cataclysm scenario, there was no way he was going to go along with it. She had an ace in the hole, but she wasn't ready to play that card, because the steps of the cataclysm scenario were best delivered in small doses. He had to believe what she was saying now before she went further.

"Look at those people who were wearing foil caps on the news today. It doesn't matter whether there is technology that can read brain waves, right? They're acting like the technology exists and they're wearing the foil-lined caps to prevent it. They believe it, because my father said it. He also talked about Shadow Technology, and he talked about the LID. Someone out there believes what he said and now they want it."

He walked faster. She had to double step to match his pace. "I understand what you're saying, but I've got more important things to do than chase another rabbit trail," he said. "In case you didn't get it from the morning news, my company's experiencing turbulence. I've got quite a few partners who want to know what my plan is to get us out of this mess, and I've got to come up with a resolution, fast. I'm not going to tell them that my plan is based on believing that Shadow and LID Technologies are real, when we've had some damn good experts working on this and they've reached the conclusion that these things don't exist."

"You spend a lot on anti-encryption technology for Black Raven, both on the software and on the personnel who oversee it, don't you? Your people are good at breaking through firewalls, right?"

The house was in view now. The helicopter had landed in the

courtyard. She stepped into the courtyard with him as he said, "You know the answer to that."

One pilot remained in the cockpit. Another was walking toward them. Apparently, she was invisible, as the man didn't acknowledge her presence, but merely looked at Sebastian as he approached. "Good morning, sir. We're ready when you are."

"Five minutes."

He glanced at Skye, opened his mouth like he was going to say something, before shaking his head. He walked towards the door of the house.

She followed. "My father not only developed the LID, he created a back door to lift it."

He turned to her when he was just a few steps from the door. "But it doesn't exist-"

"Good grief, but you're stubborn. Assume that Shadow Technology exists, and the LID exists. How much would you pay for the technology? And a way to access it? Because that's what the back door does. Once you're in the LID, Shadow Technology is yours, and every piece of data in PRISM and other government collection programs is yours to manipulate as you please."

He folded his arms across his chest and stood, silent.

"What lengths would you go to assume control of that kind of technology? Not just for your company's use, but to be the sole owner of that technology. To be able to sell it," she paused, "or not? The treasure trove of government information that is being mined all day, every day, would be yours for the taking, or the selling. Better than having warehouses full of raw information, you'd get to make sense of it." She snapped her fingers. "Like that."

"Interesting," he said. "I'll give you that. But theories that are based on nonexistent premises won't find your father. I'd just as soon put on a foil-lined cap than run with this idea." He opened the door. He had his hand on the solid handle of the front door, his foot on the threshold. "I'm going to go upstairs and tell Spring goodbye."

Her heart pounded. It was time to play her ace. She had to get to Firefly Island, now, and there was no other way she was going to get there.

Please, Dad, forgive me.

She grabbed his upper arm. "Sebastian. Wait."

Chapter Eighteen

He shrugged out of her grasp as gently as he could. He liked her enough that he felt bad for her. Bad, that she was her father's daughter. Bad, that her relationship to the man had her believing the delusional crap that he spouted. He even felt bad that he was leaving her, and he didn't want to examine the reasons why that was the case, because he knew that feeling had more to do with him than her.

Feelings had nothing to do with what he had to do next. Sebastian had followed a hunch, he'd been wrong, and he'd even apologized to her. His seemingly endless desire for Skye to have helpful information wouldn't make it so. In the search for Richard Barrows, she was a dead end street, and it was now time to move on. He turned his back to her and opened the door.

Three agents in the first floor work area were at their desks. They stood when he and Skye entered. He nodded to them and quickly climbed the stairs to the living area on the second floor. Skye was at his side, taking the steps with him, as the agents who had been outside with them entered the office area. He didn't have to look at his agents to know they were watching them. He felt their eyes on him. In a matter of minutes they'd all hear about the slap and whatever parts of the conversation had been overheard. He shook off the concern. The day had bigger issues.

"Please wait," she said, her hand on his forearm as they reached the landing.

He kept moving forward, but before opening the door to the living quarters, he turned to Skye. A bright, intense look burned her eyes as her gaze flitted around the room, to the downstairs area, where the agents were looking up, at them. Turning back to him, she stepped in closer. Close enough for him to smell the fresh air on her skin, mingled with the heated scent of vanilla and spice.

Sebastian's body reacted as if he'd been hit by an aphrodisiac-filled missile.

Time to get the hell out of her orbit.

She dropped her voice to the lowest whisper. "What I have to say is for your ears only."

Her eyes were wide, focused on everything and nothing. Her breath was shallow and fast. She looked as though her thoughts had no bearing in reality, as though she was afraid of imaginary demons. Holy shit. She looked like her father, in some of the videotaped interviews that he'd watched. She looked like she was crazy. He had to get away from her. In his ear, Ragno said, "Tell her no." He didn't need Ragno feeding him the correct response.

"I can't make that kind of promise."

She placed both hands on his biceps, gripping him as though seeking balance in a room that was spinning. The pleading gesture sent shock waves through his body. "Limit those with knowledge," she said, glancing around the office, looking down the stairs, at the agents, and back at him with eyes that burned with a feverish glaze, "Make sure you know the only people who know this."

"Right now, if you speak low enough, the only people who will know will be me and Ragno."

"I can take you," she said, tiptoeing even closer to him, her body sliding along his as he bent to her. Her voice was barely a whisper, as though she was scared to say the words aloud, "I can take you to my father's backup. It is proof that Shadow and LID Technologies exist. The backup has the data for backdoor access."

"Holy mother of God," Ragno said, as his heart did a stutter beat, "did I hear that correctly?"

"Yes," he said to Ragno, his gut rejoicing that maybe his hunch for following her had been correct after all. Profound relief seeped through his pores. It wasn't a roadmap to Barrows. Hell, it wasn't even a clue as to where the man might be.

But Barrows' backup?

If it existed, and if it was what Skye said it was, securing the backup was certainly a step in the right direction, and it sure as hell explained why someone would want Richard Barrows and his daughters.

Remembering she was a habitual liar, some of his excitement faded. "Son of a bitch, Skye. Yesterday you said you didn't know anything about any backup."

She dropped her hands from his arms, and stood flat-footed, but still too close for him to have any hope of fighting his body's desire for her. "Yesterday I was afraid for our lives and didn't know who to trust."

Standing just inches from her, he looked into her upturned face, searching her expression. He had figured out that when she lied, she stared straight into his eyes with an expression that was intense, but blank. The corners of her lips didn't curl, and she almost held her breath. Now, her cheeks were flushed, but that could have been from the cold outside air and climbing the stairs. She was also breathing hard and chewing on the inside corner of her bottom lip, things that she didn't do when she lied.

Dammit.

Maybe he wanted so badly to believe her he was seeing signs that weren't there. "Why the hell should I believe you today?"

"Be nice," Ragno said softly, directly into his ear and brain. "She's giving you something. Something potentially big, if I might add. Don't squelch it by being an asshole. What's wrong with you?"

He could give her a list. He ignored Ragno. He kept his gaze locked on the twilight-zone world that was Skye, hoping she wasn't playing a game.

"And by the way," Ragno said, "you two are on camera."

Shit.

He broke eye contact with Skye. A quick glance downstairs showed several agents watching them, while others pretended to be busy. He gave them a quelling look, and they averted their attention elsewhere.

"Why are you crowding her like that?" Ragno demanded. "Or is she crowding you? You two look as though you're undressing each other with your eyes, and by your body language, it's as though this isn't the first time." She fell silent for a second. "Sebastian?"

He didn't respond to Ragno's question, but for decorum's sake he took a couple of steps back from Skye and folded his arms. Not exactly receptive body language, but hell, considering the source, he still wasn't sure how far he could trust Barrows' daughter. She made it clear she wanted to bolt. What if this information she was finally providing was just a ruse to get her away from the security of Last Resort, where she could make a break for it?

"Well? Why should I believe you're telling the truth today when you said something different yesterday?"

"I told you. Yesterday I didn't trust you."

"Now you do?"

She drew a deep breath, looking up at him. As she gave him a slow nod, he wanted to take her in his arms. He didn't, though, because if he did, he'd be confirming Ragno's guess and he'd be doing it publicly. Black Raven agents weren't supposed to cross any of the lines he'd crossed. He'd violated the rule against lusting after a client and the rule against acting on lust with a client. He knew better, because he had written the damn rules, and there were good reasons for them.

"I've got to trust you. We need help, and you'll never find my father, if you don't believe what I'm saying about Shadow and LID Technologies. If you don't accept that Shadow and LID Technologies exist, you won't understand how critical it is that we find my father. Not," she said tightly, "because he made a jail break—which, by the way, I still don't believe—but because the knowledge and information he has is of importance to national security." Skye gave him a significant look. "At the highest level."

She sure sounded as though she believed what she was saying, but she'd also been raised by a crazy genius, who bought into tin foil hats and space aliens. "Before I even entertain any of this, there's one rule," he said, "and you've got to live by it as though your next breath depends on it."

She nodded, eyes questioning.

"No more lies."

Her face became blank. She stopped chewing on her lip and her eyes widened. "I agree. No more lies."

"You just lied."

She shook her head and gave him a half smile. *Son of a bitch. She's toying with me.* The problem was, he liked mind games. Loved them, as a matter of fact. A good mind game was like a good hunt and playing this one with her would be fun, except the stakes were too high. "Where's the backup?"

"Shhhh," she said, glancing around the office. "Not so loud."

"Where is it?"

"The lake house."

"Which one? Washington or Florida?"

She gave him a headshake. "Neither. Tennessee."

"Ragno?"

"We have no properties associated with Richard or Skye in

Tennessee," Ragno answered, "or any identities or people linked to them."

Her gray green eyes were on him, studying him with a pleading look that said 'believe me.' He was surprised at how much he wanted to. "Where is the property in Tennessee? Give me the address and the name in which it is registered."

She gave him a slow headshake. "I can't tell you until you agree that you'll take me there. I need to get there myself, and it's imperative I get there immediately. If I tell you where it is, you'll send someone else."

Her desperate, urgent tone spoke volumes. "That's where you were running to, isn't it? When I showed up yesterday, you weren't just trying to run, you were running to your father's backup."

She nodded. "Yes."

His heartbeat slowed, as he started piecing together the import of what she was telling him, and his senses became sharper. Even at an arm's length, he smelled the outdoors on her. Underneath the fresh pine scent, he detected the sweet vanilla of her anxious fear. "Is your father there?"

She shook her head, her eyes wide and focused on him. "He wouldn't go there, if people were after him. He'd never willingly lead anyone to his backup."

"What prompted you to try to go there?"

She drew a deep breath. "My father sent me a signal."

"A signal?" he asked, fighting to keep his voice calm, remembering that yesterday, Ragno and Pete had suspected that one of Skye's phones was missing. A fact that Skye had, of course, denied. "He sent you a signal?"

She nodded.

"When?"

"Yesterday morning. At 5:25."

Son of a bitch. "Don't you think it would have been helpful for me to know this earlier." His voice grew louder with each word, stepping closer to her, needing to be closer to her. He wasn't going to touch her when he was so frustrated. He wasn't his father. He didn't hit women. But, goddamn it, he had the urge to shake some sense into her. He jammed his hands into the back pockets of his cargo pants instead. "Damn helpful, because we can trace phone calls or texts or-" he took a deep breath as he stood within inches of her. "Hell, yesterday you said you didn't have another phone, and I know that you didn't get a call at 5:25 am on any line we've traced to you. Are you fucking with me? What kind of signal?"

"Calm down," Ragno said, her voice low.

"Don't yell at me," Skye stood tall, not cowing to him. She strong-armed his shoulder in an attempt to push him away. When he pushed her hand off of him and moved even closer, she punched him in his right bicep, driving her knuckles exactly along the cut line. Blistering pain radiated from the cut.

He automatically embraced the sparks of pain. He had been through much worse suck-ass moments than this one, yet now he didn't bother to keep venomous sarcasm out of his voice. "That fucking feels just great. You've got to stop hitting people, because one day," he said with lethal softness, "someone's going to hit you back."

She flinched, recovered, and looked even more defiantly at him. "You're the only person I've ever hit."

Great. Fucking great.

He noticed a fear in her eyes that he knew was due to him. A flood of emotions—fury, protectiveness, and concern crashed around him. He thought about apologizing, but stopped himself. *She lies and she hits. What the hell do I have to apologize for? Saving her fucking life? Hell.* He swallowed his frustration. Whatever he had, he had it bad. He softened his voice. Slightly. "Please tell me you're not as crazy as your father. What kind of signal did he send? Extraterrestrial? Was it a red light? A warm glow?"

"Sebastian. Breathe," Ragno said, a welcome voice of reason in his ear, as Skye glared at him. "You're losing it, and this is too important. If, and this is a big if, if Shadows and LID technologies actually exist, and the NSA has implemented those programs, there's any number of entities—and individuals—that would do anything to get their hands on a way of accessing it. We need to know what she knows."

"Stop trying to intimidate me," Skye retorted. "Because you can't. You can yell, you can crowd me, you can ridicule me, and you can..." she drew a deep breath, her eyes scanning the office, and her cheeks became bright red when she took in the fact that others were watching their argument "...forget it. He sent a text. I had a burner phone. I lied when I told you that I didn't."

He drew a deep breath. "Of course you lied. Where's the

phone?"

"Smashed to pieces. Down the toilet at home in Covington."

"Ragno, send agents there. Yank the toilet, search the traps, make sure she's telling the truth about this."

"What was the phone number?"

She drew a deep breath. "I have no idea."

"You're lying again."

"I'm not," she shook her head. "I never once used the phone. It was only intended to receive that one message. My father handed it to me. There was no need for me to ever know the number."

He drew a deep breath. "Ragno? Anything we can do with this to determine call origination?"

"Not a call," Skye said, "it was a text."

"Well, we can't tell anything without either the phone or the phone number," Ragno said. "Ask her nicely to tell us what the message was. Maybe I can back into it that way, but it's doubtful. There's too much data, too many messages, and whoever we're dealing with no doubt is using encryption for their outgoing messages, just like we are."

"Skye," he said, "what exactly did his text say?"

She shook her head. "You'll never back into finding whoever has him. There's too many transmissions, and you know they're rerouting all of their outgoing messages."

He didn't need two people telling him that he wouldn't get the answer he needed. To Skye, he said, "Just answer the fuc-" he closed his eyes and drew in a deep breath to gain control of the moment. "Just answer the question. What exactly did the text say?"

"He used a code, which basically tells me to get to get to our lake house in Tennessee and to await the next signal from him, which was supposed to come in exactly 24 hours."

"Well?"

"Well what?"

"Give me the goddamn code."

"*131441413923117208152620.*" She whispered, as though she was worried someone would hear.

His head throbbed as he watched the ease with which she repeated the nonsensical numbers. "That's how your father spoke to you. In meaningless numbers. Did he add xoxo at the end?"

"Yes, to the numbers. No, to the xoxo," she said, her eyes pained. He remembered the numbers and letters throughout Spring's tablet, and realized that both girls had been victims of Barrows-style psychiatric abuse. "But the numbers aren't meaningless. Some parents teach kids foreign languages. My father did too. It's just he created the languages, and they're based upon numbers. They're not meaningless."

Jesus H. Christ. Getting information from her was like having his teeth pulled without painkillers. "So what do the numbers mean?"

She drew a deep breath. "Cataclysm. Run. Now."

His heart pounded, both out of frustration and because he felt he was hanging onto reality by the fingertips of one hand. If he kept looking at her, listening to her, he was going to lose his grasp. "And what the hell does that mean?"

"It means to get to the lake house in Tennessee and get in position for his next communication. That's it. That's all it means. That's why I need to get there," she said. "Now. I'm late. I was supposed to be there within twenty-four hours of the message, by 5:25 this morning, and I would have been there, but you showed up-"

"And saved your life-"

"And," she paused, "yes. But if you hadn't delayed me, you might not have needed to save my life."

He chuckled, glad he could find humor in lala land. "Lady, you weren't anywhere close to leaving when the kidnappers showed up."

"Sebastian," Ragno said, "don't argue with her."

"I need to get there," Skye said. "Now. Please. Can we continue this conversation on the way?"

"I haven't agreed to take you anywhere."

She folded her arms, cocked her head to the side, narrowed her eyes in a way that told him she knew he was lying, and said, "Oh, really?"

Ragno said, "Sebastian? We need to investigate this. Don't you understand how big this is?"

Of course he did. He just didn't want to admit to Skye that she'd won. *Dammit.* If he was around her much longer, he was going to be crazier than Barrows.

"I'll go and get Spring. She won't be happy when she's right in the middle of-"

"Spring stays here."

"I won't go without her."

"She's safe here, surrounded by tight security." No way was he going to take Spring with them. Spring was his ace in the hole, and a way to keep Skye honest. Big sis wouldn't bolt, if her baby sis was at Last Resort.

"Do you think I'd take her and try to make a run for it?"

"Hell, yes." When she looked at him like he had three heads, he opened the door to the private quarters and gestured with his chin for her to proceed.

"Sebastian," Ragno broke in, "she still hasn't told you where the lake house is."

"Where exactly is it?"

"I became turned around last night, but I estimate it's approximately three and a half hours of driving from here. Maybe four."

"The address, Skye. We're not driving. I need to know the nearest airstrip."

She shook her head. "Nashville International is the closest airport. There are some private airstrips, but even when we've flown privately we've used the international airport."

"The address," he said.

"No. I walk in when you walk in, and you won't know the address until we're almost there," she folded her arms, eyes serious, and stood firm in the entryway, "and nothing you do or say will make me handle this any other way."

"Is your claim that there's backup just a ploy to get there, so you can check on whether he's sent another message?"

"No," she said, after only a second's hesitation. Something in the way she shifted her eyes off of him, to the agents who were still watching, and refocused on him, was a warning signal. "There's backup there. You'll see."

He nodded and opened the door for her. As she stepped in, he paused at the threshold of the living quarters and shook off the red-flag feeling. It didn't matter. Even if she was only wanting to go there to see whether her father had sent her a signal, that was important enough, because this time, he'd get the device and track the origination. Backup for Shadows and LID Technologies, if it existed, would be an added bonus.

"Ragno. Get Zeus on the line."

Sebastian waited longer than he should have. Ragno's silence told him she was filling in Zeus on details before connecting the call, and that she had muted her connection to Sebastian. *Great. Fucking great.* "Ragno, don't talk behind my back."

"Well, I hear Skye Barrows has given you one hell of a handful to contend with," Zeus answered, his words light, but concern evident in his partner's tone. "Are you all right, in spite of the fact that Ragno is telling me that something's off with you?"

"Zeus," Ragno said, "I was speaking in confidence."

"I'm fine," Sebastian said.

"How are your headaches?" Zeus asked, his tone serious.

"Fine. Look, can you please just focus on work?"

"Sure. Barrows' backup?" Zeus said. "It's a big fucking deal. Huge."

"I'm aware," Sebastian said, "but it might all be bullshit. We'll need to run diagnostics immediately. Want to meet me in Tennessee?"

"I'm headed out to Raven Two now."

"I'll alert the pilots," Ragno said. "She'll be ready for departure when you get there."

Traveling alone, Sebastian would have been in the chopper in two minutes, and at the nearest airport in twenty. But it took Skye a while to tell Spring she was leaving. Spring had layered smooth as paper icing on about three-dozen cupcakes in preparation for decorating them. She showed Skye fresh drawings of what she planned to put on the cupcakes. Skye did a fantastic job of appearing interested, as though what Spring was showing her was the most important thing in the world, before calmly mentioning that she and Sebastian had to leave for a few hours.

As though the dog knew Spring needed reassurance, she sat at Spring's feet and leaned against her leg. The dog's ears were erect, as they both listened intently to Skye's softly spoken reassurances. Doctor Schilling also stood close by, and Skye continually drew Schilling into the conversation, as she assured Spring she'd be gone for only a few hours.

Hell. It was even hard for him to say goodbye to Spring. Unlike Skye, he didn't know whether he'd be headed back to Last Resort, when they were through in Tennessee. With Spring's big blue eyes focused on him, he pretended he'd return. *Coward.* Before he was out the door, Spring said, "Wait."

When he turned back to her, she handed him a plastic bag full of white jellybeans. He glanced at the bag and gave her a frown, as he slipped it into his jacket pocket. "Not even one red?"

She giggled. "Are you ever going to stop asking that?"

Without warning, she stepped closer, tiptoed up to his cheek, and gave him a sweet peck. "I'll save some cupcakes for you," she said. "Yours will be the best."

As Skye reached out for one last hug with Spring, he was lost in the crashing currents of his complex feelings for Skye and his protective feelings for Spring. He didn't know what he felt for Skye. Lust? Hell, yes. Curiosity? Absolutely. Frustration? More than a little. An insane desire to know her better? Yes, that too, even though he was now worried that she was nuts.

With Spring, his feelings were simpler. He wanted to ensure that for the rest of her life, she smiled that sweet smile and only had to worry about putting icing on cupcakes, or whatever other obsession had her attention for the moment. Innocence inspired his protective instincts like nothing else, and Spring's blue-eyed brand of it made him feel like building a fucking fortress for her.

In his quick jaunt on the side of insanity, he had a fucked-up flash—the fortress he was going to erect for Spring would have to include living quarters for him and Skye. It was as simple as that, because the bond between the two of them never needed to be broken. The two of them, together. Skye and Spring. They needed to be protected from the ugliness of the world, and he was suddenly, irrationally pissed at Richard Barrows for not planning better for his daughters.

As he walked out of the house, the feeling that something was wrong came at him out of nowhere. He glanced to his side, at Skye. She wore a Black Raven issue leather jacket, which he'd pulled out of a closet and handed to her before climbing down the stairs. With her dark hair spilling over the black leather, and the snug pink sweater underneath, she looked positively vampish. Problem was, there was only one sister next to him and it felt wrong. He wanted them both with him, where he could cherish and protect them.

He drew a deep breath.

Last Resort versus travelling to some unknown destination in Tennessee?

No contest. Last Resort was safer. Too much could go wrong in a transport. Still, the sisters were meant to be together, and he was separating them. He had no option. Skye wouldn't tell him where the lake house was unless he agreed to take her there, and he couldn't torture the information out of her. Black Raven could handle the task of getting Skye there safely and returning her to Last Resort unharmed, but there was no need for Spring to go as well.

He shook off his discomfort as he helped Skye board the Bell 525 helicopter, one of several that Black Raven used for training, missions, and transporting personnel and clients between Last Resort and the airstrip that was located about an hour away by car, fifteen minutes by air. A four-man detail climbed into the chopper with them.

An hour after deciding to take Skye with him to the lake house in Tennessee, he was nodding goodbye to the Black Raven helicopter pilots, who'd transported them to the airstrip. The chopper landing pad was one hundred yards from where Raven One waited. Because of the regional airport's proximity to Last Resort, Black Raven had a hangar there. The airstrip and the terminal was public, and the airport, though nowhere near as busy as Hartsfield-Jackson, Atlanta's International Airport, had enough traffic that he was on high alert. Two private jets were landing. A fuel truck and a mechanic's truck were heading to the helicopter that has just transported them. He paused, saw that the chopper pilots were watching the approaching trucks, and they didn't seem surprised. He resumed walking.

The team of agents walked in circle formation around Skye and Sebastian, their eyes in all directions. The two pilots of Raven One were at the base of the boarding ladder. "Departure in ten minutes, sir."

Chapter Nineteen

Raven One was supposed to be taking him to headquarters in Denver, where his partners who were stateside were congregating and the ones who were abroad would call in. Brandon, their corporate lawyer and his best friend, would be at the meeting for a legal assessment. Damage control was needed, because Senator McCollum, the head of the Bureau of Prisons outsourcing committee, was a major power broker in D.C. McCollum hired Black Raven for both his private oil interests and public sector contracts, which meant he was now one of their biggest clients. The senator was now majorly dissatisfied, and Sebastian had to apprise his partners of the potential for fall out. Yet instead of heading to Denver, he was sucked deeper into the world of Richard Barrows, on the search for backup that had better be where Skye said it was, looking for a message that he hoped like hell would be there. He'd participate by phone in the conference, as would Zeus.

The jet had two cabins. The forward cabin was larger, with seats set in configurations that facilitated working conferences while flying. The rear cabin was smaller, with two seats next to each other and a long couch that ran along the length of the plane. It was perfect for sleeping, or other things. He shook away the thought of those other things that he wouldn't be doing on this flight, no matter how tempting that thought might be. A door separated the two cabins. He took off the leather jacket he wore and laid it on a chair. He reached into the pocket, took out the bag of jellybeans and then guided Skye into the smaller rear cabin.

Their accompanying agents had been in the office when he and Skye had argued and they'd been on the trail when Skye had slapped him. He thought about leaving the door open, but shut it behind them.

Fuck it. Let them compare notes and talk. I have bigger problems to worry about.

He gestured to the couch as he opened the bag and took out three jellybeans. "You should try to nap."

He sat on one of the seats, stretched out his legs, and ate one coconut-flavored bean at a time. She peeled off the leather jacket, laid it on the couch, then sat next to him, her thigh sliding against his as she settled into the leather seat. *Fuck.* Of course she wasn't going to listen to him and take the couch.

"Ragno," he said, as he put the arm rest down between the two seats, "our flying time is 50 minutes. What's Zeus's ETA?"

"He'll arrive there about a half hour before you. They're ready to go in advance of your arrival."

"Skye," he said, fishing out three more jellybeans. "We need the address."

"There isn't a street address," she said.

"Of course there isn't," he said, not trying to conceal his irritation. "I've stopped expecting easy with you or your father. Just give us the exact location."

She shrugged. "I'll tell you when we land."

"If you wait until then, you'll be wasting time, because no matter when you tell me, I'm sending a team there in advance of our arrival. We need to secure the area before you step foot there. So tell me now, or tell me later." He shrugged. "Up to you."

She stared at him for a second, before saying, "Firefly Island in Hickory Lake."

He repeated what she said to Ragno. Over the sound of her fingers racing across her keyboard, she said, "I heard her."

Skye glanced at Sebastian. "We need to call the caretaker first."

"Why?"

"The island isn't accessible by car. There isn't a bridge. Our cabin and the caretaker's cottage are the only houses on the island. Jack Graham and his wife, Posie, are the caretakers. The property's in their name."

In a matter of seconds, Ragno confirmed what Skye was saying.

"Jack always comes to get us in a boat." She rattled off a phone number.

"Ragno, heard that?"

"Yes. Give me a second."

"There's no answer," Sebastian informed Skye, after Ragno tried the number.

Her eyes widened. "That can't be."

He pressed his fingertips to his temple in an effort to ease the throbbing in his head, closed the jellybean bag, and shook his head. "Would I lie about this?"

"But Jack and Posie take care of us. It's what they do. They were carefully vetted prior to hiring. They've lived on Firefly Island for ten years. They're more than employees. He's reliable, and so is she. They always answer."

"Not today," he said. "Could it be that he's just not answering a number that he doesn't recognize?"

"No. Jack answers our calls, regardless of whether he recognizes the numbers. We change phones like most people change clothes. Remember? I'm Richard Barrows' daughter," she said. Her tone was half-joking, half-desperate, and the sudden fear in her eyes made him want to hold her, to reassure her. "My father's paranoia dictates what we do. Jack knows he won't recognize the numbers that we're using. But we always call that line. Or there are two more options. Jack has three potential numbers that we use-"

"Three?" Sebastian asked.

She nodded. "There are always three. Well, not always. Mostly always. My father's compulsions, which he's passed onto Spring, either by genetics or proximity, dictate that occurrences happen in threes."

"Give me the numbers."

She gave them to him. Ragno dialed them as he repeated them. No answer. He gave Skye a headshake as her eyes searched his.

"Especially now that news has broken regarding the prison break," Skye said, "Jack would answer calls to these numbers."

"Keep trying," Sebastian said to Ragno, as the jet started taxiing. "Send Zeus in advance to reconnoiter. Secure a boat. Call on the satellite phone while we're en route if there's any news."

"Will do."

He took off the earpiece, slipped it into his pocket, and switched off the telecommunications portal on his watch. Only a few inches separated their seats. The armrest provided a laughable barrier, one that didn't block the magnetic pull she had on him. "I was thinking that you'd try to rest on the couch."

She shook her head. "I'm not tired. Besides, I can't do anything now but worry about Jack and Posie."

"Worry won't be productive. We should know something

shortly after we land," he said. He couldn't help but get personal when he saw the fear and exhaustion in her gray-green eyes. "You didn't sleep at all last night."

She gave him a slight smile, shrugging as the jet became airborne. "It wasn't my first night without sleep," she paused, "Thank you for believing me."

"Don't thank me. I'm trying desperately to find your father, and we have nothing else to go on. I believe that you're telling the truth as you know it. To be honest, though, I'm not certain that what your father's told you has any basis in reality. Shadows and LID Technology might have just been a figment of his imagination."

"For now, you'll just have to trust me. The technology exists. Even if you don't believe me, once you have the backup, once your people assess it, you'll know. It will be up to you to find out who wants it so badly, and up to me to follow my father's instructions."

"Those instructions," he said. "All you know is you were supposed to get to Tennessee and await more instructions?" He had quizzed her endlessly on the way to the airport, but that was all she gave him.

"Yes. I'll know more when I get to the lake house." Her smile was slight, with just a turn-up to the left side of her mouth and a bit of light in her eyes. It was a sad, bittersweet smile that said, *'The world's fucked up, but damn it, I'm going to be brave and find humor wherever I can.'*

Her smile was almost his undoing, because it made him hyper-focus on her, when he had told himself that all he was going to do was sit next to her and try like hell to ignore the magnetic pull she worked on him. With his eyes on that smile, studying the nuances of it, as he inhaled the fresh, vanilla-sweet scent of her natural perfume, she became impossible to resist.

Fuck me to hell.

As the jet leveled off, he shifted his legs, readjusted himself in the seat, and glanced at the bulge of his erection, visible through the Black Raven-issue khaki trousers. He glanced at her, saw that her eyes were on his hip area, and gave a hoarse laugh that was almost a groan. "Can't help that, but don't worry. After that apology I gave you, I'm certainly not going there again."

"Would you, here?" She gestured with her chin to the door between the two cabins. "With your agents on the other side of the door?"

He chuckled. "Behind a closed door? If I wasn't working, and with the right woman, the answer would be hell yes, and it wouldn't matter who was on the other side of a closed door. I've never been very selective as to time and place. Would you?"

Some of the worry left her eyes as she laughed. "I've done it behind billowing drapes, in a crowded ballroom."

Damn.

He'd known that she was his kind of woman, from the moment he'd looked at her bare-chested pose, as she readied herself for a dive. His kind of woman, he reminded himself, but not his woman. "On a full commercial plane?"

She shrugged. "That's a rookie move."

"The bathrooms are hell."

She shook her head, with a smile. It would have been demure, but for the positively wicked gleam in her eyes. "We weren't in a bathroom."

"Holy hell."

"The hardest thing about that," she paused, "well, there were plenty of difficulties. But it is really hard to have an absolutely silent orgasm. Especially if it's a good one." He started chuckling and ended it with a deep, heartfelt laugh. "You know," she continued, "I could probably win this game, because from my late teens, until about two years ago, when I chose to become celibate, I had one hell of a lot of fun in the sex department."

"Monogamy's hell," he said, studying her eyes, her lips, the tilt of her head, "isn't it?"

She nodded, her eyes serious, her expression blank, except for a slight smile that played at her lips. "Sure is. I've never been committed to it."

"Your blank face tells me you're lying."

"No. Nothing but the honest truth."

"Now I'm wondering at what point in this conversation did you start lying?"

"I haven't at all," she paused, with a gleam in her eyes that was virtually an admission she was fibbing and having fun doing it. "What about you? Monogamy. Has it ever worked for you?"

He cringed on the inside, knowing he shouldn't have ventured down this path, yet he was intrigued by the irreverence with which she approached such a private subject. "Years ago I was in a couple of committed relationships-"

"At the same time?"

"No. Over a span of years. I actually liked it, until I figured out I'm just not the committing type." He narrowed his eyes, studying her, enjoying talking to her about a subject that, like religion and politics, would be better kept private. "You've never been monogamous?"

She shook her head. "I've never been in a committed relationship, and that is the honest truth. There weren't all that many men, but the men I did it with sure did it with a bang. You probably even know their names." She gave him a slight frown, glancing again at his hips. She recaptured his eyes with a delicious, enticing smile. "You really don't want to act on that, do you?"

He shook his head. Thank God the flight was short, and they were already a few minutes into it. "Regrettably, no."

She drew a deep breath. "Wow." Her expression turned serious. "Have I turned you off with my sexual honesty?"

"Actually, it's become torture," he said, "I'm using as much willpower as I've ever had, when what I really want to do is-" he drew a deep breath, and shut the hell up. If he described what he wanted to do to her, how hard she made him, how he wanted to rip those damn jeans off of her and slide in and out of her until she moaned like she had the night before, he was going to die. *Fuck it.* If he thought for one more second about it, he wouldn't resist.

"That's too bad." Her voice was so low it was almost a hoarse whisper, her face just inches from his. "Because when I said best sex ever, I meant it. And I know what I'm talking about."

"I can't remember better," he said, shifting in the seat, groaning as he did. "But you can change the subject. Or else I have to go hang out with my agents." *After hanging out with myself in the bathroom.*

"You don't kiss on the lips," she said, her tone serious again. "When we were having sex, you avoided my kiss." He drew a deep breath, as her eyes studied his, regretting that he had stayed seated and didn't move into the front cabin. With just inches separating them, her eyelashes were thick and dark, even without mascara. A loose one had fallen on her cheek. He lifted his index finger, touched it, and flicked it off her cheek. "Why?"

Her question opened a door that he didn't want to go

through, but the light in her eyes was so captivating, he didn't want to disappoint her desire for an answer. "How honest of an answer do you want?"

"On a scale of one to ten," she said, "give me a ten. It's the least you can do, after you've had your hackers break into notes from my therapy sessions."

She had him with that truth, which he couldn't refute. "Somewhere along the way, I got it in my head that kisses, full on the mouth, French kisses, the kind that go on..." he almost groaned, suddenly wanting to glide his tongue on hers, wanting to taste her, wanting to lock lips with her and pretend, for hours, that nothing but the two of them existed, "...and on, were promises. A promise of a future, even if that promise is just another phone call, another night together, another..." his voice trailed, "...another something. I stopped making those kinds of promises years ago. Sex is sex. That's it. Women know before we have sex that there's no future."

She shook her head, giving him a wide-eyed, skeptical look.

"Really. They know. I make sure they know. I don't get caught in the predicament I got caught in with you. Having to apologize. Having to talk about it."

She was sitting in the seat sideways, her boots kicked off, her feet curled under her, settled into the conversation. Hell. She was interested in his answer, and more than slightly enjoying his discomfort. "How do they know? Because I'm betting that they don't really understand what you're saying. You see, even when a man says he can't offer a future," she paused, "there's something about the female brain. Maybe it's all of that estrogen that runs through it. We just don't get it. We think the most impossible man could somehow become..."

He chuckled. "Prince Charming?"

She blushed, then shook it off. "If not that fantastical, then just 'the one.' The one we were meant for. So how do your women know so effectively that you're not it?"

His insides did a flip. He couldn't go there with her. Open and honest was one thing. Revealing just how committed he was to having no commitments was another. "You don't want to know the answer to that question."

"Go on. Shock me. Believe me, I've heard it all from men. You know everything about me. Tell me something about you I don't know. Tell me what you tell women in advance. What gives them no doubt that there's nothing more than the moment?" She paused. "Because most men aren't quite so honest."

He didn't want to tell her. Really didn't want to tell her, and his extreme hesitancy shocked him, because it shouldn't matter to him what she thought of him. There wasn't going to be a future for them. He didn't offer a future. Couldn't offer a future. Actually, he probably didn't even have a future, not even for himself, and, right this moment his dick wasn't the only thing that was throbbing. His head was pounding, a constant reminder of his own fallibility. *Aw hell.* He drew a deep breath. "I stopped having relationships about ten years ago. There was just one too many from which I had a hard time extricating myself."

"It's called a break-up," she said, as the plane hit a bump of turbulence, "not an extrication. Geez. And my therapists said I have relationship issues?" She stared at him, thoughtfully. "So, how do you deliver the there's-no-future-not-even-a-phone-call disclaimer? And still manage to get some?"

"Well," he paused, wondering whether he was really going there. *Aw. Fuck it. Why not?* She had asked. "Here's how that happens. I agree on a price before I show up." Her eyes widened. "X amount buys me X amount of time. It's usually a lot of money," he said, "and I usually don't go to the same woman more than once. I use reputable companies. Once the money changes hands, and it always does before sex, they know it's just a business deal. You're the first real woman I've been with in ten years. By real, I mean someone I didn't pay for her services."

Open-mouthed shock had never been quite so gorgeous.

He touched her chin with his index finger and lifted it. "There you have it. Now you know the real me. I work endless hours. When I get a break, and I want sex, I call and arrange it. I fly across the country for it, or they come to me. It's all pretty damn anonymous. I learned not to go to the same woman twice, because even then, you run the risk of emotional attachment."

"That's," she drew a deep breath, and when he thought she was going to say disgusting, because that word would have matched the look she was giving him, he put her index finger on her lips, and shook his head, not wanting to hear her answer.

"Shhhh. I know." *Sick. Sad. Disgusting. Pathetic.* He didn't need her to put a label on it and that's why he touched her lips. His action shushed her, but it did way more than that. The feel of her soft, plush lower lip sent an electric shock through him. Her lips were full and slightly moist and felt like a balm on the rough callous of his trigger finger. He skimmed the full crescent of her lower lip, unable to stop until he ran his finger along the full length of it, then doing the same with the top lip.

Holy hell. He dropped his hand, realizing how badly he had fucked-up, because if ever he was going to kiss a woman again, it now had to be Skye.

From the shocked stillness that greeted him and the uncharacteristic lack of a smart retort, he realized that if the opportunity had existed for anything between them, it was gone. Her probing questions had given her way too much information. Now she was probably more worried about disease than anything else.

Hell.

He would be. He unsnapped his seat belt, stood, and stretched the kinks out of his back. He reached for the door handle as the plane started its descent. He looked down at her before opening it. "Don't worry. I know we didn't last night, but I use condoms. I knew you were on the pill. That's why I didn't use one with you. In the last several months I've had more medical tests than I thought were possible. I haven't had sex since the accident in July. I didn't want it, until I met you. I'm clean." He stepped into the other compartment, shutting the door behind him.

Did their night together produce sentimental feelings for him? He no longer needed to worry about that. Mission accomplished.

Chapter Twenty

His revelation had shocked her into silent numbness. She shouldn't have asked such personal questions. A decade of going to prostitutes to avoid emotional attachments was an admission that was better left in the world of unspoken words. At least now she knew exactly where Sebastian stood with women.

The soft touch of the wheels on the runway made her shudder, reminding her that she had enough to worry about without thinking about Sebastian's personal life. If Ragno had managed to get in touch with Jack and Posie, she'd have called Sebastian on the sat phone. Silence on their end was not a good sign.

Dear God. Please help me figure this out. Find my father and Jen, and let Jack and Posie be safe. End this before I actually hand over my father's backup to Sebastian. End this before I have to tell Sebastian where we need to go with the backup.

The same uncertainty that prompted her prayer provoked an intense longing for her beautiful bakery. She wanted to be Chloe Stewart again, where no one knew her true identity, where Spring was safe and happy, where the weight of being Richard Barrows' daughter wasn't suffocating her, where she was ignoring men and the complications they brought into her world. She wanted all of that, and this time, she wanted it all to be permanent.

When the jet taxied to a stop near other private jets, she stood and opened the door to the forward cabin. Her eyes fell on Sebastian. Clearly not in a rush to get off the jet, he was sitting in a seat that faced the rear of the plane, facing one of his agents. His long legs were stretched in front of him, and, as usual he was talking, with one finger touching gently on his earpiece, while his hand rested on his iPad's keyboard.

"Aren't we leaving?" she asked from the doorway.

He glanced at her and gave her a headshake. "We're waiting for word from the advance team before we go."

"Did anyone manage to contact Jack or Posie?"

He gave her a slow, barely perceptible headshake no, before his eyes drifted back to his tablet. The other agents were also talking on their phones or studying their iPads. One of the pilots opened the door to the cockpit, but they remained in their seats, checking their instrument panels. The agents, Sebastian included, wore either long-sleeve t-shirts or turtle neck sweaters, all with Black Raven logos. From the five men, Skye figured that broad chests, bulging biceps, and narrow waists appeared to be as much of a Black Raven prerequisite as a pistol, which they all wore at their hips like extensions of themselves.

She yanked her hair back in the ponytail holder that she'd put on her wrist earlier, saw that Sebastian's eyes were on her movements, and her chest, as he talked to one of his agents. She wanted a t-shirt. A plain t-shirt. Something cool, cottony, and boxy. Not a pink, form-hugging sweater that barely reached the top of equally snug jeans.

"There are power bars and snacks," Sebastian said, gesturing with his head in the direction of the plane's galley. "You should eat something."

As she shrugged off the advice, he frowned. Although she hadn't eaten since Sunday night, she couldn't. Not now. Not until she figured out what to do next.

"At least have a soda."

The idea of a sugary drink made her stomach twist. His frown deepened when she made no move towards the galley, but instead of saying anything, his eyes drifted back to his iPad.

Waiting one more minute was going to kill her. She walked up the aisle to where he was sitting, folded her arms, and stared at him until he gave her his full attention. "I'm ready to go. I need to get to Firefly Island." She stamped her foot on the soft carpet. "Now."

"Not yet," he said, looking up at her, his blue eyes stern and unflinching, "the advance team will be there in a few minutes, and we're not leaving here until they give us an all clear."

"But I told you from the beginning. I need to get there and I need to do it now. I can't wait. Otherwise, I wouldn't have given you the location."

He glanced into her eyes and gave her a slow headshake.

"We're not going until we get the all clear. What are you not understanding about that?"

"And I can't wait. What are you not understanding about that? I've got to get there, and I've got to do it now." She gasped as she looked into his unreadable eyes. "You tricked me into talking, while you had no intention of taking me there-"

"No trick. Not at all." Sebastian interrupted with lethal curtness, sounding like a man whose internal powder keg had exploded. "For once in this oddball, paranoia-fueled world your father is now dragging all of us through, can you stop second-guessing me? The only reason why you're not going there right this second is because it's too dangerous. Do you have a death wish? Please. Just. Stop. Second-guessing me. Right. Fucking. Now."

Skye flinched, as absolute stillness filled the jet.

The pilots had turned and were looking at the two of them. She could feel the eyes of the agents burning into her. Sebastian's tone, the words, the depth of his irritation, when he was normally so cool and controlled, broadcast to all who were present and listening that there was something going on between the two of them that wasn't about finding her father, and it had nothing to do with protecting her.

The news coverage that she'd seen earlier in the morning had hailed him as a man who had built a company out of thin air into a leading, world-wide private security contracting force. She guessed that such unprofessional outbursts were rare for him. Like he'd said earlier, she got to him, and not in ways that were all good.

The shocked silence of the others that met his outburst confirmed what Sebastian said earlier, that he had crossed a line with her that was taboo within the company. As the silence became prolonged, the agents and pilots, thank God, started focusing on other tasks. One cleared his throat. Another coughed. Sebastian wouldn't look at her. He stood, turned his back to her, and walked to the galley. In a low voice, presumably to Ragno, Skye heard him say, "I'm fine." After a few seconds, he said, "Don't worry. I can handle this."

What Ragno and the other agents didn't know was that whatever happened between them amounted to nothing, because that was all Sebastian was capable of delivering. Sebastian had been right about her. Deep down, somewhere about twenty feet below the fibs she delivered to men, when she assured them all she wanted was casual sex, she wanted more than casual dalliances. Whether she'd ever break out of the cycle of setting herself up for disappointment was an open question. In contrast, he was a lost cause, because he'd long ago given up on wanting anything more. Why she even cared, she had no idea.

Dear God. I'm going crazy.

Twenty minutes passed, as the agents and Sebastian worked and she fidgeted. She sat, she stood, and she paced the aisle. The jet was spacious, but not large enough to accommodate her restlessness. She sipped sparkling water and tried to eat a power bar, but almost choked on the tasteless fake chocolate and peanuts.

They should have news by now.

"Say that again." Sebastian had been sitting. He stood. The other agents were all suddenly still and, for once, quiet. "Ragno, drop the other calls, but open your lines to my team. We all need to hear Zeus." Now, his tone was abrupt and deadly serious, and, when she looked at him from her vantage point in the galley, near the cockpit, his eyes were on her. He cupped his ear with his left hand. "Zeus. Go."

Sebastian pressed his lips together. His team tensed as they listened to words that she couldn't hear, through their own earphones. The news wasn't good. She knew it, even before he said anything. After long minutes, his eyes rested on her.

"Skye."

She stood still, folded her arms, and braced herself. His eyes were sympathetic, the set of his jaw solid and grim. "I need you to sit down."

Her heart pounded. *Oh God. Now what?* "What's going on?" He walked down the aisle to her, gently took her by the forearm, and sat her in the seat that he'd been using. He sat directly across from her, in a seat that faced her.

"Just tell me."

He sat on the very edge of his seat so that his knees were on either side of hers and leaned forward, getting closer to her, as he said, "Your caretakers have been killed."

She shook her head, for the moment incapable of believing the truth of what he was saying. "No. No one knows that they're associated with us. No one. Even you didn't know."

He nodded. "We're guessing it happened in the last twelve hours. We'll know more soon. Either whomever did this found the place on their own," he paused, "or your father told them about it."

"He wouldn't, unless he was pushed to the breaking point, and that wouldn't have come unless he believed Spring and I were in trouble. Or Jen. They must be using Jen against him."

He frowned, not verbalizing his thoughts. His hands rested on her knees, as his somber seriousness told her he agreed with her assessment.

"Or he's trying to give them what he wants. He's giving them the backup, so they stop pursuing Spring and me. Otherwise, he wouldn't have sent them there. As far as he knew, Spring and I were going there. That's where his message from yesterday morning was going to send us. Don't you see, if he," she drew a deep breath, and another, barely able to exhale, or pull fresh air into her lungs, "if he told them about the lake house, he was potentially leading them, whoever they are, to us. He gave them what they wanted to try to get them to stop hunting us. Do you know how desperate he must have been to do that?"

"We don't know how they found the lake house. We just know they did. Where is the backup and the device on which you were to receive a message? Zeus will secure the items, if they're still there."

"What do you mean, if they're still there?"

"The place has been ransacked."

"I've got to go there. I've got to check."

He reached for her hands and gripped them, calming her and keeping her still. He seemed to have abandoned the notion that he should keep a professional distance from her, as he pulled her closer, tightening his legs on hers and bending his head to her. They were both on the edge of their seats now, as close as they could be without her being on his lap. She reveled in his closeness, finding strength in his warmth, as he looked at her with a look of sympathy that told her he recognized her anguish. "I can't let you go there."

"I've got to see them – the house."

Frustration and sympathy in his eyes combined into the intense look of someone who desperately wanted things to be different. "Listen to me. Their deaths were just as horrific as the deaths at the safe house. I don't want you to see it. You will never be able to get it out of your mind. Please," he said, drawing a deep breath, running his fingers across her forehead, pushing back hair that had fallen out of her hastily assembled ponytail. "Please trust me on this. There was an arsenal there that your caretakers didn't get to use. Just like my men at the safe house and the marshals, your caretakers didn't stand a chance. "

His closeness felt right. As he gripped her hands, she realized that she needed his comfort. "I can handle it. I've got to go there."

He shook his head. "I can't sanitize it for you. I can't cleanse the site until the marshals get there. Can you just, for once, take my word on something, without pressing for details?"

No. No she couldn't. He should know that about her by now. "Tell me what happened to them."

He drew a deep breath, as though weighing how much to tell her. "She was hung from a tree, cut repeatedly, and he was tied to the trunk. He was forced to watch whatever those cock-sucking sons of bitches did to her."

The jet seemed to lurch forward, then sideways. She glanced out the window. No. It wasn't moving at all. She was spinning, though, like a child's top. Round and round and round. She closed her eyes for a second, trying to stop the sickening motion.

"Skye. Come on, honey." He bent closer to her, now kneeling in the aisle, at her side, holding her close against him, whispering, "Stay with me. I need your help, okay? I know you've been through hell, but I'll figure a way out of this. For you, for Spring, for your father."

She nodded, leaned into him, breathing deeply as he closed his arms around her. He smelled like the outdoors, of forests, of musky, powerful male. She opened her eyes, and saw worry and yearning in his eyes. In his arms, she knew that as long as he held her, she had a chance at succeeding. She didn't know how it would happen, but with the kind of certainty that came from being a female who had never felt complete until he held her, she knew she had to trust him. Completely.

"You're the only person who can put a stop to this, you know that, right?" he said, his voice a low, raspy whisper. "Help us shut these people down and find your father."

She gave a small nod.

"That's it," he said, still holding her close. "As much as I hate to do it, we have to at least let the marshals know how far we've gotten with this lead. Unless you want us to broadcast the real reason we were going there, we need to get your father's backup off the island, and we need to do it now."

Whatever emotion had been in his voice disappeared. In its place was the matter-of-fact certainty that came from a man who was confident that every thought he had was the right one. "Please cooperate. If your father's backup is there, if he left a message for you, I don't want the marshals to know this at the same time we do. So far, Zeus and his team have found three safes, and two lockboxes." He paused, pressed his hand against his ear, but kept the other arm around her back. "And a hidden room behind the bar in the living room. In which there are three more wall safes. All were open when Zeus and his team arrived," he paused, listening, but his eyes were on hers. "Contents are gone from all of them. Hell. The place is huge." There was another pause as he listened. "Tell me where Zeus needs to look. Tell me where you'd have looked, if we had taken you there." He paused. "And please, no games. Tell me. Honestly."

She drew a deep breath. "There are two places. One with a burner phone, one with the backup. For the phone, second floor, bedroom with the queen-size bed. There's a hideaway space, under the third floorboard from the wall, back north corner. He'll have to move the bed."

He repeated the instructions to Zeus. "For the backup?"

She shook her head. "It isn't in the main house. It's in the caretaker's cottage. Second cabinet to the right of the refrigerator. The back of the cabinet comes out, if he puts pressure at the very top. It's a false back. There's a metal box."

Sebastian repeated Skye's instructions. As he waited for information from Zeus and the advance team, his attention focused on her. He smoothed her hair, and said, "You okay?"

She nodded. The feeling that the world was spinning had passed. In its place, were numb misery and trepidation, as she waited for news from Zeus.

He looked doubtful as he studied her. "You sure?"

She nodded, realizing that the four agents were waiting, just as tense as Sebastian was, for word from Zeus's team. Their eyes were focused on Sebastian and Skye.

After a few more seconds, Sebastian tensed, at the same time one of his agents mumbled, "Damn."

Sharp blue eyes focused on her. "Whatever was there, isn't. Both locations are empty."

He stood, as she put her forehead down into the palms of her hands, not wanting to look Sebastian—or anyone else—in the eye, as her father's world crashed around her. After long minutes, she looked up. Five pairs of eyes were on her, but she focused only on the cobalt-blue pair of the man who was standing next to her. "I need to get to Charlotte, North Carolina."

Sebastian drew a deep breath. "What's in Charlotte?"

"Another set of backup. The next burner phone, where my father would let me know if the cataclysm scenario is still in play. There are two safety deposit boxes, in two branches of the First American Bank. One is a downtown branch, another is about ten minutes away. I need to get there. Now." She drew a deep breath and stood. She gripped his biceps, holding on to him, needing his solid strength. "Please. Take me there now. We can't wait. The second one was timed for twenty-four hours. But the third one could come at any second. Hurry. We have to go now!"

He reached for her hands. "Listen to me. Breathe," he said, his voice velvety, smooth, and calm. His tone was so commanding, so controlled, she had no option but to focus on him and watch him draw a deep breath, as though willing her to do the same.

She took a deep breath, even though her world was falling apart.

"Chances are whoever has gotten to the lake house, has also gotten to Charlotte."

Calmness crashed around her, like glass shattering. Even though what he said made infinite sense, she shook her head as panic seized her. "It can't be."

"I can send agents there faster than we can get there," he paused, his voice steady. "Just tell me whether we'll be able to access the boxes and how."

"There's code, formulated off of passwords."

"You don't have to be there in person for access?"

"No. My father set these up so that he could direct others to access it." She paused. "In case of an emergency, and he or I couldn't get there."

"The access codes," he arched an eyebrow. "This is information that only your father would have given them, right?"

She nodded. "Or me."

"And you haven't given the information to anyone else, correct?"

"No."

He frowned. "Would Jennifer Root have known the codes?"

She shook her head. "No."

"Ragno. Charlotte, North Carolina. Where are our nearest agents?" He paused. "Check their status." He waited for her answer. As the minutes ticked by, his eyes never left hers. "I can have agents there in under an hour, which is faster than we can mobilize and get there ourselves."

She started to say no, but reduced the word to just a headshake.

He gripped her hands tighter, but his voice remained calm. "Look, even if I agreed to take you there, we won't have an answer for at least two hours. We have to get mobilized here, the pilots have to file a fight plan, we have to get in the air, we have to land there, we have to have secure transportation, and we have to get to the two destinations, which have to be secure before we get you there. Even with all of that effort, it's likely a futile endeavor, with unknown risks. If you give me the codes my agents need, we'll have an answer in half the time, without putting you at risk."

What he said made sense. But still, she hesitated.

"Skye? I know that this is a lot for you to trust me with," he said, "but we have no option."

She nodded yes, appreciating that he used 'we' and not 'you.'

"Ragno. It's a go. Alert the agents to mobilize," he said. "Skye, give me the codes."

"I need paper. Spring can do this kind of stuff from memory," she said, "but I need prompts."

Sebastian glanced away from her, to an agent who passed them a tablet and pen. She sat and he sat across from her, resuming his position on the edge of his chair, his knees on either side of hers. Her hand shook as she wrote down the alphabet, assigned numbers to letters, then wrote three words that her father had assigned to the Charlotte bank box. She translated those words to numbers, did mathematical equations, and came up with three sets of thirty numbers. She ripped that piece of the paper from the tablet, and handed it to Sebastian. "This is for the downtown branch. Where the phone is."

She started over, formulating another code. When she had three additional sets of thirty numbers, she handed it to Sebastian. "This is for the branch where the backup is."

As he rattled off the numbers to Ragno, he held out his hand for the other half of the paper. He took it just as she was relinquishing it. He studied it, arched an eyebrow, and shook his head.

She shrugged. "That's how my father communicated with us, with the world. Everything is a puzzle to him. Even his words."

"And he set this craziness in play, counting on you to be able to drive from Louisiana to Tennessee to North Carolina," irritation evident in his voice, but also an underlying sympathetic tone, "with God knows who after you, all the while keeping yourself and Spring safe?"

"He doesn't always think through the practical ramifications of his plans," she said, automatically defending her father, but unable to come up with more than a half-hearted attempt.

He handed the piece of paper back to her. "What's his end game?"

"What do you mean?" She knew exactly what he meant, but needed to buy time. She needed to collect her thoughts before laying that bomb on him.

"His end objective. What exactly is it that your father wants you to do?" He was leaning towards her, his manner calm, his voice determined. "He sent you a signal yesterday morning, which had you running to the lake house. He was going to send you another signal at the lake house. Because the phone on which he was going to send the signal is gone, we have no idea what message was left, or what instructions you were to follow. Or, frankly, if he was capable of sending anything at all. With what I've learned about your father, he's a man who leaves nothing to chance. In the event that one or more of these messages was lost, stolen, or you couldn't make it to the location in time—what were your instructions?"

She drew a deep breath. Even after telling Sebastian about the backup data at the lake house and in Charlotte, she hadn't considered how she was going to tell him the rest of the story. Now, he was going to know the depth of her father's paranoia, and he was going to think she was crazy for going along with it, but she had no choice but to tell him. "In Tennessee," she paused, "the signal could have been that the cataclysm scenario was over. If that had been the case, Spring and I would have just gone home, to Covington. To our bakery," her eyes welled with tears, "to our life." She drew a deep breath, saw sympathy in his eyes, almost started crying in earnest, and shook her head.

"Please don't look at me like that. I'd prefer for you just to be a hard ass."

He chuckled. One of the other agents in the room did as well, and her cheeks burned with embarrassment. She'd forgotten anyone else was there but Sebastian. She looked around the jet and realized that the four agents were riveted, their eyes on the two of them, as though they were the best show at the circus.

"Well," Sebastian said, anchoring her with his calm manner, his words commanding her attention, "we know that if he was able to send a message to Tennessee, he wasn't going to say that it was over. Cataclysm has to be tied to the prison break, and we don't have him. So it isn't over."

"Another option is that he could have told me to secure the backup and wait."

"Is the backup we're looking for in Charlotte a duplicate of what was in the lake house?"

She nodded.

"So if he had told you to secure the backup, you, Candy, and Spring, were going to have to get to Charlotte?"

She nodded. "Even if he didn't tell me to secure the backup, I was going to have to go to Charlotte, if the cataclysm scenario remained in play."

"Why?"

"To await his next message."

"Then what?"

She drew a deep breath, trying to escape his razor sharp attention. She shook her head, careful not to let her panic reflect in her face. It was time to tell him the ending. *Oh dear God, help me.* "What do you mean?"

"If you would have gotten to Charlotte, and the cataclysm scenario was still in play, what were you supposed to do?"

The only sounds that registered were her heartbeat and his breathing.

When she looked down, he used his index finger to lift her chin.

"Skye? Stay with me. I need to know this," he paused and gave her a slight headshake. "We need to know this. Ragno and Zeus are listening, and they're hanging on every word that you say."

For a second she felt foolish, suddenly aware that his leaning into her was so that the people to whom he was tethered through the mic could hear, and not about any feelings for her. But in that moment, he tightened his grip on her hands, bending towards her ear, and said, "You're doing great." His lips grazed her ear as he whispered, his tone reassuring, "Thank you."

She drew a deep breath. The huskiness in his voice had nothing to do with what she was saying, or the questions he was asking. The look in his eyes, that encouraging look that was at once soft and very, very hungry, had nothing to do with cataclysm, Shadows, or the LID. It had everything to do with how he reacted to her, that inexplicable thing that led him over a line that he had never before crossed. She knew it, even if he didn't.

And even if he was only manipulating her, she had no choice. She still had to fulfill her father's directive, and without Sebastian, she had no hope of doing it. "If the cataclysm scenario is still in play, I'm supposed to alert the authorities that the data collected by the United States is insecure, and I'm supposed to do that by going to the top of the intelligence hierarchy. If someone breaks through the LID, they have Shadow Technology, and they have access to all the data that the government has collected. Everything in PRISM, everything in any mass data collection program, because Shadow Technology integrates and assimilates the programs and data."

Sebastian nodded. "So your father claimed."

"With my father's backup for LID Technology, you'll have no doubt that Shadow Technology exists. You'll be in the system. Manipulating it. You'll not only have access to all the data the government is collecting, you'll be able to implement anything you want Shadow Technology to do. So if cataclysm is still in play, I'm supposed to bring the authorities the backup data, which contains the codes for closing the back door access."

He pressed his finger to his ear. "Ragno. Zeus. Slow down. Ask one question at a time."

He studied Skye as he listened. "The backup. Is it complete?"

Please, Dad, forgive me.

She shook her head. "There are dead ends built into it. There are prompts that require input. Passwords. I can figure my way around most of it."

He narrowed his eyes. "What kind of input?"

"Some words. Mostly numbers. It's complicated and formulated through a system of words and the words lead to prime numbers. Code-cracking programs won't provide the answers, even sophisticated programs that can make trillions of guesses per minute. The words that lead to the numbers are prompted by colors and the names of the colors make no sense in the real world."

Sebastian's eyes widened as he stared at her. Surprise turned to a hard, assessing look, as though he knew what she wasn't saying. She was giving him an answer without saying the actual words. She wasn't the sister with the phenomenal memory for meaningless words to describe colors and correlating streams of numbers.

He knew everything about her and Spring, and he should know that as well. Each dead end was actually a color. Her father used colors as markers for code, and he did that by translating colors to words to numbers. Those numbers formed the codes. It was too random for anyone with a normal memory to memorize, and her father never reduced it to writing. There was no way she was going to tell Sebastian those details while he wore a mic, with others listening to every word. There were limits to her trust.

He was a smart man. After a long silence, he nodded.

That secret, the one neither of them voiced, had to be protected at all costs.

Ragno and Zeus knew enough. They didn't need to know the rest. She held her breath, praying Sebastian wouldn't verbalize what he had just figured out – that Spring was part of the key to the incomplete data set in her father's backup.

He turned, looked at the other agents, and said, "Alert the pilot. We're headed back to Last Resort. I'm not sure where this road is taking us, but I want the sisters together. Zeus, you and your team have Firefly Island?" He paused. "Good. Give the marshals minimal information. Not the whole picture. Just enough so that later we can claim we didn't knowingly obfuscate the truth."

"Your father does things in threes." Sebastian shot her a questioning glance. "Is there a third set of backup?"

"Zachary Young had a version of it, but his was an earlier version. My father was never able to figure out what Zachary did with it, or whether he did anything at all. When Zachary and his family were killed, my father assumed that someone had the backup. The problem isn't that someone has the backup. You see," she paused, "the problem is that someone is making sense of it. That's what set the cataclysm scenario in play."

"Assuming your father's cataclysm scenario is still in play, who exactly are you supposed to take this information to? The National Security Agency? CIA? FBI?"

She hesitated, not ready to voice the answer.

"Well? The end game. I need to know your father's end game."

Oh, dear God. Help me. "I'm supposed to get to Washington. Straight to the President."

She waited for disbelief. She waited for him to lose his cool. It was outlandish, she knew, but in her father's world, it all made perfect sense. The leap of faith into that world, though, was going to be a big one for this man who was so grounded in reality.

Instead of disbelief, he gave her a quizzical look, and asked, "Of?"

"What do you mean, *of?*"

"The President of what?"

"Of the United States."

Chapter Twenty One

The President of the United States?

Of course.

All great conspiracy theories ended in the Oval Office.

Why should this one—born of one of the more brilliant minds of the century— be any different?

Skye had cringed as she said it, and he didn't blame her. Her pronouncement prompted his brain to flood with more smartass comments than he could voice and an equal number of questions. All of which coalesced into silence, as he had backed away from her, because he couldn't think of a goddamn thing to say. A long minute passed, when he and his agents did nothing but stare at her. She stood, glanced at him with a look of despair, and walked to the back of the jet, taking the same seat in the rear cabin she'd occupied on the way there.

He glanced at the pilots. "Let's return to Last Resort."

One of them nodded. "We're on the leading edge of a cold front. Gusty winds. There might be a bit of a weather delay."

Sebastian stayed in the front of the plane with his agents, none of whom were saying a thing. Like children who were waiting for a parent to explode, they were eyeing him, waiting for his reaction to Skye's pronouncement that she was supposed to go to the Oval Office.

Sinking heavily into a seat, he stretched his legs into the aisle. He reached into a jacket pocket, opened a pill bottle, and took a pill that seemed to affect him more mildly than some of his others. He needed to take the edge off the headache. Popular thought in the Black Raven ranks was that there wasn't enough blood in a man's body to fuel both his dick and his brain at the same time. On him, at the moment, his head was pounding, and his balls were aching, because encouraging Skye to speak, leaning into her, holding her, and comforting her, had prompted another bout of unsatisfied arousal, and his body was rebelling. The dual areas of throbbing pain proved that while his dick and brain might not function effectively at the same time, the two certainly could hurt simultaneously.

Zeus and Ragno had heard every word and so far their radio silence was deafening. "Zeus?"

"I'm here. Not sure where we should go with this," Zeus said. "Give me a few minutes to think."

"Sebastian," Ragno said, breaking one of the longest pauses he'd ever heard from her, "did she really say that her father's instructions are for her to go to the President of the United States?"

"You heard it as I did."

"How the hell was she planning to accomplish that? Was she going to stroll across the White House lawn and just walk through an open door? Current events aside, does she really think that's how one gets in?"

If he felt that he was getting closer to finding Richard Barrows, he'd have chuckled at the thought of Skye, Spring, and the dog going through the gates of Pennsylvania Avenue. But he didn't have the reassuring feeling that came with getting close to his prey. In fact, now that Skye had finally spilled her guts, all he could do was wonder what the hell to do with the information. "I have no idea."

"We could have access, if we need it," Ragno said.

"I know," he said. "But that would require us to play some mighty big cards, and we don't call in those cards unless we're certain of what we're asking for, and equally certain of the results we're going to get."

"In this situation it certainly wouldn't be advisable," Ragno said.

"No joke," he said, watching as the pilot shut the door to the cockpit.

"I know. I'm just thinking aloud. Sorry, Sebastian," Ragno said, "she got me with that one. Let me backup a minute. According to what she's saying, the backup that was on Firefly Island provides access to Shadow and LID Technologies, and the person who has access will be able to manipulate the data collection capabilities of the U.S. government."

Sebastian glanced back to where Skye was sitting. The door that separated the compartments was open. His breath caught in his throat, when he got an eyeful of her. Skye had pulled her feet up on the seat and put her head down on her knees, hugging her legs to her chest. He ignored the tweak to his heart that her posture inspired.

Dammit.

He had to think about the implications of what she'd just told him. Not about her. If she was listening to his side of the conversation, she gave no indication. Just in case, he faced forward and dropped his voice to a whisper. "So can't the government just shut it off? If Shadow Technology is actually running, and that's a really big if, can't they just shut it down?"

"The programs are complex," Ragno said, "it could take time. Skye is saying she has to alert the authorities to a breach. It seems that what she's saying is that if someone has the code to the LID, their breach will be invisible. We now know that countries like China and other sophisticated hackers," she paused, "like us, can get in and out without being detected. What Skye is telling us is that she needs to alert the President of the potential for a breach, and hand him the backup so he can stop it."

"Let's assume that someone gets in. What's the damage?"

"Say China is behind this. If Shadow Technology does what Barrows says it does, China has now won the technological information war. Better than that, they now have the most intelligent data collection capabilities in the world. The U.S. government may be collecting everything, all the time, but all we'd be doing is handing it to China. The U.S. would have to regroup. It won't force us back to the age before the Internet, but this technology breach could force us back into the nineties."

She paused. "Back when we were just collecting data, without an effective method of assimilating it. Remember? The clues to the September 11 attacks were all there. Richard Barrows is absolutely correct on that. The U.S. just wasn't assimilating the clues," she drew a deep breath, "which proves that endless information is not helpful knowledge. We don't want other governments, or individuals, to have the tools that we use to turn information into knowledge."

"But you still think Shadow Technology and LID Technology do not exist, correct?" He silently debated which pain—headache or balls—was worse. The headache won. Tendrils of pain were shooting from his temple and forming an ice pick jab through his brain. He tried not to focus on the headache, thinking, instead, about the myriad of reasons why the jet might not be moving.

"Well, if I listen to the governmental officials we've managed to talk to since Richard Barrows escaped," she said, "I'd have to say that the technologies don't exist."

"So Barrows has Skye planning on going to the White House, telling the President that there's been a security breach on programs that might not even exist."

"That about sums it up," Ragno said, "and without the backup, this could all be one great big show on the part of Barrows. To prove his point that the government was collecting data without proper safeguards in place."

"Unless the backup is in Charlotte." Some of the throbbing in his head eased, but not because he really had any hope that the backup was in Charlotte. Thank God for drugs. Life was better with chemistry. "We'd at least know if these technologies exist."

"I'm not very hopeful we'll find the backup," she answered.

"I'm betting no, and there's no way I'm assuming that the backup—which we don't have and likely won't have—is what Richard Barrows led his daughter to believe that it was."

"Well, I'm not so sure I'd agree with you on that."

Cool. Calm. Unflappable. Ragno was all of that. Her simple statement stopped his runaway disbelief in its tracks. "Why?"

"Because he didn't lie."

"He believed in extraterrestrial life, for God's sake."

"Well, have you proven that it doesn't exist?"

"Ragno, please don't tell me you're buying the man's bullshit. You just said the technologies don't exist-"

"No. I said the government officials say that it doesn't exist-"

"But-"

"Calm down, big man. I'm just saying that I don't see a basis for believing that he'd lie about this. He was too passionate about it."

"Well," he paused, remembering what Skye had said about the legions of people who wore foil-lined caps, "someone believes the man, because they've gone to great lengths to secure his backup." He paused. "Say we buy into it all. We believe all of it. We go trucking up to the White House and tell the President our story. Does it help us find Richard Barrows?"

"Perhaps."

"How?"

"Because if Shadow and LID Technologies exist, and we know they're being breached," Ragno said, "meaning we believe

Skye, and she is correct, and the President orders the NSA to let us have access, we can find the breach, and try like hell to diagnose who is doing it."

Zeus said, "By the way, I'm agreeing with Ragno so far."

Sebastian groaned. "This just got fucking worse. Are you two listening to yourselves? I'd rather tell the President that spacemen are coming. Imagine what will happen if the systems don't exist."

"We will forever be the butt of jokes," Ragno said.

"Bad ones," Zeus added. "And we won't be anywhere close to finding Richard Barrows. Marshals are here, and Minero is calling me. I'm out for now."

"But if Shadows and LID Technologies exist," Ragno added after Zeus broke the phone connection, her tone once again calm. "It is likely you will not only find Barrows; you'll prevent one of the greatest technological security breaches of all time. You'll be saving the world."

"Fuck saving the world," Sebastian muttered. "I just need to find Richard Barrows and throw his ass back in jail."

He glanced at his watch. Almost thirty minutes had elapsed since he'd activated the agents in Charlotte. They'd know the answer to whether the backup was there soon. He glanced back, taking in the skeptical expressions of his agents who were still open mic'd to him and Ragno.

As the jet started taxiing to the runway, on the intercom the pilot said, "We have clearance to move to the queue for takeoff, but if we don't get in the air in the next five minutes, we'll have a brief weather delay. Whenever we get up, it's going to get bumpy. Make sure your seatbelts are on."

He looked behind him, past the questioning glances of his agents, to Skye. When his eyes rested on her, his heart sank. Smart ass comments and questioning arguments he was used to. Bravado when she had no right to have it? Hell yes, he admired that. Lying? Not a problem for him, especially when she broadcasted the fact. It was more amusing than irritating. The fact that she hit him? Also not a problem. He loved that she expressed her frustration with physical jabs, punches, and slaps. Each time she laid her hands on him, any way that she did, his body responded with full throttle yearning. Even absolute faith in her father's crazy beliefs, he could handle, because a woman with that much faith in another person was rare.

So much about her was absolutely irresistible that her beaten-up posture as she sat in the oversized seat, head down on her knees, hit him like a gut punch. His woman didn't need to look like the world had just beaten her up. No. He wasn't going to let that spirit be crushed. Not without whatever moral support he could give her. "Ragno, I'm signing off for a while."

"Wait. This just in. Our agents have found Biondo's body. We're alerting Marshal Minero now. Our field observations put time of death three days ago. Before the murder of his victim. You were correct last night, when you tried to tell Minero that the timing was odd. Someone else was using Biondo's murder of his victim as a diversionary tactic to split the manpower."

"Any clues as to who may have murdered the man?"

"None whatsoever."

Fuck.

He found no enjoyment in being right on this one. "Ragno, when you talk to Minero, refrain from saying I told you so, okay?"

"Will do."

He clicked the watch's phone capabilities to off and unsnapped his seat belt. Moving to the back of the plane, he shut the door that separated the cabins, and sat in the seat next to hers.

"Hey."

She didn't lift her head. "Please don't say that you think I'm crazy."

He chuckled as he buckled up. "I wasn't going to say that. I think your father is crazy. You? I still have no idea what to think of you."

Her ponytail was loose, and on his side of her shoulders. He reached for some wayward tendrils, and smoothed them back. As he dropped his hand from her head, he placed it on the armrest. His forearm was grazing the side of her leg. He wanted that contact. It was cheating, he knew, but he wanted her. Even if he shouldn't.

She turned her head to the side, still resting it on her knees. Her luminous, gray-green eyes were steady, focused on him. That deep inner light that reminded him of a gas lantern on a foggy New Orleans evening was gone. "I can't make this right," she said. "I can't keep going. I can't stand my father's world. It's all smoke and mirrors. I want reality."

He chuckled. "Like a perfect coffee house?"

She nodded. "Reality doesn't have to be ugly."

"No," he shrugged, "it certainly doesn't."

"My father's expectations are," she sighed, and her eyes welled with tears, "unrealistic for me. Always have been. I had no business being at MIT as young as I was-"

"You were certainly smart enough to be there-"

"But I was a kid. A broken-hearted one who missed her mother desperately."

She didn't have to say that she still did. From the heavy, sad look she gave him, he knew she did. "My mother made him better. Without her, I tried. But I didn't have the same influence on him. My mother told me to believe him. To have faith in him. So I always did. I still do. I've always felt responsible for him." She gave him a soft smile. "When it became too much, I'd go partying. Right now, I don't know how to make any of this right. I know what my father wants me to do, and I believe I need to do it. But the reality of what he's set in motion is killing me. Jack and Posie were wonderful. Daniel and Sarah were too. Jen is missing. God knows what's happening to my father." She shook her head. "I just can't make any of this right."

"Focus on what you've accomplished."

She shook her head. "Not much. I dropped the ball. I should've been on the road to Tennessee, long before you arrived at the bakery. I'd have the backup. It wouldn't be gone. People I care about wouldn't be dead."

"Maybe. But you could also be dead. You kept yourself and your sister from being kidnapped."

"You did that."

He smiled. "I helped. You were fighting them before I got there, and doing a decent job of it. You at least delayed them."

"But I need you to believe me, and I can't even persuade you that what I'm saying has any basis in reality. Shadow and LID Technologies exist. They really do. I've seen them. I was at his side, when he developed them.

"I can't take your word for it. I need evidence," he said it as nicely as he could, and she nodded. "You and Spring are safe now. We'll find your father. I'm still not sure how, but we will. You've got to trust me on this."

Some of the misery lifted from her eyes. He knew he should

return to the front cabin. He should at least open the door, which should prevent anything physical from happening between them. But inertia overcame logic. His butt stayed planted in the comfortable chair, and when he inhaled he smelled vanilla and fresh pine. He leaned closer to her. Seconds passed, and still he didn't move. He only breathed in her scent.

A faint pink blush formed on her cheek. The rose-pink was the color of the sweater, which was the color of her nipples, and once his mind seized upon that thought, there was only one thing that his body wanted to happen. He wasn't going there, but he gave himself freedom to touch her. He ran his finger along her cheekbone, because for some reason it made sense for him to want to know the answer to whether the pink flush had any heat in it. He didn't just want to know the answer. He needed to know the answer. Yes. There was heat. When she blushed, there was just a small elevation of temperature, one that he could barely detect, but it was there, on the tip of his index finger.

He would have stopped, but she caught her breath and licked her lips, leaving a sheen of moisture on her lower lip. Where, of course, he now needed to touch. With his index finger on the glistening pink pad of her lower lip, she breathed in, even deeper, and he was lost. She wanted reality? He didn't have it for her.

With the very last centimeter of self-control that existed in his body, he said, "You have to tell me to stop. I won't do it on my own."

She shook her head, as he traced the outline of her lips and bent forward to kiss her neck. "I'm not going to do that." She smiled a lazy, sultry smile as he tore himself from her. "Just don't apologize after."

No apology?

No problem.

Somewhere between getting her out of her seat and getting his rock hard penis into her, shoes and clothes came off. He started with her jeans, she started with his shirt. As she started to lift the sweater over her head, he gripped her hands. "Wait."

He sat her on the bench seat and knelt between her legs. Her jeans were off, her panties were somewhere in the heap. Doing something he'd wanted to do ever since seeing her in the kitchen that morning, he unbuttoned each tiny button of her sweater, then pushed it aside. He paused, admiring the way the mounds of her breasts moved with each of her breaths. He unsnapped the front hook of her bra, drawing a deep, harsh breath. Her nipples were the exact shade of the damn sweater that had been tormenting him, and he bent to her, his naked body pressed against hers, as he closed his mouth on one nipple, sucking, biting, and licking, until she moaned. He turned his attention to the other, reaching behind her and holding her tight as she arched into him.

The night before she'd been surprised by his idea of foreplay. Now, her eyes glistened as she watched him study her body. She gave him a positively wicked smile as she teased him by opening her legs, licking her lips as she did so. Turn on factor? Off the charts. He loved uninhibited women.

Over the intercom, the pilot said, "We've been cleared for takeoff. There are a few planes ahead of us."

Sebastian pushed Skye's knees further apart as the jet started rolling. "We should stop this and buckle up."

"Stop and I'll kill you."

He laughed as he eyed her tight folds and dark curls. With the same index finger that had grazed the pink flush along her cheekbone, and her lip, he touched her core, swirling his finger into her, closing his eyes at the feel of her slick heat, listening to her soft moans. He lifted the finger to his mouth, sucked her moisture off of it, and needed more.

Goddamn it, but he wanted to kiss her as he did her, the old-fashioned way, the kind of wet kiss that went with love-making sex. The kind of no-holds barred intimate touching that could go on for hours. He wanted to open his mouth on hers, slide his tongue over hers, taste her, and not stop until their lips were bruised, and make love until they screamed into each other's mouth in release.

Not an option. Instead, he bent his face towards her sex, and covered it with his mouth as he moved his hands to her hips and pulled her to him. As though he had never tasted a woman before, he groaned, relishing the salty-sweet, fresh taste that confronted him as he tongued her. She lifted her feet to the seat's edge, opening herself to him as he sucked and licked. Mostly, he feasted, coincidentally giving her pleasure while indulging in the assault of sensations that her body offered. Her hands were on his head, pulling his hair. When he penetrated her with his tongue, her restrained whimpers were just as sexy as the screams she'd given him the night before.

He moved his tongue to her clitoris and slid two fingers deep inside of her as the jet picked up speed. Thrusting with his fingers, he nibbled as he sucked. Because four men were on the other side of a thin door, her cries may have been restrained, but there was nothing restrained about the way she pulled his hair and clenched her thighs against his head. With her hips bucking, her head thrashing, and her breath coming in short gasps, she whimpered, peaking as quietly as she could while the jet gained altitude.

He lifted himself before her orgasm stopped, tearing his mouth from something he never wanted to leave. He pulled her from the couch, laid her on the floor, knelt between her legs, and lifted her knees over his shoulders. He pushed the tip of his penis into her, feeling her close around him as he buried himself, inch by inch. In the throes of an orgasm, her muscles were clenching so hard that he had to fight his way in, powering through it as he thrust up and deep. She gasped, opened her eyes, gripped his waist for balance, and shifted her hips as she tried to accommodate the full length of him.

He grit his teeth but didn't slow his pace. He needed days with her, damn it. Slow and leisurely? Maybe one day he'd have the opportunity, but not today. He pounded into her, watching her expression as he rode her, hard. She lost her breath, her eyes became glazed, and her mouth opened in a silent scream. When he became concerned it was too much for her, he slowed his pace. She shook her head and encouraged him by meeting his thrusts by arching into him. Her channel contracted around him, becoming a heat-filled, pulsing tourniquet on his penis that fueled a power-driven release. Nerve-endings sizzled from the bottom of his feet to the tips of his fingers, and everywhere in between. His orgasm was just as deep as it had been the night before, with violent and endless contractions that stole his breath, leaving him with the feeling that, for the moment, at least, his world was finally in sync.

With his last ounce of energy, he maneuvered himself and her, so that she was on top of him, holding her so that she was eye-level with him. He stayed inside, focusing on the feel of his hot semen and her juices, the feel of her full breasts, pressed against his chest, the pounding of her heart that joined with his. Her face and neck were flush with sexual energy, her eyes burned with a deep, internal light, and she gave him a full, satisfied smile as she looked into his eyes.

With the warmth that came with her radiant, satisfied smile, his in-sync feeling disappeared.

I want more.

He should be done with her, but he wasn't, and what he wanted had nothing to do with sex. Lifting his head, he planted soft kisses along her jawbone, up her cheek, to her temples, to her forehead. He moved his lips to hers. When there was just a thin space between them, he stopped.

A piece of paper could have fit between their lips, but not much more. He looked into her eyes. She was watching him. Waiting for his next move. She wasn't going to push the issue.

Hell.

He dropped his head without making lip contact, not wanting to look her in the eye. He shifted his hips, sliding out of her, and immediately wanted back in. "We should get dressed," he said, his voice harsher than he intended, irritated not because she had done anything suggesting that she expected a damn thing out of him. No. The problem was his. He didn't meet her eyes as he unraveled the pile of clothes, sorting through his and hers. He was buckling his belt as she stepped out of the bathroom, fully dressed, her hair once again in a ponytail and a loose braid.

He drew a deep breath, stricken by how pretty she was.

I am royally fucked.

His problem, not hers.

"You okay?" he asked, forcing himself to push past the feeling of dissatisfaction, that had nothing to do with her and everything to do with him.

As she nodded, he grabbed her by the arms and pulled her close. He should just return to the front cabin of the jet. But he didn't feel like it. He was stepping out on a limb by holding on to her, stepping out on a limb by asking her about her father's outlandish scenario. But as he wrapped his arms around her, he had at least one more question that needed an answer. "How exactly were you supposed to get into see the President? Did your father just expect you to knock on the front door of the White House?"

She frowned. "Of course not."

The plane started its descent, swaying through turbulence, before settling into comfortable air. He sat, heavy, in the seat, and she did the same, buckling her seat belt.

"Well?"

"A senator will get me there."

He swallowed, drew a deep breath, and asked, "Which senator?"

"Senator Robert McCollum."

He felt like someone had punched him in the gut.

"Sebastian?"

He shook his head, trying to clear the jumble of thoughts provoked by hearing the name of the senator with whom he'd negotiated the prison security contracts. "What exactly does McCollum know about any of this?"

"I'm not sure."

"Does he know about Shadow and LID Technologies? Does he know that you're supposed to be bringing the President your father's backup?"

"I have no idea. I just know I'm supposed to contact him. He's going to get me access to the President."

He looked out of the window and down. The jet had just breached a layer of clouds. He could see the ground. He touched his watch, testing whether he had communication capabilities. "Ragno?"

"Yes. Did you have a nice flight?"

Nice didn't describe it. Incredible was more like it. He didn't go there. "We're still in the air. Any word from Charlotte?"

"No backup."

Skye's eyes were on him. He shook his head. "Backup's gone."

She shut her eyes in disappointment.

Ragno continued, "The safety deposit box had a pouch of diamonds, some gold medallions, and cash. Who the hell are these people that they'd leave a pouch of loose diamonds?"

"Great question, but diamonds and gold medallions can be marked, and they're smart enough to know that. Did cameras pick up anything useful?"

"Partial faces. That's it. Nothing helpful. Our facial recognition software isn't giving us anything."

"What about the phone?"

"Also gone."

Questioning eyes were on him. He shook his head.

"Well," he paused, "Skye just gave me a bit more information." He drew a deep breath, still amazed at the idea of who Barrows had established as the D.C. contact for getting Skye into the White House. "Brace yourself. It gets better."

"Tell me."

"Skye's contact in D.C. is Bob McCollum," he said. "McCollum is supposed to get her into the White House."

"Are you kidding me?"

A chuckle caught in his throat. "Believe me, I couldn't make this shit up if I tried."

"What does McCollum know?"

"Skye doesn't know. She's just supposed to contact him. He's supposed to get her, and the backup, into the Oval Office."

"Without the backup," Skye interrupted, "PRISM and other data collection systems will remain vulnerable. Shadows and LID Technologies are already integrated into the systems. There's no shutting the backdoor to the LID without the backup. If whoever has my father manages to complete the code, they will have a key that they can use anytime, anywhere. We would essentially be asking the President to destroy years of effort and billions of dollars of capital investment, on faith."

"Ragno," he said, studying the feverish expression in Skye's eyes, wondering if what she was saying had any bearing in reality, and knowing he had to go on faith that it did. "You copy that?"

"You were right," she answered. "It got better."

"Call Last Resort. Arrange a helicopter transport, fast, for Doctor Schilling and Spring to get to the hangar."

Skye's hand was on his forearm. "I'm not sure that will work," she said. "She won't want to hear that from Agent Schilling. She's probably only about halfway though decorating the cupcakes."

"If you call her, and talk to her, can you make it work? I need to talk to McCollum and I don't want to leave you in Georgia while we do it. We don't have time for a detour. If we get the chopper up in the air now, we'll have Spring and the doctor at the airport just a matter of minutes after we land."

"I'll try," Skye gave him a slight smile. "She loves helicopter rides."

Of course she did. Wouldn't any teenager who was fortunate

enough to get in one? "Can you also work on having Candy stay at Last Resort?"

Skye nodded.

"Ragno. I'm taking the sisters to Washington. Mobilize one of our safe houses there. Figure out where McCollum's going to be in say," he glanced at his watch, figured out the logistics of how soon he could be paying McCollum a visit in person, assuming McCollum was in Washington. "In three hours. Don't alert him that I'm coming."

"There's no guarantee he's in D.C. Congress isn't in session."

Sebastian paused. "Well, make sure of it for me, but for now, assume that's where we're headed. I've known Bob for a long time, and I've never known a time when he wasn't in D.C. in the middle of the workweek. The man breathes political fumes, like some of us breathe fresh air, and there's no better place than D.C. for the fumes."

"You're not taking Skye and Spring to see him, are you?"

"No. They'll be at our safe house there."

"So why risk transporting them to D.C.?"

He swallowed. He didn't want to tell Ragno that Spring had at least part of the code to whatever dead ends might be on Richard Barrows' elusive backup. He might not have gotten Skye's unspoken message earlier, if he hadn't been so intrigued by Spring and what she was doing that morning. He had asked Spring enough questions and had glanced in the sketchbook. Then, he'd thought that it was gibberish. Now he believed that Barrows had taught Spring a coded language. A detailed, illogical, coded language.

With her savant-like ability to memorize meaningless data streams, Spring was part of the key. Skye didn't know her way around all of the prompts in the program. He'd bet that Spring could answer any prompt with the correct sequence of numbers.

He doubted that Ragno had figured it out, and while there were usually never any secrets between himself and Ragno, he didn't feel the need to broadcast the fact now that Spring was an integral part of Barrows' plan. His gut told him that Spring's importance to the project need never see the light of day.

"Sebastian? Why risk Spring's transport to D.C.?"

"Because there's something off here and," he swallowed, hard, not wanting to say the next words but knowing he had to admit going to see the President was a possible outcome. "If we have to visit the Oval Office, I want Skye right there with me and I don't want Spring to be a sitting duck, halfway across the country. I want them together."

"What should I tell our partners? The meeting is supposed to take place at three."

"Contact me by phone and see where I am. In the meantime, tell them anything you want," he paused, "except the truth. We don't need to tell them yet that I'm dabbling on the side of insanity."

Skye flinched, then visibly shrugged off his comment. She knew how crazy this sounded. He'd love for Ragno to be at his side in D.C., but that wasn't an option. Ragno never left her floor of corporate headquarters.

Never.

"Have Zeus meet me in D.C. In the meantime, while you're profiling Root, Young, and Whittaker, check for any contact any of them may have had with Senator McCollum, or for any commonality of contact."

Chapter Twenty Two

Firefly Island on Hickory Lake had been a beautiful setting for Trask's brand of fun. It was rare that he got to be outside, enjoying nature, as he gave his demons free reign. Barrows, of course, hadn't given up the precise location of the backup or told him about the phone. Jack and Posie had been foolishly loyal and stubborn, even under the most rigorous persuasion. Their loyalty required his creativity, and he'd outdone himself. Trask's aids had hung the woman from a tree. He'd enjoyed her thrashing and her screams that were muted through her gag. Sounds carried over water, and though Firefly Island was private, nearby islands were populated.

Giving his well-honed skills free rein, Trask had sliced Posie with his favorite skinning knife. Small, deep cuts. The pain was deferred as the nerves took time catching up. He had time. God only knew, he enjoyed his work. Sunlight glinting on the vivid red blood dripping from her multiple wounds gave him a high. Killing gave him a thrill he couldn't explain. Torture was an indulgent bonus he didn't always have time for.

The husband he'd left till last. Intact. Aware. Secured at the base of the tree, his wife's thrashing feet brushing the top of his head, as her life's blood leaked over him in a delightful red tide of surrender.

He'd given them the choice: *Answer the question, I'll make it quick, or take your time, and I'll take mine.*

Their screams of pain and total nonsense told him their decision. Thank God. It had been some of his best work. Absolutely brilliant, if he did say so himself.

Upon returning to headquarters at nine in the morning, as his experts worked on the backup, he'd retreated to his personal quarters, where he'd enjoyed the attention of a very young woman, who he'd specially ordered from Shanghai. She'd been trained to do things with a man that would have made most women cringe.

At three in the afternoon, showered, fresh and flush with

invigoration, he stepped into the computer lab to check on what his experts had managed to do with Barrows' backup. Dunbar was there, on the central command stage with the lead analyst, elevated above a team of twenty. Each of the analysts on the floor worked with eight touch-sensitive screens and multiple keyboards. They remained focused on their screens, as he took to the podium. One stood, backed away from his screen, glanced at the podium, and shook his head. After a minute, another did the same thing.

The lead analyst said, "Take a break for a few minutes, before taking a fresh crack at it."

It wasn't quite the celebratory mood that he'd anticipated. Cold fury surged through him as the high of the killings, the adrenaline rush he'd sustained most of the day, shattered. He had to struggle for composure, biting the side of his mouth until he tasted the coppery slide of his own blood. When he was sure he could remain calm, he said, "Dunbar?"

"So far, we've been able to confirm that the backup we obtained from the lake house and the Charlotte bank vault contain duplicate information. We also confirmed that we have more data than what was previously delivered to us."

"All encouraging," he said. *Imbecile.* He didn't care about what they had managed to confirm. He wanted results. "Are we anywhere near to lifting the LID that covers Shadow Technology? Are we in PRISM? Are we in any of the government's databases?"

"No."

What tiny speck of bliss that might have remained from his day disappeared in roiling fury, yet Trask managed to smile. "If we have Barrows' backup, why not?"

"Because even with his own backup, Barrows built dead ends into the code." Dunbar gestured to the analysts. His dark hair was curling on his forehead, which was beady with sweat. Trask's insides roiled with anger, as he watched Dunbar swipe his forehead with his goddamn handkerchief. At that moment, as he patiently waited for Dunbar to assume just a tiny bit of authority, Trask decided that when he had no more use for Dunbar, hopefully soon, he was going to peel the man's forehead off of his fucking skull.

The lead analyst was in his forties and regarded in the industry as a brilliant mind. He smelled like stale, nervous perspiration. His horn-rimmed glasses were smudged. His thin red hair was damp with perspiration and sticking to his scalp. He glanced at Trask and said, "The two who stepped away just hit such a dead end."

"What do you mean by dead end?" Trask kept his tone deceptively moderate, but his people knew him, and he saw fear in the light brown eyes of the lead analyst, that matched the fear that Dunbar was trying, but failing, to conceal.

"Words," the analyst said, pushing the bridge of his glasses up his nose. "The programs stop at nonsensical words, and we don't know the passwords that are required with each word. We suspect that each word requires us to input passwords, but we have no way of knowing the code that correlates with the words."

He reminded himself that there was going to be a cleansing when this project was over. He eyed Dunbar and the lead analyst, careful not to reveal how tired he was of all of the fucking morons that worked for him. "What about our code-cracking programs? The ones you insisted I pay two point five million for? The ones you said would be able to work around the most sophisticated encryption programs? And the technology department you both insisted I need? My overhead for this department, with the experts and programs, is twenty million a year. So far, all of it is a loss."

"We're running the code-cracking programs. They're not working. Randomness is problematic. We need to have some known inputs," the analyst said, "and right now we don't have that. We're going to have an answer. It's just going to take time."

"Time? An hour? A day?"

Now both men had handkerchiefs in their hands. Dunbar swallowed a mouthful of nervous saliva, his Adam's apple juggling up and down. "It could take months."

Not while Richard Barrows had one breath of life in his body.

"And if Barrows cooperates, how much time?"

The lead analyst shrugged. "A day. Or two. At most."

"Bring Miss Root in here," Trask said, "and let my men know that the team that brings me Skye and Spring Barrows will have their annual salaries quadrupled."

After a few minutes, Jennifer Root was led onto the podium by three of his men. Her stride was powerful, and there was no reason why it shouldn't be. Her injuries, up until he had hacked off the tips of her index and middle finger, had all been fake.

Now, sparks flew from her wildly pissed-off dark brown eyes as he gave her a cool nod. Her black pants were neatly pressed and her loafers were on, but she had missed a button at the top of her blouse and her black cardigan was hanging on her shoulders, as though she hadn't had time to fully put it on.

"Hello, darling," he said, glancing at her bandaged hand. "I hope the injury to your fingers won't be too inconvenient for you." His on-staff doctor had re-sewn the tips of her index and middle fingers onto her left hand.

"My fingers," she said. "My goddamn fingers. You sick, sadistic son of a bitch. How dare you!"

Could anyone maintain any fucking composure? "Oh come on, Jennifer," he said, "you really must take one for the team. I know what I'm doing. The cuts were clean," he shrugged, "the doctor tells me that you'll have full functioning. There will just be the faintest trace of a scar. Your next manicure's on me."

"Fucking asshole."

"There's no need to raise your voice, and your crude indignation is misplaced. We made progress, right?"

"From the beginning, I've done every goddamn thing that you asked," she paused. "I'm the one who brought you this deal."

He shook his head. "Now that's not entirely true, and you know it. You're giving yourself too much credit. The deal was rolling long before you and Young jumped on the bandwagon. What you and Young did was oversell what the two of you were capable of delivering."

She drew a deep breath. "I delivered exactly what I promised. We could never guarantee that your experts could make sense of Richard's work, and we said that from the beginning. Richard purposefully leaves out code-"

He shook his head, smiling at the sparks that flew from her eyes. "A fact that you and Young didn't bother to tell me. A fact that I just learned, no thanks to you."

"You need me, because you'll never break the LID without his cooperation," she said, "and I can persuade him to do that. Don't you forget it."

At Trask's side, Dunbar tensed. The three assistants who had led Jennifer into the room also tensed. No one threatened him. No one at all. He drew a deep breath, stared at her, and calmed himself before saying, in as normal of a tone as he ever used, "Young thought I needed him as well, and look where that got him. The only person I need here is Richard Barrows. And if we can make sense of the backup that I acquired," he said, "even that need no longer exists."

She jutted her chin out, defiant, despite his implicit admission to killing Young, something he had denied until that moment. "It shouldn't have come as a surprise that Richard doesn't do complete data sets. Even with the data that you've secured, there will be dead ends. There will be prompts that only he knows. There will be code that he will have to give you," she said, "and, unless you have his daughters-"

"We're close to the girls," he said, calmly, speaking the truth. It paid to hire good people, and he had paid top dollar when he hired men who had been Black Raven agents. Now they were his. Former Black Raven agents who were now his men, who had spent time at Last Resort were strategizing now on how to secure the sisters. It was only a matter of time before he'd have Skye and Spring, and that time was growing shorter.

"Close isn't going to cut it," she said, "and unless you show him his daughters, Richard Barrows isn't going to give you a goddamn thing without my help. He'd rather die."

"You know, she's younger than you. She also has far superior bone structure. But I think," he let his eyes travel her body, "the two of you are similar body types. I think that with a hood on, Barrows will believe that you're Skye. I might just be able to persuade him that I'm killing his daughter when I kill you."

**

2:45 p.m., Tuesday

"Skye," Sebastian said, from the front cabin of the jet. "Spring will be here in fifteen minutes." His gaze was reassuring, but something had happened after they had sex. Instead of feeling like they'd gotten closer, he'd become more distant. It happened right after he almost kissed her. Almost, but didn't.

Then she'd said McCollum's name, and he'd become all business.

Skye nodded, smoothed her hair, and tried to collect herself. She didn't want Spring to sense anything other than calmness. Raven One had landed ten minutes earlier. She'd stayed in the rear cabin, but when the wheels touched the ground, Sebastian had moved to the forward cabin. He'd left open the door that separated the two. Through it, she saw him talking on his phone, to his agents, and to the pilots, who had opened the door to the cockpit. One was in the main cabin, but the other stayed in his seat, clipboard in hand, checking controls. Sebastian seemed comfortable, the center of attention, having simultaneous and never-ending conversations.

Through the window she could see the jet had taxied into the Black Raven hangar. She counted four agents, standing at attention at the large entry doors. Beyond the huge doors, which remained open, the day had turned gray. A sleek black helicopter sat on the far side of the hangar, about fifty yards from the jet. Four men worked in an area with desks and computers.

She'd given up on wishing that they'd open the door to the jet, but she still wanted out. She braced herself for the awkward moment when the four men who made up the security team stared at her, but when she walked into the forward cabin, only one gave her a passing glance. They might have wondered what she and Sebastian had done behind that closed door, they might have even heard exactly what was happening, as it happened, but if they did, they gave no indication. The only eyes that held hers were Sebastian's, and even though he was staring at her, he was focused more on his conversations than her.

Feeling like a child who was being a nuisance—and not liking the feeling one bit—she placed her hand on his arm for attention and said, "Can I step outside the jet?"

His eyes were unreadable as he gave her a slight headshake. "Best if you don't."

"Please."

A flash of concern? Maybe. Or was it irritation? No. The irritation seemed to be gone, replaced with...something else. Something far gentler. Certainly she saw understanding there, because he had the knowledge that she hated confined spaces. "Okay, go stretch your legs for a few minutes. You've got to stay in the hangar, though. Okay?"

"Yes."

He glanced at his agents. His nod of permission was almost imperceptible, but as his chin dipped, the four agents stood. Their fast action proved that while it looked like they weren't paying attention to her, to Sebastian, to their soft-spoken words, and to the invisible undercurrents of their interaction, they obviously were.

"Give them a minute."

The door opened. A gust of deliciously cold, fresh air blew through the jet. She shrugged into the leather jacket, zipping it as she waited for the signal that it was safe for her to step out of the plane. The precautions seemed over the top-theatrical to her, and she almost told Sebastian so. After all, they were in a guarded hangar.

As she opened her mouth with a wisecrack, his eyes rested on hers. He was in work-mode, talking to Ragno, and the depth of worry she saw in his eyes was infectious. The wisecrack faded from her mind. He said, "Stay close to me."

Once down the stairs, the team allowed her to step a few feet from the jet, then stopped, becoming a human wall surrounding her and Sebastian. This was as good as it was going to get, and it was heavenly. Ice-cold wind blew her hair loose and made her cheeks tingle. Cold moisture enveloped her. She pulled the leather jacket closer as she inhaled the fresh air, saw that Sebastian's blue eyes were on her, and said, "Thank you."

His nod was accompanied by the faintest hint of a smile, which disappeared as soon as it formed. He pressed a finger to his ear, and said, "Repeat that."

He was so close to her that she could feel his body tense. He stood even straighter than usual. His uncharacteristic stillness lasted only a second, but it was accompanied by such a serious look in his eyes that her heart raced. He turned his head slightly to the right, looking up, to the open doorway of the jet. Gridiron focus was on the pilot who stood at the top of the ladder, looking down at them.

Moving in unison, all of the men took a step closer to the ladder. One bumped into her, because she was the only one who hadn't gotten a signal to get in the jet. She looked around the terminal, wondering what was prompting the urgency. Sebastian's eyes were grim and his jaw was clenched. "Activate the chopper that is here," Sebastian said. "Now. Skye. Get in the jet."

"What's wrong?"

He bent, dipped his shoulder, lifted her over it, and climbed the boarding ladder with her on top of his shoulder. His fast move stunned the breath out of her body. When he bent again to deposit her inside the jet, she stood where he placed her, about a foot in the doorway. She gasped for air, still surprised by

Sebastian's quick move. He stepped past her, into the cockpit, bending on one knee and crowding into the middle of the two pilots whose eyes were riveted on the radar screen.

"Ragno," Sebastian said, "Activate the cameras on the chopper that is carrying Spring. Call that chopper Target A. Feed the camera feed here."

He paused.

"Disabled? Impossible. It was fucking-well designed for no overrides."

Skye's heart raced as she watched Sebastian. "No," she said, fighting through the confusion, grasping only the fact that Target A was the helicopter carrying Spring and something had gone terribly wrong with it. "No," she whispered, but no one was listening.

One of the agents who had climbed into the jet ahead of them caught her attention by putting his face in front of hers. "Ms. Barrows, you need to step away from the doorway."

She barely registered that he was talking to her, much less the import of his words. He gripped her forearm, and pulled her further into the jet, as another stood in the open doorway. "Sit," the agent said, "Stay away from the windows."

She yanked his hand off of her. "Tell me what's going on. Sebastian?"

He ignored her. His back was to her, and his eyes were trained on the jet's radar screen. Deep brown, unreadable eyes of one of the agents glanced into hers, but only for a second. He blocked her view of the cockpit and Sebastian. Without an answer, the agent turned away from her, bent to look through the window. Over his shoulder said, in the direction of Sebastian, he said, "Pilots are at the chopper."

One of the jet pilots said, "Target A deviated off path three minutes ago. Now headed southeast."

The other pilot said, "We lost radio contact at deviation. No answer."

"Check with tower," Sebastian said.

"Tower's trying. No reply. Target A is still moving. Southeast. Wait," the pilot said, "They're slowing."

"Map Target A's path on land, focusing on directions from Last Resort." Sebastian snapped. "Radio it to the helicopter pilots as you tell me. Activate vehicles from Last Resort-"

"Based on present position, I estimate Target A is a thirty minute drive from Last Resort. Getting longer."

"Mobilize vehicles now," Sebastian said.

"Sebastian," she said, her voice breaking. "Please don't let anything happen to her. She's all I have." Her heart pounded and she could barely breathe. *No.*

Not Spring.

Oh, dear God. They couldn't have Spring. The agent moved away. She stood. Sebastian gave her a passing glance, barely meeting her eyes. His attention was focused on the helicopter, which was being driven to the entrance of the hangar.

"Ms. Barrows," one of the agents said, "please sit."

Not going to happen. She had no intention of sitting, had no intention of listening to the two agents who stood at her side. She needed an answer, and she needed it now.

Sebastian stood only a few feet from her, but the distance could have been an ocean, because the agents seemed hell bent on keeping her away from him. One of the agents grabbed her wrist. She clawed at his hand. "Let me go." She broke free, closed the distance between them, and, just as Sebastian started down the steps, "Take me with you. Please."

He glanced into her eyes with a look of steady, calm resolve. "I'll bring her to you. I promise. But I can't protect both of you in this situation. Stay put where I know you'll be safe. I promise I'll bring Spring back. I," he paused, gripped her shoulders, held her steady, and said, "promise."

She gripped the hands that braced her shoulders. "I've got to be with her."

"Too dangerous." As he held her gaze, she detected something more than the calm, stoic face he presented to the world. For a fleeting second, his eyes delivered a message of pain, frustration, and misery that matched her feelings. The second was gone and so was the window into his true thoughts. He gently removed his hands from her shoulders, held onto her hands for a second longer, and over her shoulder, said, "Restrain her if necessary."

One of the agents who remained with her enclosed his arms around her waist, anchoring her inside the jet. She clawed at the beefy arms that held her and kicked at his legs. He adjusted position, so that his arms encircled her arms and she couldn't fight him.

"Let me go," she said, as Sebastian took the steps at a run. Two pilots were in the helicopter, two agents were waiting outside of it, and two of the agents who had been with them all day ran alongside Sebastian. They jumped in, and it rolled outside the hangar.

The agent who held her captive pulled her back into the jet and waited until the door was shut before letting her go. "I'm sorry, Ms. Barrows. It's for your own safety."

"I'm not worried about me."

Pained brown eyes gave her a solid glance. "I know that, ma'am."

"I want my sister," she said, "I need Spring. Oh, God. She's going to be so afraid. You don't understand. She's special. She can't be taken. They can't have her," she choked on the words. "Please," she gripped the man's arms, just as she had gripped Sebastian's. "Please. Let me go. Let me out of here. I've got to get to her. She's going to be terrified, even with Sebastian there. When he gets to her, she'll need me. Please."

He freed her arms and guided her to a seat. She didn't want to sit, but strong hands somehow managed to make her body do so. Long minutes passed, when she could only fight to breathe. The two agents knelt in the aisle. The one who hadn't been in charge of restraining her offered her a cold bottle of water. She shook her head. He handed her a cold compress, which she took but didn't understand why he thought she needed it. She could hold herself together. Spring needed her to be calm. Strong. She needed to figure out a way to get to her.

"I've got to be there when Sebastian gets to her. Please. Take me there. Can't we get in a car? Drive me there."

One of the agents cupped his hand to his ear.

"What?" she asked, knowing that they were listening to updates that they weren't bothering to repeat. "Tell me."

Only silence and pained expressions greeted her.

"Please," she whispered, suddenly understanding that they were mic'd to Sebastian, knowing that Sebastian needed to think and didn't need to be distracted by her. "Please tell me what's going on."

More silence.

Finally, she drew her legs up and placed her head on her knees, resigned to the reality that these men had no intention of letting her go. At one point, she looked up, and was met with the concerned brown eyes of the agent who had restrained her. "Please," she whispered, "Take me there."

"Ms. Barrows, we can't take you there," he said. The man appeared calm, his Black Raven-style stoicism intact, but his eyes reflected compassion, worry, and unease.

He cupped his hand to his ear. The other agent did the same. The pilots stepped out of the cockpit. The men exchanged a brief look, and suddenly they were focusing on her, their expressions uniformly calm and controlled, but with an underlying gravity that told her that the unimaginable had happened. With their grim expressions, words became unnecessary. The four men exchanged a long glance, as though silently nominating who would be the one to confirm her suspicion.

"They took her," she whispered. She gripped the armrests, because the jet suddenly seemed to be lurching and spinning, when it wasn't moving at all. "Didn't they?"

Her vision spun. Unable to focus on any one thing or person that was still, their faces became a hideous blur of serious eyes and grim, unsmiling mouths. She stood, holding onto the wall for support. Standing made the spinning stop. She was marginally better.

Hold it together. Hold. It. Together.

Chapter Twenty Three

Ten minutes was enough time to make Sebastian realize that the heart of steel he'd so carefully cultivated wasn't impenetrable. The thought that these bastards had gotten to Spring pierced him with razor sharp edges that ripped open his chest, cut through his bone and flesh, and left a raw hole that served to remind him that something integral to human life was missing.

This depth of pain couldn't be blamed on his head injury. Nope. He was in nightmare world. He'd built one hell of a life escaping from it, but now he was living it. Finding Richard Barrows and returning him to federal custody was work. It was important work, and he had a hell of a lot riding on it, but it was simply a task to complete.

Finding Spring, retrieving her unharmed, and placing her in Skye's arms? As necessary to his being as his next breath of air. He'd succeed, or he'd die trying.

"I have a visual on Target A," the pilot on Sebastian's left said, "ten o'clock."

On one knee between the two pilots, Sebastian looked through the wrap-around windshield and eyed the grounded helicopter, a custom-outfitted Bell 525, as they turned and descended towards it. Radar had revealed that it had landed five minutes earlier. He was mic'd to the pilots, to Ragno, to the six-man team that was in the helicopter with him, to the agents on the jet who were with Skye, to the vehicles that were speeding to the scene from Last Resort, and to the base of operations that was at Last Resort. The never-ending babble made him feel like he was mic'd to the entire world.

His agents were trained for situations like this, and the steady calm with which everyone spoke, using minimal words, was the result of training and practice. As the helicopter began its descent, he touched the watch, muted all other voices except Ragno, and said, "Ragno, just you."

"Alright," she said. "Should Raven One depart for D.C. now?"

"Not yet."

"Let me know if that changes. I'm mapping the area where you are now. Vehicles from Last Resort are ten minutes out."

Cold air ripped through the chopper, as the pilot opened the doors. Glock in Sebastian's hand, he turned towards the open door, crouching there as they hovered over the open field. At another time of the year, there might have been green grass or a crop in the field, but now the field looked muddy and wet. The late-afternoon sky was gray. Snow flurries were floating in the air, and there wasn't a sign of life anywhere near the helicopter.

At twenty feet above the ground, he readied himself. He turned to the team. "Two of you stay with the pilots. Once we're on the ground, go back up. Look for," he paused, "anything unusual." At five feet above ground, he jumped. He ran across the field, climbed into the helicopter, immediately receiving confirmation on what his gut had told him. Bodies. Four of them. All his. *Son of a fucking bitch.*

"Spring isn't here," he said, having to fight to keep angry emotion out of his voice, both at the absence of Spring and the bloodshed that confronted him in the helicopter. Calling in official law enforcement agencies was probably a waste of time. Whoever had Spring wasn't going to step into a conventional trap.

He did it anyway. "Inform local authorities, state police, and feds. We have a kidnapping that we'll assume is spanning interstate boundaries. Get the FBI involved. We need alerts on all roadways and interstates."

The grounded equipment was a two-pilot helicopter, the same type as he had just jumped from. It had an open cockpit and four rows of four passenger seats. "Pilots seats are empty," he said, relaying information to Ragno. He looked at one of his team members, "Enable the cockpit surveillance system so that everyone can see."

The agent stepped to the flight deck. "Shouldn't I wait for forensics?"

"No time for normal protocols." He frowned, thinking through the lack of helpful information that had come from any of the other scenes, even from the bodies of the men. "These people aren't in any databases."

He gave the agent a few seconds. "Any luck?"

"No, sir. It's been effectively disabled, and I'm not sure how."

"It was not turned on as the pilots flew to Last Resort, but once Spring and her team were aboard, it was on," Ragno said.

"They knew our protocol. They knew if it wasn't on while we had a high security client in transport, we would have been alerted."

"It was disabled as they veered off course," Ragno said.

He switched the camera on his watch on, lifted his wrist, and said, "Ragno, feed this to the others. In the row of passenger seats that's closest to the cockpit, Dr. Schilling is in the seat that's nearest to the door. There's an entry wound in her forehead. Eyes open." He swallowed, remembering the light look in her pretty brown eyes earlier that day, when she had said that she'd drawn the lucky straw for the day. "To her right, there's an empty seat, presumably the one that Spring was in. To the right of that, there's Agent Reiss." Hell. He had chastised Reiss on the last day of the man's life. "Two bullets. One grazed his left temple. Another closer to the center of the forehead. There are two additional agents in the row of seats behind Reiss and Schilling. All dead."

He thought through different scenarios of how it might have happened, rejecting a few. He went to the last row of seats, the one that was furthest from the cockpit, and frowned. There was a compartment behind the seats, one of the customizations they'd requested from the manufacturer. It was for stowing suitcases, weapons, and gear. It would be able to fit two men. "Most likely scenario to me is that the kidnappers hid in the storage space. They had to get on the helicopter, while it was at the airport. While the chopper was en route to Last Resort, they killed our pilots. Do an aerial search of the route from the airport to Last Resort. I suspect the bodies of our pilots are somewhere along the way."

Black Raven body count due to the prison break? Ten.

He drew a deep breath and pushed away the mixture of rage and fury that came with that thought. Rage and fury wasn't going to find the person, who needed a brutal dose of payback.

He looked again at Dr. Schilling's body, thinking aloud. "The perps were in place, in the pilot seats, when the team boarded with Spring. It looks like the perps turned around and surprised them. It's the only thing that makes sense. The team that was in charge of protecting Spring got on the helicopter, thinking Black Raven pilots were flying them. Given the time of their deviation from course, I'm guessing everything seemed normal for the first ten or so minutes of the flight. The pilots turned around and would have been shooting together and fast to take down four of our armed agents at the same time."

He paused, watching a convoy of six black Range Rovers halt on the road. As four agents stepped out of each vehicle, he said, "Ragno. Is the helicopter that's in the air finding anything?"

"No."

"Tell them to keep looking and provide local assistance. I'll ride back to the airport in a vehicle. How's Skye?"

"She figured out that Spring was gone, even before the agents managed to tell her anything. She's pacing, but outwardly calm." The void in his heart ached so badly it stole his fucking breath. Ragno, in a quiet tone that imparted sympathy and empathy, said, "Sure you don't want me to give Raven One the green light for a departure and send her to the safe house without you?"

The idea had tremendous appeal. Nothing he could do or say was going to make Skye feel any better, and he needed to focus, not be sidetracked by Skye. He wasn't a coward, though. Never had been, and never planned to be. "Have you figured out McCollum's whereabouts?"

"D.C.," she said. "I've also figured out a few more things that make him more interesting. Two years ago, when the frequency of telephone conversations between Jennifer Root and Zachary Young was at its peak, they frequently talked to Senator McCollum. So did Barrows."

"Interesting," Sebastian said, walking in the direction of the agents who were crossing the field. "But that can be explained due to his involvement on various technology committees. Right?"

"Senator McCollum had his hands in every prestigious committee, so yes. What's more interesting," Ragno said, "is that Jennifer Root, Zachary Young, and Senator McCollum all had conversations with multiple phone numbers that we cannot identify. We're working on it."

"Well, my gut is telling me to head to D.C., and Raven One is my most direct route there," he said, thinking aloud. "Hold it for me."

The most senior agent approached him. He recognized Mack Poitras. They'd been on assignment in Syria and the man was currently in charge of training at Last Resort. "I'm leaving you in charge of the assessment here and any support we need to provide the authorities. I have two agents at the airport. I need five of your best to depart with me. Give me your five with skills that are most translatable to hostage extraction capabilities in multiple hostile environments." He had to assume there'd be an extraction. He didn't know when, how, or where, but there would be an extraction, and he hoped like hell it was going to happen soon.

"Yes, sir." He issued commands through a mic, then glanced at Sebastian. "Sir, the lead car is for you. The other car will follow."

Sebastian turned to walk in the direction of the car. "Ragno, assemble a team of ten additional agents for me from those that are in the D.C. area. Duplicate the effort in Denver, and again on the West Coast. I want teams of at least thirty ready to go anywhere within a minute of when we find out where these bastards are. Alert Denver to mobilize the C130J crew, with medical staff, fully stocked for anything they throw at us, and ready to go at a moment's notice. Parts unknown at the moment." He knew with dead certainty that he'd need the equipment that the cargo plane held. Which equipment, in particular? He had no fucking clue.

"Got it," Ragno said. "Order is issued."

He had about one hundred yards of muddy field to traverse before reaching the vehicle, where the driver and two agents were waiting to accompany him to the airport. "Ragno, put me back on a private line."

"Done."

"Double check. Get Zeus on line, but no one else. No one external, and no one internal. No one at all, but you, me, Zeus." Dammit, his insides were roiling with the thought that he couldn't get out of his head.

"Give me a second." He slow-walked, delaying his time for reaching the other agents and the vehicle so that he could finish his conversation. Snow was accumulating on the ground, and his feet were leaving dark tracks in the soft-white powder. "We're secure. Zeus is on the line with us."

"Talk to me," Zeus said.

"Either this was an inside job or someone who was in our employ recently was giving the perps intel."

"Interesting theory," Zeus said.

"Tell us your thoughts," Ragno said.

"Our fleet of Bell 525's is relatively new," he said, sidestepping a puddle of water with a fringe of ice. "They've been in use for what, six months?"

"Correct. We took delivery of six at the end of May. The two that are stationed there arrived in June."

"The stowage compartment. That didn't exist in the prior helicopters that we used at Last Resort, did it?"

"Only on the exterior."

"So there was nowhere on the helicopter where two men could hide and then access the interior, while the helicopter was in flight."

"I'm pulling up the plans now," Ragno said.

"I was in the old ones more times than I can count," Zeus answered. "And so were you. You know the answer to that without looking at the plans."

He slowed his pace. "Our customizations are kept secret, correct?"

"Yes," Zeus said.

"So how would the perps have known there'd be a hiding place?"

"Wishful thinking?" Ragno said. "I need more before I buy it. Someone with the manufacturer could have leaked our customization."

"I need more too. They could have had plan A, plan B, and plan C."

He was almost to the Range Rover, where three sets of ears would be tuned to his every word. He slowed his pace. Black Raven didn't follow a simple alternating procedure for transport vehicles. They were currently in a two-to-one approach, and it would have taken someone with knowledge of Black Raven's procedures, and someone watching the helicopter usage for the pattern at the airport, to know which helicopter was going to be the one to pick up Spring. "They knew which helicopter was flying next. They knew our usage pattern. Right?"

Zeus gave a low whistle.

Ragno said, "Well, they wouldn't have left that to chance, would they?"

"I don't think anyone in our current ranks would have done this," he said, sickened by the thought, but having to entertain it. "But we have to look at our own. More than the agents in our current ranks, I'm thinking it could be someone who's left us. One of our prior agents could have shared inside knowledge."

Black Raven hired men and women who had honor and integrity. The company was considered the crown jewel of private security contractors. Employment with Black Raven was coveted by many and offered to relatively few, and it wasn't a temporary stint. It was a career with honor. There were risks, and the job was dangerous, but the agents were highly compensated, and the benefits were the best in the business. No matter the degree of psychological testing that was employed in the hiring process and in training, or the loyalty that the company instilled, the bottom line was that he was dealing with humans, and the almighty dollar was a powerful lure.

"Zeus, any thoughts?" Sebastian asked.

"I agree with you," Zeus said. "I'll work with Ragno on establishing parameters for an internal assessment. Top priority, though, is the people who've left our employment and ascertaining whether any had knowledge of procedures at Last Resort."

Sebastian's heart thudded as he reached the SUV. "Agreed. Because we want to know where they've gone. Maybe cross-referencing to the profiles you're assembling on Root, Young, BY Laboratories, Whittaker, and Senator McCollum will ultimately give us something."

He glanced at the three agents who were standing at attention, outside the lead vehicle, waiting on him. Their eyes reflected the somberness of the weather and the events of the day. After the agents introduced themselves, he said, "The reality of losing our own is never easy. Welcome to the team that's going to find the people who did this."

The three pairs of eyes reflected his own grim feelings, showing that they were each fantasizing that they would be the one to make the perpetrators pay. Black Raven agents were not killing machines. Not usually. Today, if that's what was needed to do the job, he was going to authorize it wholeheartedly.

He stepped into the car, automatically touching the button for pushing the seat back and glancing in the rear seat to see how much legroom the agent who was behind him needed. The agent gave him a nod. "Sir, you're fine."

Another agent said, "We knew to put the shortest agent behind you."

Sebastian chuckled as the SUV pulled away, focused for a second on where they were heading, and the day became grayer as he wondered what in the hell he was going to say to Skye. "Ragno?"

"We've lost twenty seven agents in the last calendar year, thirty two in the calendar year before that. That's the easy part," she said. "When they leave, they don't typically provide a road map of where they're going. It's going to take some work."

Over the mic he heard Zeus and Ragno discussing the best method of formulating searches before Zeus broke the connection. Ragno was quiet for a second. Without the click-clack of her typing as she sent instructions to her team, he wouldn't have known that she was there. It was too much silence for him. "Mic me to the teams."

Voices flooded the mic and he felt comfortable again. As he shifted in the seat, he felt an out-of-place lump in his jacket pocket and reached for it. His hand froze as he touched the bag of jellybeans that Spring had given him. The day was only going to get harder.

I'm going to find you, sweetheart. Bank on it.

Starting now, he thought, as the airport came into view.

Once in the hangar, he stepped out of the SUV and walked, without hesitation, to the jet. Embrace the suck, he told himself. Be a man, and own up to it. He'd embraced more crap that he would have ever imagined fitting into a life. Seeing Skye right now was the last thing he wanted to do. Witnessing the hurt in Skye's eyes when he owned up to losing Spring? Unimaginable.

He climbed the ladder, feeling like it was the final leg of Everest and his tank was out of oxygen. Every single fucking job until that moment had been easy. Nights strung together in war zones without sleep, holding onto weapons for so long they became an extension of his hands, the edginess of knowing that one mistake would be fatal, picking up body parts after an explosion. Those things came with the job. Having to console Skye, having to tell her he was sorry for underestimating the capabilities of the enemy? Unfathomable.

Raven One's engines were humming. The door closed behind him and the agents who'd come with him. One of the agents who had remained with her was in the doorway that separated the two cabins. He gave Sebastian a nod, his eyes grim. She was in the rear cabin, on the couch, shoes off, legs up, and head down on her knees.

He bent to his knees as the plane started rolling.

"Skye."

She looked at him with eyes that were devoid of hope. He reached for her, but she moved away and kept her hands clasped together in front of her knees. "Don't touch me."

Sorry wasn't going to cut it. Not for him, and especially not for her. As the jet lifted off the ground, he said, "I'm going to find her. You need to believe that."

She drew a deep breath, her eyes heavy with misery. "I believed you when you said we were safe. Then you promised you'd bring her back."

Her words stole his breath, as effectively as a bullet piercing a lung.

"Negotiate with them," she said, standing. "Tell them that they can have me in exchange for her. Please," she said, drawing a deep breath as she fought for control. "Tell them. Figure out what they want me to pay for her freedom. I'll give them my last dollar."

"I can't do that." For a million reasons, and one being that the perpetrators hadn't indicated they were interested in bargaining. The perps had exactly what they wanted. An almost complete set of backup and, with Spring, great leverage on Barrows. Plus, if everything that Skye had said was true, the perps now had the missing code, because Spring knew it. His blood ran cold with that thought. He hoped to God that they didn't know what they had.

Luminous gray-green eyes, shiny with fatigue and fear, studied him. "Do you have any fucking clue as to where they've taken her?" She took a deep breath. "Please tell me that you have some idea of who these people might be, and where she is?"

Death would have been easier than being honest with Skye. But she was being brave, she had asked a damn good question, and she deserved an honest answer.

"Not yet."

She held her hand over her mouth in a silent scream before turning fast, running across the rear cabin, gripping the door of the bathroom and throwing it open. She moved so fast he had no idea what she was doing, until she was on her knees, dry-heaving into the toilet. She hadn't eaten a damn thing that he knew of, and he knew she didn't have anything to vomit. But her body was demanding that she break down, and even though her strong-willed brain had no intention of showing weakness, she couldn't stop this reflex. He went into the bathroom with her, knelt next to her, and massaged her back until the spasms stopped.

After, he lifted her from the floor, eased her to the couch, and wiped her face with a cold, damp washcloth. He handed her a bottle of water, which he was relieved that she took. The coward's way out would have been for him to sit in the forward compartment, under the guise of giving her space. Instead, he looked to the agent who was stationed in the doorway between the two cabins. "Get me the sat phone."

Normally he didn't bother with the satellite phone while in flight, figuring his flight time gave Ragno a break, in which she could digest some of the tremendous volumes of information that her team collected. On this flight, though, he needed to communicate with Ragno.

He took off his jacket, and laid it on the seat in which he'd sat earlier, when the only thing that had been on his mind had been sex. When the jacket hit the leather seat, the bag of jellybeans that Spring had given him fell out of the interior pocket and thudded onto the carpeted floor. Earlier in the day, he'd eaten his way through half of the candy, but the bag still held at least sixty-six.

Or some other increment of three.

His gut twisted at the sight of the opaque jellybeans. As he bent to pick up the bag, his mind played a trick with a flash of denim-blue eyes, shining bright with the light of her innocent smile, and the words that she'd last spoken to him drifted through his thoughts. *"I'll save some cupcakes for you. Yours will be the best."*

In response, he had failed her. Miserably.

The heartache that came with the memory was the kind of suck he could never embrace. It tore his insides apart, immobilizing him, so that he had to drop to one knee as he reached for the bag. The despair that he felt at the thought of the sweet, innocence that was Spring being subjected to the same evil that he'd seen at the safe house overwhelmed him for a long second. He'd never felt so ineffective in his life, and for this moment of failure, he had an audience of one. One was too many. She lifted her head off of her knees and was watching him with a glance of despair and fear that matched what was racing through him. As he held her gaze, she studied him, the look of compassion in her eyes telling him that she was reading him as effectively as anyone had ever done.

Shake it off, he told himself. He touched the bag, gently picked it up, placing the jellybeans into his pants pocket as he stood. Putting the emotions on the backburner.

Easier said than done, and now that his emotions were involved, the tailspin he'd been in for the last four days was uncontrollable. He fought hard to keep his face calm, as his agent returned to the cabin and handed him the sat phone. Maybe he needed to sit in the forward cabin. Emotional ineffectiveness wasn't going to find Spring. As he took a step forward, Skye said, "Please stay with me."

It all still sucked. Yet her soft voice, those few words, instantly made him feel like he wasn't losing control of the most precarious situation in which he'd ever been. He sat on the couch, next to Skye. She stayed in her self-protective, knees-up huddle, but when she placed her forehead back on her knees she leaned against him. She slid her arm across his waist as if she needed to hold onto something solid to anchor herself. Fear came off her in waves, but she was hanging tough. God he admired her. Her strength, her ability to hold it together, her understanding that there was, for the moment, absolutely nothing she could do but trust that he'd come through.

Sebastian took a moment to inhale the clean, sweet fragrance of her hair, enough of a jolt to reinforce his determination. To find her sister, to figure out what the fuck her father was up to, and to get through this entire clusterfuck without further collateral damage.

He lifted the sat phone to his ear and wrapped his free arm around her, drawing her closer. Her hand fisted into his shirt, and he felt her hot breath against his chest, right over his heart. "Ragno," he said, holding the phone to the ear that was closest to Skye so that she could hear Ragno's side of the conversation as well. "Talk to me."

Ragno drew a deep breath. "Too damned busy weaving all these threads of research together like a silkworm."

"Anything sticking yet?" His only hope of finding Spring lay in the profiles that Ragno's team was generating. He hoped like hell that there'd be some sort of intersect, some clue that would tell him where to look. And fast.

"Not yet," she said, "but the cocoon's growing. Are you really going to march into Senator McCollum's office, with Barrows' cataclysm scenario being your only roadmap?"

Yeah. With nothing more than his certainty that at least Skye believed her father, even if he wasn't so damn sure. "Absolutely," he said, allowing none of his skepticism to shade his voice. He was rewarded when Skye squeezed her arm more tightly across his waist, as some of the tension left her body. "I don't have the luxury of time on this one." He looked forward to seeing the senator's face when he told him he was acting on instructions from Richard Barrows, and that he had to see the President of the United States.

Where was that going to get him? *No fucking clue.* All he knew was that the tailspin had picked up speed, and just as he had followed his gut when it told him he needed to talk to Skye and Spring in person, his gut was telling him the same thing with McCollum.

Gut instinct aside, he needed a few facts. Something. Anything. "You're now working with developing profiles on Barrows, Root, Young, BY Laboratories, Whittaker, our former Black Raven agents, and checking for intersections, and any link to Senator McCollum, right?"

"Yes," Ragno told him evenly, without reminding him that she knew her job and was the best at what she did, and didn't need reminders from him. "Pieces and parts, integrating more data than five freaking super computers. No one in my department is getting so much as a pee break until we figure this out."

"Something's going to break soon," he said, offering encouragement, though not at all sure there would be a connection.

"Aside from our bladders?" she muttered under her breath, the click-clack of her typing not pausing. "It's a challenge, and we're all up for it. Right now we're hacking our way through the universe, and we're being damn careful not to leave footprints. This takes time, Sebastian."

"I know."

"When you get your hands on Barrows or his backup, please deliver straight to me. If Shadow Technology actually does what the man claims, my job would be a hell of a lot easier. Black Raven would rule the universe."

"Duly noted," he said, "just talk to me. Tell me what you find, as you find it."

He glanced into Skye's eyes, absorbing her pain and misery and pairing it with his own. He touched his lips to her forehead. "We'll have a safe house for you in D.C."

"Sebastian?" Ragno asked.

"Talking to Skye now."

"Gotcha," Ragno answered.

"I know you'd prefer to not be away from the search and rescue mission," he said to Skye, "but I need you to cooperate and go to the safe house without argument. You'll know what I know, as I know it. I promise. Any important developments."

Skye shook her head, drawing a deep breath as she readied herself to argue with him, but he didn't give her the opportunity to respond.

"I need to know that you're safe. Otherwise," he swallowed, not wanting to admit it to himself, much less to her, but knowing that anything less than total honesty wouldn't work. "I won't be able to function. Please don't argue with me on this. Please."

She held his eyes for a long minute, before nodding.

Chapter Twenty Four

From the peace of his office, Trask observed Barrows' youngest on the monitor, listening to her every delicious sniff through the audio system. She'd been there for an hour, and was long past the incessant screams of 'no' that had marked her arrival. She was also past the harsh sobs that had torn at her throat, so that now she gasped and choked just to breathe. Now, trussed up in the pure white straight jacket that had taken three men to strap her into, she was no longer capable of tearing at her hair or self-harming. She'd been responsible for most of the scratches on her face. Her long black hair hung stark and straight, as she rocked and mewled like a hurt animal. A beautiful, meandering rivulet of crimson blood dripped from her right nostril, past her lips, and down her chin.

He'd watched her long enough to know that a clean bullet to her fucked-up brain would be a mercy killing. Yet in the same manner that he craved killing and torture, he wanted to get closer to the beautiful girl. Wanted to touch her, to look into her denim-blue eyes, to smell her, but her uniqueness presented a problem for him. His captives never saw his face. The molded silicone mask's colorful distortions disturbed even grown men, who weren't afraid of anything. Research told him that Spring wasn't normal. By the abject, wide-eyed fear that was in her eyes, fear at her surroundings, fear with each gentle touch of his medical staff, he knew that she wouldn't be able to handle his mask.

Not that he gave a flying fuck if he put her into cardiac arrest before this was done, but he needed her right now. Later, he'd play.

The daughter was in the room that adjoined Treatment Room B, where Barrows was now positioned, once again in his wheelchair, with firm ankle and wrist restraints. The man couldn't move. All he'd been able to do, for the last hour, was listen to his daughter's cries. Thanks to the media system, they'd amplified every sound that had come out of her. He turned his attention to the monitor that showed Barrows. Eyes squeezed shut, Barrows sobbed brokenly.

She rocked with increasing power. He could watch her for hours, but time was a luxury he didn't have. He pressed a button on the intercom system, which was connected to the treatment room. "Medicate the girl," he said, to the lead doctor on his staff. "I need her to calm the fuck down. Her father needs to hear every word I say, and I don't want her hysterics to get in the way. When she's sedated, remove the straight-jacket."

The monitor that showed Barrows revealed a man who was shivering with grief and fear. Blisters from yesterday's water torture were bursting, and his skin was cracking. Trask couldn't comprehend loving anyone–or anything–as much as Barrows apparently loved this kid, but that would work in his favor. "Let's give him a glimmer of hope. Make him believe he can control the situation. Once she's calm, clean them both. Let her have her things, if that's what it's going to take to calm her down, until the medicine takes effect."

He'd looked through her rhinestone-covered backpack, seen the tablets with endless pages of numbers and words, and had immediately handed it all to his tech people. It was too fucking bizarre not to mean something. Whether the idiots who were working for him would be able to figure it out, though, was another matter entirely.

"Keep a copy of those tablets with the analysts, but make sure the originals are in her backpack. I want to see if the numbers and words mean anything, and maybe father and daughter's actions will tell me. Give father and daughter a few minutes of a reunion and then I'll go in."

He gave more instructions, staging the scene so Spring wouldn't see him, just in case the drugs didn't put her out entirely. He waited as his instructions were implemented.

Cleaning, drugging, and bandaging the two of them took his medical staff about an hour. Barrows was freed of his restraints. Bandages on his face covered the worst areas. His hair was combed, and he wore a fresh gown and a robe. Spring was calm, barely awake on the gurney that they'd use to wheel her into the room. Her backpack was on the shelf below the mattress.

Together again. At last.

These two were a living testament as to why emotions and attachments reflected weakness and stupidity.

At the sight of his daughter, Barrows became less broken. He stood as the gurney entered the room, even though his broken left leg could support no weight. He hobbled to where the aids positioned Spring, bent to her and smoothed her hair back.

"Spring, baby." Her eyes opened, and the cameras behind Barrows captured the moment. For a second, she was confused, before her eyes widened in fear. She shrank away from him. "It's me, honey," he said. "Dad. Everything's going to be..." his voice trailed off as he looked around the room. He leaned closer to her. The high-tech audio picked up even the faintest whisper, as he lied to his daughter, with remarkable conviction, "You're going to be fine. You just rest, okay?"

They were positioned exactly as he had requested. Barrows was against the wall, Spring, drugged and drowsy on the bed, was lying on her side and facing her father. Her eyes were shut. The treatment room was large, and there was enough space between Spring's bed and the door for him to do what needed to be done. They had set up a workstation for Richard, with a stainless steel table at a height that was comfortable with his wheelchair. On top of the table was a laptop computer that was not networked with anything except the lead analyst in the computer room, who was going to be overseeing each of Barrows' keystrokes.

Enough of this saccharine-sweet, fucking reunion. Time to get down to business.

Trask entered the room. His masked presence inspired Richard to assume a protective huddle, with his upper body leaning over his daughter. "Where's Skye?" Richard asked.

"Unable to join us at the moment."

"You sick fuck. I demand to see her."

"Your demands have no bearing on what happens here." He nodded in the direction of the young woman. "Count as a blessing that I have provided you with an opportunity to be with this one."

Barrows glared at him. He refocused his attention on Spring, who lay still and unresponsive, even as he talked to her. Fury on his face, he glanced up. "What did you give her, you depraved psycho?"

Barrows had no idea. *Hell.* Trask had no idea, nor did he care, what drugs the medical staff had given to her. "A strong dose of Valium."

"What else?"

"Nothing."

"She doesn't react like this to Valium."

He shrugged. "Well, she's had something else. Doesn't matter. I wanted her quiet. In my world, I get what I want."

"She can't open her eyes, you son of a bitch."

The girl whimpered.

Well, maybe she couldn't open her eyes, but she could certainly hear or sense her father's agitation. "Put on her headphones, if you don't want her upset more than necessary. And I can assure you, our conversation is about to take a turn." Barrows had enough energy to shoot him a look of pure hatred.

"She doesn't have..."

He gestured beneath the gurney. "Her backpack."

Barrows snatched up the bag, reached inside, and pulled out the pink headset, which he gently placed over her ears, smoothing her hair and kissing her forehead as he did.

Without the aid of the cameras, he couldn't see the girl's face, but she was quiet and still. He didn't give a shit if she was sleeping, drugged, or almost dead. Her role here was done.

"Here are the facts on which you need to focus," he informed Barrows. "If you do not do exactly as I say, you will lose both daughters today."

Barrows tried to lunge at him, but since he was almost as incapacitated as the kid, he didn't get close. He didn't even have the force to move himself around the gurney, which separated them. "Bring Skye to me," Barrows said.

"You're in my world, and here we play by my rules. Rule number one is the time for conversation is over. I don't want to hear you. Rule number two. If you want to live, if you want your daughters to live, you do exactly as I say. There are no other rules."

"Shadow Technology will never be yours," Barrows said, defiant, as he stroked his daughter's arm. "Even I can't break the encryption technology that I designed for the LID."

"My patience has run out. And when my patience runs out, I like to hurt small, innocent things." He cast a glance at the back of the girl. She was still. He returned his attention to her father. "Time for procrastination and playing games is over. I have the backup from both Hickory Lake and South Carolina. Even so, we need some assistance in running the programs. My world. My rules. You're smart enough to understand the very simple rules that now govern your actions. You just broke rule number one."

He walked over to the girl's bed, leaned over it, and gently stroked the curve of her hip, drawing fuel from the fear he saw in Barrows' eyes.

"Do. Not. Break. My. Rules. Again. There's a laptop behind you. We have reached a point in the program where we need a password. We've received a prompt that contains the word cardinal. We know there are words, numbers, and letters in your daughter's tablet that translate into code, but the word cardinal is not there. We will figure this out eventually, but I thought it would be more expedient to ask you the question directly. Our next option is to awaken your daughter and see what we need to do to get her to cooperate, because it is obvious to us from the material in her tablets that with her ability to translate words to letters and letters to numbers, she is a tool that will be useful to us in figuring out your passwords. If you want to spare your daughter that interaction with us, type the correct input on the laptop that's behind you. I'll know in a matter of minutes whether it works. If you make a mistake or fail to cooperate, the excruciating deaths of your daughters will be on your head."

Face gray, eyes wide, Barrows shook his head. "You can't do this."

"I can, and I am. You just broke rule number one. Again." Trask had anticipated this. "I warned you of the consequences. Bring Skye in."

His aides led a woman into the sterile exam room. The captive wore a white linen hood, loose white pants, and a white shirt that was fitted just enough to show a female shape. Her hands were handcuffed behind her back and her feet were chained together. Medicated and barely able to walk, she had a similar body type to the older daughter.

Barrows' abject horror was everything for which he'd hoped. The aides let her drop to her knees, about ten feet from Spring's bed.

His assistant handed him his Beretta, equipped with a silencer. He squeezed the trigger, firing two rounds in quick succession to her chest, in the heart. Blood splatter and flesh particles rained down on Barrows and the back of his sedated daughter.

Objective fulfilled.

Jennifer dead and Barrows mortally afraid for his other kid's life.

He loved a good two-fer.

Barrows was braced against the gurney, but it was clear he was about to collapse. Face grim, hands shaking, he hobbled across the room to the body. Halfway he stumbled to his knees, and on all fours, the last several feet. Like a pathetic mongrel, he rested his head on the shrouded head of the dead woman. An aide was at each arm, their sole job for the moment to keep Barrows from figuring out the identity of the dead woman. Barrows' chest heaved and his body shook with the force of his cries. Trask watched the outpouring of grief in a purely scientific way. In his wildest dreams he couldn't imagine caring for any one human so much.

"One down. One to go. The responsibility of her death lies squarely on you. Ready to go to work now?"

As Barrows started to lift the blood-saturated cowl, the aides pulled him away. Barrows' harsh cries of heartbreak bounced off the walls of the stark examining room.

"My world. My rules. Listen closely, because I'm adding one. Rule number one. I don't want to hear from you. Rule number two. You're going to do exactly as I say. Rule number three. Don't forget how you feel right now. Remember it every second. Be aware of the power I have over you. If you force me to kill that one," he pointed his gun at the gurney, "I assure you it won't be a mercifully quick shot to the heart. I'll give her to my men to play with for a while, after I'm done playing some unique mind games with her. I'll make fucking sure she loses every last bit of her mind and her humanity in slow, agonizing increments. However, if you do as I say, you and your daughter will walk out of here, once I have access to the LID," he said. "The word is cardinal. Type the code that will get us past it."

***

A dusting of snow blanketed the steps that led to the stately Georgetown townhome of Senator Robert McCollum. Though he had a staff of housekeepers, security, and executive assistants, Senator Robert McCollum personally opened the red-lacquered door for Sebastian and Zeus. McCollum was a tall, good-looking man, with a full head of salt and pepper, wavy hair. He had friendly green eyes, ruddy cheeks, a booming voice, and an accent that had intentional, slight undertones of good-old-boy-from-Texas. Broad-shouldered and erect, he was in decent shape for a fifty-five year old man. Being a down-home-yet-sophisticated-good-old-boy was part of his charisma, a trait with which the man was abundantly blessed.

Sebastian had long known that Bob McCollum was also an heir to an oil fortune. McCollum had come to DC with more than his share of money. He didn't need the perks that came with being a senator. Most people would have thought that made McCollum a more honest man than someone who was in political service, simply because they could turn it into a money grab. In Sebastian's estimation, McCollum's motivation for being a politician was far more dangerous than the motivation for money. He was there for power, and Sebastian had understood that about him for years. The D.C. political scene was a chess game for McCollum, and the man thrived at it, all the while running an oil company with interests that spanned from the Gulf of Mexico to the Middle East.

Ragno had provided just enough information for Sebastian to question the look of concerned sincerity that flooded the man's face. When McCollum gave him his usual firm, friendly handshake, Sebastian wondered whether anything about the man was genuine.

Darkness blanketed the city with a chilly, wintry gloom, penetrated only by headlights from incessant traffic and streetlights. The sidewalk was busy with speed-walking, bundled pedestrians. Snowflakes floated in the moist air. Sebastian followed Bob into the warmly-lit townhome, his mind clicking as fast as the constant keystrokes he heard through his earpiece. Ragno hadn't yet been able to provide answers, but she was getting closer. Linked to both him and Zeus, she fed them damning information, as the profiles of BY Laboratories, Young, Root, and McCollum began intersecting.

With the luxury of time, he wouldn't have needed a personal visit to McCollum. He had no time, though, and he was desperate enough to find Spring that he'd do anything for an answer. Anything, he reminded himself, even being calm and playing the ridiculous game of charades that came with doing business with one of D.C.'s elite power brokers.

As McCollum led them through the entry and into the living room of the spacious townhome, with its stark white, modern decorations and its museum quality sculptures and paintings, Sebastian mentally formulated questions for McCollum as Ragno fed him information. Zeus was there as a reality check, a balance to make sure that what happened in McCollum's office wasn't to the detriment of the operation or to Black Raven.

Sebastian had called ahead and told the senator that they were going to deliver a status report on the search for Barrows. Nothing more. The senator, wearing a burgundy cardigan over a crisp white dress shirt, led them into his spacious first-floor study. A navy blue tie was neatly knotted and tucked into the cardigan. Crisp navy slacks were pleated with precision. Dark loafers completed his important-man-at-home look. A fire crackled in the study's oversized fireplace. A black Labrador retriever with gray in her muzzle lifted her head when Zeus and Sebastian entered the study, came over for a good long sniff, and Sebastian petted the dog behind the ears.

"Lucy's looking good," Sebastian said, knowing that the senator adored the dog, who had recently had hip surgery.

McCollum nodded. "She's twelve this year. I'm keeping her in shape with swim therapy. Can you believe that? There's a vet in Virginia who does physical therapy for dogs. Costs a fucking fortune." McCollum waved away the aide who lingered in the doorway. "Tom," he said, "you can shut the door." As he settled into his leather chair, on the business side of a desk that was a solid, oversized plank of polished mahogany, he said, "Gentlemen. Would you like to remove your jackets and get comfortable?"

Sebastian shook his head, keeping his leather bomber on. "We won't be here long."

"At least have a seat. I have to admit," he paused, as Sebastian and Zeus sat in the large guest chairs that were on the other side of the desk, "with the afternoon's news that Richard Barrows' daughter was kidnapped while under Black Raven's protection, I'd have thought that you'd be too busy to provide me a personal update on the prison break."

"Well," Sebastian said, studying Bob's face, careful to keep his own expression calm and trying hard to do nothing to reveal the roiling urgency that was boiling in his gut, "this isn't simply an update."

The senator was too smart to reveal anything in facial features. "Oh?"

Sebastian's first goal, a strategy he had developed with Zeus and Ragno, as the information started to click, was to test how committed the man was to towing the government's official line. "When did the National Security Agency start implementing

Shadow Technology?"

"Excuse me?" McCollum's brow furrowed. Whether the puzzlement was real or not, Sebastian had no idea.

"Since September 11, 2001, you've been on three committees that had direct oversight on intelligence gathering and the workings of the National Security Agency. The Patriot Act Implementation Committee, the Foreign Intelligence Surveillance Act Implementation Committee, and the Committee for the Implementation of the Protect America Act."

"That's right, but I've been on a hell of a lot of committees in my tenure as a senator. I'm in my third term. Seventeen years here," he shrugged, "Legislation evolves. Committees come and go-"

"I'm not here to recap your career," Sebastian interrupted, dropping the pretense of formality. Out of the corner of his eye, he saw Zeus settle back to watch the show, his blacker than black eyes studying the senator. "I'm trying like hell to figure out the motivation for someone to have kidnapped Richard Barrows, and now his daughter."

McCollum sat back in his chair, arched his eyebrows, and shook his head. "And you're looking to me for the answer?"

"That's exactly right. I'm here for you to tell me whether Shadow Technology exists," Sebastian said, "and whether the government has implemented it in their intelligence gathering efforts."

"You're talking about the data assimilation program that Richard Barrows claims to have created for the government?"

"Yes. The program that's encrypted by LID Technology," Sebastian said as he began rubbing his temple with his right hand. When he saw Zeus's eyes follow his movement, he dropped his hand. *Fuck.* The pounding of his headache was a reminder of a past mistake that he'd made. He didn't have time to make a mistake now. "Barrows claims to have developed these programs for the government."

Zeus leaned forward. "It's an easy answer, Senator McCollum. Yes, or no." His tone was smooth, his voice low. As always, Zeus spoke with the quiet authority of a man who expected people to absorb his every word. His posture and expression was one of serious gravity, conveying the silent, underlying message to damn well listen to him or there would be consequences. "Has the government implemented Shadow and

LID Technologies?"

McCollum drew a deep breath, and sighed. "Sebastian, Zeus," he said, his gaze encompassing both. "How long have I known you two? I'd help you out with this, if I could. You know that. But you're asking about matters that are integral to highly sensitive operations."

"We're not seeking the official governmental line," Sebastian snapped. "And the answer to how long I've known you is years. Your family's company was one of my first clients in Iraq, and it's been a steady relationship since. Yes, I'm asking for sensitive information. What you tell us will go no further. PRISM is public knowledge. Other data-gathering efforts of the intelligence agencies are public knowledge. We know about the massive volumes of data the Government is collecting on all U.S. citizens under the guise of intelligence surveillance. We know the government has spent two billion dollars on data storage facilities in Utah, and we know there are plans to spend more. The American public may be hoodwinked, but you can't honestly expect us to believe the government hasn't come up with a method to assimilate and organize all the data it's collecting."

"There's a limit to what I can discuss," McCollum said. "Even with you, on intelligence matters and especially on PRISM."

Ragno, who was listening, said, "Well, now we know he's pretty damn committed to towing the government line."

"Okay. I'll try it this way." Sebastian reached into the pocket of his leather jacket, pulled out a piece of paper, leaned forward, slapped the paper down in front of the senator, and said, "This message is for the Oval Office, and you're the person who is to get it there. It means whomever has kidnapped Richard Barrows is within an inch of breaking the encryption codes that protect Shadow Technology. Once he does that, he'll have access to every piece of information accumulated by the National Security Agency. Banking information. Intelligence on U.S. citizens and foreigners. He'll be able to do whatever he wants with the information, including manipulating the data. He'll be capable of paralyzing commerce, with just a few keystrokes."

McCollum read the three sentences that Skye had written, and gave Sebastian a slow headshake, his clear green eyes not giving a bit of a hint as to his inner thoughts. "I've got no idea what this means, and no idea what you're talking about." He narrowed his eyes, "Are you buying into Richard Barrows' conspiracy theories?"

Ragno said, "Sebastian. Zeus. I've got it. If I have to, I can prove that the McCollum's hands are all over the deal. More data's coming in. It's a go. Start playing hardball."

Sebastian glanced at Zeus, who gave him a nod that said go for it, even though the accusations he was ready to lobby were the equivalent of throwing gasoline on a bridge that should never be burned. A clock, positioned next to the fireplace, chimed with six melodic rings. Six p.m.

Fuck. Me. To. Hell.

Spring had been missing for three and a half hours. He grit his jaw, fighting for calmness, when what he really wanted to do was wrap his hands around McCollum's neck and strangle him to within a centimeter of his life.

"I'll cut to the chase," he said with barely leashed anger. "My intel tells me that Zachary Young, Richard Barrows' partner, attempted to sell Shadows and LID Technology to the person who has kidnapped Richard Barrows."

As McCollum leaned forward, his desk chair squeaked. He dropped his hands down on his desk. "How do you know this?"

Ragno had narrowed the potential purchasers to five, and the profiles had revealed long conference calls involving Senator McCollum, Young, and Root in the relevant time frame. To complete the goal of finding Richard Barrows and Spring, five potential purchasers were four to many. He needed to know the one, and he needed to know where the one who had prevailed was currently holding Spring. That's what he needed to get from the goddamn fucking politician, who was sitting across from him and doing a damn good job of acting like an innocent man.

Sebastian leaned forward, closer to the senator's desk. He imitated the man's posture and position, placing his palms flat on the plank of smooth wood and giving the man a hard glare as he listened to Ragno's steady, calm voice, as she fed him information. "Bob," he said, dropping any formality and using the shorthand version of the senator's first name, "do you know how many times you've hired me in the past thirteen years?"

The senator shook his head.

"Sixty-seven. Mostly in contracts in the Middle East. You've hired Black Raven through your oil companies and you've also been instrumental in getting us hired through government contracts. You do it because we deliver. Black Raven isn't good. We're great. You've said it yourself. And the reason why we're great is, in addition to agents with brawn and guns, we have an entire think tank behind the scenes.

"Today's battles are won not just though a show of power, but on analyzing data. We've recreated the events that took place in the lives of Jennifer Root and Zachary Young for the last three years. Every banking transaction, every trip, every credit card transaction, every e-mail, and every phone call."

The desk chair squeaked again, and the senator's shoulders sagged. Slightly. "When Richard Barrows' oldest daughter told me you were the conduit her father had planned for the Oval Office, I had Ragno profile you as well."

Sebastian felt better when the senator's ruddy cheeks became pale. "Are you insinuating that I somehow am involved in what is going on with Richard Barrows?"

"Come on, Bob," Zeus said, a low note of humor obvious in his quiet tone. "That's exactly what we're insinuating. You knew it the moment we called."

The senator stood. Sebastian and Zeus did so as well.

Ragno's voice broke in. "Sebastian. Zeus. I'm cross-referencing data on our prior agents, who may have had knowledge of recent transportation procedures used at Last Resort. I've got two common elements with our prior agents and the five prospective purchasers. One is Trask Enterprises. Another is a Russian company. Other intel narrows it to Trask, but we still need confirmation from the senator on that."

"You knew the value of the technology, because you knew the government was implementing it. You, Root, and Young negotiated the deal with Trask Enterprises," Sebastian said. "Yes or no?"

"I did no such thing."

Sebastian felt better when he heard the tone of indignation in the senator's voice. He could smell the pine logs that were burning in the fireplace, could smell Lucy's dander, and as he leaned across the desk, he could smell the stink of nervousness that was beginning to infuse the air around the senator.

"Bob, here's where I get to educate you on the difference between me and the law enforcement officials who work for the federal government. You know that lady with a blindfold who holds the scales of justice?"

The senator gave a slow, puzzled nod.

"I don't give a flying fuck about her, or her concept of justice.

I'm hired to do a job, and that's all I care about. For this job," Sebastian said, leaning further across the desk, more into the man's space. "I'm not hired to do one thing that might tarnish your career. My goal is to find Richard Barrows and throw his ass back in jail," Sebastian said. "Understand?"

The senator nodded, his eyes intense and focused on Sebastian. "I understand that, because I hired you to keep prisoners exactly where they're supposed to be."

"You hired me so that you could say just that, to make sure no one looked to you. Ever." Sebastian said. "The truth is you hired my company to give you somewhere to point your finger, when the prison break occurred, to cover your ass when news leaked of Barrows' escape, which we all now know was a kidnapping. Let me repeat. My goal is only to find Richard Barrows. Now, that includes his youngest daughter. It also includes finding the sick sons of bitches who killed my agents. For the moment, I'd like to think you weren't involved in that. I'd like to give you the benefit of the doubt, that you were only the driver of this deal. That you left the details to others. Well, those others are going to pay for what they've done," Sebastian drew a deep breath. "Unlike you, if I meet my goals, I don't need to point fingers anywhere, and I don't plan on pointing my finger at you, unless you give me a reason. Do you fucking understand that?"

Cheeks that had been pale were now flushed with red. "Are you threatening me?"

"No," Zeus said, his voice low, his tone matter-of-fact. "Not at all. What Sebastian is telling you is that he has your balls in his hand, and it's up to you how hard he squeezes."

Double-teaming the senator with his new reality would have been fun, if the stakes weren't so high, if Sebastian had never seen Skye and Spring in person, if he hadn't fallen for the sisters as hard as he'd ever fallen for anything in his life. This wasn't fun. It sucked. And he didn't have the time that it was going to take to negotiate a deal with this devil.

He swallowed back his impatience and said, "The way I see it, right now Black Raven has two choices. One, all the crap Black Raven now knows about you and your involvement can be shared with the marshals and any other federal agency involved in this investigation. Or two, it never needs to see the light of day. If your involvement gets exposed, it won't be through Black Raven. Your fucking choice, option one or-"

"Sebastian, Zeus, the talking head on the news this morning,

Whittaker," Ragno interrupted, and he paused, staring at the senator as he listened to Ragno, "was paid large amounts by a company that has connections to Trask. This week. Wire transactions occurred yesterday. Contributions from that company have also been made to the Committee to reelect Robert McCollum, as well as other companies owned by Trask. Many, many contributions."

Ragno's news resulted in a new problem. He glanced at Zeus, whose dark eyes were intense as he nodded to Sebastian. They both knew of James Trask, the man behind the conglomeration of companies under Trask Enterprises. Black Raven had provided protection in South America to oil interests, where the threat was discovered to be from people associated with Trask Enterprises. Trask was known to be a brilliant, ego-driven narcissist, whose ideas weren't always based in reality. He was also a recluse, seldom seen in public. His companies had properties all over the world, with hundreds of properties in the U.S. alone. "Location?"

Not able to hear the mic'd convo, the senator looked puzzled. "Wh-"

Sebastian put up a hand to quiet him.

"We need that from the senator. I can't pinpoint it yet," Ragno said. "Maybe not for a while. However, I know McCollum, at the time the negotiations with Young, Root, and Trask were ongoing, spent a good bit of time in Norfolk, Virginia, at the east coast headquarters of Trask Enterprises. The senator's security detail and aides love Waffle Houses and strip clubs in their time off. Lots of credit card transactions at both of those places. Among other things."

"Your choice, Bob," Sebastian said. "Option one or two? One, do I spoon feed everything I've got to the FBI or whatever Senate subcommittee might be tasked with focusing on impeachment targets, or, two, do I pretend it doesn't exist and," he paused, sweetening the deal, "if the opportunity to make you look good presents itself, seize it."

The marked silence between Sebastian and Zeus gave the senator a moment to invent options for himself that did not exist. With his face beet red, the senator cleared his throat. "Does your option two include destroying the data that you have that links me to Trask?"

Sebastian exchanged a glance with Zeus. Black Raven didn't usually destroy data. They didn't broadcast it, but that was a far cry from destroying it and potentially interfering with investigations by law enforcement agencies. The senator lifted his hands to his temples and squeezed, hard. "If you agree to my terms, I can tell you exactly where James Trask is holding Richard Barrows."

"Our option two does not include destroying data," Sebastian said, sinking into his chair, readying himself for the negotiation. "We may not broadcast it and we may not deliver it to the FBI with a bow on it, but we don't destroy it. I'd prefer to admit failure and lose Richard Barrows and his daughter. I can assure you of one thing. If that happens, I will take you down with me. I will destroy you."

Sebastian and Zeus had planned the negotiation strategy. While he wanted to fly over the desk, knock the man down, and pound his head against the floor until his thick skull cracked and brains leaked out, Sebastian curbed the impulse. Once he received the go-ahead nod from Zeus, it took ten minutes of time that he didn't have, but after painting a picture of political, personal, and family ruin from which the senator would never recover, Sebastian and Zeus walked out of the townhouse with exactly what they had hoped for.

Chapter Twenty Five

Within minutes of McCollum pinpointing the location, the twenty-agent mobile tactical force that Sebastian had on stand-by in Denver was en route to Norfolk, Virginia. The C130J was stocked with weapons, ammunition, explosives, parachutes, night-vision goggles, bulletproof vests, thermal imaging equipment, rappelling equipment, and any and all additional equipment necessary to outfit fifty agents. The cargo hold also held two armored vehicles and a combat-ready chopper, equipped to handle medical evacuations. A physician and four paramedics completed the unit.

Like a good Boy Scout, Sebastian was prepared for all sorts of shit to hit the fan. Problem was, this wasn't about fucking merit badges. What the plane didn't carry was an answer to the question of the safest, most efficient, foolproof way to extract Spring and her father. That fell to him. While he'd love to rush in and grab her, the one thing his experience had taught him was a hastily-planned extraction was a surefire way to lose her.

In the background, Ragno continued to assemble the forensic information, bringing all the threads together. Sebastian's mind raced through options as intel streamed in. Flight time from D.C. to Norfolk was two hours less than the flying time for the Denver-based team. As he stepped off the jet and into the private, secured hangar, Ragno said, "The sum of all of this is Trask wants for nothing. I'm not sure what you can offer."

"No negotiating," Sebastian said. "He's got what he wants. He has the backup for Shadows and LID Technologies and with Spring there, he's going to have the remaining code. He'll use her to get it out of Barrows." *I hope to hell that's all he's going to use Spring for.*

He stepped into a nondescript sedan with Zeus. Sebastian, riding shotgun, Zeus in back, and Agent Stan Black driving, did recon past Trask Enterprises. As they approached, he signaled for Agent Black to go slow.

The sprawling property spanned a city block, and was bordered on three sides with a ten-foot-tall, wrought iron fence.

Trask Enterprises was housed in a white granite, ten-story building, that spanned more than half of the property. Money there. A lot of it. Small, rectangular windows were on most of the floors. The top two floors had larger, floor-to-ceiling windows. All the windows were tinted, lit uniformly. It was impossible to tell by glancing at the building where people were located on the interior. The team on the ground had reported that distant thermal imaging revealed significant heat sources on the sixth through eighth floors, with minor heat sources spread throughout the rest of the building.

The parking lot was half full of cars. There was only one guard station, with only one official entryway though the fence. Three guards manned the station. At least two additional guards roamed the ground-level parking lot. Those two had Dobermans on leashes. On the fourth side of the building, the side that fronted on the Elizabeth River, there were docks and boats, all owned by Trask.

It wasn't snowing, but the gusty air was damp and chilly. The quiet streets of the warehouse district were slick. Billowing, dark clouds covered the moon and stars. A pile of leaves blew in a swirl down the street.

"Gusty." He turned to glance at Zeus. *Not good for a night drop.*

Zeus nodded in response to Sebastian. "Cloud ceiling's questionable."

"If you decide on a targeted parachute jump onto the roof, the wind and clouds will be problematic," Ragno offered.

"HALO?" Sebastian asked. A high-altitude, low-opening jump might be their best bet. The technique would prevent detection of the plane and jumpers if they decided to access the building from the roof. Trask was no fool. He'd have high-tech tracking systems to notify security if the perimeter was breached.

"What I was thinking," Zeus said. "Extreme accuracy will be a bitch with this wind."

"It might be our only op-"

"Too dangerous. HALO onto a ten-story building under these conditions? I'm analyzing parameters given wind and cloud ceiling," Ragno said. "With freefalling to 3500 feet before opening your chutes, that's a terminal velocity-"

"Ragno," Sebastian said. "We know. Just check out the weather for a HALO drop in approximately two hours, with the understanding that it won't be a cakewalk."

Of the agents who had arrived with him from D.C., four were on the ground, nearby. The bum huddled in a doorway a block down was theirs. A guy who appeared to be sleeping off a drunk in his car about a third of the way into the block was theirs. Two others were unseen, but they hadn't yet stepped onto the property. Two other agents were doing recon by boat on the water side of the building, looking for a weakness there.

"That was Mike Jackson, and Soams guarding the front entrance," Zeus said, his tone grim as they passed the midpoint of the block.

Up until a year ago, both men had been trusted Black Raven agents. "Yeah. Saw them." Sebastian indicated to Agent Black to continue forward. Best not to pass in front twice. His agents—ex-agents—would notice the vehicle if they drove by twice. "Begs the fucking question; how many more of our people now work for Trask?"

"How much of us did they take to him?" Ragno snarled. Sebastian heard her fingers going a mile a minute. Closing gaps, he knew.

"One situation at a time," Sebastian said

"I can multitask," Ragno answered.

Yeah, she could. Like no one else. "Remind me to recommend you get a raise."

"Thank you. I gave myself one last month."

Sebastian grinned. "Hope it was substantial."

In reply, all he heard was her soft breaths and the clacking of her keyboard.

"Back to the hangar?" Agent Black asked.

"Yeah. Hot coffee, energy drinks, and strategies. We'll be ready to fill the others in as soon as they land. I want a foolproof plan in place when they get here." Foolproof, meaning Skye's family would be reunited. As hard as he tried not to think about her, she was in his mind as he raced through scenarios. Each option was viewed with the importance of making sure collateral damage—meaning damage that would affect her—was avoided at all costs.

He'd seen enough of the property and Trask Enterprises building to know that he needed to use all agents who were headed his way. Ragno's team was pulling every satellite map, every public-record plan of the building, and any and all information they could find on James Trask, who had purchased the property three years earlier. After months of extensive renovations, it became the East Coast headquarters of Trask Enterprises. Much of Trask's labor-intensive operations were in Third World countries. Sebastian, having firsthand experience in how much easier it was to work in countries other than the United States, could guess why.

Planning time was torture, yet Sebastian considered, and rejected, multiple methods of attack and extraction. Given the manner in which Trask had brutally killed the marshals and his own agents, he knew he had to be careful. In this situation, to fail to plan was to plan to fail. One false move, and both Spring and Barrows would be dead.

If they weren't already.

"Sebastian. Three of our current agents have prior experience working with Trask," Ragno said. "Two of them are in Syria at the moment and one of them is in Russia. One was perfectly clear with us at the time of hiring, that he's operating under a false identity. Agent Zane Axel."

They didn't often hire agents who were under assumed identities, but it happened when there were good reasons for it. "What are the reasons for the assumed identity?"

"He worked for Trask for seven years. Said he needed to change his name when he left Trask. He's been with us five years. Exemplary record. A valuable agent."

"What were his references, because I'm assuming we didn't call Trask?"

"None. He tested in."

Sebastian was impressed. Very few agents were hired by Black Raven without references. Testing in meant that he went through six months of rigorous exams, mental and physical, without getting paid anything but a subsidence salary. "Find Agent Axel first. While I talk to him, find the other two and talk to them."

"Will do."

With a moment free from Ragno, and a few minutes before they reached the hangar they were using as a staging area, Sebastian called the agent who was in charge of the D.C. safe house where, he knew, Skye was restless, scared, and doing her damned best to hold it together. "How is she?"

"Calm," the female agent said, "but pacing."

"Put her on."

He heard Skye draw a deep breath in the slight pause before she spoke. He visualized her collecting herself, her right hand at her collarbone, tapping at it with her index finger, trying to be calm when she felt anything but. "Please give me good news."

"I know where they are," he said, "and I'm assessing extraction options."

She drew a deep, shaky breath, the kind that pulled every nerve in his body taut. His mind ached to reassure her, while his body ached to hold her. Even now, she wasn't the type to cry. God. She was exactly the kind of woman he had always hoped to find. Before he gave up looking.

Her next question was simple and direct. "How long?"

He glanced at his watch. The C130J was still an hour and a half from landing. He'd have a plan by the time they landed. It wouldn't take more than fifteen minutes to organize the agents. "Not more than four hours. Maybe less."

Silence.

He didn't know what else to say.

"I'm afraid I'll die without them," she whispered. Her tone wasn't accusatory. It reflected that she was staring into the pit of despair, was desperately afraid, and she didn't have a damn soul but him to confide in.

"I know," he said, understanding the stakes long before she voiced them. *Not on my watch.* He wanted to tell her that, but he couldn't. *No one else is dying today.* He couldn't promise that, either. "And that won't happen, if I can do anything in my power to stop it."

Lame beyond words. But honest. Anything else amounted to false assurances, because he didn't have control of the situation. Not yet. While confident in his ability to rescue Spring and Barrows, he had no idea what shape the two were already in, nor did he know what the hell was going to happen the minute Trask became aware that his property was breached. He added, "I'll call the minute I know more."

"Thank you," she said, her voice firm. "Be safe."

"Sebastian," Ragno interrupted, and the connection to Skye was gone, "I've got Agent Axel on the phone. I've given him the facts."

"Sir," Agent Axel said. "I was in charge of Central American security operations for Trask Enterprises. I left before Trask acquired the Norfolk, Virginia property. Trask is a paranoid, sadistic son of a bitch. He loves to torture."

Not something Sebastian wanted to hear. "Why did you leave?"

"I understand chain of command, and I understand the need for blind obedience. With Trask, though, I witnessed one too many arbitrary killings."

"Arbitrary?"

"James Trask kills managers whose factories don't meet quotas. Beheadings are not unheard of. He's got handlers who make sure none of his more heinous acts are traced to him. He's nothing but a rich and powerful terrorist, fighting for the glory of nothing but James Trask. I didn't sign up for that, sir."

"You felt compelled to change your name?"

"Yes, sir. I was on the fringe of Trask's inner circle in Central America, working with men who do not have the option of leaving. They're highly paid. Staggering amounts. More than I can ever hope to make as a Black Raven agent."

That said a lot, because Black Raven's pay scale was astronomical. "So he pays for silence and loyalty."

"And he kills people who aren't loyal. Hence my name change. I'm sure he expended significant efforts hunting me down," Agent Axel said. "In his Central American headquarters, several rooms were reserved for Trask's aberrant behavior. His all-consuming need to torture. He called them treatment rooms. They looked like hospital rooms. He had medical staff. The top floor of his building was his private living quarters, and nothing else. He likes his rooms large and spacious, with views. Below his top-floor living quarters was his private office, where only a few people were ever allowed. On the floor below his office were the treatment rooms, with a private stairwell between the floors. I'd suspect he has the same set up in Norfolk. He's a creature of habit."

Agent Axel drew a deep breath before continuing. "Sir. This man craves torturing others. He's a freak. When he's in his torture chambers, or when he's going to kill someone, he wears a strange sort of mask. It distorts his features. Changes colors. In general, it's horrifying. I can't describe it any other way."

Sebastian's stomach twisted. "Anything else?"

"Yes. When I worked for him, he always had an exit strategy. The man didn't so much as drive to one of his own factories, without having his security detail know exactly how to extricate him from any adverse situation that might arise. His overseas holdings are extensive. From Norfolk, he can easily disappear into any number of countries that wouldn't extradite him to the U.S."

Sebastian glanced into the visor mirror. Zeus was also listening to Agent Axel. Their eyes locked. Carefully orchestrated exit strategies indicated that Trask was not the type to stand and fight. Cowards ran. A man worried about saving his own ass might not stop to kill his hostages. A sadist might, however. The security detail in charge of the man would also have other priorities, and those priorities would revolve around saving Trask, not killing hostages, or taking them with him.

Maybe.

He sure as hell hoped so.

"Ragno, Sebastian," Zeus said. "Give me a few minutes."

Sebastian nodded, as Zeus clicked off the shared communication line.

"Hello my sweet angel," Zeus said. "How was school today?"

As they drove back to the hangar, Sebastian's mind focused on extraction scenarios while listening to Zeus talk to his daughter. As always, Zeus's voice was calm and controlled. Yet when he spoke to six-year-old Ana, a soft lining in his tone revealed something the man didn't often show the world-an attachment to something other than Black Raven's work, an attachment that encompassed emotional depth and intense caring. Concern, love, and empathy were evident as he talked with his daughter about her day and her homework, then ended the call with, "I'll talk to you in the morning. Love you, baby girl."

***

Four hours after McCollum gave them the location, Sebastian and Zeus were standing before forty Black Raven agents in the hangar. There were thirty-seven men and three women. Some of the agents had backgrounds in military combat arms, others had SWAT experience. All had excelled in Black Raven's rigorous training programs for firearms skills, problem-solving ability, and team compatibility. Sebastian knew the experienced, elite agents by name, and he was familiar with most of their backgrounds. Anything he didn't know, Ragno and Zeus fed him as he talked. They split into ten four-man teams, with Sebastian and Zeus each taking a team. The other teams were led by the agents with the most experience in hostage rescue and urban warfare.

"Ragno, get McCollum on the phone."

When McCollum answered, he said, "The operation will be noisy. I need you to mobilize a naval team to secure the perimeter and keep local law enforcement away. You might want to prepare after-the-fact press releases that it was a military drill. You're good at bullshit. Think of something. Call me back ASAP with the name of the person who'll be in charge."

To the agent he had singled out, he said, "You're in charge of the liaison effort. Naval personnel are not to get involved or have access to the premises. Perimeter security is their only role. Got it?"

He gave a curt nod. "Yes, sir."

"You are operating under orders of Senator Robert McCollum, who is reporting directly to the President. That is all you know. If there's any issue, tell them to call McCollum. He'll provide further support for keeping them off the property."

"Yes, sir."

"Ragno, mobilize a team of Cleaners. We'll need men here to deal with the fall out."

To his agents, he said. "Goals. One, rescue Spring Barrows. Two, rescue Richard Barrows. Three, James Trask is not to escape. Ragno, stream their photos."

She did.

"Now stream the photos of our former Black Raven agents who currently work for Trask."

As their photographs appeared on a large monitor to his left, and individual iPads, he watched his agents. "Remember these faces. You may know them. They were once Black Raven agents. If these men are in Trask's inner sanctum and if you encounter any of them, feel free to thank them for compromising the integrity of our operations in a manner that led to the death of our agents. Thank them in any manner you see fit and that is warranted by the situation."

He didn't need to be more explicit.

"Sebastian," Ragno said, "That's not-"

He spoke over her. "Sorry, Ragno. Now's not the time for leniency. The teams with Zeus and myself are parachuting onto the roof." The weather wasn't optimal, but a HALO jump was possible. They could handle it. "Omega team will follow us. Omega team will remain on the roof and provide sniper coverage on the action on the ground and be on watch for Trask to attempt an air escape. Omega team will have surface-to-air missiles for use, if necessary.

"We don't know what kind of alarms are in place," he continued. "Landing on the roof may trigger them. The moment alarms are in play, we're engaging in full assault with all teams. Alpha Team is my team. Beta Team is Zeus's team. There are four potential rooftop entry points. Here. Here. Here. And here."

Analysts on Ragno's team were streaming images as Sebastian spoke. Close-range satellite imagery revealed rooftop details. "We'll assess when we get there. We'll make as much progress as we can into the building. The goal is to get to floors seven, eight, and nine, the floors that thermal imaging flagged for us, without setting off alarms. It's highly unlikely we will make it there," he said, acknowledging and embracing the uncertainties they were facing. "Once the penetration by Alpha, Beta, and Omega teams produces an alarm, we'll use all other teams for the mother of all diversions at ground level. Goal is to draw all Trask security to ground level."

"Two teams are to breach the property via water, disable all watercraft, and access the property that borders the waterfront. Two other teams will access the property in armored vehicles. The signal is go, go, go. Upon hearing that, from me or Zeus, go straight through the guard gate and into the doors of Trask Enterprises, using whatever force is necessary."

Ragno interrupted, "Excuse me, Sebastian, but you're authorizing all-out combat. Aside from the Geneva Convention, you're operating on domestic soil. You can't go in shooting to kill anything in your way."

"Sorry, Ragno," he said, "can't hear you-"

"Sebastian-"

"I'm going to turn you off for a while."

More instructions followed. Sebastian didn't intend to let Trask, or anyone of importance, out of the building alive, and he made his intentions clear to his agents. By the steady, focused looks his agents were giving him, he'd bet that none planned on showing mercy. Their own had been killed. It was time for retaliation.

A half hour later, under cover of cloudy darkness and using

night vision goggles, he and twelve other agents parachuted out of the C130J, the cold air enveloping him. He landed on the roof, unsnapped the parachute's bindings, and pulled off his oxygen mask. He listened to nothing but a distant airplane, traffic on a nearby interstate, and the quiet steps of his agents as they assembled into their teams and readied themselves for the extraction. No alarm. At least none that he could hear.

He had reestablished connection with Ragno, and all team leaders were mic'd to her. "HALO successful, Ragno."

"Fabulous. Good luck, all."

Sebastian gave Zeus a nod when they isolated the best entryway, a service stairwell for air-conditioning units. Three shots, fired with a silencer-equipped Glock, took care of the lock. An agent opened the door, and he was in, his M4 Carbine hoisted. Seven cement stairs led to a door wired with an alarm. In the perfect world, he'd have time to disable it. He eyed the mechanism, figured that tampering with it at the door would only trip it. To disable the system, he had to go to another location, and they couldn't get there from where they were. Time they'd lose by backtracking and attempting to disarm the system? Too much.

Team leaders were poised for his command.

"Go, go, go."

Alarms rang. Short bursts of gunfire could be heard, as his men moved forward. Progress was reported in short, clear words and phrases. "Delta Team has docks clear and secure."

"Three guards, at gate. Dead. Two in parking lot, weapons raised. Dead. Armored vehicle through plate glass windows. Two front desk security guards. Dead."

"Two guards, lobby rear. Dead."

"One guard running, North side of building. Running away."

"Do not give chase," Sebastian said. "Focus on building. Perimeter agent will take care of him."

"Fifteen Trask guards, from stairwell, far right of lobby."

As a barrage of gunfire filled the communication airwaves, Sebastian and Zeus and their teams made progress onto the top floor. They parted ways, Zeus down a hallway and Sebastian into the only door on the tenth floor. It led into spacious living quarters, with floor to ceiling windows. No one there. Moving as a unit, he and his team descended a spiral staircase to the ninth floor, into a large, sterile office. Television monitors displayed several other areas of the building, but he focused on only one, a monitor that showed what looked like a hospital room. There was one hospital bed, and a man lay on his stomach on top of it, arm draped down the side. Sebastian recognized Barrows.

There was no telling whether he was alive.

There was no sign of Spring.

Heart in his throat, he descended the circular stairs, leading his team. In room clearing formation, they entered a hallway. Empty. He pointed at the ceiling-mounted cameras. One of his men went ahead and disabled them with gunfire, as they moved stealthily down the length. There were eight doors.

Fuck.

They systematically opened each door and determined that each room was clear. In the seventh room they found Barrows. No Spring.

He ran to the bed.

"Barrows. Found," he said. The man's complexion was gray, his lips tinged blue. "Eighth floor. Unconscious. Sebastian felt for Barrows' carotid, feeling profound relief when he found it. "Faint pulse. Bullet entry in shoulder, another in his back. Doctor?"

"Roger," the doctor responded. "Heading in."

"No. Stand by for clearance from Zeus." He glanced at his agents. "Two of you stay with Barrows. Defend and keep alive. Field dress. Pressure. Get more instruction from doc."

"Omega team," Omega team leader's voice was calm, but barely audible over the whir of an engine. "Foreign helicopter approaching roof."

"At first positive ID that it is for Trask," Sebastian said, "blow it out of the sky."

"Roger. Still only assuming it's Trask's."

He gestured to one of the agents on his team to follow him, then for the remaining two to stay with Barrows. Sebastian ran as he retraced his steps through the eighth floor corridor. The lone team member who was accompanying him ran in stride with him. There'd been no sign of Trask since entering the building. With the helicopter approaching the roof, Sebastian had his first clue as to where Trask was going. Exit strategy. Helicopter. Roof. Enough said.

"Omega under fire."

"Activate missile."

"Done."

Within seconds of hearing the word, Sebastian heard the explosion and felt the repercussions as he ran.

"Sir. Eight Trask personnel. Exiting stairwell. Roof, eastern side. Spring Barrows is hostage. She appears unconscious."

He reached the circular stairwell. Three floors to climb.

"Sir. They have the advantage."

"Beta Team remains on seven," Zeus said. "We do not yet have control of six and seven, but we will prevent their reinforcements from heading up. Copy?"

"Roger," Sebastian said, taking the steps three at a time, not pausing to breathe, running through the ninth floor penthouse, and into the same air conditioning service area through which they had entered the building. He paused at the door, knowing he and his team member had the advantage of surprise on Trask and his men. They thought they only had the four-agent Omega team to contend with.

"Omega, talk to me."

"They're demanding we drop weapons." The response was terse and whispered. "They've got us, two to one. Plus, they have the hostage."

"Our chopper's in the air," Sebastian said, "Three minutes out."

"Too long."

"Tell me location of the hostage and the location of Trask. I'll exit the stairwell on the western side of the building." Same way he'd gained entry. He visualized the roof. He'd seen it in aerial shots, as he parachuted in, and when he'd been standing on it. "From there, will I have a clean shot at Trask?"

"Yes. Position is your ten o'clock. Ten yards. He's fifth from your right. His back is to you. He just took Spring from the man on his right. She's slumped."

"I'll take Trask, the man on his right, and the man on his left. You and your men handle the rest. Open fire as I do. Do not fire if there's any danger of hitting the girl."

Sebastian looked at his team member as he lifted his Glock. "Open the door on my nod. Omega, reconfirm position of Trask."

He shut his eyes for a second, breathing deeply, as he listened to the verbal instructions. It wasn't the first time he'd emerged from cover with an operation's success riding on the accuracy of his bullet. The difference now was he saw Skye and Spring when he shut his eyes and the sight jolted him like an electric shock.

He could not fail. Could not even think the word failure, yet there it was, more than a thought. Failure was suddenly a tangible thing, inspiring the harsh reality of what would happen if he did not succeed. It was an f-word that had no business intruding into his thoughts, yet it was rocking him to his core, twisting his gut, making him realize with laser-sharp clarity why crossing the line in his line of work was something never to be done. He opened his eyes, shook off the f-word and the split-second of hesitation it had inspired, caught the puzzled glance of the agent who was watching him, and took a deep, calming breath.

Fuck.

The whole operation had been a nightmare. It needed to end, and when it did, he wasn't looking back. He needed to feel like himself again. Another deep breath. One more, and he felt normal. One more, and Sebastian was in kill zone, where the world stopped spinning, and all that mattered was the precision with which his shot met its intended target. When he could hear the whump-thud of his heartbeat, when he felt blood crawling though his veins, he was ready.

Following the directions given to him, he emerged from the doorway and took aim. Finger on the trigger, he took only the edge of a second to confirm that Trask was in the position that he'd been told. Sebastian fired two shots in quick succession—bam! bam!—into the back of Trask's head. Bam! Bam! Two, into the temple of the man on Trasks's left, and two more rapid-fire shots into the forehead of the man on his right. His men took advantage of the element of surprise and killed the others.

Without pausing, he ran to where Spring lay, face down on the ground. Trask had fallen over her, face first, lying sideways across her. She wasn't moving. He kicked Trask's body off of her, bent to her, feeling for a pulse behind her ear. When he felt the flow of blood through her body, he was able to draw a deep breath. He gently turned her head so he could see her face. It was drained of color, a trace of blue veins beneath her pale skin. Her hair was matted and filthy. A bruise smudged her jaw. She was dressed in a flimsy hospital gown, wearing only panties underneath. Clear fingerprint bruises on her upper arms and legs showed that she'd been manhandled.

Rage pulsed behind Sebastian's eyes. He glanced at Trask and made sure he saw no sign of life. "Spring? Honey? It's Sebastian. You're safe. I have you. Can you open your eyes?" Into his headset, he said, grimly, "Doctor. Location?"

Spring's eyes remained closed as Sebastian smoothed her hair off her face.

"Still trying to get to Barrows on eight. I'm on five. Getting ready to head through the fighting on six and seven."

"Zeus here. Western stairwell." Over Zeus' words, Sebastian heard three pops of gunfire, and then, "Is now clear for you Doc."

Spring's breathing was slow, but like her pulse, the rate was steady. Though her body was limp, there were no gunshot wounds, no blood. For Spring, he knew the trauma would be mental, if not physical. Her hair blew wildly, as the chopper landed on the rooftop nearby. He sheltered her with his body, picked her up, and cradled her against his chest. He ran, hunched over to avoid the spinning rotors. He shielded Spring with his body from the rushing, cold air, as the helicopter landed.

Two paramedics, about to jump down, gave him a nod. The chopper was equipped with the latest medical personnel and equipment, yet he was reluctant to hand over his burden. His arms tightened around her before he handed her up.

"Take a stretcher to eight for Barrows," he instructed, as two other men jumped onto the rooftop and ran to the stairs. He watched for a moment, as the paramedics strapped Spring onto a gurney and administered oxygen and an IV.

Sebastian stepped away. "Doctor?"

"Just getting to eight." He was out of breath.

"Timing issue. Stretcher's on its way to eight. How long before Richard is ready for travel, because I'll send the chopper to the hospital with Spring, if it's more than 15 minutes."

"Not there yet." He heard heavy breathing as the doctor ran the remainder of the way.

"Doc, you sound like you're out of shape."

"I'm ignoring that, asshole."

Sebastian chuckled. He waited, while every fiber in his being hoped that Richard Barrows wasn't bleeding out.

"He's lost one hell of a lot of blood, but the agents here seemed to have managed to stop the flow. Damn. Pulse is weak. We don't have the luxury of keeping him here one second longer.

He'll be up in five minutes. Four if we're lucky. That includes travel time to roof."

"Will he live?"

"Looking grim."

Answer enough.

To the paramedic, who was slipping an IV needle into Spring's arm, Sebastian said, "Prognosis?"

Dark brown eyes held his for a second and the paramedic gave him a nod. "She's sedated. Not sure with what, but she should be fine."

Two agents from Omega team remained on the roof, which was littered with the bodies of Trask and his men. Two Omega agents walked the perimeter, ready to provide rooftop support for any ground action and keep the rooftop secure, in case any other Trask personnel made the mistake of trying to evacuate that way. At the moment, though, there was no action outside. All remaining agents had descended into the building to help the fight on seven and eight.

"Zeus," Sebastian reluctantly moved away from the chopper. Spring was in excellent hands, and she wasn't his only priority.

"Copy."

"Where's the most resistance?"

"Eight. Southeastern corner. Gunfire in stairwell. We're in the computer lab. Fuckers started a fire."

"Headed there now." Sebastian jogged down the stairs, passing the ninth floor as they communicated. "Any sign of Barrows' backup?"

He heard a round of automatic gunfire, as Zeus answered. "Fighting gunfire and fire as I search."

"Omega agents on the roof. When you can, search any bags that Trask and his men were carrying. Ragno. Get me Skye." He wanted to tell her himself that her sister was safe.

As Sebastian went into the western stairwell, the agents and the paramedic went by him, carrying Richard Barrows on a stretcher. The doctor, who was running alongside them, flipped Sebastian the middle finger. He and Doctor Richard Williams had been friends for years. Dick was a slender six-feet tall and, when he wasn't working, he participated in ultramarathons. He regularly trained other agents in physical fitness drills. "That's for saying I'm out of shape. I'll challenge you to a 10-mile drill, course of my choosing, anytime."

Sebastian chuckled. "You're on."

"Get your head fixed, Sebastian." *Fuck.* He didn't need Dick reminding him of a pending date with a neurosurgeon. "Then call me."

He was ten steps from the door that would lead him to eight, when Ragno said, "Sebastian, here's Skye."

She said, "I'm here."

"Spring and your father are on their way to the hospital. Spring is sedated. She should be fine." He paused before opening the door, and softened his voice, but knew Skye well enough to know that she would want to know what he knew, without sugarcoating. "Your father isn't doing as well. He was shot. Twice. He's lost a lot of blood. There are other wounds from his time in captivity. We're not sure of prognosis."

Silence.

"Skye? You okay?"

He heard her draw a deep breath. "Thank you," she whispered. "I've got to get to the hospital."

"Raven One will take you. You're leaving now. Ragno will keep you informed of their progress, as you're en route."

He broke the connection, pausing before entering the firefight in the computer lab.

Done.

The job of finding Richard Barrows was over. Spring was safe. Trask was dead. Mission? Almost complete. The rest was details. He shook off his personal worry and concern for Skye and told himself he couldn't do a damn thing about whether her father lived or died. All he was left with was a nagging, pissed off feeling at himself, that he'd let the job get under his skin.

Done, he reminded himself.

It was fucking done, and it was well past the time for him to shake off the emotional crap the job had produced. With Trask dead, and the Barrows family on their way to being reunited, there was one loose end that needed his immediate attention. "Ragno?"

"Yes?"

"That profile on Minero. Did it turn up anything?"

"Nothing at all."

Good. That meant he could focus his attention on ending the

firefight at Trask Enterprises. He hoisted his M4 Carbine, drew a deep breath, and opened the stairwell door on eight. The shitstorm was ending. *Now.*

Chapter Twenty Six

Spring was drifting in and out of consciousness. They knew she'd been medicated, but weren't sure with what. She was still in the trauma unit of Sentara Norfolk General Hospital, in a room that was down the hall from where her father was in surgery. Skye was sitting by Spring's bedside, when Sebastian walked into the room, a nurse in scrubs at his side. The redheaded nurse was part of her father's surgical team and had given her two updates, since she had arrived at the hospital.

The look on Sebastian's face was grim. The nurse's features didn't reveal anything. Skye stood, drawing a deep breath, and bracing herself.

"It's good news," the nurse said, her voice low. "Would you mind stepping outside, so I can give you a report on how your father's doing?"

The lights in Spring's room were dim, with the shades drawn. Aside from the soft hums and beeps on the equipment monitoring Spring's vitals, the hospital room and the long corridor immediately outside of it were quiet. Down the hallway, two marshals stood guard outside the doors that led to the operating rooms. She'd met them, and a few others, including Marshal Minero, who she'd done the phone interview with the morning before at Last Resort. They'd all been polite, reserved, and seemed relieved that the ordeal was over.

"They successfully removed the two bullets," the nurse informed her, seemingly oblivious to Sebastian, who stood back, listening. "Now they're repairing the damage. His vitals have stabilized. We're confident his condition will improve, once he's out of surgery. The goal will be as soon as he's not critical, we'll move him to the same suite as your sister." The nurse smiled. "That'll make your visits easier, won't it?"

"Thank you," Skye said, relief pulsing through her. The only thing holding her together now was the tension that bound every nerve. She couldn't collapse. Not now. She needed to be strong when Spring awoke, which could be any minute. She needed to be strong while her father recovered from major surgery. Most immediately, she needed to hold herself together, while she confirmed what she saw in Sebastian's serious gaze. He was about to say goodbye. She knew it. He knew it. It was all over but the telling and watching him walk away.

"Your father has approximately another hour of surgery," the nurse informed her in a soft tone. "I'll come find you, if there's news."

"Please." As the woman walked away, Skye focused her attention on Sebastian. Profound relief and happiness at seeing him was immediately snuffed by her self-preservation instinct, as she took in his intense blue eyes and the grim set of his jaw. There was no smile. No dimples. He carried with him the gravity of a long night and the fall-out from it. "Has Spring woken up yet?"

"No," she answered. "She's resting. Sleeping, really." No one knew yet the long-reaching ramifications. Skye was optimistic, but braced for that conversation with the psychiatrist and the doctors treating her sister.

"The room next to hers is empty. We can talk in there." He wore black cargo pants with pockets, a black t-shirt, a leather bomber jacket, and black shoes with soles made for running. Which he was getting ready to do. She choked on the laughter his shoes inspired, as she caught a glance at the grim look in his eyes. He didn't touch her. Didn't look as if he wanted to touch her, and Skye's mouth went dry as her heart beat hard in her ears. This was it. *I saved your ass, and your sister and father. I'm done here. Nice knowing you. Bye-bye.*

He opened the door for her, waited as she went by, and left it half open.

Braced, she turned to lean against a table that held a vase of silk flowers and a fanned out pile of magazines. She felt a deep longing to be in his arms, with her face pressed against his chest. His formal, erect posture told her he wasn't offering a hug, and the hard, distant look in his eyes warned her that throwing herself against him wouldn't be a good move. He hadn't shaved since the morning before, and the stubble of his beard added to the look of a man who'd been through hell, and conquered it. He ran his fingers through his short, dark brown hair. He stood, just a few feet in the room, with his arms loose at his sides. He smelled faintly of smoke and the outdoors, and his musky-sweet aroma enveloped her. His gaze held hers.

"Ragno, give me a few minutes." He pulled the earpiece, slipped it in his pocket, and gave her all his attention. "I have information, if you want it."

"Yes." Her instincts had been dead-on accurate. This wasn't a comfort call.

"The mastermind behind what happened to your father and Spring was a man named James Trask." He gave her more details, painting a picture that chilled her.

"Is he still-"

"Dead," he said, his tone matter-of-fact, his eyes unreadable. "As are a good many of the people who worked for him."

"How did he get involved?"

He studied her, his eyes intent, the faintest trace of a smile at his lips. "I knew you'd want to know more. This is what we know now. As soon as your father perfected Shadow and LID technology, as soon as he claimed that the NSA would be implementing it, which, by the way, no one with the government has ever confirmed, Zachary Young and Jennifer Root went behind his back and auctioned the technology to the highest bidder."

The two people who her father had trusted over anyone else. She shook her head. "No. I don't believe it."

He arched an eyebrow. "Data is unmistakable. The lawyer and his partner were the impetus. We have phone calls, text messages, and locales for meetings. There were several potential bidders. Trask had inside intelligence and knew exactly what he was buying, because he had inside help."

"Inside? Meaning inside BY Laboratories?"

"No," Sebastian said, with a frown. "Inside the government."

Her heart pounded. "Who?"

He hesitated.

"Who?"

"To get to your father and Spring, I had to make a deal with the man that his name would be left out of this. I'm trusting you would have done the same thing and won't break my word. Can I count on your silence?"

She nodded.

"The same person who your father trusted to get you to the

Oval Office. Robert McCollum knew exactly how vital the technology was and he knew exactly what Trask should be bidding for it. He was well aware of the power it would give Trask. But you didn't hear that from me. As a matter of fact, you will never hear that fact again, and, even though I know you'd probably like nothing better than to see him rode out of Washington on a rail, you can't repeat it. There will be no public airing of the evidence of the senator's involvement."

She drew a deep breath, holding her right hand, palm flat, below her neck, while her thumb touched her right clavicle, her index finger thumping at the left clavicle. His gaze fell on the gesture, then rose, seemingly reluctantly, to her face. "Thank you."

He shrugged. "Not the first time I've had to agree to a distasteful compromise to do a job the right way. Senator McCollum will screw up one too many times, and fail. That's what ultimately happens to men who abuse power. Trust me. I'll be waiting for it and applauding when it happens. In the meantime, I'll enjoy watching him worry about whether I really am going to keep my end of the bargain." The deep undercurrents in his eyes, coupled with his words, chilled her.

"Jennifer?" she asked. "Did you find her?"

He nodded, with a slight frown and, for a moment, a look of concern for her flashed through his eyes. "Dead."

"She caused so much harm. To the people who trusted her the most. I can't wrap my brain around this. I can't switch so fast from caring about her and treating her like family, to knowing she'd trade a family that loved her for money." Skye rubbed her upper arms with both hands, feeling chilled and hot, at the same time as her mind reeled with the reality of what Jen had set in motion. "I don't know how to feel right now."

For a moment she thought he'd close the few feet between them, but instead he shoved his hands into the pockets of his jacket. "I vote for ecstatic. In the long run, your father was correct not to trust her," Sebastian said. "Brilliant move on his part, and it saved you and your sister. Jen was working with the monster, until he decided that he had enough leverage on your father with Spring. Trask recorded everything. The fucking bitch tried to trap your father into revealing your location to Trask. Trask killed her in a manner that I am sure your father will never, not for one day of the rest of his life, get out of his mind."

"How?" she whispered.

"He claimed she was you. In the heat of the moment, with her head covered, your father couldn't know the lie," he frowned, "he threatened to do the same to Spring. From what we can tell from the tapes, your father thinks you're dead."

There was a long pause. The look in his eyes said that he had more details, but her stomach immediately twisted into a knot, as though she'd eaten something rotten, when she hadn't actually eaten in hours. No, she hadn't eaten anything substantial in days. She didn't want to know more details. He was silent for a second, eyes on her, as she stood there, shocked.

He moved a step closer, and suddenly looked like the man she'd been with for the last two days. There was concern in his eyes, compassion, and an understanding that she was barely holding herself together. He suddenly seemed more human than the machine telling her of death and backstabbing. The moment disappeared with a knock at the door.

"Come in," he said, with a shrug and a headshake, physically transforming himself back to the cold, aloof man who was keeping himself an arm's distance away from her.

One of his agents pushed the door all the way open, then stepped closer, and whispered something to Sebastian.

"Two minutes," he answered, "I'll meet you at the ER drive."

Well, now she knew how long he was staying. "Thank you," she said, "for bringing my sister and my father back to me."

"No need to thank me. I was only doing my job."

Only a job.

That was it. The words resonated, filling the room with a meaning that was unmistakable. It explained his aloofness. Everything that she'd been through with him—everything—was only a job to him. Now, he was doing what anyone who had finished a job did. He had already mentally moved on to something else, which meant he had moved on from her.

She'd been a job. That was it. The thought had an immediate, physical impact on her. Deep inside, where her heart was, there was a slow burn. It came with a disappointment that she hadn't allowed herself to experience in years. It stole her breath, scorching through her flesh, leaving a raw hurt, the depth of which took her by complete surprise. She'd given one hell of a lot of tough girl talk.

Once with me won't count.

Hah. He hadn't fallen for it, but she sure had fallen for him.

She'd fallen for her own line, and now she realized just how stupid she'd been. Once with him, no, she reminded herself, thinking about being with him on the plane, twice, and she was going to have to work hard at getting over him.

He was giving her no indication that he was going to have the same problem.

Don't think about it, she told herself. Do not think about it. "Did Trask manage to make sense of my father's backup?"

He gave her a slow headshake and a slight frown. "We're searching now and doing diagnostics on all servers and computers. It's a slow process. There were casualties. Identifying bodies and dealing with authorities takes precedence. Plus, there was a fire at the site. That's making the technical diagnostics more difficult. It's going to take some time.

"Your father will receive medical care here until he's stable. When it's safe for him to travel, he'll be returned to the custody of the Federal Bureau of Prisons. Marshals are already here. You and Spring are under the continuing protection of Black Raven. The Senior Agent in charge of your detail is Agent Katherine Scott. She'll be checking in with you this morning and over the next few days will work out the parameters." He paused, as she started to feel queasy. He was saying goodbye, without uttering the word. Wrong. He'd said goodbye some time ago. She just hadn't realized it. "You'll have my agents with you at all times. If you need anything, just ask them."

Them.

Not him.

Message received.

He stood within touching distance, yet seemed a million miles away, more machine than the man with whom she'd spent the last two days. Rather than stepping closer, he left, without so much as a look of pain, or regret, or any damn thing to acknowledge that they had shared anything, much less something special.

Loneliness cloaked her, suffocating her. He shut the door, and when it clicked shut, the harshness rattled her. She drew a deep breath. The twisting ball of pain that was now her stomach travelled up. She ran to the bathroom, fell to her knees at the toilet, overwhelmed with the need to puke. There was nothing but water to vomit, but that didn't stop the gut-wrenching heaves that wracked her body. When they subsided, she sat down, hard, cross-legged, and held her face in her hands.

Seconds became minutes. He had warned her. To avoid relationships, he'd gone to prostitutes for the last ten years, for God's sake. All to avoid a break-up, which he had labeled, 'an extrication'. He may have been colossally bad with good byes, but he had just delivered the most effective one she'd ever received.

The door opened. *Sebastian?* Her foolish heart leapt.

"Oh, honey."

Her hopes crashed as she looked into the kind, worried eyes of one of her sister's nurses. "Your father is about to be taken into recovery, and your sister is fine. Too much stress, and I bet you haven't eaten since you got here, have you? Come on, let me help you up. There's a girl."

Numb, Skye allowed the nurse to help her out of the bathroom and to a nearby chair. "Sit here for a moment and take deep breaths. Everything's okay now. It really is."

"I'm fine," she whispered, shaking off the very edge of the misery that had enveloped her, as the nurse stood beside the chair to take her pulse. If she said she was going to be fine enough, she'd start to believe it. Once she believed it, she'd feel it. She touched her hand to her cheek, only then realizing that tears were free falling.

"Just fine."

***

11:00 a.m., Friday

"Can we eat pizza for lunch?" Spring's question interrupted her thoughts.

"Of course," Skye smiled at her sister, as she shook off the heavy mood that came with remembering Sebastian walking out of the room two days earlier. The only thing that had made his absence palatable was that she was with her father and Spring. He'd saved them, and when she focused on that, she was better.

The cataclysm scenario was over, and the three of them were safe.

Spring's residual physical injuries amounted to minor scratches and bruises from her struggles against her captors. She remembered some of what had happened in the helicopter and when she had first arrived at Trask Enterprises. For the first twenty-four hours of their stay at the hospital, Spring had drifted in and out of a sedative-induced sleep. Skye had alternated between watching her sister sleep, and watching their father, in the adjoining room, sleep. Spring was going to be fine. Her father was going to recuperate.

The evening before, he'd been conscious long enough to realize that Skye and Spring were both with him, alive, and he was no longer Trask's captive. His relief had been profound. The reunion of the three of them had helped lift the veil of inexplicable misery that had fallen over her with Sebastian's departure.

Over.

Their lives could return to Barrows-style normal.

Now, Spring had anti-anxiety meds prescribed as needed. So far, the morning had been good. She hadn't needed anything, thanks to Black Raven. The supplies that had been collected for Spring while they were at Last Resort had arrived earlier that morning, along with the clothes that they had there. As Spring finished breakfast, an orderly had come into the room, a puzzled expression on his face as he wheeled in a long, rectangular table. "I was told to set this up near the windows."

Spring had already organized five pounds of jellybeans into clear glass bowls. Using a new sketchpad, she was drawing a cake. She held up the sketchpad, and Skye nodded, but barely focused on the drawing of a three-layer cake. "That's pretty, honey."

"You think so? I'm thinking maybe we should have four layers of cupcakes instead of a cake. I just haven't decided what to make to celebrate, when we all get home."

All.

Skye hadn't told Spring that their father wouldn't be leaving with them. When he left, he'd be returning to federal prison to serve the remainder of his term. Skye didn't feel the need to tell her sister that. Not yet.

She gave her sister a soft smile. "We can have whatever you want. And if it's cupcakes, we can find someone nice to give the extras to."

"And I've got to do something Sebastian will like, too, because he's going to be there, right? Do you think he'll visit us today? I really, really can't wait to see him again."

"Maybe," Skye said, turning away from her sister as her smile faltered. It was the second time that day Spring had asked about

Sebastian. Every time one of the Black Raven agents, with their broad chests and logo'd shirts, were visible to Spring, she asked them about Sebastian. Dear God, she had to figure out a way to make her sister forget him.

That might be easy, once she figured out how to do it herself.

"Tell me what flavor the cupcakes will be."

Instantly diverted, Spring flipped the page and started over, from the beginning. The wintery weather event was over, replaced with clear blue skies and crisp weather. Skye had raised the blinds in both rooms as high as she could and opened one of the louvered windows in Spring's room. Light was streaming into the windows of both rooms. She had pulled her chair next to Spring's table, close to the open window so that she could feel the fresh, cool air.

The nightmare was over, she reminded herself. While Spring was focused on drawing, she stood, walked into the hallway, walked the few steps to her father's room, and, when the marshal who stood guard at his doorway moved aside, she peeked in. She was wearing socks, jeans, along with a t-shirt and sweatshirt that she'd gotten in the hospital gift shop. Her soft, silent footsteps made no noise, but somehow, her father sensed her standing by his bed. He opened his eyes and lifted his hand to her, before falling back asleep with a soft smile on his face. Color was returning to his face. So far, he'd been too drowsy, even when awake, to talk about anything that had happened. All that had mattered to him was that she and Spring were together. That they were fine.

She walked back into Spring's room, resumed her position in the chair, pulling her feet up, and resting her arms on her knees, as she watched Spring draw what would be one of many, many cupcakes for the elaborate celebratory cupcake-cake she was planning. "That's beautiful, honey."

Over. The nightmare was over.

She'd had almost forty-eight, no, she glanced at her watch, saw that it was a little past eleven, and she corrected herself. She'd had more like fifty-one hours to process the reality that whatever she and Sebastian had shared when she'd been on the run with him had fizzled into nothingness, the minute his attention was directed elsewhere.

Silly girl, she chastised herself, reminding herself of the life lesson that had been rammed down her throat when her mother died, years before Sebastian had ever walked into Creative Confections.

People leave.

It's what they did. If not physically, emotionally.

Her remedy for the lesson?

Toughen up.

Don't get close. If they didn't leave on their own accord, she'd be happy to lead them to the door with a smile. If she had no expectations, she couldn't be hurt.

Sebastian had saved them. Wasn't that enough? Yes. It was. But seeing how easily he'd become distant hurt her, deep inside, in a place she'd long ago closed off. He'd opened doors that she had kept under lock and key. Or maybe she had opened the doors to him. It didn't matter who had opened that place where hurt lived. She had to close it.

For a second, she tried to tell herself that Sebastian was no different than any man she'd ever come across, but the thought was so preposterous that she almost laughed out loud. She'd have to do better than that, because actually, he was very different. Unique. She'd never fallen so hard before. Hard and fast.

Shake it off, she told herself. *Don't be stupid.* She'd known the moment that she had laid eyes on him that he was unavailable, and he hadn't done one damn thing to mislead her.

"Skye?"

She forced her mental focus to return to her sister. "Yes?"

"Pizza?"

Skye nodded. "That's a great idea, honey. I'm starving myself. We can order plenty for the nurses and for the agents who are helping us. What kind should we get?"

"Pepperoni, mushroom, extra cheese."

"Okay. Let me figure out where we're going to order from," she said, "and we need to talk about where we're going when we leave here." Under the circumstances, she and Spring were going to remain at the hospital, until her father was discharged to the custody of the marshals. How many days that would take was an open question for the moment, but she still needed a plan.

"Home."

She'd been about ready to stand, but that one, simple word kept her there, seated, her arms around her knees. *Exactly where the hell is home, or where should it be?* Skye had no clue. All she knew was that home was where she and Spring were, and the fact that she and her sister were together was all due to Sebastian's tenacity.

Gratitude.

That's what he deserves.

The job was over, and he had moved on, but he deserved a big thank you, as he took whatever road he chose that led away from her. She placed her arms on the armrests and stood, as someone gave a powerful knock on the door. The medical staff usually gave a soft courtesy knock before walking in, without a signal from either her or Spring. The agents, however, waited for her signal.

"Come in," she said.

The door opened fast. A four-legged, caramel-brown blob ran into the room, her pink leash trailing on the floor. Candy leapt the last several feet through the air, landing on Spring's lap. Sebastian stepped into the room, his broad frame filling the doorway, his blue-eyes resting upon her, Spring, and back to her. Fifty-one hours had passed since she'd last seen him. It now felt like only a minute.

"Sorry," he said, though there was an underlying laugh in his voice that suggested he was anything but. He walked into the room, shrugged off a black cashmere overcoat, and laid it on Spring's bed. He wore a charcoal gray business suit with a tie that had a palette of blues and gray. His dress shirt was crisp and white. With a full-dimpled, beautiful smile that matched the light in his eyes, he was so cover-model handsome he stole her breath away. Any progress she'd made on getting over the hope that something existed between them immediately evaporated. "I didn't think she'd attack."

The reunion of Spring and Candy was met with squeals of joy on the part of girl and dog. Spring unsnapped Candy's leash and got down to nose level with the dog, by sitting cross-legged on the floor and wrapped her arms tightly around the furry neck. She glanced up at Sebastian with adoring eyes. "I knew you were going to come here this morning. Skye told me you saved us. Me. My dad. I don't remember that part. Not at all," she beamed. "But, thank you."

"I had to get one of my favorite girls, didn't I?" He shrugged. "Just doing my job."

"Well," Spring said, catapulting herself off the floor and into his arms, with a broad smile that tore at Skye's heart, until she saw that Sebastian returned it. "You're really good at it."

"Thank you." Over Spring's head, his eyes were on Skye's. His expression now turned slightly more serious, more thoughtful. "How are you doing?"

"Fine," she said, answering honestly. Almost honestly. The jolt to her senses brought by his presence there told her that shaking off the feeling of being with him for two days was going to take a while. He didn't need to know that, though, and she'd die before she told him. *Gratitude*, she reminded herself, that's what he deserved, because a less tenacious man, someone who wasn't as committed to his job, would have failed.

"You look really handsome when you're all dressed up," Spring said, slipping out of his arms, resuming her position on the floor with an arm slung around her dog. "Where are you going?"

He chuckled. "Washington, D.C. To meet with a whole bunch of politicians about what has happened over the last few days. I stopped by here on my way. Wanted to make sure you and your sister were okay. I'm glad that I did, because my agents were having a hard time persuading the hospital administration that Candy is a therapy dog." He gave Skye a pointed look. "Ragno doctored something up in the National Registry of Therapy Dogs. She's sending you an e-mail with the certificate."

Skye laughed. "Thank you."

"It might help if she started behaving," he said, his tone serious, but his smile suggesting that it didn't matter one bit whether Candy was obedient. To Spring, he said, "Good to see you up and looking so perfect."

"I'm designing a cake," she said, "for when we all go home. All you need to tell me is what flavors you want for your cupcakes. My dad's going to want chocolate."

He glanced at Skye with the mention of their father going home. Skye gave him a slight headshake. He nodded.

Spring continued, oblivious to the message that had passed between them. "So Dad's will be chocolate with butter cream icing. I'll decorate them with," she paused, "well, I haven't decided that yet. But I was thinking of multi-colored crystals, like amethyst geodes."

To Spring, he said, "With you making it, it's sure to be

beautiful and spectacular and taste amazing." He paused, "Do you mind if I take your sister away for a minute?"

Skye's stomach twisted, as his attention shifted from Spring to her. This is where he was going to tell her he was moving on. Oh, God. He felt the need to actually say the words, as if his visit two mornings earlier hadn't given her enough of a hint. Why he might feel the need to do such a thing was part of the reason it was going to be so damn hard to get over him, because underneath his bulletproof, hard-shell of toughness, he was a nice guy. She shook herself. Maybe this had nothing to do with what had happened between them. Maybe he was just going to tell her about her security detail. After all, she had hired his company to provide security and threat assessment. Agent Scott was the agent in charge of her team, yet all the agents who worked for Black Raven worked for Sebastian. She was considering whether to change her name, and she needed advice. Plenty of it. Maybe that was it.

"Of course not," Spring said, "but hurry back. I want to talk to you some more. I'll pull out the daydream jellybeans for you. Didn't know you were coming, or I'd have done that already."

"Oh, come on," he said, indignation in his tone, but a full smile, framed by deep dimples, was on his face. "Can't I at least have the cherry-red ones?"

Spring stood and gave him a slow headshake. "We've been through this a million times. The answer's no. It will always be no. You only get the daydreams."

He laughed, but his laughter faded as he opened the door of the room and walked Skye across the hallway, to the interior, windowless hospital room that his Black Raven agents and the marshals were using as a staging area. Two agents who were working in the room stood at attention, told Sebastian good morning, exiting as they entered, leaving the door to the room open.

"Best if you don't go outside today," Sebastian said. "There's a large group of your father's followers keeping vigil on the front lawn. News broke of his location during the night. Agents on your detail will walk Candy in the interior courtyard."

She nodded. "Agent Scott informed me about them." The hospital bed had been removed from the room. There was a table, with four chairs. She walked to one of the chairs, decided she didn't feel like sitting, and turned to him. He stood near the doorway, his posture indicating a desire for a fast exit. "Thank you for bringing Candy here. I didn't expect that."

"I thought it would make Spring happy." He fell quiet, studying her. "A lot is going to happen in the next few days. As soon as your father is stable for a twenty-four hour period, the marshals are going to transport him. You and Spring will leave when he does."

"Thank you for that information."

There was another of his long silences. She fought the urge to say anything, just to stop her growing discomfort. His frown and his prolonged silence told her that he was struggling, internally, with something. What and why? Not her problem. He touched his fingertips to his temple, dropping them when he realized what he was doing.

"Headache?"

"Yes, but it won't be the biggest problem of the day." If anything, his look became even more serious as he held her gaze. "Have you decided where to live?"

"No. Spring wants to go home." She gave him a slight smile and a shoulder shake. "I'm not really sure where that should be for us. I always thought that Firefly Island could be a refuge, but not with what happened there," she shuddered. Sebastian hadn't given her all the details, but she knew enough. "Besides, Spring needs interaction. The bakery was perfect, because it gave her something to do. I just don't know if I have the energy to recreate it somewhere else, and if we go to Covington, there's no way around being Skye and Spring Barrows, thanks to the media." Over the last forty-eight hours, the media had created a detailed chronology of post-prison break events. "And I'm not sure whether we should do that." She drew a deep breath, folded her arms to her chest, and mentally shook herself. "Sorry. None of this is your problem. Agent Scott is great. She's helping me assess the options." She paused, before adding, "The idea of being in that town and in our beautiful bakery is heavenly."

"My agents have made sure there's no sign of what happened there," he said. "And after a while, the media attention will disappear."

"Spring's backpack didn't catch up to her," Skye said. "If you can mention that to your agents who are still at the site?" She tried not to tell him too much, but added. "Those tablets with all of her drawings are important to her." *And I want to destroy them.*

He nodded.

Hell. He knew.

She knew he was remembering when he had asked Spring about the drawings in the tablet. "We have the tablets. They're safe."

"Not all the code is there. But there are enough answers that would enable extrapolation. It would take a highly skilled analyst to figure it out," she said, "or a damn smart computer program. Still, those tablets shouldn't fall into the wrong hands."

He interrupted her, a serious look in her eyes. "I know that. We have control of everything that was at Trask Enterprises. That's part of why I'm headed to Washington. There's a push and pull going on. Right now they're pulling, but I'm pushing, and I'm doing it with McCollum's help. He's got a personal interest in my success right now, because if I fail, he's going down with me. Believe it or not, the official line with the government is still that your father's Shadows and LID Technology has not been implemented by any government agency."

Cool, calm blue eyes assessed her. "No one with the Government wants to publicly admit the degree of citizen surveillance that is taking place. " He shrugged. "Until the government admits to me that I've got custody of state secrets, they're not getting a damn thing from me. Officially, I took nothing from Trask Enterprises. Unofficially, Black Raven is safeguarding your father's data for him."

She stared at him with a sudden certainty, brought on by an awareness of how shrewd he was, how everything he did had a purpose. "You've found my father's backup, haven't you? You have her tablets and you're trying to make sense of the codes, aren't you?"

"Officially, no," he said. "Everything was destroyed. Unofficially, Black Raven has custody of what might ultimately be a very valuable asset. We haven't made sense of anything yet."

"It isn't yours, though. It belongs to my father."

"I'm aware of that. But your father now has options. The government's re-arrest of him is a formality. Because of what happened to your father while he was supposed to be under the care of the federal bureau of prisons, he may have leverage that he didn't have before. Simply put, the government should have known that due to the sensitive nature of the data that your father had created, he was likely to be a target. Yet they did nothing to protect him. That type of callous disregard for risk could be actionable, and could give your father some degree of leniency. There are some things in the works on your father's behalf that will require his input. Zeus will be here by the end of the day to provide your father some advice, the minute he's able to focus. At a minimum, your father will need to hire a lawyer, and he'll need Zeus' help and your help with that. We have a few names in mind for him, but that's his decision.

"I'm already doing some behind-the-scenes negotiations regarding a reduction to your father's sentence. I can't discuss details. His re-arrest, though, is certain. There will be plenty of press coverage highlighting his return to prison, even if all they're doing is wheeling him into a prison hospital. You need to prepare yourself and Spring for that."

She nodded. "Will do."

"Once he decides on a lawyer, the lawyer will file a motion for a sentence reduction, that, based on the negotiations that are now underway, the government will not oppose, and a federal judge will greatly reduce the remainder of his sentence." He paused. "I plan to offer him the best job offer he's ever received. Ragno has now drunk the Kool Aid. She's persuaded me that he's an asset Black Raven cannot live without. What Ragno wants, Ragno gets. But a lot has to fall into place for all of this to happen." There was another long silence. He drew a deep breath. "Look. I really came here to tell you that I'm sorry. I shouldn't have-"

"Don't." She held her hand up, shook her head, and said, "There's nothing you need to tell me that begins with an apology."

He squared his jaw. "But-"

"No. Please," she folded her arms against her chest. He wasn't going to hug her, so she had to hug herself. *Today is just another day in the life of Skye Barrows. I'll figure out a way to cope. I always have.*

"I mishandled the operation by letting it get personal, and I shouldn't-"

"I asked—no," she corrected herself, "I told you not to apologize again. Consenting adults, and all that." She shrugged. "Don't look back. I'm not. Job's over. You did a great job. Thank you for rescuing Spring and my father. Thank you for bringing them both back to me. Check in with your agents in the future if you have concerns, but we're not your personal responsibility any longer. I understand that you have to move on." She did understand, even though it felt as though she was being ripped apart on the inside, even though he was studying her with a serious look of concern in his deep blue eyes. What he was thinking, she couldn't tell. Whatever it was, though, it ran deep, equally intense as the turbulent emotions she was now feeling.

"Well," he said, his voice low, his tone concerned. "Can I at least tell you that you deserve better? You should stop settling for nothing."

Her jaw hurt from clenching her teeth. "You're not the first man to say that-"

"Maybe not. The fact that I can't do anything to have a future with you has now become one of the biggest disappointments I've ever experienced."

"Damn. How the hell do you manage to be so stoic in the face of such a disappointment? Because I've spent a lifetime acting cool and calm when I feel anything but, and I can tell you, the major disappointments hit me harder than this one looks like it's hitting you."

He frowned. "You're special, Skye. But-"

"But. There's always a but." She heard the bitterness in her tone, and didn't fight it.

"I'm dying to take you in my arms," he said, "but it's just going to prolong the inevitable moment when I walk away."

"Please stop," she said, cringing on the inside, folding her arms tighter against herself. "I'm barely holding on here. Don't you understand that?"

He nodded as his blue eyes held hers. His jaw was grim, and a pulse beat at his temple. For a second, the look in his eyes matched the misery she felt, until his eyes became guarded again.

"If the only reason you're coming to see me is to say you're sorry, or to tell me you wish there was something there, or to tell me I'm special, I don't need that. Your agents can handle the business details of protecting us. Black Raven's deal with my father will be between my father and you. I'll communicate with Agent Scott and Zeus. I don't need visits from you, and Spring doesn't either."

He nodded, with a slight frown. "I'll tell Spring goodbye."

Not a good idea, she thought, but he walked out of the makeshift conference room and across the hallway, before she could voice a protest. He lifted his coat on the bed, draped it over his arm, and said, with the same soft smile he always gave to Spring, "I have to go now."

She was sitting at the table, a pencil poised in her hand, eraser side down on the paper, as she worked on a drawing, "But you just got here. Can't you stay a little while longer?"

He shook his head. "No."

"Well, tomorrow, right? I'll see you tomorrow. Won't I?"

Lie, Skye thought. *Please lie. Tell her you'll be here tomorrow. Don't tell her no.*

His smile slipped and he suddenly had the same serious look he'd had when they'd been across the hall, the look that screamed of a man who was fighting, with tremendous effort, a deep inner struggle. Odd, how she hadn't recognized it when his focus was on her, when the words he had said were all about her. Now, through the paper thin veneer of stoicism he presented, she saw heartache and heaviness and misery, all in the crystal-clear, blue-eyed gaze that he was giving to Spring, whose overly-developed sense of empathy picked up on it immediately.

Spring dropped the pencil and stood. "Please stay, Sebastian," she whispered, her eyes wide, her gaze focused on him. Candy, who'd been snoozing at her feet, rose with her, yawning as she did so. "You have to stay with us. Just a little while longer."

"I can't."

"Well, you're going to come back tomorrow," Spring said. As her sister pleaded, Skye's heart twisted. "Aren't you?"

He cleared his throat. "I'm afraid not," he said, his voice barely a whisper.

"I don't understand," she said, shaking her head, her eyes wide, "Don't you like us?"

Skye wanted to scream at him to lie. Didn't he see what he was doing to her? *Oh, dear God,* she prayed silently, as fervently for this as for anything she'd ever prayed for in her life. *Please let this end.*

His glance fell on Skye. It was the heavy look of a man who was waging an internal war with demons that were too strong to defeat, because they were of his own creation.

"Spring," Skye said, drawing upon reserves that she didn't know she had, her voice calm, as she said, "Sebastian has to leave."

As usual when her emotions started to run and she became agitated, Spring didn't pay attention. Instead, she reached for a bowl of bright red jellybeans, counted three, and, with them in the palm of her hand, said, "I'll give you these if you stay. You can always have the red ones if you stay."

"I'm sorry, I-" he was responding to Spring, but his eyes were on her, his message unmistakably directed at her. "I hope that you'll forgive me."

For hurting her, maybe one day. If he tore her sister's heart out for one more second, there wasn't going to be forgiveness.

Spring walked closer to him. "Please, Sebastian. Stay."

"Go," Skye whispered. "Just go."

He heard her, and nodded. Instead of listening though, he drew a deep breath, froze for a second, then turned to Spring.

Spring's eyes were wide. Tears flowed down her cheeks and dripped to her chin. With her free hand she tugged on the coat that was draped over his arm, while with the other she had her palm outstretched, the three red jellybeans an offering that spoke volumes. Skye had to fight back her own tears, knowing that if she dissolved, it was only going to hurt Spring. "Please stay."

"Spring, he has to go, now," Skye said, her voice trembling. She drew a deep breath, walked closer to Spring, and gently placed one hand on her sister's shoulder, the other on the hand that was tugging at Sebastian's coat. "Spring, let him go."

He finally looked into her eyes again. He was winning the war with his emotions, and now he looked more like he had earlier, in the conference room, when he'd spoken to her without Spring present. Strong. Stoic. Removed. As though he was already miles down the road that was going to lead him away from them.

"Now," Skye whispered, over Spring's sobs, managing to be calm when she wanted to cry just as loudly as Spring. "Go. She'll never understand."

He slid his hand underneath Spring's, and gently closed her fingers so that the jellybeans were no longer visible. "You keep the red ones for yourself." Bending, Sebastian gently touched his lips to Spring's forehead, and whispered, barely loud enough for Skye to hear. "Goodbye, beautiful girl. You take care of your sister for me, okay?"

Without glancing at Skye, he was gone. His absence immediately created a void through which her heart fell. When her sister rushed into her arms, crying as though her world had shattered and would never be whole again, she knew exactly how Spring felt. For once in her life, Skye bent her head on her sister's shoulder, and cried with her.

"I know, honey. It hurts," she whispered after long, long minutes when they held each other. "But we'll be okay. I'll make us okay."

If she said it enough, she'd believe it.

Chapter Twenty Seven

One Week Later

Sebastian stood for a moment in the doorway of Raven One. A few lights shone from a nearby hangar at New Orleans Lakefront Airport, and in the distance the city lights shimmered against the black night. The headlights of Brandon's black sedan turned on, as Sebastian walked down the stairs of the jet. He'd told his friend the 4:30 a.m. pickup was unnecessary, but Brandon had insisted on being there. The air was damp and chilly. Tiny drops of moisture fell on his black leather jacket, as he walked across the tarmac. After placing a small duffel bag and his backpack in the trunk of Brandon's car, Sebastian opened the door to the passenger side of the sedan, dropped into the seat, pressed the button that would push the seat back, and sank deeply in. "Thanks for the lift."

Brandon said, "You're welcome. You doing okay?"

"Never better," Sebastian said, sarcasm flag high in his tone.

His friend shot him a worried glance, studying him before putting the car in drive. Seeing his own unease reflected in Brandon's eyes bothered the living hell out of him.

"Save the empathetic looks," Sebastian said. "I'm either going to be fine, or I'm not. I'm okay, either way, as long as you and Zeus don't leave me hanging somewhere in between, unable to do a goddamn thing for myself."

Brandon nodded as he drove out of the parking lot. "Doctor Cavanaugh says there's going to be some tests this morning, you have to sign consent forms, and you get to meet your surgeons. By nine, you'll be done with the preliminaries. You're going to have some time on your hands until the surgery, which is scheduled for two p.m."

"Correction," Sebastian said, as Brandon stopped at a red light on Downs Road. Sebastian glanced at a bar with a full parking lot and patrons spilling out of it. The area was five steps below skid row and known for drug deals. It hadn't changed in

Sebastian's lifetime. He doubted it ever would. "Surgery's at 10 a.m. I want it done and over. ASAP."

"Well," Brandon said, "I just talked to him. Five minutes ago. He's on his way to Ochsner now. I told him you had actually arrived, when I saw Raven One's landing lights. I don't think he was really counting on you to arrive, until I gave him confirmation. He gave me the tentative schedule, which he's now firming up."

"Son of a fucking bitch-"

"It's brain surgery, Sebastian. Not an annual physical-"

"I'm aware-"

"Given that you decided on this yesterday, and you've cancelled at the last minute before, you're lucky he was able to pull all of this together so quickly. Cancel this time, and he's sworn to give you that lobotomy he's threatened."

"Hell." Leaning his head on the headrest, he stretched his legs, exhaled hard, then inhaled again. *Hell, hell, hell.* For the last week, the frenzy of activity involving the aftermath of the prison break and the operation at Trask Enterprises had been nonstop. Equally pressing was the logistics of what he and Ragno had dubbed Operation Acquire Barrows. Constant attention on high-urgency projects had been required, and the steady, unending work had been the only thing keeping him on course.

Yet it didn't matter how hard he focused, or how serious the problems were, he had wants, needs, and aspirations. All intensified the more time he spent with Skye. He wanted her so badly he could imagine how her body would feel, when he wrapped his arms around her.

What he had wanted to do, with every fiber of his being, was go to her and tell her that he needed her in his life. He wanted to build a life with her. Wanted to hold her at night, and wake with her curled in his arms in the morning. He wanted to smell her skin and see her smile. Every fucking day. Not only when they were on high adrenaline alert. But in the quiet, calm times, too. He wanted it all.

And his "all" contained Skye Barrows.

When he slept each night he dreamed of her, what they could be if they were together, how his life would change with Skye in it. Each day, he expected the need to become less palpable, less urgent, but his dreams—ridiculous dreams of starry nights, making love in front of a fireplace, celebrations with Spring's colorful creations, laughter, and having children, the kinds of things other people had but he had never craved—played tricks on him, because each morning the need to see her had intensified.

Maybe the surgeon could cut out that part of his brain, because seven days after seeing her for the last time, when he'd delivered the dog to them, he'd never felt so much like he was making a mistake, that he was slamming a door he never should have shut.

She was less than an hour away.

The thought rattled him, but proximity hadn't been the reason he had stayed away. He was mobile. Could be anywhere, in just the stretch of time it would take a fast car or Raven One to get him there. The problem was deep within him, a fear of getting close to women. That fear was borne of a bad childhood and an abusive father, a deep-rooted belief that he had inherited from his father a toxic capability of hurting others and, in the process, destroying something that should have been enduring and beautiful. Even with knowing he'd made a mistake by walking away from her, he had no plans to do a damn thing about it. An hour away? Irrelevant.

"Anyway," Brandon continued, not realizing that all of Sebastian's needs, wants, and love life were being mentally debated. "Think about what you'd like to do in the downtime. Michael and Taylor want to see you," Brandon said. Michael was Brandon's one-year-old child, who was Sebastian's godchild, and Taylor was Brandon's new wife, "Zeus will be here later this morning."

As Brandon pulled onto the interstate, Sebastian glanced at the distant lights of the New Orleans skyline. "I don't need you guys to babysit me."

"Leaving you alone and giving you time to worry about this surgery wouldn't be the friendly thing to do," Brandon said. "Especially when you're in this situation because of me and Taylor."

"I'm not worried about the surgery."

"Well, what the hell are you worried about? Each time I've talked to you this week, you've sounded less and less like yourself."

"My agents died. I had funerals to attend."

Brandon nodded. "I know. I'm sorry. You've done that

before, though. You're the one who always counsels the rest of us. Have for years. It's part of the job. A part we all acknowledge every day."

"It never gets easy."

"I've known you all your life. There's something else," Brandon said. His eyes reflected the lights of the dash as he shot a glance over at Sebastian. "I think it involves what happened between you and Skye."

"Drop it." Apparently Brandon had gotten an earful from Ragno. Brandon had asked him earlier in the week what had happened with Skye. Sebastian had brushed it off.

"Oh, come on, Sebastian. This is me you're talking to. I know how monumental it was for you to cross that line."

"Yeah. And it never should have happened."

"Then why did it?"

"Proximity, the rude awakening of a dormant libido," he paused, "she's gorgeous and," he paused, "hell. She was willing. A gunpowder situation. High-stress situation. Mutual attraction. One spark set it off. That's it."

"You sure that's all? Because the stress is over and I know you well enough to know you're still thinking about her, because I've never seen you this cranky in your life." Brandon paused. He added, in a quiet, gentle tone, "You're not your father."

Sebastian's heart raced at the mention of that man. Brandon and Sebastian had bonded as children, in part, because Brandon's house had provided a refuge from the horrors that went on in Sebastian's home. "Why the hell are you bringing him up?"

"Because you're not him, and there aren't many people around who would dare to bring him up to you and remind you of that fact."

"Fucking bastard destroyed everything he ever loved," Sebastian said.

"And he's been dead for years. You've won, Sebastian. You're protecting the world from anyone who resembles him. Don't you see that? You're doing a damn good job of protecting others, but he's still getting to you. Don't let your father do his number on you." Brandon shook his head. "Don't let him win this one. Have some faith in yourself. Don't be afraid of falling head over heels in love. Figure out a way to make it work between you and Skye."

"Fuck off," Sebastian said. "I'm not talking about her."

Brandon shrugged as he turned into the hospital's valet stand. "Fine. For the record, though, I'm not buying your explanation about her. By the way, congratulations. Black Raven now officially has the brainpower of Richard Barrows. It's either a great move on your part, or, considering the amount you're agreeing to pay him over the next decade, insane."

"He's worth every penny, I assure you. My gut says it's one of the best moves I've ever made."

Brandon reached in the backseat, grabbed a briefcase, and handed the keys to the parking attendant. "You think so? A brilliant, paranoid conspiracy theorist who now has a mother lode of post-traumatic stress?"

"Well, Ragno and Zeus agree wholeheartedly," Sebastian said, grabbing his bags out of the trunk, then eyeing Brandon. "Aren't you just dropping me off and going to work? I'll be in tests for a few hours."

Brandon waved his briefcase at Sebastian. "I'm going to work from the hospital, to make sure you don't run away. Most of what I'm doing this morning is Black Raven work, anyway; talking to Barrows' attorney and looking at the terms of the employment contract. Ragno's given me strict instructions not to involve you in any way. She's worried that if you focus on work, you'll change your mind about the surgery."

Barrows had followed his advice and hired an attorney, who had immediately secured a reduction to his remaining prison term. Sebastian and Zeus had met with Barrows the morning before, before his release from Sentara Norfolk General Hospital. Ragno had been with them via a conference call. Richard Barrows had been profoundly grateful to Sebastian for rescuing him and Spring. Denim blue eyes that were the exact shade of Spring's had given him a once over, and said, "Spring told me all about you." In the face of his silence, Barrows had added, "Odd, but Skye wouldn't say a word about you."

Given his abrupt departure from their lives, Sebastian didn't know what to say about that. The man had given him a pointed, assessing look, then his hard gaze softened. "You saved my family. In exchange, you not only have my profound gratitude," he paused, "you'll have my brainpower. There are limits, of course, as to what I will do for you. I need to explore your views on surveillance, on the depth to which you will go-"

"My view is we do enough to get the job done," Sebastian had interrupted. "Like what we did in your case."

"Well, there are gray areas that you might not see."

"Then I'll let you educate me with your considerable brilliance."

Barrows had chuckled. "My brainpower is not quite something that's ever been regarded as a national resource, but," he had smiled, and his eyes lightened, "perhaps it should be."

"It will be at Black Raven," Sebastian had answered.

After their meeting, the marshals had transferred Barrows to the U.S. Medical Center for Federal Prisoners in Springfield, Missouri, where he'd be for at least one month. News of Barrows' reduced prison term had coincided with news of his official transfer into federal custody. Footage of Barrows' fans, with their foil-lined caps on their heads along the road leading to the medical center, had streamed throughout the day on news shows. Once the techno-scientist was released from the hospital, his term of imprisonment would end and a two-year term of supervised release was to commence. During his supervised release, he'd start working with Black Raven's technology team.

Ragno was ecstatic.

***

Four and a half hours after arriving at Ochsner, Sebastian had been poked, prodded, imaged, tested, and had signed his life away on more consent forms than he could count. When he had shaken the hand of the man who was going to be cutting into his brain, the reality of it left him momentarily speechless, then clarity hit him with a lightning flash.

One life.

He had countless opportunities to fuck it up, but all he was ever going to get was one life. Skye had something he needed in his one life, and if he died on that fucking table she'd never know how he felt about her. He shouldn't have run from her. He had treated her like all the other men in her life had treated her. She deserved better from him. She deserved to at least know how profoundly she had affected him.

He'd have loved a few moments by himself, but Zeus and Brandon were waiting on him in his private hospital room. Their heavy silence as he walked in after the battery of tests, told him exactly what they'd been talking about before he opened the door. "Have you decided who'll deliver my eulogy?"

Zeus gave him a slow headshake, his dark eyes serious. "Not

funny."

"I thought you weren't worried about the surgery," Brandon said.

"I'm not. You two, though, look like you're figuring out where to scatter my ashes. Crescent Beach on Compass Cay." He gave Brandon a smile at the mention of the island in the Exuma region of the Bahamas that he and Brandon had discovered years earlier. "You'd at least get a boat trip out of it."

Sebastian ignored the hospital gown and a blue cap folded neatly on the bed. He wasn't putting that shit on until the last possible minute. Though he'd tried to move things up, there were some things Sebastian couldn't control, and surgery was still scheduled for two p.m. Technicians were going to start working on him at one. He glanced at his watch. It was nine thirty. He had three and a half long, long hours to kill.

"I talked with the chief neurosurgeon, when I first arrived this morning," Zeus said, surprising Sebastian. "You're going to be fine. I'm confident."

"You two know what to do if I'm not," Sebastian said. He'd talked to both of them earlier, when he first learned that the surgery was looming. It was the biggest favor he'd ever asked of anyone. The windows of the room overlooked the Mississippi River and the gray, cloudy sky. A ship glided upriver, in the direction of River's Bend, the town in which Brandon and Sebastian had grown up. The tanker gave him something to focus on, other than his friends and the heaviness in the room. "I'm not afraid of dying. Brandon has the medical power of attorney." He gave his friend a hard look. "I'm trusting you with this. Do not hesitate. Do not leave me helpless."

"Don't worry," Brandon said, "We'll treat you exactly as we'd want to be treated."

Sebastian turned from the window in time to see Zeus touch his hand to his ear, then press a button on his watch. "Ragno," Zeus said, "what was that?"

Sebastian tuned in, his mind craving his connection with Ragno and the constant stream of information involving Black Raven operational issues. He couldn't hear a damn thing from her side of the conversation, because Zeus didn't put her on speaker. Sebastian and Ragno had said their goodbyes at midnight. He'd been finishing business in D.C. As always, she was at corporate headquarters in Denver. She'd told him to focus on getting himself well and refused to talk with him about business until after the surgery. Her tone had been strained, as though she'd been one step removed from crying. The thought of Ragno breaking down with worry over his surgery had rattled him so badly, he agreed not to talk to her until afterwards.

Zeus had taken over Sebastian's role that morning. Zeus was now handling all business matters that would have normally been directed to Sebastian, until Sebastian was well enough to resume work. Whether it would be one week, two weeks, longer, or never, was an open question.

"Okay," Zeus said, turning his back to Sebastian, "Put on Scott."

Sebastian's ears prickled at the mention of the agent in charge of Skye and Spring's security detail. They'd returned to Covington three days earlier. Skye, the brave woman that she was, had decided not to live under an assumed identity. She was testing the waters, knowing that with Black Raven's assistance, she and Spring could disappear again if needed.

Zeus frowned, glanced at Sebastian, then walked out of the room as he said, "Scott, we've been through-" The door shut and he couldn't hear the rest of Zeus' words.

Dammit.

Sebastian crossed the room, opened the door, and almost walked straight into Taylor and Michael. As always, Taylor looked beautiful, with her long, honey-golden hair free flowing in waves down to her waist. Her hazel-green eyes reflected her soft smile as she stepped back, avoiding Sebastian. He bent to kiss her cheek, and accepted the transfer of Michael into his arms. Michael was almost one year old, and a wriggling bundle of a heavy, blue-eyed, laughing baby. "Hello, Gorgeous."

"Me, or Michael?"

"Both."

Taylor gave him a soft smile and a concerned look. "Back at you. How are you?"

"Fine, and I will be. Don't you jump on the worry train as well." He pressed his lips against Michael's forehead, and was rewarded with a string of gurgles and coos. "And how's my favorite godchild?"

"Wonderful," she said. "We're looking forward to you recuperating at our house. I know you'll be on your feet in no time, but I'm hoping you'll be with us at least long enough to work on him saying Sebastian."

With Michael's plump, sticky hand on his cheek, he walked to where Zeus stood. Zeus glanced at him, and said, "Ragno, send two more agents to Scott."

"What's going on?"

Zeus glanced at Sebastian and walked back into Sebastian's room. "You're not supposed to be worrying about work."

"I'll worry anyway. Just tell me," he said, his eyes falling on Brandon, who had his arm casually draped around Taylor's shoulder. He glanced back at Zeus, shifted Michael from one arm to the other, and said, "Well?"

"Media's breaking the news of where Skye and Spring are. Reporters from national networks are in Covington. "

"Dammit," Sebastian said, moving the baby's chubby index finger from his left eye. "Scott was supposed to be prepared for that."

"She is."

"Then what's the problem?"

Zeus studied him for a second. "There isn't a problem."

"Then why does she need two more agents? The team is six. That's plenty enough, unless there's a threat. So what the hell is happening?"

"A few of Barrows' supporters got advance scoop. They're on the street in front of Creative Confections. It's peaceful," Zeus shrugged, the expression in his dark eyes unreadable. "We're just getting prepared for larger numbers."

"Wait. She's not supposed to open the bakery until tomorrow."

"Bakery's not open. She and Spring are there, doing prep work. Don't worry. We're not talking Syria, Sebastian, and we're not talking terrorists. We're talking about peaceful demonstrators, who wear aluminum foil on their heads and who are likely arriving there to show support for Barrows." Dark eyes held Sebastian's for a long minute, studying him. "We have this. Don't worry."

"I'm not worried." He paused with the automatic words, because he was worried about Skye and Spring and how they were going to cope with this new wrinkle. "It's just-"

"Sounds like someone's worried to me," Brandon said. For a second, the only sound in the room was Michael's gurgles.

Taylor's hazel-green eyes, Brandon's jade-green eyes, and Zeus' black eyes were all on him.

His friends knew exactly what he was thinking. He walked over to Taylor, handed her Michael, and said, "Give me your car keys, Brandon."

"No," Brandon said. "No way. She'll be fine. If you want to talk to her, call her."

Calling her wasn't going to be good enough. "I'll be back in time."

Over his shoulder, he saw Zeus walk to the door, the only exit, and block it. Sebastian turned to him. "It's going to take more than that to stop me."

Zeus folded his arms. The man was huge. Sebastian had never won a physical fight with him. "We'll only let you go if we drive you there," Zeus said. "That way we're sure you'll come back."

Chapter Twenty Eight

Skye was on a ladder writing the menu for the next week on the hanging chalkboard in fat, pink chalk. They were keeping it simple until they hired help. With Black Raven's assistance in vetting applicants, finding the perfect couple who could fulfill the many roles that were needed was going to be relatively easy. Spring was in the kitchen with two of the agents, the younger ones on the team. Both had been selected by Scott based upon compatibility measures that indicated that they would be good with Spring's needs. One had cooking experience, one had none. Both were taking directions from her on how to ice cupcakes. The other four agents were outside. Two were on the front porch, watching the ten demonstrators that had gathered on the sidewalk. Sunlight glinted off their foil-lined caps. So far, they hadn't done anything but stand there.

Out of the corner of her eye, she saw Candy stand and wag her tail as she looked out of the glass windows of the French door. No one was supposed to enter the front yard, but someone was walking into the gate just as freely as if the place was open for business, which it wasn't.

What the hell?

Black Raven was better than this. With the demonstrators on the sidewalk, no one was supposed to get in the gate. As she saw who was walking up the path, her heart paused. *No. Not him, not now.* There was no mistaking Sebastian with his long-legged, purposeful stride and broad shoulders. No wonder the agents hadn't stopped him.

"No," she muttered, dropping the chalk and climbing down the ladder so fast she slipped off the last two rungs. Her ankle rolled as her feet hit the ground, sending a shock of pain up her left leg and into her back.

"Damn."

She glanced into the kitchen as she righted herself. Spring's back was to the wide window that faced the public area of the bakery. She hadn't seen him.

Skye had only one sudden, urgent goal.

Sebastian was going to turn around and leave before Spring saw him. Skye tested her ankle. It hurt, but the pain only gave her resolve. She made it to the French doors as he did, unlocking them so that she could tell him to leave. He pushed the door open and stepped in.

"Leave," she said, "You're not welcome here."

His eyes were serious. There was no smile, and no dimples. As her body started reacting to the fact that the man who haunted her dreams was standing in front of her, she fought the urge to physically push him away.

"I've got to talk to you about us."

Us.

The word hit her with such force it stole her breath, because 'us' was something she'd never been with a man. She shook her head. *Do not fall for this. He's good, remember? He knows what you need to hear. Knows everything about you. Probably read all about how lonely you are in some report made by some psychologist, when you were feeling vulnerable.*

"Us? Are you delusional? Doesn't matter. Please leave before Spring sees you," she said. He stood firm, without backing away. "There isn't an 'us'. Will never be an 'us'. You made that perfectly clear. Go. Now."

He gave her a half smile, but no light made it to his eyes. "That's why I have to talk to you."

He was a man who did nothing lightly. He spoke with purpose. Every action backed by deliberate intent. She knew that. While her heart screamed at her to listen, her protective instinct told her to get him the hell away from Spring. If anything, the man could turn his emotions off as easily as one flicked a light switch on their way out of a room. The onslaught of desire that came with seeing him didn't make her forget that horrifying reality. He was emotionally unavailable. She wanted no part of him.

"Please," he said, his tone serious and his eyes heavy with a message of sincerity. "Just listen to me for a few minutes. That's all I ask."

She inhaled, and that was her undoing. She smelled the outdoors and the fresh aroma of a wooded forest, every scent she associated with him. All she wanted to do was burrow into the warm comfort of his strong arms. She glanced through the kitchen window. Spring was leaning on the table, her back still to the window, talking to one of Sebastian's agents.

"I'll listen, on one condition."

"Go."

"When you're done, you leave, and never return."

"If you ask me that again," he said. "Yes."

"Upstairs. Go. Now. Don't let Spring see you."

He glanced over her shoulder, into the kitchen, and nodded in understanding. He moved fast, disappearing up the circular stairway. Skye collected herself and walked into the kitchen, only slightly limping. "Honey, how are things going?"

"Great. We're going to start decorating in a little bit. They're going to look like a night sky with fireworks exploding."

"Perfect."

Both agents were mic'd to Agent Scott, and probably had advance warning from Scott that Sebastian was walking into the coffee house. She pulled one of the agents to the side and said, "Keep her occupied. I'll be upstairs for a few minutes. Do not let her see him when he is on his way out."

He gave her a nod.

She climbed the stairwell, taking the time with each step to breathe. She needed resolve. She needed to be strong. Being her father's daughter had made her dig a deep inner well of resilient strength in handling difficult men and the problems they produced. She drew upon those resources now, and when she reached the door, she was confident that she wouldn't falter.

He turned to her when she entered the office. He was standing in the middle of the office, in precisely the same position he'd been in when he had knocked her to the ground nine days earlier. A slight smile played at his lips. "At least this time you're not pulling a gun out on me."

She shut the office door. "You took mine. Which reminds me," she paused, realizing he was only an arms length from her, remembering the feeling of being underneath him, and suddenly longing for his touch. *So much for being strong.* "I want them back."

"I'll mention it to Agent Scott. But you need some lessons."

She folded her arms, and stood her ground. "Here's a newsflash. You don't get to tell me what I need."

"I know. But I do get to talk about us," he said.

Though her heart pounded, she shook her head, "Obviously, it bears repeating. There is no us."

"I'm here to change that."

"You can't."

He gave her a full, rare smile. The power of that smile shot straight to her foolish heart. "Then I'll get to the point. I'm having brain surgery this afternoon. Odds are fifty-fifty that I'll survive. I'm not afraid of dying, so the odds aren't bothering me."

She closed the distance between them, lifted both hands to his shoulders, and shoved him backwards. He moved maybe an inch. Barely. "God, Sebastian this is so freaking unfair! You walk in here, claim to want there to be an us, then tell me you're about to have brain surgery and could possibly die? In a few hours? What the hell is this?" Her heart fell to the floor with the horrifying reality of what he was saying and the calmness with which he delivered his message. "What the hell am I supposed to say? Please don't die. Thanks for the damn head's up?" *Hold me. Kiss me. Tell me that we have something.*

He stood there, feet planted, eyes serious, his jaw set. "Even if everything goes well, I'll be in a medically induced coma for a while. The length of time depends on how the cuts go. It could be a few days, or longer. None of that bothers me." He shrugged, then stepped closer to her.

"Leave," she said, furious. "Leave now."

"I can't," he said, reaching for her.

She swatted his hand away. "I can't believe you've come here to tell me that you could be dying this afternoon."

"That's not at all what I came here to tell you. I know it's a lot to digest, but I needed to give you some context, because here's where I get to the 'us' part."

"Let me get this straight," Skye wrapped her arms tightly around her waist so that she didn't hit him. "There's an 'us' because there's a chance you'll die, therefore you have nothing to lose, and no commitments to make, because—Gee, you might be dead in a few hours? What do you want? A pity fuck before you go under the knife?"

"No. No fucking involved. What is scaring the living hell out of me right now, the reason I couldn't wait to talk to you, is my fear that too much time will have passed between right now and when I'm well again." He drew a deep breath. "I'm afraid that I'll wake up and be fine and you won't be a part of my life. Or worse,

I'm afraid that I'll die and you won't know how much you mean to me."

He touched his fingers to his temple, then dropped them with an annoyed shake of his head. He was silent, staring at her. He broke eye contact with her, drew a deep breath and looked back. She'd seen him do all kinds of things. None of which had made him nervous. Now he was uncertain, and when she realized that, her anger evaporated. In its place, hope was born. "How much I mean to you? What does that mean?"

He frowned. "I'll do better. What I'm trying to tell you is that I cannot imagine my life without you. Cannot imagine it, because even though I tried to turn off all the switches you turned on, all I've done for the last week is think about you and what we could be if I worked on us. And I had to come here now and tell you, because if the worst happens and I die today, you would never have known. You don't realize how special you are, do you?"

She folded her arms, fighting back sudden tears, unsure what to say.

"I want us to be together for now and for the rest of my life. Whether it's for the next few hours, or fifty years. However long I've got. I want there to be an us. Give me a chance, and I'll make us so damn good that you..." he paused, searching for the right words, "...you won't regret it. Us. Come on. Let me try. Let me start over."

He lifted his hand to her cheek, and traced her cheekbone with his index finger. "I know what I did earlier this week was abrupt. You see, in the past, that's what I always did the minute I started getting close to someone. The difference is this time it's been killing me not to be with you. I know now that by walking away from you, I made the biggest mistake I've ever made. It won't always be easy. My job will require me to leave. I'm not the kind of guy you're going to wake up with every morning, not the kind of guy you'll see every night. But I will always come back to you and I will always be loyal. I'm so," he drew a deep breath, "scared that if I don't tell you this now, you'll never understand that one of the biggest regrets of my life has suddenly become that I didn't kiss you. That I didn't open the door that could lead to the infinite possibilities of what we can become, if I, if we, let there be an us."

His eyes had a question. Though she suddenly knew her answer could be nothing but yes, he was taking his time asking it, his gaze on hers. He pulled her close, so that Skye could feel the hard wall of his chest against her soft breasts. It was good that he was strong enough to hold her up with just one arm, because as his warmth seeped through her, her knees suddenly felt weak. His right hand cradled her face in a soft caress, then, with his index finger he traced the outline of her lips. This man, who never kissed women because it signified too much, was making his intent perfectly clear, and she was barely able to breathe with the reality of it.

Her eyes fluttered closed as, with agonizing slowness, he brushed a gentle kiss across her lips. The whisper soft contact of his mouth instantly warmed her.

It has been worth the wait, and he is only beginning.

With agonizing slowness, their lips met and pressed together. He groaned, but still, he took his time. His lips drifted away from hers. He placed a path of tiny closed-mouth kisses, along her upper lip and then her lower lip. She stood on her tiptoes, wrapping her arms around his neck as he traced another trail of fire along her lips. Her breath caught as he nibbled, each touch of his lips and teeth followed by a soft caress of his tongue.

When he made it to the center of her lower lip, he pressed both lips against hers. Her mouth opened to his and her head fell back as his tongue glided over hers. Long minutes fell away, as they did nothing but kiss like two people who were starved for each other. Gentleness gave way to passion, and, when they were both breathing heavily, he kept going, holding her so tightly she knew that the kiss meant as much to him as it meant to her. She opened her eyes as he slowly pulled his lips from hers. He rested his forehead on hers, his eyes dark with desire.

"I was just going to kiss you," he said, his voice husky.

Desire for more had overcome her need to breathe. "No," she whispered. "Don't stop."

He chuckled as he moved forward. His lips found hers again, but he only hovered against her lips. His eyes became serious. "What was that you said about me leaving and never returning? Still a request?" He punctuated his sentence with a deep kiss, then broke away for her response. "Well?"

"No," she whispered. "I figure we have ten minutes before Spring comes up here."

"We?"

She nodded.

"As in us," his eyes held hers, "and everything that word

entails?"

His intense look told her he meant 'us' in a manner that was much more than a fleeting thing.

"I want us to last forever," he said.

"Is that supposed to be a romantic proposal?" she laughed, still in his arms.

He was studying her, at first serious, then a slow smile lit his face as the reality of what he was saying hit him. Her laughter trailed off, but she couldn't keep herself from smiling.

"There," he said. "That's what I wanted to see."

She turned serious as she looked up at him. "What?"

"That smile. It's pure magic. It transforms," he paused, as though searching for the word, then settling on one, "life. Come on. Tell me there'll be an us. Today. Tomorrow. Forever."

"Are you proposing, Sebastian? Shouldn't we take some time..." Her words trailed. Time? He might not have any more than now.

"Time?" He paused. He lifted his hand to her forehead, smoothed away her hair, then lifted her chin with his finger. "I live by snap judgments and fast decisions. This will be the most important one I've ever made. In going through you to find your father, I learned things about you that you've probably forgotten."

"But I don't know everything about you."

He frowned. "Given what you already know about me, this might be enough for you to make a decision." He paused, took a deep breath, and gave her a nod. "I fell in love with you even before we said hello. Before I walked into Creative Confections, Ragno was feeding me information about you and fast-streaming photographs of your life to me. What captivated me in those photographs wasn't your beauty. It was your smile, and I couldn't stop looking at how it lit up every room you were in, how everyone who was with you was drawn to it. When I saw your smile, in photograph after photograph, you had me. Then, when I saw you in person, and saw the deep, inner light in your eyes, I knew that you were the only woman I'd always return to. When I heard your voice, my first thought was that your voice could guide a man through hell. The last week has given me enough time to know that if I walk away from you, I'll be making the biggest mistake of my life."

"So this is what you need to know about me now, in order to

answer my question." He backed away from her, and then lifted her right hand and held it in both of his. "I want there to be an 'us' so I can know that for the rest of my life there's a chance I'll get to see your smile, even if there are times that it's as elusive as the green flash on the horizon. I want to spend the rest of my life creating a world for you, for us, that is so wonderful that every morning when you awaken there's the possibility that the day will bring you something to smile about, and that I'll get to be there to enjoy it." He lifted her hand, kissed the back of it, and with all the charm of his smile pouring into the radiant light of his eyes, he said, "Skye Barrows, will you marry me?"

His words rocked her world, but they were nothing compared to the intense emotion that was pouring out of his serious eyes. She had never imagined such a heartfelt proposal would come her way. "I don't know what to say," she whispered. "That's so-"

"Say yes," he said, "and I'll make certain you're never sorry that you did."

"It won't just be me you're getting. Spring and I come as a package deal. It won't be easy."

"Of course Spring is part of 'us.'"

"Then I guess there's only one more thing for me say."

He smiled. "I do?"

"Before that. I love you Sebastian Connelly. I will always love you. I'll be there when you leave for a job, and waiting for you when you return. I'll be your rock when the world around you shakes. I'll be there for you. Always. Us," she whispered, closing her eyes as his lips found hers, "yes."

***

Sebastian floated in a dark abyss where he had no grasp on time. He didn't know where he was, and was barely aware of who he was. Filmy tendrils of thought-zapping clouds shrouded his brain and fogged his thoughts for hours, or maybe days. Against what little will he could muster, forces that he couldn't fight pulled him into a netherworld that had the finality of neither heaven nor hell, and nowhere in between. He was on a never-ending, spiraling journey, one where his mind and soul couldn't find either eternal bliss or damning hellfire.

Hours later—maybe days—he was aware enough to recognize the sound of a door opening and was finally able to recognize voices.

"Skye, did you stay all night?" Brandon asked.

"Yes," she said, her voice soft and steady. "I want to be here when he awakens."

But I asked you not to come until I'm on my feet. I don't want you to see me like this.

"He's totally off sedatives by now, right?" Brandon said.

"They weaned him slowly. He's been off them since yesterday evening," Zeus said, worry heavy in his voice.

"He should be awake by now," Brandon said.

He wanted to tell them he could hear them. That he'd be up, soon.

"You're right." Zeus said.

Why can't I speak? The clouds that enveloped him not only fogged his brain, they placed suffocating weight on his chest, rendering him speechless.

"Doctor Cavanaugh said to give it time." Brandon's tone was even. Measured. Cautious.

"That was last night, and Cavanaugh seemed worried when he said it." Zeus whispered, but Sebastian still heard it.

"Hell." Brandon dropped his voice, adding words that Sebastian couldn't decipher, but he recognized the tension and worry.

Zeus responded, in a low whisper. Then louder, Zeus said, "Sebastian, you're fine. The surgery was a success."

"He'll wake up when he's ready," Skye said, her voice soft and steady. "And he will be fine." The sweet scent of vanilla and pine enveloped him. Her scent. He felt a soft, warm touch on his arm, and, before his mind slipped away again, into the land of murky, dark gray fog, he was able to focus on her. Soft lips traced kisses along his cheekbone. "Hey, Sebastian," she whispered. "Sleep. Rest easy. Don't let us rush you. We're right here, with you."

Now that he knew she was there, something shifted. Yes, he had asked her to stay away until he was on his feet. He hadn't wanted her to see him helpless and weak. He should've known she wasn't going to listen to him. Now, he was damn glad she was there, because her voice, her touch, became a lifeline.

I need you. Here. I'm somewhere worse than hell. Stay with me. Hold on to me. Be my anchor. Keep talking to me. Please.

"You're fine, sweetheart," she said, gripping his hand. "You have plenty of time to wake up, and I'm going to stay with you until you do."

For the first time in days, knowing that she was next to him, he slept without being in a disorienting, sickening fog. His brain and his body rested. He listened for her voice, soothing and gentle, as every now and then she'd touch his hand, his forearm, smooth the sheets around him, and murmur something in his ear. He had no idea how long it took, but eventually he found the strength to reach for her hand. When he finally fully awakened for the first time post-surgery and opened his eyes, slate green eyes, gleaming with light, glanced into his.

"Oh, my God," Skye said, "he's awake."

He heard a rustle. Chair legs moved. From over her shoulder, Brandon and Zeus appeared, looking down at him. A flurry of activity ensued, with medical personnel and tests.

It was hours before he was alone with Skye, who rewarded him with the most beautiful smile he'd ever seen. He didn't need more medical tests to tell him he was going to be fine. When he looked at Skye, he knew that he would be.

STELLA BARCELONA

JIGSAW

A Black Raven Novel

Coming in Spring 2016

BLACK
RAVEN

Prologue

Ana slipped her small hand into her father's. His daughter's soft touch pulled Zeus Hernandez from his conversation with two senior Black Raven agents, reminding him that the purpose of this gathering wasn't work. "Daddy, hurry," she said, pulling on his hand. "They're getting ready to cut the wedding cake. Come with me."

Zeus looked down, into velvety-brown eyes shining with the unfiltered excitement of youth. He bent to one knee and planted a soft kiss on her cheek. With his free hand, he straightened the bow on her red hair ribbon. Loose tendrils of silky black hair had escaped from her ponytail and fallen across her face. He pushed the wayward hair back, gently tucking the strands behind her ears. She let go of his hand, then draped her arms over his shoulders and pressed her forehead to his so that their noses touched. He inhaled her sugary sweet, girlish scent and stared into her eyes, as she asked, "Don't you want to see?"

"Of course, my sweet angel."

He let her lead the way through the courtyard of New Orleans' City Park, towards the Pavilion of Two Sisters, where the wedding reception for his partner, Sebastian Connelly, and Skye Barrows, was taking place.

Accompanied by his daughter, Zeus opened the door to the reception venue. His eyes scanned the guests, before resting on Sebastian, who was talking to Skye and her younger sister, Spring. Zeus was happy for his friend. Barely eleven months earlier he had been on the operating table, having life-threatening brain surgery following a week from hell.

The Black Raven job that had involved Skye and her father, Richard Barrows, was completed before Sebastian went under the knife. But even while Sebastian was down, the world was still filled with bad guys. In the ensuing months, London, Miami, Bogotá, and Paris had been rocked with large-scale terrorist acts, leading to the inevitable conclusion that the terrorists were winning. People were afraid, waiting for the next horrific event. Economic markets were in turmoil. The global fall out was great for Black Raven's security business, but not for one other damn thing.

Sebastian had recovered from his surgery with none of the troubling aftereffects they'd all dreaded. He was back to normal, at the helm of Black Raven with his partners where he belonged. Guests at their wedding were the inner circle of Black Raven agents, partners, and friends. The father of the bride, computer software genius Richard Barrows, the man whose kidnapping from prison had brought Sebastian and Skye together, was there. Upon his official release from imprisonment, he'd started work with Black Raven at their Denver headquarters. Zeus had been working with him, along with Ragno, the head of their data analysis unit. Zeus and Ragno had concluded that Barrows was brilliant when focused, his ordeal had done nothing to diminish his brainpower, and they were damn glad he was now working for Black Raven instead of a competitor.

Partygoers were gathered at one end of the reception hall. Screens were being wheeled away and, as the cakes came into view, the room became a collective gasp of oohs and ahhs.

"Daddy, I can't see," Ana tugged at his hand, as they stood at the edge of the crowd.

He lifted her, and settled her on his hip. At seven, Ana would soon be too big to hold like this, and too old to want her father to carry her, but today she wrapped skinny arms around his neck and held on. "How's this?"

"Wow," she said. "Look at all the birds on the groom's cake. And the flowers. Dad! I've never seen so many flowers on a wedding cake. The colors are weird, aren't they? But it's beautiful. Wow."

Zeus watched Sebastian bend to his bride and give her a lingering kiss. At this wedding, the groom revealed none of the hesitation that had marked Zeus' own wedding day. None of the second thoughts. Not one bit of doubt. Zeus had pretended to be just as happy as Sebastian really was. Now, watching Sebastian's genuine, heartfelt reactions to the moments that marked his wedding day, Zeus wondered whether he'd fooled anyone.

Skye led Spring to the cakes for photographs. For a moment, Spring looked overwhelmed by the attention, but she managed a smile for the photographer. Sebastian, who was hanging back and allowing Spring to bask in the attention given to the cakes she'd created, approached Zeus. His eyes changed from happy groom to serious Raven. "How are operations going?"

Zeus shook his head. "Not today. You've got a gorgeous new wife to focus on." His eyes fell on Richard, who stood a few feet from the cake tables, smiling at his daughters. "A ready-made family. Besides, things are fine. Nothing unusual."

Zeus and the other Ravens who were at the wedding reception were mic'd to Ragno, who was at headquarters in Denver. Sebastian was not. For the last two hours, in deference to the celebration, Ragno had maintained radio silence.

"Zeus," as if she'd read his thoughts, Ragno's voice came through the mic, as clear as though she was standing next to him. "You spoke too soon. I'm talking only to you, and it can't wait. Understand?"

"Got it," he said, as Sebastian walked away from him and toward the cake tables. The band picked up their instruments, a signal that soon he wouldn't be able to hear Ragno. "Give me a second."

For Ragno to drop the other Ravens and speak directly to him meant that attention was needed, immediately, and the matter involved him, personally.

Zeus walked over to the Black Raven agent who had full-time duties over Ana. Agent Victoria Martel was Nanny Vick to Ana, a beloved sitter, friend, disciplinarian, and confidant. To Zeus,

Vick was a caregiver with a Glock, his insurance for Ana's safety when he wasn't at home with her in Miami. Overkill? He hoped so. With his daughter, there was no such thing as being too careful.

Ana wriggled out of his grasp and stood firmly on the ground, next to Agent Martel. She was used to Zeus' sudden transitions to business mode. "Want me to get you a piece?"

"If one of those cakes is chocolate on the inside," he said, touching her cheek, "absolutely. I'll be right back, baby. Stay with Vick." He turned from them and walked outside. "Ragno. I'm all ears."

"Richard Morgan, Chief Amicus Counsel for the United States at the newly convened International Terrorist Tribunal, died six hours ago in Paris. His death looks like insulin overdose in a diabetic. Initial reports indicate it was accidental."

"Okay," he said, walking across the brick courtyard, the lone person outside of the reception hall. Zeus knew a bit about the International Terrorist Tribunal, ITT for short. Hearings were just beginning in France. The world was watching. The ITT had one month to conduct four proceedings in four countries, then reach a verdict regarding recent terrorist acts in France, the U.S., Columbia, and England. The world needed an answer. Something. Anything. From his point of view, the current ITT proceedings were too ambitious, convened too hastily, and promised to be a clusterfuck of epic proportions, fueled by a news-thirsty media that was in a feeding frenzy on the public fear of terrorism. Zeus had no doubt that terrorists, whether they were affiliated with an established group or random wannabes, would find targets among the proceedings. The media was thirsty for the first shots to be fired.

"Although there's no indication of foul play," Ragno said, "Morgan's death has caused shockwaves about security concerns in at least one person, who has made a hiring call to us for personal security for the person who is stepping in to fill Morgan's shoes."

"Wouldn't there be government-agency security for the judges from the United States and participating parties who are there on behalf of the U.S.?

"Yes. Marshals. DHS. Plus, the ITT has its own security forces in each country."

"So someone is trying to circumvent the security that's

already in place?"

"Yes. The person who is hiring us believes that Morgan's death was not accidental. He believes that drugs were administered that caused his death. Having low confidence level in the existing security, he wants Black Raven. Specifically, he has requested that you provide on site protection to the new Chief Amicus Counsel."

"Did you happen to mention that I no longer do bodyguard details?" Zeus asked as he walked across a brick courtyard and stopped at a pond where gold and white koi swam lazily below lily pads. It was three in the afternoon, and the January sun had warmed the mild winter chill out of the air. He pulled off his suit jacket as his eyes followed the fattest koi in the pond.

"I explained that, but this man does not take no for an answer. Plus, his companies have been existing clients of Black Raven for some years, though he isn't the one that usually makes the hiring calls."

"Well, the answer is no. I don't care who he is."

"You're the originating partner on his files, which over the years have produced millions in revenue."

Zeus paused. The big fish shimmered with red and gold, with white spots, and it was a bully. When smaller fish crossed its path, it swam fast and nudged the others out of its way. Zeus bent down, picked up a few pebbles out of the garden that bordered the pond, and dropped one near the bully as he started an attack. "Tell him we have a number of highly qualified agents who can handle the job. I'll oversee the operation and be personally involved from afar, but I'm not going to be on site, day in and day out."

"He told me you wouldn't say no, even after I had accounting provide a rough estimate of the daily fee, which included a ridiculous rate for you. It's an enormous job. Multiple countries. High profile. I'm estimating you'll need twenty agents. Minimum. Worldwide transports. Accounting factored in outrageous profit levels on every conceivable contingency."

As Ragno rattled off astronomical numbers, Zeus dropped another pebble near the bully, wondering if the aggressive fish was smart enough to learn that his own actions were creating the threat. "Even with that kind of figure thrown at him, and a warning that the estimate will only go up, he said no one other than you is acceptable as lead agent. He insisted that I call you, tell you about the job, and ask you to do it." She paused. "So that's what I'm doing."

Son of a bitch. "Who is he?"

"Samuel Dixon."

The name carried an out-of-the-blue gut punch, one that he hadn't seen coming. For a man who was seldom surprised at anything, a man who had trained himself to react calmly to almost every conceivable situation, the adrenaline rush that came with hearing Dixon's name resulted in a jolt to his very being. Zeus exhaled. He looked up, at the bright blue, cloudless sky, and waited for the words that would seal his fate. The sun's heat warmed his exterior, while internal trepidation chilled his insides.

If he was right, 'no' was the only answer that made sense, but he knew he wasn't going to say it. 'No' was not a word he was going to articulate, because Samuel Dixon would only be making this request on behalf of one person, knowing that, like a goddamn moth driven to light, for all the reasons Zeus' answer should be no, Zeus was going to say yes. He'd been on a road leading away from her for years. It was a painful turn he'd taken willingly, resulting in a sharp, regret-filled detour that could never be undone.

Ragno continued, "Dixon believes she's in grave danger and insists that you lead the protective detail. You saved his life once. No one else will do."

Let me be wrong. "She who?"

"The ITT's new Chief Amicus Counsel for the United States is Dixon's daughter. Samantha Fairfax Dixon."

Not wrong.

Of all the variations of hell Zeus had confronted in his life, this one would be the hardest to navigate. It was a hell that defied reason, a scorching inferno that he'd created. He tried to think of a way out, but couldn't, even though walking through this fire-filled cauldron was going to test him in ways he didn't want to think about, and that was even without worrying about the risks the job would present.

Samuel Dixon was right.

Zeus couldn't refuse.

Fucking hell.

Dear Reader,

Thank you for purchasing and reading SHADOWS. Please help spread the word about SHADOWS by telling your friends about it and by writing a review at AMAZON, BARNES & NOBLE, and/or GOODREADS.

For me, actually being in the writing chair is the best part of the writing process, but a close second is the interaction that I have with readers. I love to hear from you, so please like my Facebook page and be on the lookout for posts, and updates on contests and appearances at facebook.com/stellabarcelona. I also can be reached via email at mail@stellabarcelona.com and, if you are interested in even more, you can join my mailing list at stellabarcelona.com/newsletter. Don't worry, I'm too busy to send out frequent newsletters, and I promise I won't share your email address. My website, stellabarcelona.com, has blogs that I update from time to time, some book related, some not. Please comment and let me know what you think of my blogs. If you'd prefer to contact me through the U.S. mail, I can be reached at P.O. Box 70332, New Orleans, Louisiana, 70172-0332.

Stay in touch!

Stella

ABOUT THE AUTHOR

  Stella Barcelona has always had an active imagination, a tendency to daydream, and a passion for reading romance, mysteries, and thrillers. She has found an outlet for all of these aspects of herself by writing romantic thrillers.

  In her day-to-day life, Stella is a lawyer and works for a court in New Orleans. She lives minutes from the French Quarter, with her husband of seventeen years and two adorable papillons who believe they are princesses. She is a member of Romance Writers of America and the Southern Louisiana Chapter of the Romance Writers of America. Her first novel, DECEIVED, was inspired by New Orleans, its unique citizens, and the city's World War II-era history.

  Her third novel, JIGSAW, a Black Raven novel, will be released in 2016.